"In WITCH SONG, Amber Argyle makes a riveting debut, creating a fresh new world full of wonder, peril and splendor. I found WITCH SONG to be positively engrossing from the first page to the last. I'm convinced that this is just the first book in what will be a long and prosperous career!"

David Farland, New York Times Bestselling Author of the *Runelords* Series

WITCH SONG

BOOK I OF THE WITCH SONG SERIES

Starling Publishing

Second American Paperback Edition

This is a work of fiction. Names, characters, places, and incidents either are the product of the author's imagination or are used fictitiously. Any resemblance to actual events, locales, or persons, living or dead, is entirely coincidental. The publisher does not have any control and does not assume responsibility for author or third-party Web sites or their content.

Copyright ©2011 by Amber Argyle

Editing by Kara Klotz
Author photo by ShaunaLee Johnson
Map by Robert Defendi

Cover art by Eve Ventrue. Contact Eve by visiting her Web site at http://eve-ventrue.weebly.com/

ISBN-13: 978-0-9857394-5-4
eBook ISBN: 978-1-936850-17-4

Library of Congress Control Number: 2011920942

Printed in the United States of America
10 9 8 7 6 5 4 3 2

Visit Amber Argyle at her author Web site:
http://www.amberargyle.com

Dedication

For Kent and Alice Argyle
Because you loved me first, best and always.

URWAY CITY STATE

DRYSDEN
MOUNTAINS
PERCHANCE

HARDEN CITY STATE
BRUSENNA'S HOME
GONSTOWER

ENDIR CITY STATE

ORDIN

NEFALIE

TRESSALAY

CORRIETH

DARKWELL
SEA

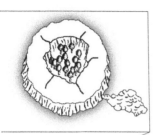

HAVEN

TARTEN

ENDALL SEA

SENNA'S LANDING

KAEN'S FARM

SHIOK

ICAR MOUNTAINS

CARPEL

EPAL

ESPEN'S REALM

ZAEN

SHIPS GRAVEYARD

WITCH SONG

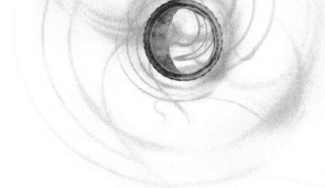

BOOK I OF THE WITCH SONG SERIES

BY AMBER ARGYLE

1. WITCHBORN

Brusenna's straw-colored hair felt as hot as a sun-baked rock. She was sticky with sweat that trickled down her spine and made her simple dress cling to her. Her every instinct urged her to run from the glares that stung like angry wasps. She had already put off her trip to the market for too long.

The merchant finished wrapping the spools of thread in crinkling brown paper. "Twelve upice," Bommer said sourly.

A ridiculous price, no doubt made worse by the drought. Had Brusenna been anyone else, she could have bartered it down to half that. Even though the villagers only suspected, it was enough. Careful not to touch her, the man's hand swallowed the coins she dropped in it. She wondered what marvelous things he ate to flesh out his skin that way. Things like the honey-sweetened cakes she could still smell in her clothes long after she'd left the marketplace.

As Bommer mumbled and counted his money, Brusenna gathered the packages tightly to her chest and hurried away. She hadn't gone five steps when a heavy hand clamped down on her shoulder. Fear shot through her veins like a thousand nettles. Here, no one ever touched her.

With a wince, she craned her neck back to see the merchant looming over her. "You tryin' to cheat me, chanter?"

This close, the smell of his stale body odor hit her hard. She swallowed the urge to gag. Her mind worked furiously. She'd counted twice. "I gave you twelve," she managed.

He yanked her around, grabbing her other arm and bringing her face next to his. She cringed as his large paunch pressed against her. Somewhere, a baby squalled. "You think I can't count?"

Brusenna tried to answer, but her mouth locked up. She should have been more careful. She should have stayed until he had finished counting her coins, but she had been too eager to escape. He shook her, his dirty nails digging into her skin. Her packages tumbled from her hands and hit the ground.

Taking shallow breaths and arching away from him, she squirmed, desperate to be free. "Please," she said, finally finding her voice. "Let me go!"

He laughed, his eyes gleaming with pleasure. "No. I don't think so. Not this time. You know what the punishment is for stealing?"

The stocks. Brusenna swallowed hard. Trapped for an entire day with the whole village taunting her. They'd throw things. Rotten food. And worse. She looked for help in the crowd that had eagerly gathered around them. Satisfaction shone plain on every face. She was suddenly angry with her mother for letting her face this alone. For refusing to come because someone might recognize her.

"I didn't steal," she whispered, already knowing no one would listen.

"You callin' me a liar?" Tobacco spit splattered her face. He backhanded her. Her vision flashed white, then black with stars, then red. She tasted blood. Her eyes burned with tears. She clamped her teeth shut against the pain, refusing to cry out.

Bommer half-dragged her toward the center of the square, where two thin blocks of wood were connected with a hinge. Three holes, one for her neck and two for her wrists. Remnants of rotten food, manure and rocks littered the base.

The sight of the stocks shocked Brusenna into action. She squirmed and struggled.

His hand on the back of her neck, Bommer shoved her throat into the largest, center hole. She tried to rear back. He pushed harder. The wood cut into her windpipe. She couldn't breathe.

"You let that child go, or you'll sorely miss your brain, my friend," said a feminine voice that was somehow soft and commanding at the same time.

Brusenna felt Bommer freeze, his arm still pinning her neck. She strained against Bommer to see who had spoken. In front of her, sitting astride a glossy black horse, a woman glared at the merchant down the barrel of an expensive-looking musket. The wind picked up and her gleaming hair shifted like a field of ripe wheat. The woman's cobalt eyes met Brusenna's golden ones.

Brusenna gaped. She'd hoped for help, but never imagined it would come from someone both rich and powerful.

"What'd you say to me?" he asked the stranger.

The woman cocked back the hammer. "You heard what I said." Bommer didn't respond. Brusenna felt him shift uncertainly. When no one moved to support him, he growled deep in his throat. He pushed once more on Brusenna's neck, hard. But then she was free. She collapsed, clutching her throat and coughing violently.

When the spots stopped dancing before her eyes, she glanced up. The woman was watching Brusenna, fury burning in her eyes. The stranger let the barrel drop. "Where I come from, merchants ask for the missing coin before they accuse their customers of stealing. Especially a child."

A child? Brusenna bristled as she rose to her feet. She was nearly fifteen. Then, from the corner of her eye, she saw Sheriff Tomack pushing through the crowd. All thoughts of defiance flew out of her head. She tried to slip through an opening, but the press of bodies tightened into an impregnable wall. Arms roughly shoved her back to Bommer.

She shuddered as his hand clamped down on her shoulder again. "Sheriff, this girl stole from me and this," he worked his tongue like he had a bad taste in his mouth, "woman is interfering."

"I already heard it, Bommer." Sheriff Tomack studied Brusenna with an unreadable expression. "You trying to cause trouble, girl?"

Digging her toenails into the packed dirt, she shook her head adamantly.

He grunted. "Well then, give Bommer his upice or spend your day in the stocks."

Anger flared in her chest and died like a candle flame in a windstorm. It didn't matter that she'd already given Bommer twelve upice. It didn't matter that he was lying. She couldn't prove it and her word meant nothing to the villagers. Scrabbling in her money bag, she found an upice and held it out for Bommer.

The merchant slowly shook his head. "I don't want her money. I want her time in the stocks."

Brusenna's hand automatically moved to her bruised throat. Tears stung her eyes. She quickly blinked them back.

"Why?" Sheriff Tomack asked.

Bommer snorted. "You know why."

"You got proof?"

Bommer spit in the dirt. "None of us needs it. We all know what she is."

No one said it, but the word echoed in Brusenna's head, *Witch*.

"Has the girl ever stolen from you before?" Sheriff Tomack asked cautiously.

Bommer took a deep breath. "Her punishment is my choice."

With a click, the woman on the horse released the hammer on her musket. Dismounting, she strode forward. The crowd parted, half in fear and half in awe. She threw a handful of coins at Bommer's chest. The gleaming silver bits bounced off and scattered across the ground. Brusenna's eyes widened in disbelief. The woman hadn't tossed a few dirty upices; the coins were silvers.

Looking both beautiful and terrible, the woman straightened her shoulders. "Take your money, merchant. If you give this girl more trouble, I'll see that no one ever buys from you again."

Bommer spit a stream of tobacco juice dangerously close to the woman's foot. "Who're you to make threats?"

She smiled, a mere baring of her teeth. "Would you like to find out?"

Glaring, Bommer rolled his chaw around his mouth. Finally, his glower shifted to Brusenna. "You ain't worth it, chanter." He scooped up the coins and stomped back to his booth.

Hate filled Brusenna. She hated that Bommer's lies allowed him to abuse her without cause—had earned him ten times his due. She hated the crowd for hating her. Still, it could have been much worse. She could be in the stocks. Grim relief washed through her, cooling her anger. It was past time to be heading home. She twisted to disappear in the crowd. But the strange woman gripped the back of her dress with an iron fist. Knowing better than to fight, Brusenna stifled a groan. *Not again,* she thought.

Sheriff Tomack gave the woman a small nod before moving away.

Brusenna turned a pain-filled glance to the marketplace. Though the crowd had grudgingly moved on, people still shot suspicious, hateful glances her way. Their tolerance of her had taken a dive since the drought had worsened. They blamed her and her mother for their dying crops, simply because they were Witches.

She forced herself to unclench her fists. The breeze felt cool against her sweaty palms. She turned toward the woman, though she dared not look at her face. "Thank you," she murmured.

The woman cocked her head to the side. "Why do you buy from him?"

Brusenna shrugged. "The others won't sell to me. And Bommer needs the money."

"So he resents you for it." She released her grip on Brusenna's dress. "What's your name, child?" Her voice was as sweet and lingering as the smell of the honeycakes.

"I'm not a child. My name is Brusenna."

The woman sighed in relief. "Ah, Sacra's daughter. I thought so."

How could this woman know Brusenna's name? Her mother's name? Her ears buzzed. She managed to bob her head once. She began gathering her scattered packages. The paper scraped loudly against the packed dirt.

The woman crouched beside her. Picking up the last package, she brushed it off and handed it to Brusenna. "My name is Coyel. Will you take me to your mother?"

Brusenna's stomach clenched. There were two iron-clad rules—one: never let them hear your song; two: never lead them home. She swallowed hard. "Thank you, Coyel, for helping me. But I'm not ... I mean, I shouldn't ... I mean—"

Coyel cocked an eyebrow and pitched her voice so no one else would hear, "I'm the eldest Keeper of the Four Sisters."

Brusenna blinked in confusion. Coyel's statement seemed to hold a deeper meaning, but for all her searching, she couldn't understand it. "I ... I'm an only child. My sister died before I was born."

A look of disbelief crossed Coyel's face and Brusenna knew she had missed the mark entirely. "Take me to your home. I must speak with your mother."

She bit her bottom lip. Coyel had saved her from the stocks, so if she wanted to speak with her mother ... well, Brusenna owed her that much. With a nervous glance at the townspeople, she nodded then scurried through the streets. Almost as soon as the village thinned behind them, they crossed into fields flanked by deep forests that grew over the gentle hills like a furry blanket over sleeping giants. Usually, those forests were deep green, but the drought had caused weaker patches to give up the season, trimming themselves in golds and reds.

Brusenna's shoulders itched for the cool, comforting shadows of the trees. She felt naked out in the open like this, where hateful villagers could scrutinize her. She felt even more vulnerable with the echoing clop of the horse's hooves to remind her of the woman and her cobalt eyes.

Nearly a league from the marketplace, Brusenna waited while Coyel tied her horse to a nearby tree. The path wound through thickets as dense and tangled as matted cat fur. She and her mother made it this way to keep strangers out.

Just as she moved to enter the forest, Coyel placed a hand on her shoulder. "This is your home. You should be the one to sing the song."

Brusenna's eyes widened in disbelief. Another Witch? It couldn't be.

Coyel lifted an eyebrow. "Unless you'd prefer me to sing?"

Brusenna didn't understand. Coyel was beautiful and powerful. Not skittish and weak. How could she be a Witch? "At the marketplace, you knew what I was. How?"

Coyel shot a glare in the direction of the village. "I heard someone saying the Witch was finally going to the stocks."

Brusenna folded her arms across her stomach. It made sense. Who else but another Witch would have helped her?

Coyel must have sensed her hesitation. "Are you unable?" There was simple curiosity in her gaze. As if she wanted to see if Brusenna could do it.

Of course she could sing the pathway clear. She'd been doing it for years. But Brusenna hesitated. It went against years of training to sing in front of a stranger. She was nervous to perform in front of another Witch who was everything Brusenna wasn't.

Before she could change her mind, she squared her shoulders and started singing.

Plants of the forest make a path for me,
For through this forest I must flee.
After I pass hide my trail,
For an enemy I must quell.

The underbrush shivered and then untangled like it had been raked through by a wooden comb. As they walked, Brusenna continued her song. As soon as their feet lifted, the plants wove behind them, tangling and knotting themselves into a formidable barrier nearly as tall as a man's chest.

What was nearly impossible without the song was fairly easy with it. In no time, they left behind the last of the forest. Brusenna stepped aside, giving the woman a full view of her home. Drought left the whole countryside brittle. And yet here, their lush gardens thrived. The house and barn were neat and well tended. The milk cow lazily munched her cud under the shade of a tree. With a fierce kind of pride, she watched for Coyel's reaction.

Coyel took in the prolific gardens with a sweep of her gaze. But the woman didn't seem impressed. As if she'd expected no less. And maybe she had.

Brusenna wanted to ask why Coyel had come, but her tongue dried in her mouth. Her mind shouted it instead, *What do you want with us?*

Bruke, Brusenna's enormous wolfhound, noticed them from his position in the shade of the house and bounded forward, the scruff on the back of his neck stiff with distrust. They'd purchased him as a guard dog after someone had shot their old plow horse. His wary eyes shifted to Brusenna in question.

Brusenna blinked rapidly. She suddenly wanted to explain why she'd broken the rule before the stranger breezed into their house. She darted past Coyel and up the worn path. "Bruke, heel."

With a glare at the stranger, Bruke glued himself to Brusenna's side.

She pushed open the door to the house. "Mother!" she called, pulling some clinging hair off her sweaty forehead.

Sacra's head popped up from the floor cellar. "What is it, Brusenna?"

"A woman named—"

"Coyel," the woman finished as she stepped up behind her.

For the longest time, the two women stared at each other. The charge between them made the tiny hairs on Brusenna's arms stand on end. Coyel stepped into their home. To Brusenna's knowledge, she was the first outsider to do so.

"It's been a long time, Sacra," Coyel said.

Brusenna's gaze flitted back and forth between her mother and Coyel. That they knew each other went beyond her comprehension. In her fourteen years, Brusenna had never seen her mother converse with anyone other than an occasional trouble-making villager—usually one of the adolescent boys who had taken on the challenge to kill one of their animals as a dare.

Sacra stepped out of the cellar and lowered the door as gently as if it were glass. Slowly, she straightened her slender back.

"Brusenna, leave the things on the table and g

Brusenna's disbelief rose in her throat, n

"But, Mother—" At her mother's glower, s

words, dropped her purchases on the table a

door. Bruke followed. Careful to keep her striu̶ᵉ ᵛ.ₑₗ

until she had rounded the corner of the house before peeking

back. The way was clear.

"Bruke, stay," she whispered. With a disappointed whine, the dog sat on his haunches.

Hunched over, Brusenna retraced her steps. The soft grass felt cool under her hands and the sun was hot on her back as she crouched on one side of the doorway. There were no sounds from within. She waited until her knees were practically numb. She'd almost determined to chance a peek through the window when their voices halted her.

"What brings you, Coyel?" her mother asked warily.

"The Keepers need you, Sacra. There are precious few of us left and signs of the Dark Witch increase daily. The Circle of Keepers must be complete if we are to recapture her and stop the drought."

Brusenna's eyebrows flew up in wonder. It had never occurred to her that Sacra could have been a different person before she became her mother. Mustering every ounce of bravery, she peeked through the corner of the window.

"Calling Espen the Dark Witch only increases her power over us." Sacra's gaze remained fixed on the floor. "Find another Eighth."

Coyel pressed her lips in a tight line. "The others are gone."

Her mother's head came up slowly; she blinked in surprise … and fear. "I have a daughter. You have only yourself."

Coyel pointed toward Gonstower. "They call us Witches. But long before that, the Creators named us Keepers. It's what we are. Keepers of the Four Sisters—Earth, Plants, Water and Sunlight. And as a Keeper, you can't deny that all are floundering. If we don't act now, it'll be too late."

Sacra stood rigid and immovable. "No."

yel's voice flared, "You know what the Dark Witch will
if she succeeds? Your daughter is Witchborn; even worse,
she's the child of a former Head of Earth." She shook her head
in disbelief. "She doesn't even know our signs."

Her mother turned away and stared blankly at the trees behind
the house. "The less Brusenna knows, the safer she is."

"Safer?" Coyel spat. "You haven't taught her to protect herself.
She's terrified of those *villagers*." The last word sounded like
her mother's voice after she'd found rats in their oats. "What
chance do you think the girl will stand when Espen finds her?"

Her head in her palms, a moan escaped her mother's lips.
Coyel stepped forward and rested her hand on Sacra's shoulder.
"I've heard her. When she's fully come into her own, I wouldn't
doubt she'll be at least a Level Four. But right now, she's …
immature. And not just her song. Keeping her isolated will only
make it worse. She needs to be around other Keepers her own
age. Learn."

Brusenna's cheeks flamed with shame, partly because she
suspected Coyel was right about her immaturity. Whenever she
was around strangers, her tongue dried up in her mouth and her
stomach felt full of writhing snakes.

Her mother jerked away as if Coyel's touch had burned her.
"Coyel, no. Espen won't find her. I've been careful. Gonstower
is isolated. No one knows I'm here. And we're not completely
without friends."

Friends? Brusenna mentally flipped through the faces of the
villagers who would have gladly seen her in the stocks. What
friends?

Coyel's gentleness vanished, replaced by disbelief and anger.
"I found you. And if you think those villagers will protect her
identity, you're deceiving yourself. The ignorant fools would
gladly turn her over. Never understanding the very Keepers they
hate are all that stand between them and—"

"I said no!" Sacra shouted. Brusenna jumped. She'd never
heard her mother shout before. "Get out!"

Coyel backed away, her jaw working as if she might chew through Sacra's resistance and then her head dropped. "We're gathering at Haven. I'll wait in the village for three days." Her fervent gaze met Sacra's smoldering one. "Please, Sacra. We can't do it without you."

Not daring to linger another moment, Brusenna scampered away from the door and pressed herself flat against the smooth boards on the other side of the house.

"Please, Sacra," Coyel asked again. And then all Brusenna could hear was the sound of footsteps that grew fainter within moments.

She barely felt Bruke nudge her with his wet nose. Her chest rose and fell as her mind reeled with unfamiliar names. Circle of Keepers, Level Four, the Dark Witch? Surely her mother had no understanding of such things. Surely she'd lived here for generations.

Hadn't she?

2. OF SILVER AND SHADOW

The stairs creaked. A moment later, the kitchen door groaned and slapped against the frame. Having been unable to sleep, Brusenna padded to her window.

Sacra trailed through the waist-high corn as if wading through water, her palms skimming the tops of the plants. Witch song drifted in the air as the moonlight cast everything in silver and shadow. Brusenna watched until her mother disappeared into the dense forest. Before she could change her mind, she snatched her wrap from its hook and flung it around her narrow shoulders.

Telling her dog to stay, Brusenna scanned for her mother before bursting free of the house. Darting from one shadow to the next, she halted at the sound of her mother's song. Pure, beautiful, enchanting. Closing her eyes, she concentrated on the words only a Witchborn could understand—words sung by a Witch in the Creator's language, the language of authority, with the correct melding of melody and rhythm.

Following the sound, Brusenna paused at the edge of the forest and peered into the dappled darkness. The wind played with her cotton shift, pressing it against her body before billowing it out then twisting it around her. She shivered as the wind's fingers painted her skin silver with moonlight.

Gritting her teeth, she gathered the hem of her shift in her fist and plunged into the ever-deepening shadows. She'd lost count of how many scratches she'd accumulated and how often she'd stumbled, when the path before her suddenly cleared. Startled, she found herself in the shadows that edged a perfectly formed circle. One she hadn't known existed. Scrambling, she ducked behind an enormous tree and peered inward with awe.

Her mother stood, arms outspread and her Witch song commanding and sure.

Wind, lift me high,
That my words reach to'rds the sky.

All around Sacra, the trees swirled as if caught inside a slow whirlwind. Her face upturned, she repeated the song one last, heart-stopping time.

A current of air snatched her off the ground, twisting her hair as it caught her next words.

Oh, Wind, to Haven carry my song,
For the ears of the Keepers must hear it 'fore long.
Of the Keepers, how many remain?
Upon how many has the Dark Witch laid her claim?

With a roar, a gust swirled the song into a tight cocoon and hurtled it away. Sacra's song faded, even as the wind lowered her to the ground. She continued staring into the night sky, as if waiting for a response.

Her entire life, Brusenna had witnessed her mother singing. But never like this, with so much power. Shivering, Brusenna sat down and hugged her wrap around her legs. She considered confronting her mother, but anger stopped her. There were secrets here. Secrets Brusenna had been ignorant of her entire life. Secrets she was determined to find the answers to. Time passed. She'd grown so accustomed to the quiet that she started at the sound of another song—one that wasn't from her mother, but distant, as if little more than an eerie echo.

Eight Witches remain.
The rest are in chains.

Sacra bowed her head. "Coyel spoke true," she whispered.

Brusenna stretched out her stiff, cold legs and rubbed her numb hip. She waited a long time to see if anything more would happen. But her mother showed no signs of leaving. No signs of anything.

Afraid she'd already stayed too long, Brusenna eased to her feet and backed up a step. Something cracked beneath her weight. She froze. Her mother's gaze snapped to the tree Brusenna hid behind. Holding her breath, she stood perfectly still, her blood pounding in her ears. For what seemed an eternity, her mother stared in her direction before she turned her gaze back to the night sky.

Brusenna exhaled in a rush and slunk away from the clearing. She stepped into the bright light of their corn field. The moon's position revealed how long she'd spent in the forest. She turned as another faint song brushed her ears. But she didn't want to trek through the woods again. Nor did she think a new song would provide more answers than the last had.

Besides, her eyes burned with weariness and her whole body felt numb. She stumbled up the stairs to her room and into her bed.

The next thing she knew, dawn teased her through her curtains. Throwing back her quilt, she thundered down the wooden steps. There was her mother, mixing breakfast as always, her customary smile in place. Brusenna wondered what else hid behind that smile.

"You'll need to start bringing the vegetables in. It's going to freeze early this year," her mother said as she dished up Brusenna's oatmeal.

Brusenna plopped into her chair. In the morning glare, she could almost believe last night had been a dream. But the stinging scratches on her shins didn't lie. The certainty of it made Brusenna feel even more unsettled. Normally, she'd have come right out and asked her mother. They didn't keep secrets from each other ... or at least, Brusenna hadn't thought they did. Coyel's arrival seemed to have shattered that assumption.

Coyel's arrival seemed to have shattered many assumptions. Brusenna glanced up to see her mother staring into the oatmeal as if it might hold the answers to all of their problems. "Mother?"

Her mother's head snapped up, a dark glower in her eyes.

Brusenna shrank back. Things were happening. Things she didn't understand. "Mother, what's going on?"

Sacra looked away. "Why did you follow me last night?"

Brusenna's chest tightened. She scuffed her calloused feet against the worn wood floor. "You knew?"

Her mother chuckled dryly. "Yes, Brusenna. I knew you were watching me."

She clenched the sides of her chair. "Why didn't you say anything?"

Sacra shrugged. "In your place, I would've done the same." She pressed her lips in a thin line. "It's called the Calling Song. It must be performed in the Ring of Power—a circular clearing, ringed with tall trees. At least eight Witches are required to perform the most powerful of songs ... the kind of songs that could end the drought. There aren't enough of them at Haven."

"To fight the Dark Witch?" Brusenna blurted before clamping her hand over her mouth.

Sacra inhaled sharply. "How could you ..." Her eyes narrowed. "You listened to Coyel and me, didn't you?" The tiny lines around her eyes deepened as she pressed them shut. "I'd hoped you'd never have to hear of Espen." She clutched the sides of the table as if it was the only thing keeping her upright, yet her voice remained surprisingly calm, "Yes, Brusenna. We're going to fight her. But there are eight of us and only one of her. So you shouldn't worry."

"What's she done?" Brusenna asked cautiously.

The sinews in her mother's hands stood out against her clenched knuckles. "She's a murderer! One who should've been stopped long ago."

"Who—"

"I'll speak no more of Espen!"

Brusenna drew back as if she'd been slapped. She'd never seen her mother so angry. The realization dawned on her that whatever existed between the Dark Witch and her mother was personal.

Sacra pinched the bridge of her nose. "Maybe Coyel was right. Maybe I should've taught you, but I never thought it would come to this. Perhaps ... well, perhaps I should've done

things differently. But after your sister and your father died ...
I had to keep you safe. Nothing else was more important than
that." She took a deep breath. "There are a few things I need to
tell you before I leave."

Brusenna's entire body went as rigid as a tree stump. "Leave?"

Her mother didn't seem to hear her. Standing, she withdrew a
large tin of beans from the shelf and poured them into an empty
container. They sounded like hail as they bounced and settled.
When they were nearly gone, she reached inside and withdrew a
worn blue book. "I wrote this in case ..." She sighed. "Everything
I should've taught you, I wrote in this journal. Read it. Study it.
Keep it with you. And don't forget your voice practice. A Witch
with a weak song is barely a Witch at all."

Brusenna reached out to steady herself against the table.
"When are you leaving?"

Her mother's gaze seemed to search for something inside
Brusenna's eyes. "The day after tomorrow."

Brusenna's hand went to her mouth. "When will you return?"
Sacra half-shook her head. "I don't know."

3. CHAПTER

Brusenna woke to a cold hand against her cheek. Her mother was fully dressed in heavy winter clothing and she smelled like the wind. She held out a folded piece of paper. "If something … bad happens, I want you to read this letter and do as it says. Do you understand?"

Brusenna nodded. The chill seeped through her clothes as soon as she left the warmth of the quilts to follow her mother into her room. She watched as her mother tucked the letter away in the money box; the same box that contained her dead father's wedding ring. A sense of foreboding filled Brusenna, leaving her body numb with dread.

"I know you think I'm abandoning you, but I'm not. I've asked Sheriff Tomack to look out for you. He's a good man. I've known him for many years."

Tomack's help in the marketplace suddenly made sense. "Is he one of the friends you told Coyel about?"

"One of the few." Sacra started down the stairs, "There's something else I need to show you." Kneeling before the kitchen stove, she wiggled one of the corner bricks. It gave way easily.

Brusenna gasped at the gold glinting beneath it. Dropping beside her mother, she picked up a warm coin and brushed off the soot with her thumbs. In all her life, she'd never held a gold piece before, only the cheaper metal upice. "Where'd you get this?" Betrayal and hurt mingled inside her. How many lies had her mother told her?

Sacra took the piece and replaced it under the brick. "There's gold under the hearth bricks and buried under the hay in the barn, too." She met Brusenna's accusing stare. "I had my reasons for keeping this from you. I'm trusting you not to use these coins—"

"Why not?" Brusenna burst out. "I could wear shoes all year, new clothes, so many of the things I've always wanted!"

"What do you think the villagers would do if they thought we had anything worth stealing?" Sacra's eyes clouded over and she looked away. "There are other reasons. Reasons I'll not tell you. Know this, Brusenna: everything I did was to protect you. Only take the gold if you must leave. Then and only then. Do you understand?"

Brusenna refused to meet her mother's gaze.

"Brusenna?" Sacra chided.

"I understand," she answered coldly.

The log in the fire snapped and Brusenna jumped. Sacra stood quickly. "I have to go. When I return, I'll tell you everything." She pulled a knit cap over her chestnut hair and kissed Brusenna's cheek. "Be safe." She turned quickly, but not before Brusenna saw the tears glistening in her eyes.

Brusenna wanted to cry out, *"No! Stop! Don't leave me!"* But the words wouldn't come.

Her cheek still tingling from her mother's kiss, Brusenna watched Sacra jog across the field, leaving dark footprints in the frost. She stepped into the forest. The trees swallowed her whole.

Brusenna stood in the doorway until her skin was blotched with cold, but she couldn't seem to shut the door. If she did, her mother would truly be gone and she'd really be alone.

But she couldn't leave the door open forever. With a shiver that shook her to her bones, she pushed it shut as warm tears streamed down her cold cheeks.

***

Taking the tin of salt from the shelf, Brusenna pulled back the cover and stared at the light dusting that remained. Her heart fell. She had to have salt. And the only way to get it was to go into town. Swallowing the bile that rose in her throat, she looked down at Bruke. "There's nothing to help it. I have to go."

Changing into her best shin-length dress, she went into her mother's room. It was hard to believe Sacra had only been gone three weeks. It felt longer. Much longer. She'd spent her fifteenth birthday alone. All day, every day, Brusenna had spent canning and drying their harvest—an overwhelming task without help.

Opening the lid to the money box, she couldn't help but run her finger over her father's wedding ring. How might her life have been different if her father Rend had lived? If her sister Arel had? She studied the crisp outline of the letter her mother had left her. She had a sudden urge to throw it in the fire.

Trembling from the effort of restraining herself, she withdrew the money pouch and poured some of the upices into her palm. Silently, she stared at the dull, worn pieces.

She clenched her hand around the coins until they left circular imprints on her palm. "By the Creators, I'm done with it!" She dumped the coins back into the money box. She deliberately turned her back on her mother's room and kneeled before the hearth, her heart racing and her brief flare of courage failing her. "Lies. My entire life, she's told me nothing but lies."

She realized her fists were pressed into her thighs and she slowly relaxed her fingers. Tugging the brick from its place, she took one of the gleaming coins stamped with the imprint of some long-dead war hero and stuffed it in her pocket.

"We'll see if Bommer calls me a thief after I give him this," she whispered to herself.

As she eased through the heavy woods, she sang the song that simultaneously cleared her path and made the forest grow dense around her.

Plants of the forest, make a path for me,
For through this forest I must flee.
After I pass, hide my trail,
For an enemy I must quell.

As she walked, she was aware that she was doing something she'd never done before—deliberately disobeying her mother. But she couldn't turn back. A small part of her wanted to, but something larger tugged at her and she was powerless to stop.

When she finally reached the road to town, she realized Bruke was still following her. She sighed. He was lonely, too. "Stay." She hated leaving him. He gave her a measure of protection. But a dog wasn't much good against a musket. Besides, people wouldn't approve of a dog the size of a small horse in the marketplace—especially if he was with her. Her encounter with Bommer had taught her one thing—the villagers would lie to hurt her.

Though it was obvious Bruke didn't like it—he'd been trained from puppyhood to obey and protect—he went back to the shadows under a low-growing bush and sat on his haunches.

After leaving the cool forest, the sun seemed unbearably hot. Sweat glistened on her forehead. She wiped at it with the back of her hand. The weather was certainly odd. To freeze as early and hard as it had and then turn hot again? Not to mention the three-year drought. She sighed. So many things in her life were in upheaval. Why not the weather?

The town loomed before her like a dirty sore on the Earth's crust. Tucking her golden hair behind her ears, she took a deep breath and plunged in. She had to endure the villagers' stares before she finally reached the market. She froze in front of Bommer's booth. The shutters hung askew from rusted hinges. Peeking inside, she saw sun-bleached shelves where once tins and parcels of goods had sat.

She staggered back as if Bommer's ghost might come screeching out at her.

Had Coyel kept her promise, even though Bommer had dropped the charges?

Trying to swallow the lump in her throat, Brusenna turned to the next merchant and met his gaze. He shook his head in disgust. Her cheeks flamed as she dropped her gaze and made her way to the next. He chuckled. "I don't think so, Witch."

A bead of sweat trickled down her back. With every ounce of courage she had left, she looked up.

A young man she'd never seen before. He flashed a smile, his white teeth straight and even. She'd never seen such beautiful teeth. "What does the lady need today?"

Lady? Startled, Brusenna looked behind her. But there was no one else. Could he really have just called her a lady? She stared at the blond man and tried to make her tongue work—to say something friendly and witty, but all that came out was, "Salt."

He looked her up and down. "You're probably old enough for a woman's full-length dress, wouldn't you say?" He pulled out a beautiful sky-blue bolt. "This would look wonderful with your soft yellow hair and ..." He ducked to look under her lowered lashes. "Golden eyes. Like wheat that's almost ready to harvest—hints of green. Hmm."

She felt the color rise to her cheeks for the second time. "No. All I need is salt."

He chuckled as he measured the cloth. "Salt is well and good, but a beautiful woman should have a beautiful dress."

Beautiful? No one had ever called her beautiful before. She thought of the glittering gold piece in her pocket; money enough to pay for the salt and the fabric, with change to spare. Her mother would never miss one coin. Not with as many as she had hidden under the hearth. What could it hurt to spend one little piece?

He met her gaze with a questioning look.

Feeling suddenly bold, she nodded.

She watched in fascination as he cut the cloth. Finished, he held it toward her. Their hands touched. Instead of jerking back in revulsion, he let the contact linger. Her stomach jumped into her throat. No one—no one—ever touched her. Not unless they wanted to hurt her. Flustered, she handed him the gold piece. He reverently turned it over in his hands. A smile crept across his face, making the skin wrinkle like wet paper around his pale blue eyes. "My name's Wardof. I haven't seen you around before. Where do you live?"

Amazingly, Brusenna found herself meeting his gaze as she hugged the butter-soft fabric to her chest. "In the forest."

Counting out his coins, he dropped her change into her hand. "Well, your husband's a lucky man."

"Oh, I'm not married," she said quickly, part of her pleased he thought her old enough for a husband. She dropped the change in her pocket. "I live with my mother."

He gestured to his plethora of goods. "Perhaps she'd like something?"

Brusenna suddenly felt unsure. No doubt he knew what she was. The other merchants would have seen to that. So why the kindness? And the questions? Feeling suddenly cautious, she shook her head. "No."

"Oh, come now. I'll throw in something free, just for her."

Brusenna dug her toes into the dirt. Was she so paranoid as to construe cruelty from kindness? "Maybe when she comes back."

"Oh," he said. "Of course. When she gets back from …"

She shouldn't have said that. Brusenna looked away. *Back from fighting the Dark Witch*, she thought. *If she comes back at all.* The soft cloth suddenly felt unnatural under her calloused hands.

Wardof gave an easy laugh. "Well, whenever she does, send her down to pick out something."

Brusenna gave him a small smile and turned to go. He grabbed her hand. "Wait! You forgot something." He held out the salt and placed it gently in her hand. "There."

But he didn't let go.

Without taking his eyes from her, he reached underneath his counter and pulled out a necklace. Dangling from the black cord was an amber pendant shaped like a crescent moon. "It matches your eyes perfectly."

Brusenna's eyes widened in shock. "I couldn't."

"Sure you could," he said easily. "I'll make you a deal. The rest of your change for the necklace. I'm still trying to establish myself as a merchant. A good deal is sure to buy your loyalty, no? Besides, I'm certain you'll make it up to me someday."

Brusenna gazed longingly at the necklace. She'd never owned a piece of jewelry before. And it was so beautiful. But he was giving her more than a good deal. Even she knew that. She bit her lip. "I don't know."

Without asking, he moved behind her and brushed her hair over her shoulder. Drawing the necklace around her neck, he fastened the clasp. The amber felt cool against her sweltering skin. Lifting it, she rotated the pendant, watching as it caught the light. "It's lovely." Before she could change her mind, she dug into her pocket and shoved the rest of the coins into his hand.

"So are you." He squeezed her shoulder and stepped back around the counter.

Her shoulder still felt the pressure of his grip. She cradled her hand against her body. She couldn't remember the last time someone other than her mother had touched her ... and after three weeks, even her mother's touch seemed dreamlike and distant. "Thank you."

"Perhaps you'll come see me another time?"

To see his smile and speak to him again, Brusenna might do that. Nodding a shy goodbye, she was surprised at the tears stinging her eyes. Not wanting anyone to see them, she pushed them from her cheeks and darted down a narrow side street that led out of town.

She stopped short as a group of boys blocked her path. "You're the chanter, aren't you?" the one with the crooked nose asked her.

Dropping her head, she tried to duck past him. He stepped in front of her, close enough she could smell his greasy hair and unwashed clothes. She stepped quickly to the other side; he matched her movements as if they were partners in some kind of dance. Unable to bear being so close to him, she took a step back.

He spread his feet and folded his arms over his chest. "Chanter! Why don't you cast one of your Witch spells?"

Knowing a reply would only make things worse, she tried again to slide past them. Crooked Nose easily blocked her. "Look at that, boys—she's scared." He shoved her.

She suddenly understood. Her silent acceptance would never appease this boy, or any of the others like him. Their cruelty would never stop. Never end. The strange feeling she'd experienced earlier that day washed over her. She squared her shoulders and leveled her gaze. "Let me pass." She was pleased that the demand rolled off her tongue without a tremor to betray her fear.

He only laughed. "How's a little, bitty thing like you going to make me?" Before she could process what he was doing, he gave one of her small breasts a squeeze.

Something inside her snapped. By the Creators, she was finished with it! Her mouth opened and a song from mother's journal erupted from the most primal part of her.

Plants, hear my song,
An enemy wishes to do me wrong!

All the seeds and plants with in range of her voice burst into life, trembling in anticipation of her next command.

Plants, stop the boys who'd halt my flight.
Bind them though they fight.

Weeds, grasses and vines shot around the boys' legs. Crooked Nose shrank before her and would have kept going, but vines twisted around his ankles, stopping him. She repeated the song, this time with more determination. His face drained of color as the plants edged up his legs and the legs of his companions. Any vines they kicked free were replaced with three more.

"Here now!" a voice cried from somewhere behind Brusenna. Snapping her mouth shut, she whirled to see Sheriff Tomack coming around a corner at full speed. What would he do to her? An image of herself locked in the stocks—these boys gathered around her—shot through her like a wildfire. She desperately wanted to run. But she was through running.

She would stand her ground, like Coyel did. Like her mother wouldn't.

But to her surprise, Sheriff Tomack's glower settled on Crooked Nose. "Corwood, you've done it now! I'll have you locked up for a fortnight for that!"

"But she's a Witch!" Corwood shouted, his face red with outrage.

Sheriff Tomack's gaze flicked to Brusenna before returning to Crooked Nose. "That ain't no secret, boy." He nodded to her without taking his eyes from Corwood. "Best be getting home now, Miss Brusenna."

She gaped at the sheriff. Even though her mother had said he was a friend, she'd been unable to believe it. He took a step toward her, his gaze shifting to the villagers who had been drawn to a conflict like flies to dung. "You best hurry."

Giving the sheriff a curt nod, she started down the road, but she couldn't help but pause as she drew even with Corwood. Under her breath, she hissed, "Never touch me again."

She felt like an abandoned seed in her breast had suddenly found water and sun. Swollen with newfound strength, it had started to spread roots. Now that the seed had begun to grow, she knew her life would never be the same again.

She was so busy with the changes within herself she didn't notice the pale blue eyes watching her with a knowing look in the crowd of merchants.

4. WITCH HUNTERS

As soon as the village was out of sight, Brusenna broke into a run. Her golden hair swished behind her as her feet flew over the packed Earth. When she reached the turn-off in the road, she dove into the trees and collapsed next to Bruke. Drawing in her knees, she marveled that she didn't feel terrified. Quite the opposite. She felt powerful. Even so, tears plunged down her cheeks.

"Why are they so cruel? I've never done anything to hurt them!"

Bruke whined and licked her face. He froze and a low growl erupted from his throat. He bit the pendant and pulled back. The black leather thong strained against her neck. "No Bruke! You're going to break it!" She pried it from his teeth.

Wiping her face with her palms, she darted into the forest, singing the song to hide her path from any who might follow.

Trees and plants, hide my way.
Let no one come unless I say.

The entire way, Bruke whined beside her.

When she yanked open the door to her house, the light was beginning to fade. She stood, breathing hard on the doorstep. But she couldn't seem to go inside. The house was hollow and empty. One look back at Bruke and she stepped aside. "Come."

Bruke trotted inside as if it were the most natural thing in the world, though he'd never been allowed inside before. After making a round, he sat on the floor in front of her as if to say, "What next?"

Brusenna let out a nervous laugh and suddenly realized how hungry she was. "Next is supper." Lighting a lantern, she busied herself fixing a meal for the two of them, but Bruke didn't seem interested in eating. She took a hearty bite and moved the food to her cheeks so she could talk. "Come on. Eat your supper."

Instead, Bruke jumped up and placed his paws on her thighs. His eyes fixed on the pendant, he growled.

The tiny hairs on Brusenna's arms stood on end. She swallowed. "All right, boy. I'll take it off." Reaching behind her, she undid the clasp and took the necklace to the money box, placing it beside her father's ring. "Satisfied?" she asked as she came down the stairs.

With a contented groan, he settled down to his meal.

Grunting, Brusenna plopped back on her chair. When she'd finished her dinner, she tried to memorize more songs from her mother's journal, but she couldn't seem to keep her eyes open. Giving in, she eased into her bed, with Bruke lying down at the foot. Almost immediately, she fell asleep.

A wet tongue in the palm of her hand and a soft whine brought her around. Glancing out the window, she saw the velvety blackness of deep night. Rubbing her eyes with the pads of her fingers, she sat up. "What?"

Bruke went to her closed door. He growled softly, as he'd been trained to do if strangers were sneaking around. The hairs on the back of Brusenna's neck stood on end. Could Corwood have found a way through her forest? She threw off the blankets and peeked out her window. She saw nothing out of the ordinary.

Carefully, she padded to his side. That's when she noticed a soft glow coming under her door. Had she left the lantern burning? She strained to listen over the sound of her heart thudding in her ears. The light moved! Someone was here! Pure energy surged through her veins. Bruke let out another whimper. Holding her hand on his nose, she shushed him. "Stay."

Brusenna pressed her ear to the door. "The pendant is in the room on the left," a voice whispered.

"How do we know she's in that one?" another voice responded.

"We'll check that one first," replied the first.

Brusenna heard her mother's door creak open. If she wanted to escape, her best chance was now. She stared at the doorknob, unable to make herself turn it. *Quick!* she thought. *Before it's too late!* Forcing herself not to dwell on it, she flung her door open and burst into the hall. Right into a man's arms.

"Well! Here's our little Witch!" he exclaimed.

Brusenna looked up into Wardof's vibrant blue eyes. All the kindness was gone, replaced by hatred and cruelty. That he had pretended to care made the betrayal so much worse.

"Let me go!"

He chortled. "I don't think so, little Witch. You're worth a lot of money to me."

She pounded her fists against his chest. He laughed at her.

"Bruke!" she screamed.

With a snarl, Bruke bit into Wardof's arm. He cried out in pain.

Brusenna was free. She flew down the hall. She felt coarse fur next to her as Bruke rejoined her.

"Don't let her get outside!" Wardof cried from behind her.

She shoved the kitchen door open; it cracked against the side of the house. Her legs pumped as she hurtled through the corn. It whipped her bare arms and left a stinging welt on her cheek. Without meaning to, she found herself heading to the circular clearing. She chanced a glance behind her. His shirt torn and bloody, Wardof and a lumpy man pounded up the row behind her. Steel glinted in Wardof's hand.

She had to make it to the forest to hide in the shadows of the trees. She tried to run faster, but she could hear their footsteps coming closer. She wasn't going to make it. The realization hit her moments before a pain tore into her scalp. She was on the ground, fists of her golden hair in Wardof's grip. He jerked her hard with his good arm as he pointed his blade at Bruke. "Call off the dog!"

She opened her mouth, but Bruke lunged before the words could pass her lips. The impact of the wolfhound's enormous body knocked Wardof off her.

"Stop her mouth, Garg! Stop her mouth!" he screamed as he tried to hold Bruke's snarling muzzle at bay.

Those words, more than anything, unstopped her voice. Another song from her mother's journal poured free.

Corn, stop the men who hold me tight,
Bind them though they fight.

Bruke nimbly jumped off as, in a blur of motion, the corn wove around all but the men's heads.

Brusenna sang hard and long for the corn to be strong and sure. Soon the men were trapped like bugs wrapped in a spider's silk.

Growling menacingly, Bruke leaped on Wardof's chest, daring him to move.

"Filthy Witch!" he cursed her. Bruke snarled and snapped at Wardof's cheek. Blood shone in the moonlight.

Her scalp on fire, Brusenna collapsed on the ground and sat there dumbly. If not for Bruke, they would have taken her in her sleep. He'd saved her. She shivered. Rubbing her arms, she suddenly realized she wore nothing but her sleeveless shift. And it was freezing. Self-conscious, she crossed her arms over her chest.

"You said it would be easy money," Garg whined loudly.

"Keep your tongue!" Wardof snapped.

"I don't understand." she said.

Wardof fixed his hateful gaze on her. "I'm a Witch Hunter, girl!"

A shaky, uncontrollable laugh erupted from her mouth. At first, it sounded more like a cough, but then she took a deep breath and let it free.

"What? What's she laughin' for, Wardof?"

Brusenna held her sides. "Not a very good one!"

That bought her a string of the most creative and vehement expletives she'd ever heard. When he'd caught his breath, Wardof said, "If not for that blasted dog, I'd have caught you in your sleep, or at very least inside that house! Lot harder to sing with a gag over your mouth! Next time, I'll—"

With a sigh, she ordered the corn over their mouths, too. Only their noses showed, their breathing making sharp, wheezing sounds as they struggled to draw air through the small openings she'd left them. "Thank you, Sisters," she sang to the corn.

Watching the men's pitiful struggle to free themselves from their cocoons of corn, Brusenna realized she had complete control. The realization left her awed and a little overwhelmed. But what did she do now? Thinking hard, she realized someone had sent these men after her. Only two people knew she was in Gonstower. And one of them was her mother. The other was Coyel. With a sinking feeling, she rose to her feet. "Bruke, come."

The dog shot her a pleading look.

"Bruke," she said sternly.

He whined and came to her. Burying her hands into his wiry hair, she took a deep breath and sang the corn back from their heads. "If you don't answer me, I'll wrap you back up and leave you." She nodded to Bruke. "I'm sure he'd love to have you alone." Garg and Wardof shot looks of concern Bruke's way.

"Ask us what?" Garg said.

Her mouth went dry. Ask them what, indeed. Brusenna knew just enough to understand how painfully ignorant she really was. Still, best not to let them in on that. "Tell me everything. Leave anything out and you'll be Bruke's next meal."

Wardof clamped his handsome mouth shut. Garg was not so inclined. "Come on, Wardof."

Wardof shot Garg a look of disgust. "Clamp it you, or I'll—"

"What! What are you gonna do? Tied up in corn like an overripe ear, you are!" He shifted in his sack. "I'll tell you everything I know, Witch, if you'll let me go."

"Traitorous lee—" Wardof began.

Brusenna sang and the corn wrapped tightly over Wardof's nose and mouth. Over his muffled cursing, she considered Garg. He was clearly terrified of her—even more so than the dangerous man at his side. The realization shocked her. "I guess that depends on what you tell me."

Garg shot an anxious look Wardof's way before swallowing hard. "He came into town a few months ago. Met him over drinks, I did. Said he wanted to know if there was any Witches hereabouts. 'Course I told him of you and your ma. Got all interested. Said there was money in it for me if'n I help him. 'Course times been tight with the famine and all." He shot a look of contempt at her corn.

"Don't know how you managed to grow all this like you have," he muttered, squirming uncomfortably in its bonds. "So I helped him run the merchant you use outta business. He set up shop and waited for you whilst I rounded up some local boys to harass you."

"Local boys ... Oh!" She hugged herself tightly. "You sent Corwood to ... do that to me?"

He cleared his throat awkwardly. "They was just supposed to scare you. I swear it on my father's land and my firstborn's head—even though she's only a girl." At the look on her face, he tried to wriggle away from her. "I'm an honest man! It's just times been tough and all. I needed the money. What with a wife 'n kids 'n all. I wouldn't of let 'em hurt ya!"

She straightened her shoulders as her anger rose. "Scare me? Why?"

He jerked his head in Wardof's direction. "He wanted to make sure you was one. Said when Witches get cornered, even the most careful will take to chantin'." He chuckled. "You scared them boys good."

So it had been a trap and she'd played right into it. "What exactly were you going to do with me?"

He shrugged. "Wardof didn't say and I didn't ask. I didn't know about the knife until after. I swear I didn't!"

Brusenna felt certain Garg was lying—at least about some of it. The man was coward enough to lie his way to freedom. But Wardof ... she'd seen murder in his eyes. A Witch Hunter. Whatever he wanted her for, it wasn't pleasant.

But what to do with the two of them? She couldn't kill them, though she had to admit a part of her wanted to, and she couldn't leave them here to die of exposure. She pursed her lips in frustration. She needed help. But who would help a Witch?

Then she remembered. Sheriff Tomack. Her mother had said she could trust him. And he'd helped her once; perhaps he might do so again? But did she dare leave these two alone that long? What if they escaped? If only she could contact Tomack without leaving them. Her gaze snapped to Garg. A plan took shape in her head.

Kneeling next to him, she studied him until he was sweating and squirming like a boy with a pocketful of stolen candy. She kept her voice soft, for she'd learned from her mother that mildness felt like snow shoved down one's back on a winter's day. "Here's what you're going to do, Garg. You're going to the village to tell Sheriff Tomack this man threatened to do me harm, and you followed him here. He tried to hurt me, and you stopped him. He'll haul him off to jail, and it will be in your best interest to make sure he stays there."

Wardof pitched about and yowled like a cat in a bag, muffling indistinguishable threats and cursing. "You'll be the hero. Or…" she paused for effect … "I'll leave you tied up and get the authorities myself. Then you can do your time in the cell with Wardof. Though it seems to me he'd make a pretty rough cell mate."

Garg looked at Wardof, struggling like a madman, and then back at the mild-mannered Witch. "You won't curse me?"

Brusenna swallowed her laugh and leaned in close. "If you don't do this, nothing will ever grow in your soil again. I'll personally see to that."

Her threat had the desired effect. Garg's eyes widened in horror. He licked his dry lips. "All right. I'll do it. But you better make it clear I've never had dealins with you before. I'm a man of status. Can't be philanderin' around with Witches."

Brusenna stood and brushed the dirt from her shift. "Man of status, my eye," she muttered under her breath. "Dirty low-life thief is what you are. A drunkard too, by the looks of you."

He squinted at her. "Huh? What'd you say?"

Brusenna smiled with false sweetness. "I'm going to release you now. If you're not back with the sheriff by morning, I'll put a curse on your land forever." She sang the song to release him.

Garg scrambled to his feet. "How'm I to bring 'em here? No one but Wardof's ever been able to find you and then only 'cause he had the other half a that necklace."

An unprecedented amount of pitching erupted beside from the corn cob that was Wardof.

Finally, a bit of useful information. She pointed at Garg. "Hold him." The dog went into a crouch, his muscles coiled to spring. Garg swallowed hard and held perfectly still.

Brusenna sang the corn back, revealing pinpoints of hate emanating from Wardof's eyes. She shivered uncontrollably. "What does the necklace do?"

"Witch!" he said it like it was the vilest insult imaginable.

She sat on her heels next to him. "Answer me or I'll leave you here. The plants won't weaken. You'll die within days."

"Don't threaten something you can't finish, Witch."

The courage that had taken Brusenna over earlier waned under his blazing hatred. Could she? Could she really leave this man to die? But looking into his eyes, she knew he wouldn't hesitate to kill her. And if she let him go, he'd do just that. For long moments, she searched herself. What she found surprised her. A hard lump of brutality that fed off the mistreatments she'd endured her entire life. Its ferocity frightened her. "Yes, I can finish it."

For the first time, her words seemed to affect Wardof. His eyes widened in shock and he looked to Garg for help.

"I wouldn't count on it," she said. "I bet Garg wants nothing more than to pretend this didn't happen. If you don't tell me, he might."

"Every piece of information you collect from me will cost you."

Brusenna shrugged. "You'll kill me regardless … if you get the chance."

For the first time, Wardof stopped fighting his bonds. "The necklace comes in pairs. One half leads to the other. It's the fastest way to find a Witch lair."

"Where's the other half?"

Wardof's mouth hardened, but Brusenna saw Garg's eyes flick toward Wardof's pocket. When she reached for it, Wardof bucked and twisted. With help from Bruke, she managed to pin him down. Recognizing her, the corn shifted away. Trying not to think about how thin the fabric was that separated her skin from his, she reached inside and withdrew another pendant. This one wasn't a crescent moon like the one Brusenna had in the money box, but a waning gibbous moon. The two together would make a full moon.

All the breath left her body.

The sign of the Witches.

Trembling, she rounded on Wardof. "These necklaces were made by Witches. Where'd you get them?"

He shrugged nonchalantly. "From the first Witch I captured." How many had there been? Had her mother been one of them? She tossed the gibbous necklace to Garg. "Use that to make your way back. Be here by morning."

"I swear you'll die a most unpleasant death if you take that!" Wardof screeched. "Garg, take her!"

"She'll send the dog after me, Wardof," Garg whined.

"That pair is worth more than your village makes in a year!" Wardof threatened Garg.

"One more word," she said calmly, "and I'll only leave you one nostril to breathe through."

He clamped his mouth shut, but his eyes shot daggers her way.

Garg turned and ran like a mouse released from a cat's mouth.

Turning her back to Wardof, Brusenna asked, "Why do you hunt me?"

She heard the corn squeak as he settled back. "I'll wait for my captors. I'll escape and then I'll kill you."

Fear. Brusenna tasted it in her mouth, felt it coursing in

her veins. Somehow, she managed to conceal the terror from her voice. "Then you might as well tell me. Sounds like the knowledge won't be with me long."

He grunted, pleased with himself. He clearly wanted to frighten her. Wanted her to be terrified of him. "The Dark Witch has captured all the others. She sent me to chase after a rumor. That rumor turned out to be you."

Brusenna felt the blood pounding in her temples. She turned away so he couldn't see her face. "Captured?"

"Yes, captured. Are you deaf as well as ignorant? She captured the last of them days ago. But it was rumored one of the Witches had a daughter, so she sent me to make sure. It won't be long until she realizes I've been caught. Then she'll set me free. No matter where you go, we'll find you and you'll join your Keepers!"

Brusenna couldn't bear to hear any more. She sang the corn back over his mouth and stumbled back to her house. Mother and Coyel? Whatever they'd intended to do, they'd failed. The Dark Witch had captured them.

Could she really be the only Witch left?

Trudging up the stairs to her room, Brusenna sank to the floor, buried her face in her quilt and sobbed. When all her tears were spent, she slowly stood. Something had to be done. But what?

Then she remembered her mother's letter. The one she'd nearly burned.

Rushing into her mother's room, she emptied all the contents of the money box onto the floor. Brusenna found the letter. She broke the wax seal. But it was too dark to make out the words. Flinging open the curtains to let in a shaft of moonlight, she tried to read it. But her hands were shaking too badly. Smoothing the paper on the floor, she crouched over it.

My dearest Brusenna,

If the worst happens and the Hunters find you, you must take the gold and flee to Haven. It's the only place you'll be safe from them. To find it, face the rising sun

and sing the Dawn Song. It's in my journal. Follow that
path, no matter how impossible it may seem.
   I'm with you always,
   Mother

For the briefest moment, Brusenna could feel her mother's presence. Almost immediately, the feeling started slipping away. She tried to hold onto it, but it was as fleeting as a startled songbird. Sacra wasn't here. She was the prisoner of the Dark Witch. As were all the other Witches—a whole community of Witches Brusenna hadn't even known existed. Tears again streaked down Brusenna's face. Flinging them away, she folded the letter and pushed it in her pocket.

Just as she was turning to leave, a glint caught her eye. The pendant. Hesitantly, she traced the crescent with her fingertips. Making a sudden decision, she pulled it out and clasped it around her throat.

She pulled open her mother's drawers and hauled out a large satchel. She hadn't had time to sew herself new clothes, so she tugged one of her mother's heavy dresses over her head. She stuffed a second inside. Not knowing if it might turn cold again before she found Haven, she grabbed her only pair of shoes, a warm, but lightweight blanket, bedroll, flint and striker, one pot and soap. She wished she could take the time to bake travel bread, but there was no point in staying that long.

She kneeled before the stove, wiggled the brick free and grasped handfuls of sooty gold coins. Taking her new needle, she sewed them into a hidden pocket in the satchel. Last, she stuffed food in every remaining space. Seams pulled taut, Brusenna slung it over her shoulders, testing the weight. Would it be enough? She sighed, wishing she had a horse.

She looked around her home. "What am I forgetting?" she asked Bruke. He only looked at her with his dog eyes.

The Dawn Song! She went to her mother's journal and flipped through the pages. Settling down at her kitchen table, she found the song and began practicing.

5. THE LAST WITCH

Brusenna was slumped over, her chin bunched up on her chest, when Bruke woke her with a whine and a warm tongue. With a start, she took a deep breath and passed her hand over her face, smearing her nose with slobber. "Ew!" She wiped it dry with her sleeve and peered blearily out the window. She felt suddenly afraid. What if Wardof escaped last night?

She rushed to the beginning of the corn row and breathed a sigh of relief to see the bundle still securely wrapped. She glanced up and saw the first hints of light on the tree tops. Dawn would be here in moments. The journal said to wait until the first rays touched her face before singing. Not wanting Wardof to hear even the slightest bit of the song, she ran to the far side of the pumpkins.

She squared her shoulders and opened her mouth.

Oh morning light, hear my cry,
To Haven I must fly.

As she sang, mist rose up from the ground. It congealed and thickened. The moment the light hit the mist, it turned golden and flashed with small sparks. Brusenna watched in awe as the mist trailed toward the northwest—the opposite direction of Gonstower. Then, as quickly as it appeared, the mist vaporized. Brusenna let out all of her breath in a rush. "Northwest."

To the northwest was Perchance, capitol of the Harden City-State, of which Gonstower was a small part. Beyond lay the next City-State, Urway, which held Nefalie's capital, Tressalay. Beyond that, Brusenna's knowledge was scant. She knew Nefalie was a small country, with Gonstower in the middle and it had a long coast line, though she'd never seen the sea and couldn't imagine how tired her eyes would be if the view went on without end.

Back at the house, she added the journal to her overflowing satchel. No sooner had she set it by the door than Bruke's ears lifted and his growl morphed into a bark. Brusenna stiffened. The trees and brush parted. In all her life, only Coyel had openly entered the clearing around her home. But now, a horde of men emerged from the trees. She blinked in disbelief, but they were still there, lead by Garg.

She placed a hand on Bruke's head. "Stand down."

With a groan that ended in a whine, the dog sat on his haunches and glared at the intruders.

She surveyed the men invading her fields. At least twelve of them; Garg in the lead. In his hand, the leather thong trailed behind the floating pendant. The pendant steered directly toward her. Unconsciously, her fingertips found the pendant inside her dress. Smooth and hard, it felt warm to her touch.

When Sheriff Tomack caught sight of her, he put a hand on Garg's shoulder and motioned to one of his men to stay with the fat man. Then, the sheriff snatched the pendant and held it in his large fist while signaling for all but two of his men to leave. Once his men had left, the Sheriff stepped closer to Brusenna. "In front of my witnesses, please describe the events."

Brusenna watched with delight as all but Sheriff Tomack's face went green as she told of binding Wardof with the corn.

He held out the other half of the amber necklace, the waning gibbous. "I figure it should be yours after the trouble Wardof put you through."

Brusenna studied the pendant as it twisted and twirled, catching the sunlight as it strained toward her. She'd forgotten about it until now. She reached out. At her touch, it went limp. She rubbed the stone beneath her thumbs. After only a moment's hesitation, she eased the thong over her head. Laying them side by side, she pushed. The pieces fit together with a click. Her eyes widened as the pendant began to glow. Thin streamers of light swirled away from it. All plants the light touched grew and turned a richer shade of green. Slowly the light faded to nothing. Her heart beating in her throat, she stared at the now-full moon—nothing but a thin curving seam showed where the two pieces parted.

Strangely, Sheriff Tomack didn't seem surprised by the show. He leaned and whispered, "Miss, if you ever need anything again, you come to me. Understand?"

Tears stung Brusenna's eyes. Perhaps her mother had been right about them having friends. "Thank you."

"What happened to your mother? She dead?"

Brusenna cringed. "I don't know."

He studied her. "What else do you need?"

Brusenna sniffed and wiped her nose. "I'm going to look for my mother, but if I leave everything ..." she gestured to her home.

Sheriff Tomack looked around. "I can look after things while you're gone, if you like?"

Brusenna nodded. "If I'm not here, the forest will forget in about a week. You should have no trouble finding it then. My livestock ... I don't know what to do about them."

"Tell you what I'll do. I'll take them to my place. As payment, you let me keep all they produce. When you come back, you take them back fair and square."

Brusenna nodded. "And all the food that will sour?"

He crossed his arms. "We could trade."

She thought about that for a moment. "I need a horse."

"Show me what you have then."

She took him into the cellar. He surveyed her stocked shelves in awe. "With the famine the way it is, I'd say this is well worth a horse. There's enough here to feed my family for a year or more." He turned back toward her. "One horse, a saddle and a pack. Whaddya say? Do we have an accord?"

He stuck out his hand. Brusenna hesitated. The last person to touch her had tried to kill her. But her triumph last night made her feel bold. She stuck her small hand in his large one. "Deal."

"Have you any paper and ink?"

She retrieved some and he went about writing a note. "My brother, Wittin, lives in Perchance, the next city northwest of here. Runs a horse business. This note'll get you anything you need; I'll pay him next we meet."

Brusenna took the paper and quickly scanned it. It said exactly what Sheriff Tomack had said. She glanced nervously at the Sheriff. She'd never really trusted anyone before. The closest she'd ever come was Wardof. She had no idea if this place even existed. How did she know he wasn't lying?

Sheriff Tomack must have noticed her hesitation. "Wary, I see." He pulled a gold pocket watch from his vest. He caressed the face before handing it reluctantly to her. "Give this to my brother when you see him. It's well worth a horse and saddle and he'll recognize it as the one Father gave me when I left home. The Creators know, we fought over it enough."

Brusenna took the watch shyly, dropping it and his note in the pocket that held her mother's note. He gave her an encouraging smile. "I don't claim to understand the ways of Witches, but I know if you help one in need, you'll be repaid a hundred fold."

She stared at him in awe. "If I don't come back in time, you can keep the rest of the harvest. Just save us plenty of seeds."

He grunted. "See, you've already more'n paid me."

She started past Tomack but then paused. "Make sure Wardof doesn't know where I'm going."

He gave her an even look. "He won't be getting out any time soon, I can promise you that."

"He said when the others," she deliberately left out the name Dark Witch, "found out, they'd release him."

"Oh he did, did he?" Sheriff Tomack rubbed his beard. "Well, I'll think of something." With a nod, Sheriff Tomack left to feed her stock enough to last for the week it would take for the forest to forget. She turned to the northwest. "Well Bruke, I guess we're going to Perchance. Have you ever been there before?"

As if he knew exactly where he was going, he bound off in front of her. At the edge of the clearing, Brusenna turned back. Her home. Memories like drifting snowflakes swirled in her mind. She pushed them aside. The other Witches needed her. "I'm coming, Mother."

6. Guardians

In the early morning light, Brusenna carefully separated the branches of the bush she was hiding behind and peered at the city in the distance. Her breath made a small cloud as she exhaled, momentarily blurring her view. Her gut clenched and bile rose in her throat. Towns meant people. And people had never been good to her.

But she needed a horse. Plus she'd been traveling through virgin forest for two days and she'd eaten all her food. She needed more supplies. Shifting her satchel to ease the ache between her shoulder blades, she steeled herself before leaving the cover of trees to step onto the baked, yellow path. "I don't think I should use my real name anymore," she said softly to Bruke. "From now on, I'll use Senna."

Like Gonstower, Perchance had the same frame houses with split-shingle roofs. The poorer parts of town were a dull, cheerless gray, while homes in the richer parts gleamed with white paint and dark trims. But as Senna drew nearer, she realized that was where the similarities ended—Perchance was easily four times the size of Gonstower.

She nearly turned and fled back the way she'd come. But if she couldn't even face strangers, how could she fight the Dark Witch? "They don't know you're a Witch," she muttered to herself. "Just keep your head down and stay out of trouble.

It wasn't long before Senna started passing people. She felt the hard lump in her gut soften as the bustling people continued to pay her no mind. For the first time in her life, no one was glaring or pointing or whispering. "Anonymity is a wonderful thing," she whispered to Bruke.

Bruke, who had glued himself to her side, looked up at her and whined.

Upon entering the marketplace, she noted that instead of just outdoor booths, Perchance also had buildings with elaborate signs indicating everything from shoe cobblers to master looms.

Senna stopped at the first money changer she found. The man behind the counter bit her gold, weighted it and turned it over several times before announcing his price. "One silver, ten upice."

Determined to get a fair price, Senna snatched it back. "I'll go somewhere else with it then."

"Wait now! Wait!" He hustled to come between her and the door. "All right, two silver and ten upice."

She gave him a look of exasperation.

He snorted. "Two silvers, twenty-five upice and not one single coin more!"

"Done." She handed over the coin with a flourish. Her pocket jingling with lesser money, Senna bought Bruke a dozen dried fish. Then she ordered herself a breakfast of hot squash with cream and sugar and a slice of thick, soft bread to eat it with. And because she couldn't resist, a dozen honeycakes.

She saved the honeycakes for last, savoring every tiny bite. At first, the honey was strong and sweet, but it also dissolved earliest. When it did, she was left with the medley of citrus and nuts. When nothing but a bit of doughy bread remained, she finally allowed herself to swallow.

When she'd licked every bit of sticky goodness off her fingers, she reluctantly wrapped up the rest for later. She found a bathhouse. After scrubbing her skin pink, she washed her clothes, donned a clean dress and braided her hair. With her wet clothes hanging over her satchel to dry, she bought her supplies and made her way back to the friendly merchant who had sold her the honeycakes—a pleasant-looking woman with a beautiful, curly-haired daughter.

"Don't tell me you want more!" the woman exclaimed upon seeing Senna.

Senna patted her stomach. "Unfortunately, no. I was actually hoping you knew of a man by the name of Wittin."

The woman's brow puckered as she tapped her chin with her finger. "Wittin, Wittin. Ah, yes, the horseman. Lives on the north side of town." She pointed and gave directions.

Senna weaved her way through the richer part of town. A fair distance from the village, she saw a small house—at least compared to the stables beside it. Along the path, horses of every breed and color played, ate or rested. She looked from one to another and felt her uncertainty grow. The only experience she had with horses was their plow horse that had been shot by a boy on a dare. Draft horses were too slow and cumbersome for much riding.

At the stables, she stepped up to the half-door. The paint was shiny and it looked as clean as a barn could. "Hello?" Nothing. She looked down at Bruke. "You know where they are?"

He snuffed the air and looked back at her. "Well, let's see what they've got. Maybe we could pick one out by the time they get here." She swung open the door and stepped inside. The air was heavy with the warm smell of horses, manure, hay and dirt. Shafts from the windows caught bits of dust, illuminating swirls of air currents.

The first few stalls she passed, the horses snorted indignantly at Bruke. He didn't seem to notice. Senna looked at each and every horse. Black, bay, palomino, sorrel, buckskin. Some were large and squarely built. Others had fine bones and delicate features. Each was different and yet so much of the same. "I have no idea!" she exclaimed as her head swung from one stall to the next.

Then she paused at one of the stalls. A sorrel akin to chestnut. On his forehead, a sliver of a moon; on his muzzle, a snip. Brusenna fingered her necklace as she looked him over. His eyes were gentle and inquisitive. She reached out. He dipped down, allowing her to scratch under his forelock. "Hello," she murmured softly. "What's your name?"

"Knight." The answer came from behind her. Senna whirled around to see a boy—no, a man—no, a boy. Well, at any rate, a boy who was nearly a man, coming toward her.

"Something I can do for you, miss?"

He wasn't handsome, necessarily. His ears stuck out a bit and his chin was a little too soft. But the longer she looked at him, the more she decided maybe he was. He was tall—head and shoulders taller than her. Thin, but in a strong way. He had a crop of brown hair that hung low over his forehead. His legs bowed out at the knees—probably from riding so much. He had a permanent wrinkle around his eyes, as if he never stopped smiling long enough for the lines to smooth out. He was smiling at her now. Unable to help herself, she smiled back. "I want to buy this horse."

He folded his arms across his chest and leaned against the stall. "Well, Knight is an expensive kind of horse. He's young, with plenty of vinegar, but he's also gentle. Not many horses are both."

"Vinegar?"

He chuckled and she liked the easy way he smiled. "It means he's got a lot of energy—a lot of kick." He stuck out his hand. Senna stared uncertainly at it before reaching out. She felt the calluses on his rough skin. "Name's Joshen."

"Senna."

"Well, Senna. If you're still interested, I could saddle him and you could take him for a ride."

Senna looked back at Knight. "I'd like that."

Joshen retrieved a halter and caught the horse. He opened the gate wide and stepped out. "I'd have to check our books for certain, but I'm sure Knight is worth at least three gold coins. We've a lot less pricey stock that'd work just fine."

Senna knew Joshen was trying to make sure she could pay. But she decided the less she said the better. "I'll need tack as well."

At this, he stopped and turned to her. "Depending on the saddle, that's another two."

She folded her arms across her chest. "You think I can't pay you?"

Clearly uncomfortable, he rubbed his jaw. "Well, I don't mean to be rude, Senna, but not many girls have that kind of money."

She reached inside her pocket and pulled out the Sheriff's note and gold watch. Without a word, she handed them to him.

As Knight stole a mouthful of hay from another horse's feeder, Joshen scanned the note. Halfway through, he glanced at her in astonishment. When he finished it, he held it tight in his hand, as if afraid someone might snatch it from him. "So you're Brusenna?"

The blood drained from Senna's face. The note didn't mention her full name.

Without another word, Joshen led Knight to a post and tied him off. "Wait here. I'll be back."

Grabbing the straps of her satchel, she considered slipping away. Before she could, Bruke trotted over to a pile of hay and lay down, his head between his paws. The dog seemed to have an innate sense of who was an enemy and who was a friend. He'd known the necklace was trouble. But since she'd taken the other half from Wardof, he hadn't given it a second glance. Senna slowly shook her head. "All right, if you trust him, so will I."

Finding a brush, she started working the dust from Knight's coat. Hair and dirt flew everywhere. She turned when something blocked the light. A burly man stood in the doorway with Joshen at his side. Letting the brush drop, Senna faced them.

"Name's Wittin. Joshen here tells me you brought this note from my brother, Tomack."

Senna glanced at Bruke. The dog still didn't seem concerned. Gritting her teeth, she answered, "Yes."

Wittin's eyes narrowed. "You've had trouble with Witch Hunters."

It wasn't a question. Senna unconsciously took a step back, bumping into Knight. She felt cornered … and very, very alone. "How did you know that?"

He turned to his son. "Joshen, why don't you go catch Stretch." After glancing at Senna, Joshen grabbed a halter and a bucket of oats and headed toward one of the pastures Senna had seen earlier.

Wittin took a few limping steps toward her. "There were things your mother never told you. I'm one of them."

She was glad for Knight's solid presence behind her—she wasn't sure she would be standing otherwise. "You knew my mother?"

Wittin rubbed his stubbled jaw. "For nearly twenty years. Her and Coyel came to see me a while back. Said if I saw you, I was to tell you the things you'd need to know."

All the breath left her body in a rush. "What things?"

Wittin inhaled deeply. "About the Witch War."

Ever since Coyel had appeared in her life, Senna had wanted answers. But now, she was afraid. And she wasn't sure she should trust Wittin. "Why didn't she just tell me herself? She could've written it in the note."

"Not the kind of thing you write down. And she was hoping to protect you."

Senna thought of all the times she'd been bullied and ridiculed. "Protect me? Like she protected me the day I was thrown in the stocks! How is that protecting me?"

Wittin's gaze hardened. "You should pray to the Creators you never experience the pain your mother has."

He turned away, staring out the barn door at the house and pastures beyond. "You have to understand, a good many people don't believe the Witches' powers are real. Take this blasted drought. They think it's just a twist of fate, that the seasons rule themselves. But they don't. The Witches control it.

"And a good many of the ones who do believe … well, they blame the Witches for every failed crop, every early frost. They don't realize that handling the seasons is more like controlling a half-wild colt than ordering a side of beef from a butcher.

"Then there's another group—they see the Witches' power and resent and fear them for it. It's what started the war. A group of Witches grew tired of being snubbed by men. They decided to sell their songs for money and power. But the other Witches, the Keepers, believed everyone had the right to their songs. The dissenters broke away from the main group. Called themselves Espen's Servants. Each Witch took a side."

Senna couldn't picture her mother caught up in a war.

"Many, many Witches died. Eventually, the last of the Keepers went into hiding at Haven—except your mother and you." Wittin's voice caught. "Do you understand now why your mother hid you away? Why she thought Gonstower's prejudices were a minor inconvenience?"

Senna kicked at the dirt. "She didn't want me to be a real Witch."

Wittin turned to face her. "I wouldn't say that. She just wanted to keep you as far away from danger as possible. I didn't necessarily agree, but you weren't my daughter. She did the best she could."

Tears leaked from Senna's eyes—tears of anger and betrayal as much as sadness. "But I was born a part of it."

Wittin didn't look away. "If she'd stayed with the Keepers, you'd have been brought up training to fight Espen. She didn't want that for you."

"She could've at least taught me to defend myself!"

Wittin didn't respond. Senna understood he'd run out of answers. Only her mother had the rest. And she was gone.

He shook his head, sadness in his eyes. "Your mother said it was bad—there were only eight fully trained Witches left, the rest nothing but girls. But, if the Hunters are after you—an untrained girl ... My guess is you might be the only Witch left."

Senna took a deep breath. "And the Witch Hunters ..."

"A division of Espen's Servants." Wittin rolled up his sleeve, revealing a green tattoo about the size and shape of a round pebble. "But Espen isn't the only one to use men."

Unable to help herself, she reached for it, but stopped short of actually touching him. "The full moon is a mark of the Witches." She was surprised by the hint of warning in her voice. But she was sick of people misusing Witch symbols.

Wittin fingered the raised edges. "They mark us as a Guardian when we've proven ourselves worthy. Sacra marked me and my brother long ago, but then Espen snapped my leg and I couldn't be much help, so Tomack's been keeping an eye out for you and your mother—as much as she'd let him, anyway."

"I thought you got bucked off a horse!" Joshen joked as he came into the barn.

His father smiled as he tugged his sleeve down. The older man watched his son tie the leggy bay to the post. "I'd go with you myself." He shot a look of exasperation at his leg. "But I wouldn't be much good to you." He reached out and patted Knight's neck fondly. "I'll miss this one. He's the type of horse that makes my job worth it."

Senna looked at the horse and then back at Wittin, not really understanding.

"You two do what you must to keep safe, you hear?"

"Why would you help me?" Senna blurted.

Something like anger flashed in his eyes. "Because I know better."

His comment was vague and she knew it was meant to be. Then it dawned on her that he'd said "two" and Joshen was readying another horse. "You want to come with me?"

Joshen and Wittin exchanged incredulous glances.

"Do you mean to go alone?" Wittin asked.

"Well, yes." The two men exchanged glances again and Senna began to think she was missing something.

Wittin rubbed his jaw. "I don't think you understand, Brusenna. You're not just here to pick up a horse. Your mother meant for Joshen to come with you."

Senna stared at Joshen in disbelief.

He stood up straighter. "I'm not a Guardian yet, but I've been training for it my whole life. I'm one of the best horsemen around and a right good shot with a musket."

Senna shrugged. "I'm not so bad myself." She immediately regretted her words. She'd never shot a musket in her life. Never even held one.

Wittin thumbed his nose roughly, no doubt noticing she didn't actually have a musket. "Now don't be gettin' all prideful on me. You're going to need help before you're through."

"I'll manage," she responded. The thought of being alone with any man, even one as friendly as Joshen, seemed oppressive.

Some silent communication passed between them. Wittin jerked his head "no." Joshen pursed his lips in frustration.

"All right then, Senna," Wittin finally said. "But if you change your mind, we're here."

She rested a nervous hand on Bruke's head. "Thank you." With another exchanged glance and a nod her way, the two men brought out squeaky leather tack from a locked room. When Knight was fully outfitted in a soft-hued calfskin saddle, his coat seemed even deeper. Senna stroked his neck appreciatively before turning to the two men. Tomack had been kind to her and she'd seen how much this watch meant to him. She wanted him to have it back, but she didn't want to deny Wittin his payment. "In addition, I'd like to buy Tomack's watch back."

Wittin pulled the watch from his pocket and caressed the gold back. "Keep it." He handed it to her and limped back to the house.

Joshen studied her carefully. "My father and uncle fought over that watch after Grandpa died. Take care of it."

With that, he too, strode away. When they were gone, Senna slipped the watch and five gold pieces under the locked tack room door. Then she led Knight outside, stepped into the stirrup and pulled herself up. With a gentle nudge from her, Knight moved eastward.

7. A Taste of Foolishness

Fanning herself with a heavily starched piece of cloth, Berlie watched over her honeycakes and bread with half-closed eyes. She had spent the predawn hours in her sweltering kitchen and the remainder of the day at her booth. Cooking wasn't so bad, but she didn't enjoy watching her wares spoil in the sun. No one, it seemed, had bought much today. She turned to her young daughter, Dall. "Maybe we should just call it a day."

"Do I get to eat some honeycakes?" the child clasped her small hands under her chin and leaned eagerly forward.

Usually, they only ate the bread that went stale or moldy. Berlie opened her mouth to say no, but stopped at the crestfallen look on Dall's face. "All right. You may have one now. One more when you finish your supper."

Interlocking her fingers, her daughter squealed in delight and bounced from her chair to the honeycakes.

Berlie started packing up when a voice startled her. She jumped and turned.

"Oh, I'm sorry ma'am," a man said.

He was about Berlie's age. And oh, he was handsome. She pressed her hand against her chest and took a deep breath. "Oh, that's alright. What would you like to buy?"

He shook his head gravely. "Unfortunately, I'm not here to buy. I'm looking for a young girl who may have passed this way."

Berlie crossed her arms over her chest. She remembered all too well the thin girl who had devoured her honeycakes as if she'd never tasted one before. "And who might you be?"

He leaned forward. "She's a runaway, you know."

Berlie knew that look. The look of a man after a girl who had shamed him, not someone he was worried about. "You should've never married one so young," she said through clenched teeth, remembering her own wedding day.

He quickly backtracked and, she thought, changed tactics. "No, no. She's not my wife. She's my sister."

Berlie pursed her lips. "I can read a lie on a man's face as easily as decipher a sign above a shop door. I've nothing to sell to you; and if you don't leave, I'll summon the sheriff!"

The man took a menacing step forward, but Bloy, from the booth next to Berlie's, spoke up, "You alright Berlie?" Bloy wasn't looking at her. He was looking at the man.

She gave Bloy a small smile. He was as ugly as a mule, but as gentle as the softest breeze. He'd asked her to marry him more than once. Perhaps next time, she'd say yes.

With a wide smile, the man turned into an amiable stranger again. "I'll just be on my way."

Wringing her hands to steady their shaking, Berlie nodded appreciatively to Bloy. Her daughter's sticky face had lost its grin. Bending down, she kissed Dall's forehead. "It's alright, sweetie. Let's go home and get some supper so you can have that other honeycake."

That was all it took for Dall to forget the exchange. Berlie finished loading her cart and pulled it up the hill to the poorer side of town.

When she reached her run-down house, she hauled up the cellar door. She could still sell her wares for half price to her neighbors when they returned from their day's labors. Descending the ladder, she shut her eyes and took a moment to enjoy the delicious coolness. A sound made her start. She'd half-turned when a hand clamped over her mouth and pulled her down the last two stairs. She bit down hard on a pair of fat fingers.

"Ow!"

Berlie rushed for the ladder, but a hand seized her ankle and hauled her back. She cracked her head on a rung. Hot blood ran down her forehead. But she'd been in scuffles before. Her husband had been that kind of man. Rushing her attacker, she buried her knee in his crotch. With a groan, he doubled over.

Heaving herself out of the cellar, she slammed it shut and gripped the table to pull it over the door. But what she saw stopped her cold. Her beautiful daughter sat wide-eyed on the lap of the man from the market. He took a bite of a honeycake and smiled. "Delicious."

Berlie couldn't move.

He set the pastry down and roughly stroked Dall's blonde curls. "I wonder how you would feel if you lost someone you love, all because you wouldn't tell a man where his sister was?"

Berlie heard sounds from below. A second later, the fat man pushed open the cellar door. "How come I always get the nasty jobs?" he grumbled as he hobbled up the ladder.

The man holding her daughter didn't answer his companion. "Come now. This isn't hard. Tell me where she went. I'll tie up you and your daughter. Someone's bound to come looking for you, eventually."

Berlie felt trapped. As trapped as when her father had insisted she marry the "wealthy" baker at fourteen. As trapped as when he'd backed her into a corner and beat her to a bloody pulp. As trapped as when he had died and left her with a new baby to look after at fifteen. "She went to Wittin's to buy a horse."

The man smiled broadly and took another bite of the honeycake. "There now, that wasn't so hard, was it?"

After he'd tied them both up, he patted her shoulder as the other man stuffed a gag in her mouth. "It's too bad innocent people have to get caught up in this sort of thing. But I assure you, it's for a good cause."

Berlie glared at him as he picked up the last honeycake, lifted it in farewell and shut her door behind him. It took some doing, but she finally managed to break herself free. Poor Dall had fallen asleep with a gag in her mouth. After releasing her, Berlie scooped her up and laid her in her bed. She woke the instant Berlie crossed the threshold. "Mommy, they ate all the honeycakes!"

Berlie managed a smile. "I'll make some tomorrow, just for you. How would that be?"

Dall smacked her lips. "Fresh ones?"

"Still hot."

"Okay, Mommy."

Berlie kissed her forehead. "Mommy will send a neighbor to look after you; I need to tell the sheriff about those bad men."

Dall's eyes narrowed. "You tell them, Mommy. He won't get any honeycakes in jail!"

***

Joshen tossed another forkful of hay into the feeder and stepped back to survey his work. All along the barn, the line of horses munched their supper contentedly. Resting the pitchfork against the wall, he picked up some saddle oil and opened the door to the tack room. "What in the ..." He bent down and retrieved the gold coins and pocket watch. He shook his head in amazement. "Help a Witch and you'll be repaid tenfold," he murmured.

"What was that?" He heard from the other side of the door. Stuffing the coins and watch in his pocket, Joshen peeked around the door. A stranger, he'd guess in his mid-twenties, stood next to a heavy man. "Be right with you." He couldn't understand the sudden urge to lock the tack room door, but he was a believer in instinct. "What can I do for you fellows?" he asked as he turned the lock and slipped the key in his pocket.

The taller of the two men smiled warmly enough, but it was the smile of a man coming to steal your wife. "I'd like to buy a couple of horses."

Joshen gestured for them to walk ahead of him down the row of horses—he'd rather not turn his back on either of them. "Anything in particular?"

The man stopped to stroke a buckskin's cheek. "Something with speed and stamina." He turned to him. "You sold anything like that recently?"

Why did Joshen get the feeling the man was asking about Senna? "We sell a lot of horses, mister."

"Course you do," the man replied as he continued down the row. He stopped in front of one of Joshen's best geldings. Opening the stall, the man ran his hands over the bay's legs and studied his confirmation. "I think I'll take this one. My friend here, the buckskin I saw earlier."

Joshen nodded and reached for a couple halters. He caught both horses and led them to the hitching posts. He started picking their hooves when the man spoke again. "Have you seen a young girl come this way? She would've had a big dog with her."

Joshen froze, the pick still wedged under a dried bit of manure. Were these the two Hunters after Senna? By the Creators, she was in more trouble than she knew what to do with. He surveyed the men with an expert eye. The fat one, he could take easily. But the other one ... he looked like he knew his way around a fight. And between the two of them ...

Joshen didn't like the odds. Not unarmed, anyway. He released the horse's hoof and slowly straightened. "I'm sorry, mister. I just realized these horses aren't for sale."

The man's eyes narrowed. The shorter, fatter one leaned in. "We can take him, Wardof."

"Garg, I told you not to use my name. Idiot! If I wasn't stuck with you, I swear, I'd have killed you already." Wardof took a menacing step forward. "Why do you want to protect her?"

Joshen thought fast. If he could just get outside the barn, his father would see what was going on. He edged toward the door. "I don't mean to protect her, but I won't get involved either. Witches make bad enemies."

"I make a worse one."

Joshen shook his head. "Can you make it so my land never grows another living thing?"

Wardof's voice went low and deadly, "No, but I know someone who can. If you live long enough, that is."

Joshen's palms were slick with sweat and his mouth felt as dry as flour. He'd been in fights before, but not with Hunters. He'd been taught to ignore his pride and do what he had to do to win. "I didn't see which way she went, but my dad might have. I'll go get him."

Wardof's hand clamped down on his shoulder. "It wouldn't make much sense for you to even out our numbers, would it?" Joshen tried to twist away, but then the fat fellow gripped his other arm. He was faster than he looked.

Joshen dropped to the floor, trying to use his weight to throw them off. Both Hunters stumbled. Joshen wrenched his arms free and side-swiped Wardof's legs out from under him.

"Jump on him, Garg!"

Before Joshen could scramble to his feet, Garg threw himself over him. Wardof buried his fist into Joshen's belly. Joshen doubled over as all the air was forced from his lungs.

Two sets of hands hauled him up and shoved him roughly into the tack room door. Joshen felt the knob bruise his back.

"Where is she, boy?"

Hunched over, he tried to catch his breath. "I'm not telling you dung-lickers anything!" His whole body tensed as they came at him, fists balled. But he wasn't going down easy. He ducked to the side, trying to create enough space to use his longer reach.

He didn't make it very far. They shoved him into the wall and pummeled him. Joshen curled up, his arms raised to protect himself, only occasionally managing to get a jab in. The horses were going crazy, whinnying and kicking in their stalls. Over their racket, he heard a mighty bellow. He looked up as both men were yanked off of him and tossed like bales of hay. His limp barely noticeable, Wittin heaved Wardof up by his shoulders. His meaty fist landed in the man's pretty face.

Proud to the point he was almost giddy, Joshen scrambled into action, tackling the fat man just as he reached his feet. They rolled in the hay and dirt until Joshen pinned him.

Garg tried to wiggle free. "Lemme go! Lemme go!"

Joshen gripped tighter, wondering what he was going to do with Garg now that he had him in a choke hold.

Wardof wasn't doing too well with Joshen's father. Wittin pummeled him like he was a pillow in need of a good fluffing. Wardof hit the ground and lay still. Wittin stood over him, his breathing ragged and rage still smoldering in his eyes. He turned to Joshen. "All right, son?"

"Been better."

Wittin grunted. In three strides, he had a halter in his hands. His limp more pronounced now, he surveyed the hold Joshen had. "Let's roll him onto his stomach. Put your knee into his neck. If he tries to move, push down for all you're worth."

Joshen released his grip slightly. The man scrambled. Joshen squeezed again. His father buried his knuckle in the man's temple. Garg went limp in Joshen's arms.

"So much for trying to be gentle-like about the whole thing," his father said gruffly.

They hog-tied both men and then dragged them into a corner of the barn. Joshen's mother, Qarin, came from the house, wiping her flour-white hands on her apron. "What is all this confounded commotion going on down here?"

Wittin motioned to the two unconscious men. Qarin's eyes widened.

"I heard the horses," his father explained, "and come in from the pasture to see Hunters poundin' Joshen."

The fat man moaned and moved. Wittin jerked his head toward the door. The three left the barn and stood next to the house, where neither man would overhear them.

"Suppose they were after Senna?" he asked Joshen. Gently rubbing his tender abdomen, Joshen nodded.

His father's eyes formed a question as they met Qarin's. "Mother?"

With tears in her eyes, Qarin nodded. "You're right. The safety of the Witches is everyone's responsibility. And if she really is the last, she's going to need all the help we can give her."

His father grunted as he rubbed his bad leg. "We both knew he'd have to take over someday."

Joshen glanced suspiciously at his parents. "But, you let her go!" Wittin shrugged. "A Guardian protects his Witch—even from herself. Brusenna refused to let you go with her. So you'll follow behind."

Excitement surged in Joshen's chest. Senna had left a couple hours ago. Her trail would still be fresh. And she hadn't seemed like much of a rider. He would catch up to her easily. He would finally be able to prove himself a Guardian as renowned as his father.

The sound of rushing hooves brought them around. A dark formation of horses pounded up the path in the growing twilight. As they came closer, Joshen recognized the sheriff and his volunteers. The sheriff nodded a curt greeting as he pulled up his horse. "Berlie, the baker, told us some men tied her and her daughter up before heading this way. You seen them?"

Wittin jerked his thumb over his shoulder, toward the barn. "They're tied up in the stables."

The sheriff's eyes widened as he glanced at Wittin's bum leg and Joshen's gangly build. "You two took them both?"

"Course we did!" His father crossed his arms over his chest, clearly insulted.

The sheriff held up a hand. "Well, all I meant is they seemed like pretty rough men ... according to Berlie," he added quickly.

"They tried to steal our horses. When Joshen didn't let them, they started thumping him. I evened out the numbers some. They tumbled pretty easy after that."

The sheriff brought out some parchment and scratched furiously as Wittin spoke. Joshen, Wittin and two of his volunteers signed the document as witnesses and rounded up the now-conscious men, slung them over their horse's backs like sacks of potatoes and waved goodbye.

Wittin watched them go with a wary eye. "Them two won't be in prison for long." His gaze fell on Joshen. "I think it's time you joined the cause, boy."

**

Wardof tossed his stale bread back on the tray. "We wouldn't be here if you weren't such an imbecile."

"Wha'd I do?" Garg cried.

"You used my first name."

Garg shrugged. "So? Not like it made any difference. The horseman would'a still pounded you raw."

"You didn't do any better with that gangly kid," Wardof shot back.

"You're supposed to be the Hunter. You should'a had that Witch at the house. Then we wouldn't be searchin' the whole city state lookin' for her!"

Wardof shook his head in disgust. "I told you, there's only two ways to capture a Witch—catch them in their sleep or manage to cover their mouths before they can start singing. How was I supposed to know she'd have a dog to wake her?"

"You should'a watched the house longer," Garg replied.

"How'd a half-wit like you come to be over Perchance district anyway?"

"No one else wanted to live in Gonstower," Garg grumbled.

"That explains it," Wardof sneered.

Garg shot him a look of hate. "Don't call me no more names."

Bringing his bruised face closer, Wardof beckoned Garg toward him. "You wanna do something to stop me, you dull, fat, laughable excuse for Espen's Servant!"

Garg lunged at him. The tray and its contents went flying, covering both men with split pea soup. Wardof had just managed to twist Garg into a headlock when the door creaked open. Flowing black folds swept into the room.

"Stand up, you two incompetents!"

Wardof knew that voice. Releasing his grip, he and Garg clambered to their feet. Wardof took in her wavy hair and green eyes. If he didn't know her, he would have thought her beautiful.

"Espen," he began. "I know I told you I'd have her by now, but—"

"I told you to find her," Espen interrupted. "A simple girl. Untrained even." She began pacing, eyeing them like a hawk circling its prey. "And yet you have failed me. Twice. Both times, I've had to save you from the law. Both times, I've had to leave my charges." Her eyes flashed as she stepped toward them. "I'd find her myself, but the new captives are still fighting me and I can't leave them until they are more complacent." Whipping around, she pinched their noses and yanked hard.

Awkward as it was, Wardof didn't fight her grip as she dragged them from the cell. He saw enough of the guardroom to know both of their guards were wrapped in poison barbus. Gorgeous orange blooms filled the whole room with a heady scent that made Wardof's eyes heavy. Only his nose being pinched shut and his fear kept him moving as the vines coiled around the sheriff's men like fat snakes. Within hours, the barbus would dissolve their flesh.

When they reached fresh air, Espen released them and glided forward. Rubbing his nose, Wardof took his place ten paces behind her. As they walked past a tavern, he groaned inwardly. Inebriated men rarely missed Espen's beauty.

He certainly hadn't. And now look where he was.

Sure enough, an appreciative patron stepped out and called, "Hey, lovely! Care to come take a drink with Tomund?"

Espen kept walking.

Garg shot the man a warning look. Not surprisingly, the man didn't catch it.

Tomund took off, jogging to catch up with her. "Come on now, I'll buy you some ale."

Espen whirled on him. Wardof and Garg instantly backpedaled. "If I had any desire for a …" she looked him over and spat, "man, I would've responded the first time. But seeing you are persistently foolish, I'll give you a taste of foolishness." Taking a small container from her belt, she coated her mouth with a waxy substance and, singing softly, brought her full lips toward his.

Delighted, the man leaned down, but the moment their lips met, he backed up and looked about in confusion. "Who am I? Who are you?"

She smiled. "I'm your mother and I'm telling you that you must jump. Jump all day and all night. Forever and ever."

With an expression of grim determination, the man started jumping as high and as hard as he could.

Wardof exchanged an ominous look with Garg. Had her mood been as foul when she'd "recruited" him, that could have been his fate. They both knew the power Espen held over them.

At the edge of the forest, Espen sang a Ring of Power into existence—the trees groaned as they obediently circled. She called upon the wind. She'd leeched enough power from her captives that the wind lifted her up and away. In less than an hour, she'd be back in her domain.

Wardof fingered his own crescent moon pendant, almost wishing he could break it off and throw it in the sea, bury it deep within the Earth, or melt it in a blacksmith's fire so Espen could never find him again. But that was foolishness. She'd find him. And she'd make him pay.

Besides, a little Witch was out there. Somewhere.

He mustn't keep her waiting.

8. THE DAWN SONG

For the next few days, the Dawn Song directed Senna northeast. She moved quickly, choosing roads far from towns and people. At some point, she seemed to pass an invisible barrier that turned back all the storms Perchance should have had—doubly dousing Urway and causing endless flood damage.

Everything Senna had was soaked through. And even when it wasn't raining, she felt damp and cold. A few days ago, she'd moved into a constant fog and that she liked even less than the rain. It darkened the world like a sodden blanket, smothering her while denying the warmth and comfort of the sun.

To keep her mind occupied, she practiced her scales, paying special attention to her range, tone and control. Bruke's warning bark brought her out of her miserable slump to sit up straight in the saddle. Lifting her rain-soaked hood, she squinted at his hazy form through the fog. "What, boy?"

He barked again. With a whine, he took off.

"Come!" She urged Knight to a faster walk. She stood up in her stirrups, straining to see through the fog. "Bruke, you silly kitty cat, come!" What if he didn't come back? He always came back. She felt a flash of heat course through her. She started sweating. "Bruke! Come!" She nudged Knight into a teeth-clattering trot. What if he left her? Like her father and her sister … and her mother. The void inside her swelled until it threatened to swallow her whole.

She buried her heels into Knight's sides. He shot forward. The sudden motion threw her back. Desperately fumbling for the horn, she barely managed to pull herself upright. With every wrenching stride, Senna was jerked back and forth like a rag doll. Finally, she managed to gather a fistful of reins and pull Knight to a stop.

Without thought, she abandoned the saddle. But her foot caught in the stirrup. Off balance, she lurched forward. Her hands shot out to break her fall. Grit dug into her palms. The impact jarred her wrists. Afraid Knight would take off, dragging her to her death, she scrambled to a sitting position.

But he just sniffed her leg and looked at her with his liquid eyes. Senna got to her feet and finally managed to untangle her foot. Before Knight could wander off, she looped the reins over her arm. With a groan of frustration, she cradled her hands into her chest.

And then Bruke was there. Kneeling, she wrapped her arms around his neck. The sobs came. "Don't you ever run away from me again. When I say come, you come!"

Bruke whined and licked her face.

He was all wet and smelled funny. She pushed him back. She looked up at the saddle and spoke to Knight, "Thank you for taking care of me, but we are never going that fast again. Ever."

Senna dug dirt out of her skinned palms and brushed off her dress. The wind combed its fingers through her hair. She heard a rhythmic, scraping sound. She couldn't see anything through the detestable fog. Taking the reins, she led Knight forward.

The wind picked up, blowing hard enough to whip back her cloak. The sound grew louder. Suddenly, she stepped through the last of the fog. Then she caught sight of the ocean. "The sea," she said breathlessly. The black-green waters stretched so far she could decipher the gentle curve of the Earth. Bruke was already trotting down the slope to the water.

Carefully, she came closer. The rounded stones felt hard through her boots. Senna cautiously watched the water rushing toward her feet before retreating back in on itself. Bending down, she let the waves splash over her hand. By the Creators, it was cold! Tentatively, she brought her dripping fingers to her mouth. "Salty!" So the stories were true.

Shaking off the droplets, Senna stood. Night was coming on. She needed to find a place to camp and there wasn't much for Knight to eat here. She walked down the beach until she found a place where the sheer face retreated to form a little alcove. A few trees and some grass padded the rocky ground.

Thanks to the rain, the driftwood was too wet to burn. Eating a cold, dry meal from her pack, she watched as the fog slowly rolled back in. The cold Earth leeched heat from her already-shivering body. Tipping her head back, she sang a song from her mother's journal.

> Oh kind Ash tree,
> Wilt thou make a nest for me?

By the time she'd repeated the song a dozen times, the tree above her had woven its branches into a concave bed. Pleased it had worked so well, she turned to Bruke. "You want to join me?"

He looked at the tree, then at her and back again. He pasted himself to her side. She sang another song. With a stiff groan, the tree eased a branch around them and set them gently on the makeshift bed. "Well, that should keep us off the wet ground, at least." She spread out her bedroll and curled up next to Bruke's warmth as the cold air brushed across her exposed cheek.

But she couldn't sleep. She was too saddle sore and wet. And while the tree was dry, the knobby branches weren't exactly comfortable. She'd just rolled over for the tenth time when she heard the unmistakable sound of hooves clipping stones. Propping herself up on her elbow, she squinted into the darkness.

She could just make out a darker shadow. She felt Bruke's inaudible growl vibrate against her arm. Pressing herself flat, she peered over the rim of the tree, hoping whoever it was wouldn't choose this alcove.

She could make out the form of a man leading a horse. What little light the moon gave was behind him, casting his face in shadow. He was staring at the ground, moving forward deliberately. He stopped when Knight's sharp whinny of greeting rang out. Senna held her breath. Whoever it was, he'd know she was here now. If it was Wardof, she was in for a fight. But someone else could be just as dangerous. What if he tried to take her horse?

The man slowly started backing away. But when he turned, the light caught his face. Before Senna could stop herself, she blurted, "Joshen?"

He whipped around, his head swinging from side to side—he obviously didn't know to look up. "Senna?"

Though she'd only met him once, she knew that voice. "Joshen?"

He came closer. His brow creased when he didn't see her. "I'm up here." Startled, he glanced up at her. She blinked. But he was still there. "What are you doing here?"

"I-I ..." He took a deep breath. "I've been following you." She sat bolt upright. "Following me?"

He crossed his arms over his chest. "I'm your Guardian—or I will be. It's my job to keep you safe."

She opened her mouth to argue, but he spoke before she could. "Wardof came to the barn after you left. We managed to tie them both up. The sheriff took them to jail. But they've probably escaped by now."

Her heart pounding, she threw off her blankets. "Wardof," she squeaked. He'd escaped already? She'd thought she had a few more days at least.

Joshen nodded. "Still want to be alone?"

Senna looked at Bruke's intelligent eyes. Somehow, the dog seemed to know friend from a foe and Joshen didn't even merit lifting his head off his paws. She looked back at Joshen. "No."

Joshen nodded and glanced around the cove. His eyes landed on Knight. Eagerly licking his lips, he ran his hands over the horse's coat. Eventually, he grunted. "He looks good." Turning to his own horse, the one he called Stretch, his practiced hands undid the saddle and laid it on the ground. Senna watched as he pulled a crumbled mass from his pack and began devouring it.

She tried to keep her lip from curling in distaste. "I have some supplies in my pack."

Joshen shrugged as he stuffed the last handful in his mouth. "This'll work for tonight." Brushing his hands on his trousers, he looked up at her. "Where'd you get that dog anyway? He's huge."

Senna rested her chin on her fist. "Mother bought him as a puppy after some boys shot our plow horse." Unconsciously, she began stroking his shaggy coat. "He looks after me."

"Anybody said anything about him?"

"A few funny looks, but no one's said anything." She shrugged. "I'd like to see any of them try to hurt him."

A strange look passed over Joshen's face, but he quickly covered it. Grabbing blankets from his packs, he started arranging them on the ground.

Feeling guilty, she said, "You could sleep in the tree, too." Joshen's brows wrinkled as he studied her bed. "No. I prefer the ground to a bird's nest. Thank you."

"Suit yourself." Senna replied as she squirmed inside her nest.

At dawn, Senna sat up and wrapped her arms around her legs. The rain had started again. She sang softly, so as not to wake her slumbering companion. Again the mist gathered. Only this time, it pointed directly north. She sang a different song and the tree set her gently on the ground and unwound itself.

She shook Joshen's arm. "Come on." One bleary eye peeked out at her. "Let's get going."

Taking a lungful of air, Joshen yawned and stretched. Neither of them spoke as they ate breakfast. Senna was overly conscious of his presence. It made her uncomfortable to have him there, but at the same time, his companionship was like the rays of spring after a long, desolate winter.

She wasn't alone anymore.

"How did you find me?" she asked.

"Knight is shod. It wasn't too hard to follow his tracks."

Wardof's hateful words dribbled over her. "I'll escape and then I'll kill you." She closed her eyes. "If you found me, so will he."

Joshen heaved his saddle on Stretch. "Until he manages to buy another horse, he'll be afoot and the rain will eventually wash away our tracks. We should be able to keep ahead of him." He swung into the saddle and looked at her. "Where are we going?"

Stretching to put her foot in the stirrup, she swung up and started north. Excited to finally get moving, Bruke bound ahead. "Northward to Haven."

He eyed her dubiously. "Never heard of it. How do you know where to go?"

Senna turned a wary eye toward him. "I just do," she finally answered. She could tell he wanted to press the issue, but he seemed to know better. He didn't seem to mind the silence either, which was a relief, because Senna wasn't good at making conversation. Eventually, she started her voice exercises. She was so wrapped up in stretching her range, it was a while before she noticed Joshen gaping at her.

Her voice cut off.

He blinked. "Don't—don't stop."

She blushed.

He looked awkwardly out over the water. "I didn't know it was possible for something to be that … intense."

She ducked her head in her hood so he wouldn't see her smile. Then, instead of practicing, she sang a Nefalien ballad. She sang song after song until both of them spotted the dark outline of a town through the fog. After her singing, the silence seemed heavier. "Do you know the name?" she finally asked.

Joshen squinted into the vapors. "Probably Corrieth. It's a trading port."

"And how do the people of Corrieth feel about Witches?" she asked cautiously.

Joshen turned to her, his eyes seeming to understand much more than Senna meant to reveal. "I don't know, Senna."

She felt her stomach growing cold. After the warmth and kindness of a few, the chill of many stung more.

9. SIGN OF THE WITCHES

Senna gaped at the size of Corrieth's walls looming over her. She knew they were meant to keep those inside safe, but it felt more like a cage.

"It's easily ten times the size of Perchance," Joshen said.

Senna gulped and cast a worried glance at Bruke. "What do you say, Bruke?"

His tail twitched anxiously back and forth, but he lowered his head and moved cautiously forward. That was enough for Senna.

She was relieved when the gate's guards barely looked up as they rode by. Within moments of crossing into the city, foreign spices assaulted her. Her mouth watered at the thought of a hot meal.

Joshen smacked his tongue, his eyes forming a question.

With a half-smile, Senna dismounted and moved toward the smell. It didn't take them long to find the marketplace. As they entered from a side street, she froze in amazement. Foreigners. Lots of them. The subdued hues of her people's clothing seemed bland compared to the colors and fabrics she thought only possible in flowers.

And the people! Senna hadn't known humans came in such a wide range of colors and adornments. People with charcoal skin that contrasted with the whites of their eyes and teeth. Golden skin with slanted eyes and thick black hair. More people with frightening blue marks on their flesh, their heads shorn. Others with jewels in their noses, glinting rings in their ears and blankets draped over their bodies like robes instead of trousers and shirts. Senna squirmed. People pressed in on her from all sides and the smell of food mixed sickeningly with the odor of animal feces and unwashed bodies. From all directions, sounds and colors inundated her remaining senses.

She found herself clinging to Joshen's side like a frightened toddler. He bought the three of them a small feast. Either Joshen noticed her discomfort, or he was feeling some of it himself, for he led her away from the market and toward the ocean. They managed to find a quiet spot on one of the piers, not far from a small group of sailors who sat idly next to a boarding plank.

She'd forgotten how hot food warmed hands. How it steamed when exposed to cold air. How it filled her stomach with warmth and pleasure instead of simply filling her. She devoured three steaming, stuffed rolls before starting on the honeycakes. She'd become so engrossed in her meal that Joshen's solid elbow to her ribs startled her. Her mouth still open in anticipation of her next bite, she looked at him.

He tipped his head toward the sailors.

She leaned around him to get a better look at the men, but Joshen elbowed her again. "Don't look," he whispered. "Just listen."

Taking a nibble of her honeycake, she heard one of the sailors say, "No, haven't seen any of them for months now. And I tire of this damnable fog."

Senna exchanged a glance with Joshen and leaned around to get a better look at the sailors. A dark-skinned man answered, "Perhaps they've business somewhere else, Cap'n Parknel."

"Their headquarters are 'round here somewheres," said a dark-skinned man with crooked teeth. "They'll be 'round to fix things 'fore long."

The first man, Captain Parknel, grumbled. "Mark me. The ocean feels it first. This fog might keep us all shore-bound, but it won't end there. Storms of the kind to bury a ship with a single wave'll be next."

"I hear of bad droughts inland, too," said the bald sailor.

Captain Parknel took a swig of something from a tin. "If those Witches don't come back, won't be haulin' merchandise on the waters no more."

Senna and Joshen exchanged glances. "We must be close," she whispered eagerly.

Joshen's brow furrowed and he said loudly, "You mean you don't know exactly?"

"Shh!" Senna leaned in as the sailors cast glances their way. "I've never been there before."

Joshen lowered his voice. "Then how'll you find it?"

"I'll find it," she assured him.

He shot her a dubious glance before shrugging his shoulders. "Witches."

Senna smiled. He'd said it like a grudging compliment instead of an insult—like a friend might. Swinging her feet over the water, she handed Bruke a piece of her roll.

After they finished their meal and replenished their supplies, Senna and Joshen agreed to put a little more distance between themselves and the Hunters before nightfall. They'd traveled about half a league north of the city when darkness fell. They ate their food while a chilly wind blew the smoke from the fire into their faces.

Finished, Senna laid her bedroll on the ground next to Joshen. His brow furrowed in confusion.

Her cheeks flamed scarlet. She spoke quickly, her words tripping over each other in her embarrassment. "There aren't any trees to sleep in. And I thought it might be chilly. Plus, people wouldn't be as likely to stop."

His eyebrows rose higher. "So ... you want to share blankets?"

Her mouth fell open. Had there been any ground cover nearby, she'd have gladly sung it over her head. She tried to speak, but it came out as a croak. Shaking her head, she realized showing him might do more good than stammering around.

She dug a hole in the ground and filled it with a seed the size of a small plum. After she'd replaced the dirt, she sang.

Oh shelter seed, I sing to thee,
Take up thy boughs and cover me.

A tiny, gray shoot burst forth. It grew flat, like the blade of a shovel. Yawning wider, it stretched until it encased them both in a tight shelter, like an overturned dish.

She smiled weakly. "It's called a Shelter Seed. It takes on the characteristics of the landscape to hide the inhabitants and provides instant shelter. But if you want, I can sing an opening and you could sleep outside."

Joshen stared at her in a mixture of awe and fear.

She felt hot and uncomfortable. What if he said no? She hadn't meant to flirt with him. She'd only thought he'd want to be out of the wind. "I should've asked," she said.

He swallowed. "I'd like to stay. If that's alright."

She nodded and flopped down, banging her shoulder on the hard ground. Suppressing a groan, she lay perfectly still. Eventually, their body heat warmed the shelter and she relaxed. Joshen's breathing deepened. She exhaled the last of her tension. She didn't know why, but though he wasn't much older than her, there was a sort of undeniable strength about him. A strength that shielded her like a warm blanket. After she was sure he was asleep, she finally whispered, "I'm glad you're here."

"Me, too," Joshen surprised her by responding.

***

At dawn, she awoke to Bruke's furry body warming her stomach and Joshen warming her back. His arm was thrown over her shoulder. She lay there, reveling in the strange, wonderful burning that emanated from Joshen's touch. Although she loathed to leave the warmth of their shelter—or Joshen—she carefully moved his arm and pushed herself up.

He looked so beautiful; she wished she could reach out and touch his face. She bit her lip and wondered if she had the courage. No. What if he awoke and caught her? He might think she meant something by the touch and she was pretty sure she didn't.

Even if she did, he'd never reciprocate.

The thought brought a pang deep in her chest and tears to her eyes. Pushing herself up, she sang softly for the shelter to split and pull back, like a wooden curtain rolling to the side. She crawled over Joshen and outside. Immediately, the cold wind slapped her skin and she was glad for their shelter.

Shivering, she rubbed her arms and blinked away the tears the wind tugged from her eyes. Within moments, light struck her from behind, casting her shadow across the stone strewn ground and into the freezing water. She sang.

> Oh morning light, hear my cry,
> To Haven I must fly.

The mist gathered and led east—through the water. "I don't understand," she whispered.

"So that's how you know where to go!" She whirled to see Joshen peeking through the shelter with a look of amazement.

Strangely enough, she didn't care if Joshen knew. Somehow, she'd grown to trust him and trust loosened her tongue. "East! There's nothing east but more water!" She plopped down and chucked a rock into the ashes that covered the coals of their fire like a fur coat. "Do they expect me to swim there?"

Joshen settled down next to her and nudged her with his shoulder. "Come on now. The golden fog thing pointed east. So east we go."

Senna glowered at him. "And how do you propose we do that?"

He tipped his head in the direction of the village. "We just came from the piers, didn't we?" He stood and offered her a hand.

She took it grudgingly. "A whole day wasted and now I have to go back to that place."

Bruke whined in agreement.

After traveling back the way they'd come, they skirted the city and headed for the wharves, near the place they'd eaten earlier. Joshen approached the red-bearded sailor they'd overheard yesterday. "Captain Parknel, isn't it?"

The Captain nodded, his eyes flicking to Senna.

Joshen glanced at the sailors standing behind the Captain. "Where would we go to buy a small boat?"

The Captain scratched his beard. "What you need a boat for?"

Joshen shrugged, "Fishing."

"Fishing, huh? In this fog." He eyed Senna suspiciously. "Well, if that's all you want, Mcbedee's has a couple that'll float, but you'd best be careful. The sea isn't herself these days." He pointed and gave them directions to one of the side streets.

Joshen thanked the man and started off.

Senna started after him but felt eyes watching her. She glanced back to see Captain Parknel studying her with a knowing look. With a sinking feeling, she realized he knew what she was. Her gaze flicked to Bruke for any sign of mistrust, but the dog was too busy staring at a pallet of fish.

"Don't you dare," she warned him.

With a high whine, he trotted toward her.

Casting one last glance back at the Captain, she turned and hurried after Joshen.

At a dilapidated building with a boat and lathe sign marking it as a boat maker's shop, Joshen held the door for her. The moment she stepped inside, she sneezed. Everything was covered in sawdust mixed with regular dust. She sneezed again and peered out the greasy windows. Holding her hand over her nose, she wondered if she preferred the overpowering smell of fish to the stale, dusty air of Mcbedee's shop.

A dark-skinned man appeared from the back. Flecks of wood dotted his unkempt, graying hair, which bore a striking resemblance to a bird's nest. "What can I do you for?"

"Captain Parknel told us you had fishing boats for sale," Joshen said.

The man grunted. With an impatient wave, he gestured for them to follow him. "I take old boats and make 'em serviceable again," he said as he opened the door.

Senna quickly saw what he meant. A few rickety old boats with fresh patches of wood were scattered haphazardly across the floor. She cast a dubious glance at Joshen. "Captain Parknel warned us about the sea."

"They'll float," Mcbedee said as he cleaned some dirt from under his fingernails.

She eyed the boats. She thought they resembled hollowed-out corn husks more than boats, but she doubted they could buy more without raising real suspicion. "But that's about all they'll do," she whispered to Joshen.

He leaned in and spoke softly in her ear, "It can't be too far. How could a Witch make it without a crew, otherwise?"

Senna hoped he was right. She knew nothing about boats or the sea.

Mcbedee scratched his scalp and studied Senna with a knowing look on his face. "I'll even sell you a watertight drum. Store all your delicate items inside. I have a feeling you're gonna need it."

Senna licked her lips. Joshen stuck out his hand. "Deal."

Mcbedee sold them the boat, but now they had the dilemma of how to get it and the horses back to camp. They didn't think the poor thing would survive being dragged across the rocky shore, so they finally decided to stable the horses and paddle the boat back to camp.

By the time they had it all arranged, it was well past midday. Forgoing the chance for a hot meal, they carried the cumbersome boat to the docks. Joshen held it steady while Senna climbed in. The thing rocked and skittered like a drunken horse. She breathed a sigh of relief when she had her seat.

But then Joshen placed a foot inside. Hoping it would hold the two of them without falling apart, she held her breath. He eased down. It groaned in protest but seemed determined to hold together. The two dipped their paddles in the sea and pulled. The boat did a neat circle by the dock. "You have to paddle on the other side, Senna," Joshen said.

She blushed as she noticed a group of sailors watching in amusement. "Sorry." She put her paddle on the other side of the boat and they managed to meander in the general direction of their camp. Just as they built up momentum, the next dock appeared.

"Senna, we have to turn. Put your oar on the same side as me," Joshen said.

She could tell Joshen was trying very hard to be patient with her and it only made her feel that much more inept. She switched sides and they very narrowly avoided colliding with the solid dock—a collision she doubted their corn husk would have survived. Luckily, she had mostly figured out rowing by the time they left the dock.

Sharp pain dug between her shoulder blades and night had completely overwhelmed them by the time she finally spotted their old campsite. Exhausted and wet, they ate bread and cheese before falling onto their bedrolls. In fact, she'd have missed dawn entirely had it not been for Bruke nudging her with his cold nose.

As it did yesterday, the mist pointed east. Shoulders and arms weary and sore, Senna helped Joshen heave the boat into the water. She dipped her oar in the shining water. Finding a rhythm, she pulled at the sea. It wasn't long before cold puddles pooled about her feet.

"I don't want to lose sight of the shore," Joshen cautioned.

She looked back at the shrinking coastline. "We'd never find our way back."

Joshen laughed. "Sure we would. We'd just have to wait until I could see the stars to do it."

She glanced down at Bruke, who cast an unhappy look at the water. "Don't worry. We'll be okay." But the words were more for herself than him.

About the time the shore was small enough she could cover it with her forearm, something black appeared on the horizon. Senna and Joshen exchanged a glance and pulled for it. As the last of the coast disappeared, an island took shape. "That has to be it!" Senna exclaimed. But as they drew near, imposing cliffs jutted out of the water and pointed ominously skyward.

"We won't be going ashore here," Joshen said.

"We could try and climb it," she suggested.

Joshen pointed to the base of the cliffs. "Those waves would pull us in and dash this little boat to pieces. Then the undercurrent would suck us down. We have to find another way."

Though it took most of the day, they circled the entire island. On the farthest side, Senna noted rising smoke. "Look Joshen, maybe someone's camped on shore!" Digging in their oars, they came around the bend and froze. Smoke rose from a cone that gaped at them like a hungry mouth from the cliff's face. The water swirled with a reddish tint. Black rock steamed and gurgled as the water splashed against it. Holding his oar across his lap, Joshen stuck his hand in the water before jerking it back. "It's warm!" He frowned at the hissing rocks. "That's not a campfire, it's a volcano!"

Senna's eyes widened. "Maybe we should make a wider berth?"

Joshen nodded and they moved back out to sea.

Other than the volcano, the shoreline never strayed from impassable cliffs. Her arms and shoulders felt hollow and weak. "Joshen, I'm not sure I'll be able to row back if we don't go soon."

"This can't be it," he finally relented. "There must be another island somewhere." He started turning the boat.

Senna paddled behind him, pushing the little boat up to speed. She turned to look once more at the island. "Wait." She saw something green on the cliffs. Some plant that grew in the shape of an—"Oh no! It can't be."

Joshen followed her gaze, "What do you see?"

Carefully, Senna studied it. In one spot, the jagged cliffs lined up. "On the face there! The moss grows in the shape of a crescent!"

His eyes widened. "The mark of the Witches?"

"In part." She sat down and pulled her necklace out of her shirt. "I read about it in my mother's journal. The Witches believe we are all parts of a whole. Like the phases of the moon. Together, we complete the circle and bring balance."

"Unity. We are stronger together than apart," he grunted. "So where's the waning gibbous?"

Excitement danced in Senna's eyes. "Let's get closer."

With careful strokes, they came as near to the cliff's edge as they dared. With Joshen back-paddling to keep them from being sucked forward, Senna scoured every inch of the cliffs. But there was no waning gibbous. "Maybe it's below the water line." She stood to peer at the space left by the retreating waves.

"Careful, Senna!" Joshen cried.

A crashing wave tipped the boat. Senna lurched forward. With no time to catch herself, her chest slammed into the bow. The impact left her whole body limp. She slipped forward. The frigid water slapped her hands. She was falling. Joshen grabbed her ankles before she went over. The boat tipped precariously; he threw his weight to the other side, still holding on to her leg.

They were being sucked toward the cliffs at an alarming rate. "Don't stop paddling!" she cried, fumbling for a grip on the boat.

Releasing her, Joshen back-paddled.

Bringing her knees under her, Senna winced and rubbed her chest as she pulled herself up and away from the water. Forgetting about the pain, she leaned forward and squinted into the water. A hazy, near-circle of green grew on the sea floor. "There! Below the boat!"

Joshen peeked over the side and looked back up at the crescent on the cliffs. "I don't understand."

Senna scrutinized each crevice in search of an opening. Nothing. "There has to be a cave or an opening. I know this is it!"

"Then how do we get in?" Joshen said. Senna turned toward him. His face flushed with the effort of keeping the boat from inching toward the deadly cliffs. "I can't hold it much longer. My arms are dead."

She looked back at the island. "But we're so close." She took a turn paddling. "Maybe there's an entrance just below the waterline and we have to swim in?"

Joshen looked at her as if she were mad. "Do you have any idea how cold that water is, Senna? We'd both cramp up and drown, or die of exposure and that's if the waves didn't smash us to pieces against the cliffs." He looked back at the island. "Maybe we should try again tomorrow."

Senna sighed and her weary shoulders drooped. "All right. Tomorrow, we find our way in."

10. BETRAYAL

"You're sure a boy and girl purchased the boat?"

"Said they were doing some fishing," the man at the boat shop replied.

Wardof grunted. "Where exactly were they going to fish?"

"You're more than welcome to look over my books and see if I marked that detail," Mcbedee said as he scratched his scalp.

Wardof clenched his fists. His bruises had healed; perhaps it was time to make some new ones.

Garg shifted from one foot to the other. "C'mon. We don't need no more trouble."

Wardof shot Garg the glare he'd been using to no effect on Mcbedee. With a growl, he turned toward the door.

"'Spect me to keep tabs on his sister … He can't even keep her under control and 'spects me to …" Mcbedee grumbled.

Wardof slammed the door behind him. "At least we know she came this way. My bet is she's looking for Haven. If she bought a boat, the island must be around here somewhere."

"Yeah, but nobody but Witches get in that island and she could change the location 'fore we find it."

"That's why we have to find her before she gets in! Besides, she's an ignorant little Witch. She doesn't know how to move it, you idiot!" Wardof turned in frustration.

"I told you to stop callin' me names!" Garg scowled.

Wardof rounded on Garg, pleased for the excuse to use his fists. "I'll call you whatever names—"

"Hello there, boys," a voice interrupted from behind. Wardof whirled and squinted against the bright sun. Out of the corner of his eye, he thought he saw a man who looked an awful lot like Mcbedee dart behind a building. He brought one hand up to shade his eyes. But the man was gone.

A balding man and one with a red beard leaned against the weathered boards of a tackle shop. "You lookin' for a girl?"

Instantly, Wardof was alert. "Yes, shoulder-length dark gold hair, amber eyes, skinny, a little on the short side, fifteen."

Both men nodded.

"That be her," the one with the red beard said. "Whatcha lookin' for her for?"

Wardof gave the same story he'd been using all through Nefalie.

The sailors exchanged glances. "Sister, huh?"

Both men seemed amused, though Wardof couldn't see why. "She's a bit muddled in her mind. Would've been looking for a hidden place?"

The red-bearded Captain smiled. "There's an island. Only one way in and I'm the single soul that knows it. My bet is they're headed there. I run merchandise up and down the coast, but there isn't much business now. We could take you there for the right price."

"Name it." Wardof felt happier than he had in years.

**

Senna sat on the beach, staring across the water and thinking of the green crescent on the cliff's face and the gibbous beneath the waves. "We have to get past the cliffs. But how? We can't get any closer and we can't swim in."

Joshen handed her some salted fish and biscuits before plopping down beside her. "Did you see any signs the island is anything but cliffs? I mean, how do we know if there's even anything inside?"

Senna reached down and scratched behind Bruke's ears. He groaned contentedly beneath her fingertips. "My mother said if

I followed the signs of the Dawn Song, I'd find safety. I can't believe she meant I should scale the top of a barren cliff and live out my life on lichen and crabs."

She glanced at him askance. He stuffed a fistful of food into his mouth. "Do you always eat like that?" Senna said in disgust.

He swallowed and she watched the knot of food bob down his throat. "Like what?" He scooped up another mountain of food and shoved it in.

"Like you haven't eaten in four days."

After minimal chewing, he swallowed. "I'm hungry."

"You're going to choke if you don't chew better."

He gave her a dark look. "You're sounding a lot like my mother."

Senna blushed. "Sorry. Eat on. I won't watch."

He grunted and shoveled in more food. "There 'as to be 'ome way in. May'e a 'igger 'oat? Un wid a crew?"

Trying her best not to comment on his garbled response, she shook her head. "No. I can't see the Witches letting anyone else know their secret." She rested her elbows on her knees and dug her palms into her eyes. "Think, Senna, think!" If her mother didn't explain how to actually enter Haven, then it had to be fairly obvious. She must be over-thinking it. What would any other Witch do in her place? Senna jumped to her feet. "That's it! The one thing Witches can do that no one else can. Sing!" Then her face fell. "But sing what?"

She ran to her satchel and pulled out her mother's journal. She dropped next to Joshen. Shoving a bite of biscuit in her mouth, she looked for the section on sea songs.

"And you think I'm a sloppy eater," Joshen chortled.

Senna ignored him as she skimmed through the songs. And then she found it. Jumping to her feet, she paced up and down the rocky shore as she studied the book. She hummed the tune, trying to perfect her pitch and cadence before she tried the words.

Oh, Sister Sea Plants, I ask of thee,
Take me to the place none but Witches see.

She didn't know how to explain it, but the song felt right. She grabbed the side of the boat and pushed. "Come on, the only way to find out is to try!"

Joshen's swollen cheeks deflated as he swallowed. He choked and coughed. He pounded his chest with his fist. "It's almost dark!" he managed.

Senna glanced around. "Oh, right," she groaned. "I guess that means we're waiting for morning." Deflated, she sat down to practice the song.

***

It was early. Very early. Eyes closed, Garg swayed as the movement of the ship began to lull him to sleep again. Wardof dug an elbow in his ribs.

Garg winced. "Ow!"

"Well, stay awake, you idiot! We have to keep watch."

"I thought that was the guy in the crow's nest's job?" Garg replied as he rubbed his bruised ribs.

Wardof glanced at the plethora of sailors and said under his breath, "I don't think they're that intelligent. I mean, how do they think my so-called sister found this hidden inlet anyway?"

Garg shot a knowing look behind him and then resumed his vigil. A moment later, he lifted his finger and pointed excitedly. "Is that it? Is that the island?"

Wardof squinted into the salt spray and looked back at the red-bearded Captain for confirmation. "That'd be it," Parknel said. "We should have your sister any time now."

A wicked smile lit Wardof's face. "You say you know a hidden way?"

Captain Parknel looked down his nose at Wardof. "You don't plan on sharing this place with everyone do you? The sealin' is excellent."

"No," Wardof replied. "Your secret is safe with me."

The Captain looked him over dubiously.

Wardof held up a gold coin. "I promised you another dozen of these, remember?"

Parknel's eyes lit up at the sight of the gold. "That you did!" He turned the wheel sharply to the south. "We'll set you down in the hidden lagoon. You can wait for them there."

"We got 'er this time, boss!" Garg chortled.

Wardof rubbed his hands together in delight. Espen would be so pleased.

The sailors threw anchor a good distance from the rocks, then Captain Parknel dropped a boat. One of the cliffs jutted out farther than the others and another cliff feinted toward it, so what appeared as a small chink in the cliffs was actually hiding a narrow, zigzagging passage. Wardof's excitement swelled within him. No passing ship would ever notice this channel.

After a good bit of rowing, the passage opened to a small beach covered in seals. When they were close enough, he leaped from the boat into the icy water. He and Garg waded to the rocky beach.

He looked around. The seals shot him huffy looks before slipping into the water. There were no buildings or signs of humans. It wasn't what he'd expected, but perhaps the power of the place had faded after the Witches were captured. Or maybe it was a front to hide the real city. "Are you sure—"

"Yes, yes, yes," Captain Parknel assured him. "This is the beach. There's a cave over yonder. Light a fire and wait for her there. We'll come back to check on you tomorrow."

Wardof and Garg watched as the sailors pushed the boat back into the water. "Remember, you get the other half when you come back to get us!" Garg called anxiously.

Captain Parknel's mouth opened in a throaty laugh. "You'll see me tomorra', good sirs!"

Wardof turned and jogged forward as Garg lumbered behind. When he saw the cave, he increased his speed. And then he burst inside. It wasn't very big and it looked … well, not at all what he'd anticipated. After all, the Witches were well off. Couldn't they spruce it up a bit?

A plop of something warm dripped on his head. He rubbed the slimy substance between his fingers and brought it to his nose for a sniff. "Uck!" He glanced up to see the ceiling crawling with bats. If the Witches thought bats would drive him out, they were wrong. He flicked the droppings off his fingers. "A fire will clear you out," he muttered as another dropping dripped down his shoulder.

***

Senna stood at the bow of the little boat as it bobbed on the high waves. Her stomach writhed like a net full of fish. If this didn't work, she didn't know what would. She watched the sunlight dance on the water and felt the spray from the crashing waves dampen her face. It calmed her. Closing her eyes, she sang.

Oh, Sister Sea Plants, I ask of thee,
Take me to the place none but Witches see.

Beneath the waves beating mercilessly against the rocks and the gentle lapping of the water against the boat, Senna listened hard for anything. She was fairly certain she'd sung the song correctly, but perhaps one of her notes wasn't perfect? She tried again. And again. Still nothing. A circling gull called to them from overhead. She watched its lazy flight and then turned back to Joshen. "I guess it didn't work."

He opened his mouth to reply when a finger of green kelp erupted behind him. And then another. Senna tried to scream, but no sound came out. The air filled with green kelp. Somewhere, at the back of her consciousness, her mind told her not to fight it. Terrifying as it was, Senna fell back to the bottom of the boat and watched as green surrounded them, blocking out the cliffs.

Bruke and Joshen were not so inclined. Bruke struggled and bit as his ingrained wildness erupted. Joshen produced a knife and started slashing. "Be still!" Senna ordered. But the two either didn't hear or were too afraid to stop themselves. The plants reacted by binding them both, gripping the boat and jerking them toward the cliff.

Faster and faster they raced. She must have sung it wrong. The kelp was going to smash them into the rocks! She opened her mouth in a wordless scream.

As if in response, kelp roared from the water, weaving itself around the boat until it blotted out the sun. Only the sound of the crashing waves told her they were coming closer to the cliffs. The traces of light grew fainter by the moment, proof the kelp surrounded them. Faster and faster they raced toward the churning sea. "The Creators save us!" She braced herself for the impact.

The boat pitched stern downward, throwing her into the kelp. She threw her hands out to steady herself against the waterlogged plant. The watertight drum Mcbedee had thrown in with the boat slammed into her, forcing all the breath from her. If not for the kelp, she'd have been tossed into the ocean. At least it kept her companions steady, though they wriggled and fought like snakes in a bag.

Then the sound went wrong. Muffled. Like they were underwater. Wide-eyed, Senna stared at the kelp as it bulged inward beneath her.

They were under the water!

She scrambled back. All around her, the timber groaned as if the boat were a creaky old man. Every muscle tense, she held so tight to the boat seat that her hands went white as driftwood. *Creators, please let this corn cob hold!* she silently begged.

Movement to her right. Her head swiveled in time to see Joshen's hand free, his knife pale and silver in the dimness. "No!" She lunged for him as the blade disappeared in the wall of green.

Water roared into the boat like a wild animal, clawing and biting her with bitter cold teeth. Her mouth open in shock, Senna gasped for air. Her clothes swirled around her as the water rose up to her knees. Gripping what she thought was Joshen's arm, she heaved him out of the water.

She felt Bruke struggling beneath the surface. She lunged for him, straining to lift his head out of the water. She clenched her teeth against the cold. Her hair clung to her face.

With an ominous ripping sound, the kelp heaved and water roared into her ears. The world darkened. Her hair floated free and her ears buzzed. With a pop, the pressure dug knives into her brain until Senna couldn't feel the cold. Only the pain. Writhing, she tried to fight her body's desire to breathe in the water. How long could she hold her breath?

When she thought she couldn't bear it any longer, Senna felt the pressure lessening. They were rising. Up. Up. Up.

Like a bobbing cork, they erupted above the water. Her face and lungs felt like they would explode as she waited an eternity for the water to drain away. When she couldn't stand it anymore, she gasped for air. But it was too soon. Water invaded her lungs. She leaned forward as wracking coughs shook her thin frame. She vomited. It mixed with the water around her. Senna felt the boat settle back into the water. Fighting for air, she watched the kelp retreat.

The light was soft. Not like the light from the sun, but the warm, yellowish flicker of fire. She glanced around. They floated in a pool of water inside a cave. Her senseless companions lay still beside her. But they were breathing. Even as she slumped back into the puddle of water, she was aware of the boat landing against something soft. The last thing she saw before the points of black joined was someone peering down at her and a strange laugh grated her sore ears. The voice said something, something like there was an easier way to … Senna couldn't hold on. She drifted away.

***

The fire might have cleared out the bats, but it did nothing for the smell or the guck at Wardof's feet. In his rush to find Senna, he hadn't brought much water or food. As far as he could tell, the only fresh water on this cursed island was the small cave pool coated with a thick layer of slime.

The longer the day wore on, the more he began to think the sailors must have tricked them. No Witch would call this nasty hole in the ground a refuge. Or hidden, for that matter. If any common sailor could find it, surely Espen wouldn't have searched for years.

Singing a sailor chantey off key, Garg rumbled back into the cave with a handful of clams. "Espen gonna be so happy when we catch that little Witch!"

Wardof lurched to his feet and stormed out of the cave. Garg watched him go. "Don't you like clams?"

Wardof scooped up a handful of rocks and hurled them at Garg. "They tricked us, you idiot! This is a cave! Not Haven!" He turned and stumbled on a seal. With a bark of indignation, the animal bit his leg.

Teeth ground against his bone. "Ahhh!" Tripping, Wardof hit the rocks hard and scrambled away.

Hunching its back, the seal scooted for the water.

Snatching a handful of stones, he hurled them at the seal.

Garg grabbed Wardof's arm and tried to help him up. "Sure this is it, Wardof. We just have to wait a bit longer."

"Get off me!" Wardof jerked away. He launched the biggest stone he could find at the seal, but it splashed harmlessly in the water. He wanted to sink his knife into the animal, but it was out of his reach. Just like his little Witch. Holding his injured leg a few inches above the ground, Wardof clenched his fists to his sides and roared in frustration. "I'm going to get you, you little Witch!"

He was sitting in the same spot when the boat came to a halt a little way from shore. The red-headed Captain looked around, a smile plastered on his smug face. "Well, did you find them?"

It took every ounce of Wardof's control to keep his voice even. "You know very well we did not."

Captain Parknel shrugged. "You asked me to take you to a place no one knew about. No one really knows about this cove. Unless a course you're countin' the seals." He pointed to Wardof's bloody leg. "Bad night?"

Wardof struggled to his feet. Garg reached out to help him but Wardof fended him off. "You'll pay for this—"

Parknel tipped his face to the sun and roared in laughter. But the sailors around him didn't so much as crack a smile. Wiping his eyes, the Captain cleared his throat and continued, "In reality, you're the one who's going to pay. You owe me the second half of our agreement."

Wardof's expression was pinched. "You want more money? I want the money I paid you back!"

The Captain shrugged and motioned for the sailors to bring the boat around. They pulled at the water with their oars.

"Hey, where you goin'!" Garg shouted. "You can't just leave us here!"

The Captain smiled. "Maybe you can tame the seals, convince them to give you a ride to shore. Maybe another ship will come by—someday. Maybe it really is the Witches' island and you've only to wait. At any rate, I hope you enjoy seals."

Wardof charged them, water erupting around him. He splashed next to the boat, heaved himself up and lunged for the Captain with his knife, but he stopped cold when he saw a pistol trained on his face. "You don't have the manpower or the weapons to make any threats, sea slime. Witches are the Keepers of the sea and we do them reverence." He sniffed the air above Wardof in repugnance. "Now you get your stinking Hunter carcass away from my boat before I make you shark bait."

Wardof released the boat and backed away. With a look of disgust, he reached inside his jacket and flung the remaining amount of money at the Captain. "Fine! Here are your coins!"

Parknel picked up the dripping money bag and pulled out its mate. With a jerk, he chucked both bags of gold. Wardof watched them twist and twirl in the air. They landed with a clinking sound. Gold spilled out, catching the light and standing out against the dreary stone shore. "Keep your money." The mirth was gone. "Come on, boys. Let's take her in."

The other sailors pulled on their oars as Wardof watched them growing smaller.

Garg splashed into the water beside him and howled, "You can't leave us here!"

No one in the boat looked back.

Garg kept going past Wardof, but he was a good head shorter. When he was standing on his tiptoes, he flung himself forward and flailed pitifully before going under. Wardof watched in revulsion as Garg clawed helplessly from under the shallow water. "Just push yourself back one step, idiot." When he couldn't stand any more of Garg's floundering, he swam forward, gripped his collar and dragged him to the shore.

Garg, spitting and sputtering, gargled, "They can't leave us!"

Wardof glared down at his lifelong companion. "They just did."

11. HAVEN

"Pogg takes good cares of you. Yes. Yes. Pogg keeps you life."

Pogg? Who? Senna thought. Disconnected pieces of information swirled in her head until she became dizzy. She felt a soft bed beneath her, but hadn't she been in a cave? She struggled to open her eyes. Thin slits of blurry light appeared with a black blob in the middle. She blinked and the blob became a … thing.

She blinked again, but the problem wasn't her focus. Senna looked at him—she thought it was a him—up and down with a mixture of fear and revulsion. His gray-green mottled skin was as smooth and slick as a dolphin's hide. His triangular teeth sat below a flat nose. He blinked and a thick, oily substance smeared across bulging, fishlike eyes. His hands were shaped like hers, except for a thin membrane that connected his fingers like the skin of a bat's wing. He wore only a thin, greasy sack with holes cut out for his appendages.

"What are you?" Senna asked.

Something that she hoped was a grin erupted on the creature's face. He patted his chest. "Pogg, Mettlemot. Frog people."

She shrank deeper into the bed and looked for a way to escape. But what she saw brought her up short. She was in a home, but not like one she'd ever imagined. Windows that were shaped like a spinning top, with peaked ends and bulbous centers. Walls that were impossibly smooth in some places and yet appeared knotted or even woven together like the branches of a willow tree in others. There were no seams, corners, or angles—only soft curves as the wall melded into the floor or ceiling. Everything was the color of rich cream scraped from a pail of fresh milk. "Where am I?" Before he could answer, she suddenly remembered Joshen and Bruke. "Where are my friends?"

He made a high-pitched trilling sound of displeasure. "Pogg not lets hairy one in house." He jerked his head toward a bed on the other side of the room. "Other does worses. Takes longer."

Joshen lay under a mound of blankets with only his disheveled head visible. "Joshen," Senna cried. She launched herself from the bed to the knotted wooden floor. The world swirled and dimmed. Her feet smarted like a million bee stings. With a groan, she closed her eyes and dropped onto the soft mattress. Gripping the sides to keep herself upright, she waited for the flashing lights to pass. When she could, she stood carefully, her arms splayed for balance. Tottering like a baby calf on new legs, she worked her way to Joshen's bed and collapsed beside him.

His ashen face and pale lips were nothing in comparison to the jagged rattle in his lungs. Tears stung her eyes. "Will he be alright?"

Pogg waddled to her side. "Sea goes in. Pogg gets somes out and boy breaths, but nows he hot."

Senna pressed her hand against his forehead. His skin felt like sun-baked rocks. "Very hot." She tried to remember all the herbs useful for healing. "Pesnit. I need pesnit for his fever. And some garku for strength wouldn't hurt."

Pogg started toward the door. "Comes. Pogg shows."

Reluctantly, Senna stood, but her dizziness was quick to return and slow to pass. Outside the door, she looked down, a long, long set of stairs. She swayed as they seemed to rush toward her. Closing her eyes, she reached out to steady herself.

A gurgling sound of disapproval reached for her from far away. Pogg waited for her at the bottom of the stairs, his cheeks twitching with what she guessed was impatience. She teetered down the stairs.

Pogg opened the door and darted back with a high-pitched yelp.

With a bark, Bruke lunged toward her, knocking her to the floor. Ignoring Pogg's furious babbling and shoves, the dog licked her furiously, his tail wagging as fast as he could make it.

She pushed him off. "Not now, Bruke."

With a delighted yap, he jumped up and sprinted out the door. Rolling to her knees, she pushed herself up and looked outside. Below her, more stairs sloped like water frozen over rolling stones. From the open door, the heady smell of flowers, green and damp dirt spilled into the room. A sound like the symphony of colorful birds added an undercurrent to the smell.

Already, she felt stronger, rejuvenated.

She stepped outside. Below her, the woven walls of the building forked to bite into the rich, brown Earth. Leaves sprouted from the roof. "It's a tree!"

Pogg looked at her as if she'd suddenly sprouted mushrooms from her nose. "What else woulds it be?"

She gaped in awe. She was in the midst of a forest of tree houses—some taller than the tallest buildings she'd ever seen. Between them, plants grew fat and tall, as if stretching to devour the very air. From each tree, a worn path wound through the dense foliage toward a larger, center path—like feeder streams into a river. It seemed overgrown and neglected now.

There was no doubt about it. She'd made it to Haven.

Joshen, her mind was quick to remind her. "The garden?" Dropping from two legs to four, Pogg scurried past the network of roots beside the tree faster than she'd have thought possible.

Singing quickly to clear the plants, she followed. At the back of the tree house, she stopped suddenly. An enormous garden was filled with every kind of medicinal plant she could imagine and many others. It had the look of long neglect, but neglect someone had recently tried to remedy.

The plants called hungrily to her. She answered.

*Take in light, Take in air,
Stretch thy roots, thy leaves grow fair.*

The garden practically sighed in relief as she repeated the song.

Snatching herbs for Joshen, she rushed back, singing the whole while. With groans of relief, the plants and trees around her stretched their limbs and shook out their leaves.

She hurried up the stairs to the house, Bruke glued to her side.

"Hairy one not goes in house," Pogg cried.

Senna stopped abruptly. He resented her presence on the island. That much was obvious. But she didn't have time to find out why. Joshen didn't have time. "I need him. Where's the kitchen?"

Pogg let out a gurgle of disapproval, but pointed. Searching through cupboards for a pot, she quickly boiled tea and hurried back up the seamless stairs. Sitting next to Joshen, she felt his forehead. He was still so hot. If she didn't get the fever down and soon, it might be too late. "Pogg, I need a bucket of water."

Standing again, Pogg padded out the door, but not before shooting a warning glare at Bruke.

Using a perfectly shaped wooden spoon, she parted Joshen's lips and ever so slowly dribbled the tea into his mouth as he swallowed reflexively. Hoping for even the slightest improvement, she felt his forehead. She pulled back in shock.

His fever was worse.

What if he doesn't make it? she wondered. Her arms began to tremble. She forced them to still. Tears slipped down her face. It was too much. Her sister and father before her birth. Then her mother. And now Joshen. "Joshen, please don't. Please. Everyone I love leaves me. Please."

Bruke whined and nudged her hand. She patted his head. "I know, everyone except you."

His ears alert, the dog faced the door. Beneath her palms, his body vibrated with a low growl.

Pogg stumbled into the room, a bucket of water tipping and sloshing with each step. With a grunt, he set it down beside her.

Seemingly unable to control himself, Bruke barked.

Pogg arched his back and trilled sharply.

Senna covered her ears. "Stop it!"

His face twitching, Pogg straightened his back and shot her a piercing look. Without another word, he scrambled to the opposite bed and climbed up.

Senna glared at Bruke. "Sit."

Bruke plopped on the floor.

She nodded to Pogg—after all, he'd saved their lives. "Thank you, for the water and … well, thank you." Turning quickly back to Joshen, she peeled off his stiff shirt. She dipped a cloth into the cool water and traced it across his skin. Gooseflesh bubbled beneath her touch. She studied the muscles that had begun to fill out his lanky arms. "He will be as muscular as his father, if he lives long enough," she whispered to herself.

"Forbiddens for any males to comes unbidden to Haven! Forbiddens!" Pogg practically shouted.

Senna jumped. "Why is it forbidden?"

His strange fishy eyes peered at her. "Only Witches."

Senna shifted, unconsciously putting herself between Joshen and Pogg. "Well, you aren't a Witch!"

He trilled again, but softer this time. "Last of Mettlemots, Pogg is. Last. Last. Last. Witches takes pities on Pogg. Lets him stays if he fishes for them." He unwrapped himself and ambled over. Bruke growled. Pogg ignored it. "Pogg takes pities on boy. Lets boy stays."

"Thank you," she managed. She wondered what she'd have done if Pogg had said otherwise?

"Keepers," he continued. "Dark Witch comes. Catches them. Takes them alls way. Only Pogg lefts."

Mechanically, Senna bathed Joshen's arms and chest. "If you help me—teach me what you know, I'll fight her. I promise you."

Pogg eyed her dubiously. "Dark Witch, Head Witch once. She calls meeting. Tells all Witches theys rulers of world. Man bows to them or they kills plants and stops rains 'til man listens.

"Other Witches says no. Some join Dark Witch—Servants.

Some join Witches—Keepers. Witch fight! Horrible!" Pogg swayed to the rhythm of his words. "Keepers loses Witch fight. Banishes selves! But Dark Witch not finished. No! Not finished! "Sacra has little Brusenna then. Sacra hides; not wants Brusenna dead like father and sister."

"But Dark Witch takes Keepers from Haven. Moons forgettings to change the tides. Fogs rollings in, but not rollings out. Rain comes when not supposed to. Soon winter comes in summer and all dies. Then men bows to Dark Witch. She bes queen then! No Witch stops her then!"

Pogg shook his head. "Pogg shows you. Then you frees Witches. This time, Keepers kills Dark Witch!"

12. SECRETS

Senna pulled at the collar of her shirt. Sea salt had settled into the fabric, making her itch like she'd rolled in hay. And worse than the itch, she smelled of vomit. She longed to change her clothes, but if she left and something happened … With a sigh, she worked the rag down Joshen's long arms, across his chest, down his stomach, neck and forehead. She wrung water into his hair. Smoothing it back from his face, she fanned him.

How many times had she repeated this process over the long night? Fifty? A hundred? She'd gone through all her scales and practiced the Witch songs in her mother's journal until her voice went hoarse. But at least she still had the journal. She had Mcbedee and his watertight drum to thank for that.

Pressing her ear to his chest, she listened for any sign of the rattle. She closed her eyes in relief. Still gone. With a moan, Joshen tossed beneath her. Senna's face wet and hot, she watched him squirm, like he was trying to twist away from the fever and pain. He groaned again, the whites of his eyes showing, before finally settling back to his unnaturally deep, harsh breathing.

If he didn't start getting better and soon, he'd die. A tremor shook her to her bones. Tears slipped from her eyes faster than she could wipe them.

At the sound of Pogg's floppy feet on the steps, she turned toward the door. The Mettlemot had a limp fish clamped between his jaws. The fish fell to the floor with a dull thud. "Senna eats."

She shook her head. "I can't leave him 'til he's a little better."

Pogg made a disapproving gurgle as he jerked a sheet from the bed and dunked it in the bucket of water. He draped it over Joshen, crouched on the end of the bed and started awkwardly fanning.

Senna blinked in surprise. "Wish I'd have thought of that." Pogg didn't answer, but she hadn't really expected him to. All of a sudden, she couldn't bear to be here another moment. At the door, Bruke's head swung between Senna and Joshen. Finally, he let out a frustrated whine and hurried after her. After finding some wood and lighting a small fire in the stove carefully surrounded by bricks, she cooked the fish quickly, practically burning it in her hurry. Bruke was still working on the head and tail when she hustled upstairs to check on Joshen.

Pogg hadn't moved from his crouch. His eyes shifted her way. "Senna takes bath. Smells like fish. Witches not likes that."

She was too tired to be offended. Besides, she knew she smelled worse than fish. Rubbing her eyes, she nodded. "Where?"

"Fresh water." He pointed, the webs between his fingers crumpling like wet laundry. "Senna finds it?"

She nodded.

She raided the house for soap and found some relatively clean yet slightly musty clothes and headed off in the direction Pogg had indicated. As she walked, she studied her surroundings. Unimaginable lushness surrounded the barren houses with windows as black and lifeless as the eyes of a corpse. She shivered. So beautiful ... and so empty.

Near one of the cliffs, she found a shallow pool filled with emerald water that felt luxuriously warm—probably heated by the volcano. After she'd bathed, she started back, shivering as her wet shift clung to her and the scrubbed laundry dripped from her arm. She arranged the clothes over the plants outside and hurried upstairs to find Joshen tossing again.

Pogg studied her with an unreadable expression.

With her arms crossed self-consciously over her breasts, she took a deep breath. "Thank you."

He handed her the fan and waddled out the door.

She worked over Joshen, her arms heavy with fatigue and her back sore, long into the night. The entire time, she sang, as if some part of her hoped the songs she sang to strengthen plants might do the same for Joshen. At some point, she noticed sweat beading on his upper lip and hair line. Tossing the rag into the nearly empty bucket, she touched his forehead.

He was cooler!

Over the next hour, she watched as Joshen sweated out the last of his fever. His body relaxed. Finally, he let out a long, deep sigh.

"Thank the Creators," she said with relief. Too tired to feel anything but a numb joy, she collapsed beside him.

***

Senna awoke to find sunlight drenching the room in gold. As though pulled by some unnatural force, she rolled over and her gaze met Joshen's. She swam in the sea of his gray-blue eyes. "Joshen?"

His brows wrinkled and he sounded battered, as if he had been dragged behind a horse. "Senna?"

She threw herself onto his chest. "You're okay," she sobbed.

He weakly embraced her, his arms patting her bare shoulder. "Well, of course I am. Hungry as a half-starved horse, but other than that ..." he trailed off as Senna's sobs increased. Gently, he pulled her back. "Senna, what's the matter? And why are we in the same bed?"

She shook her head, wiping her tears. "You've been sick."

His brow creased. "For how long?"

"This is the third day."

His eyes widened.

She smiled and pressed her palm to his cheek. She felt giddy, like she could dance and sing and cry all at once. "You said you were hungry. I'll go make you something."

Outside, she threw on one of the borrowed dresses before hurrying to the kitchen to prepare an herb stew.

Pogg came in dripping wet, a fish wriggling between his clamped jaws and a starfish tucked under his arm. The Mettlemot grinned broadly at her. She winced. It wasn't like a human smile. Pogg must have known people widened their mouths to show they were happy. So he did too. But it didn't have the same effect. Feeling guilty for her reaction, she smiled weakly back. Even still, he seemed genuinely happy as he handed her the fish. "Other does better. Fish makes strong." He tossed the starfish to Bruke, who immediately tore into the chewy treat.

Senna figured Mettlemots must be like a seal or walrus, hunting in the seas but living on the land. She felt a surge of fondness for the creature. "I'm not sure Joshen should have meat yet," she said gently.

Pogg looked at her oddly. "Fish makes boy strongs. Gives him strengths."

She debated. Joshen hadn't had solid food for days. Better to start small. But perhaps some fish broth would help. She cut the meat into chunks and dumped it in a pot with the herbs.

"Fish," she mumbled as she set the entrails on a plate for Bruke. "I'm so sick of fish I could eat a whole steer." But as far as she could tell, the island had nothing else. Not even chickens.

She strained meat from Joshen's bowl but left hers alone. Joshen slid eagerly back on the bed as she came into the room. She handed him the bowl and sat beside him. One look at her soup and he traded his for hers. Before she could argue, he gulped down half of it. With a sigh he leaned back against the wall. "Senna, I'm sorry."

Examining his broth with distaste, she set it down on a side table. "For what?"

"For using my knife on the kelp. I didn't understand, I—"

She pressed her fingers to his lips. Her skin tingled at the contact. "Shh. You didn't know. No real harm done."

Joshen nodded and gulped a few more swallows of soup. Already, his eyelids drooped heavily.

Senna stood. "Rest for a while. By tomorrow, you should be able to move around."

Finishing the rest of the bowl in one gulp, Joshen nodded and scooted down in the soft covers.

Senna made her way quietly toward the door. When Bruke started to follow her, she shook her head. "No, stay."

His tail hanging between his legs, Bruke trudged over to Joshen's bed.

Downstairs, Senna dumped the broth back in with the rest of the stew and made herself another bowl. As she ate, she fidgeted under Pogg's watchful eye. "Would you like me to get you a bowl?"

"Pogg eats them in water," he informed her.

Imagining him swallowing fish whole, she shuddered. But he continued to stare at her. "What?"

"Senna comes with Pogg."

Casting a nervous glance upstairs, she finished her soup and followed Pogg out of the tree house and deeper into the island. The bleak windows seemed to stare back at her. She imagined the Dark Witch watching from the shadows. "Will the Dark Witch find me here?"

Pogg shook his head. "Only Keepers can find Haven. When Dark Witch imprisoned, Witches took Dawn Song from her."

"Then how did she find it?"

Pogg bared his teeth. "Betrayers!"

So, one of the eight remaining Witches was a traitor. But who?

The trilling sounded in Pogg's throat again. "Espen."

"Espen," Senna rolled the name around her tongue. It tasted bitter. Her mother had reacted with loathing at the mention of it. But why?

Senna's thoughts were interrupted when the houses ended in a circular clearing—much like the one Mother had used at home. The clearing rose into a gentle hill, the highest point of the valley. Lifting her green dress, she climbed the rise. "Is this where they sing the songs to control nature?"

Pogg stared over the rolling green grass. "Yes. Ring of Power."

From the top, she had an unimpeded view. Like a bird's aerie, the island nestled inside a ring of jagged cliffs. Waterfalls cascaded at even intervals along the faces. "The Four Sisters." Senna breathed as she pointed, "Water, Plants, Sunlight and on the outside, the volcano makes Earth."

"Comes," Pogg gestured. "You sees Ring of Power. Now you sees books."

Still in awe, Senna followed Pogg to the other side of the clearing to an enormous tree house. Inside, she found walls covered from floor to ceiling with books. Pogg refused to go inside. "Pogg not goes. Only Witches. Pogg cares for Joshen. Senna learns to kills Dark Witch."

Senna opened her mouth to protest, but Pogg dropped to all fours again and ambled away. A strange feeling pricked the back of her neck as she surveyed the shelves. All around her, signs of habitation, yet the buildings stood empty. She wandered through the library, feeling overwhelmed. A book lying open on the table caught her eye—as if someone had left it in the middle of reading.

She traced the pages, leaving a trail through the dust. Rubbing the residue between her fingers, she stooped down and blew. Dust erupted around her, making her sneeze. Using her hand, she wiped the chair and sat down. Her eyes skimmed the page. Handwritten. This was no book. It was a journal.

Her name jumped out at her. Eagerly, she read.

Brusenna,

If you're reading this, then know you are the last. Even now, she's here. We've lost. She'll find me soon and imprison me with the others, using our songs to feed her own. There we'll stay until we give her our loyalty. Then she will have her unwilling army. An army to hold all men hostage. We'll hold out until our last hope is gone. That last hope is you. I'm sorry I didn't teach you the songs. I only wanted to keep you safe. I was wrong. Stay here, for here you are sheltered. Even now, the betrayer's blood cools in death. I wish—

There was nothing else. Senna hadn't realized she was crying until a drop splashed the page, smearing the ink. With a corner of her sleeve, she blotted it. She blinked to keep others from falling.

So it was true. Her mother was a prisoner. She'd suspected for months, but now it all seemed so sickeningly real.

How could she save them? She thought of Coyel, so powerful she need not even sing for the plants to part before her. And the eight of them combined hadn't stood a chance. How could she, an untrained girl, succeed when the others had failed?

She closed her eyes as the fear caught fire within her. Witchcraft was passed from mother to daughter. And she was the last Witch left. If she remained here, the Witches would die. Espen would win. If she fought and failed, the whole world would be thrown into chaos. Climates would cross hardened boundaries. Seasons would fail to shift. Seeds would rot in the Earth. Her mother and the others would remain prisoners or be forced to become slaves.

Something soft turned to stone within her. She had no choice. She had to fight. She had to win.

Senna stared at the books lining the shelves. She would read them—to the last. She would learn. And then she'd free them.

Or join them.

***

Bruke shifted at her feet. Senna followed his gaze to the doorway. Joshen lumbered up the path to the library, his breath coming in wheezing gasps that clouded the air around his head. The sight brought a pang to her chest. He'd almost died trying to help her. The one person in the world who cared about her and she'd nearly got him killed. She sighed. "Winter's coming early this year."

He leaned against the door frame. "Senna, where've you been?"

She stared at the words in the book without seeing them. "Hasn't Pogg taken good care of you?"

"Well, yes." He hesitated. "But it's been three days since I've even seen you."

Senna slipped her mother's journal out of the stack of books she'd already read. Wrapping a light shawl around her shoulders, she stepped out of the library and into the sunlight. Settling onto one of the natural benches made by the roots of the library tree, she caressed her mother's journal. "My mother left this for me in case the worst happened."

Joshen reluctantly sat beside her as she read aloud Sacra's words.

Espen has a secret. Somehow, with every Witch captured, her strength grows. By the end, she'll have no rival. If the last eight of us cannot unearth this secret, you must find a different way. Something we've all failed to see. Or you must live your life in hiding.

Senna traced the loops and whirls of her mother's handwriting with her fingertips. "I have to find a way to stop Espen. Preferably one that doesn't involve dueling her."

Hearing the sadness in her voice, Bruke tried to nudge under her arm.

"And what way is that?" Joshen asked.

Senna nodded toward the library. "I'm going to search the books. Somewhere, there must be an answer."

Joshen's eyes widened. "All of them?"

Senna stood and brushed off her skirt. "Until I find the answer, yes. In my spare time, I'll train myself for a duel."

Joshen gripped her arm. "You don't even know where Espen is. Or the first thing about dueling. Or how she caught the others. You think you can just read a few books and beat her? If that is all it took, your mother and the others would've done it."

Senna's cheeks flamed. "You don't need to make me more afraid. I'm already terrified."

Joshen released her. "Father told me about Espen. She's evil, Senna."

Senna let out a heavy sigh and walked briskly away. Joshen hustled to catch up with her. "Let me help you. I want to be a Guardian."

She didn't slow.

"My father was one, as was my uncle—Tomack, the sheriff of Gonstower. They sent me to keep an eye on you—to make sure you're safe."

"There is no need, Joshen. Espen can't come here unless another Witch brings her. There aren't any left to do that."

Joshen was already panting and white-faced, though he tried to hide it. "I'll wait with you. When we leave, then I'll keep you safe."

Senna suddenly felt much older than Joshen. He was still a boy and she'd become a woman overnight. He wouldn't willingly leave her. And if she let him stay, he'd die. And leave her. As everyone else did. She could stand being alone, if she knew Joshen was alive and safe. But his death … better to push him away than have him forced from her side. "You can't stay." She'd familiarized herself with the island over the last week. A cave loomed before her. She entered the darkness, Joshen close behind.

"Senna, I know you think I can't help you, but I can."

She rounded on him, her arms folded across her chest. "You won't be able to find Haven again. Not without a Witch. So don't look."

His brows furrowed. "I'm not leaving you."

"Get in the boat, Joshen."

"I'll not! I …"

Before he could finish, Senna sang.

Plants of the sea,
Take Joshen away from me.
To the shore,
That he comes no more.

Joshen ran for the cave mouth. She changed her song. Trees sprang up to block him. She sang to the sea plants again. Kelp snaked around his ankles. "Senna no! Listen—" She sang the kelp over his mouth. Still, he mumbled through it.

"Stop fighting," she begged. "You've been so sick. You'll only wear yourself out."

He stopped struggling. Senna sighed and moved to the side of the boat. "I'm sorry. But I can't ask you to involve yourself any longer. She won't kill me. She needs me."

At least Senna hoped that was true. She cleared the tears from her throat. "But you, she won't hesitate to destroy. And you're no match for her."

His eyes shot white-hot needles at her. She flinched, unable to bear the look of hatred on Joshen's face. "Please don't hate me. I can't lose you, too," she whispered.

Avoiding his gaze, she sang away some of the kelp and kissed his cheek. Slipping a handful of gold coins in his pocket, she sang again. The kelp encircled the boat and hauled him down. She watched as it shrank beneath the water. She stared at the dark pit until her eyes burned with the need to blink. But if she did, he'd really be gone—and she'd really be alone. Finally, she turned to Pogg. "The kelp will take him ashore. Can you make sure he reaches Corrieth?"

Pogg nodded. "Pogg can finds his way back."

Long after the Mettlemot had left, Senna stood in the flickering light of the cave, staring into the dark gray water.

How long would she be here? Alone.

13. Unbinding

Shivering, Senna drew her shawl closer as she stared at the rain pounding her window. She made out Pogg's warped shape slogging through the soggy grounds. Putting her book down, she rubbed her tired eyes. Two months had come and gone since she'd sent Joshen away.

Pogg dropped his catches at Senna's feet before stomping up the stairs. She watched him go and shared a look of concern with Bruke. Though she had only been on the island a few months, she had learned Pogg's volatile moods were often associated with the sea's turmoil. As Bruke tore into another chewy starfish, she lifted her long green, velvet-like dress that she thought might be a Witch uniform and eased up the stairs. At Pogg's room, she leaned against the door frame. "What's Espen done now?"

A shrill trilling erupted from Pogg's mouth. Senna forced herself not to flinch. She hated when Pogg did that. It grated her ears and frayed her already tattered nerves. It ended abruptly and she found herself unwilling to breach the silence for fear of triggering his keening again.

To pass the time, she counted the number of times Pogg rocked back and forth. She'd reached thirty-eight before he spoke, "Pogg not wants to scares Brusenna. Pogg angry because Dark Witch hurts sea." He clicked his tongue. "Meddler! Meddler! Meddler! Changes things not to be changed! Ocean rivers not flowings in right places. Sea turtles not reaches beach for eggs. Baby turtles dies! Warm water turns cold; cold water turns warm! Meddler!"

Senna shook her head. "How do you know all this?"

"Turtles tells me."

She straightened up. "Turtles?"

"Yes. Yes. And whales says warm water too colds for babies, cold water too warms for food."

Senna felt an epiphany creeping along on the edges of her mind. "You can speak to the other sea creatures?"

"Yes. Yes. Creatures speaks."

"All?"

"Air breathers speak. Not water breathers."

Her heart pounded inside her chest. "Do they know where Espen is? Where she's keeping my mother?"

Pogg's eyes went wild. On all fours, he scampered past her as fast as she'd ever seen him move. Hiking up her skirts, she flew after him. Outside, she didn't even pause to pull her shawl over her hair. Water sheeted down on her head and slogged up from the ground as she ran.

The wet made everything cling to her—clothes, hair, shoes. Within minutes, she was as drenched as if she'd dunked herself in the ocean. Thinking it some kind of game, Bruke raced ahead and then waited for the two of them to catch up before taking off again. Senna reached the cave in time to see the ripples from Pogg's plunge in the water. She paced at the edge of the pool. Waiting. Waiting.

If Pogg was right, the sea creatures might know where Espen was. Maybe she could sneak up on the Dark Witch and immobilize her before she could retaliate. Water dripped from her hair and rolled down her face. She brushed it away in annoyance. Wringing out her shawl, she draped it back over her shoulders and wished she'd worn something warmer and more watertight. Finally, she resorted to practicing her songs.

Bruke had long ago given up any hope of fun. He curled up at the edge of the cave, only an occasional whine escaping him as he dreamed. Senna's stomach growled as the light began to fade. Still, she couldn't bring herself to leave the pool.

Pogg appeared suddenly, triumph on his face. "Whales says evil songs comes from land of red flags."

Senna closed her eyes as a flame of hope flickered, warming her. But it didn't last long. The men of Tarten bore red flags. The color of blood. The color of the conqueror. They were no friend to her country—hadn't been since they failed to conquer Nefalie decades ago. Hiding among them was brilliant.

But how could she cross the sea Espen was very much in control of? Pogg seemed to have no problems navigating the raging storms, but he'd said the shipping had all but ceased. She froze. She'd read of a complicated potion few Witches had attempted.

Ioa.

Pulling her shawl over her hair, she ducked back into the onslaught. The cold and wet was even more miserable now. At the library, she threw her soggy shawl on the floor and flipped through the ancient potion books with as much care as she could.

She found the concoction in an emerald book with black writing. Her eyes widened at the complex instructions. She startled when thunder rang so loud she was afraid the lightning might peel apart the library like a knife through a raw egg. Bruke scrambled under the table, shivering and cowering. The rain sheeted down harder.

She imagined the chaos at sea. "She's not giving me much time, is she?"

***

Senna was dreaming. It was night. But not dark. The light from the moon cast everything in blue-black and silver. Senna stepped forward, her slippers silent on the soft grass. She paused at the edge of the clearing. The shadows were her companions. Her friends. If she stepped into the light, she could hide no more.

The wind tugged at her dark green cloak as if begging her to run. But in the dream there was no choice. Her feet automatically carried her into the circular clearing, toward the center. Almost immediately, she saw her—the Dark Witch, striding out to meet her. "I've waited many years, Brusenna."

Instead of replying, Senna studied the trees behind Espen. Hundreds of them. All heavy with fruit. There was something ... unnatural about them.

"Do you like my little grove?"

Senna fixed her attention back to the Dark Witch. She'd traded the traditional dark green cloak and lighter green dress for a black cloak and red dress—life and growth for blood and death. "I've come to end it. One way or another."

A slow smile spread across Espen's face as she reached inside her black seed belt that held her dueling seeds.

Senna mirrored Espen's movements, removing a handful of seeds. Seeds her life depended on. They threw them to the ground. And then both sang, their Witch songs as deadly as the plants snaking toward each other.

As Espen's vines crushed Senna's and snaked around her ankles, she knew. She wasn't strong enough. Just as all those before her had not been.

Senna gasped and sat bolt upright. Bruke's head jerked up beside her. "I had the dream again." She ran her fingers through her damp hair. Clasping them behind her neck, she leaned against her bent knees. "It always ends the same. With her defeating me."

As she'd immersed herself in her studies, she'd become more attuned to Espen's interference. She concentrated on that interference now, feeling the air pressing on her as the wind whipped through the valley. Thunder shook her tree house. The rain sheeted down even harder and for a moment, lightning bleached the night. Espen was at work again—changing the rules of nature, unbinding the barriers that held the world in order. When it was this bad, the dreams came ... dreams of failure.

Bruke rested his head on her thigh. She scratched behind his ears. Usually, he was one of her few comforts, but right now, she wanted to be alone. "Stay."

His eyes followed her as she swung her bare legs over the side of her bed and wrapped her cloak around her shoulders.

Easing open her door, she glanced back to make sure he was obeying her before hurrying outside.

She took a deep breath before plunging into the storm. She was free. Her feet flew across the waving grasses of Haven. As it always did, the cold and wet seeped deep inside her. She raced on, her heart pounding warmth through her. At the center of the Circle, she paused, her breasts rising and falling with her every breath. "How very much like my dream," she whispered. She thought of Espen, of her dark songs. "Somehow, we are connected, you and I. Opposite ends of the same rope."

In a few more months, it would be a year since she sent Joshen away. She was sixteen and he seventeen. A deep ache spread through her at the thought of him. His warmth. The safety of his presence. She shook her head to clear the memories, wishing they would stay buried deep inside her. That they'd stop hurting after all this time.

As she'd seen her mother do so long ago, Senna spread her arms and sang.

Wind, lift me high,
That my words reach to'rds the sky.

The violent wind slowed, like a herd of raging colts pricking their ears to listen to her song. She sang again. Slowly, it bent and circled her. As she continued the song, it became a lazy whirlwind that twisted her hair up and made the trees at the edge of the circle sway as if entranced. The air thickened, testing her weight.

She sang one last time. And this time, the wind lifted her. Her feet dangled above the ground. "Higher," she sang. The wind obeyed, twirling her skyward as easily as a handful of dandelion fluff. She didn't stop until she could see the churning sea beyond the island walls.

When she'd reached the apex, the wind carried her voice over the world.

Though Espen's curse that nature break,
I beg of thee hold thy stake.
Seasons stay in thy place,
Winds blow in pace.

Weather hold thy climes,
Plants keep thy times.
Not to break but bend.
Until at end, I bring thee mend.

She repeated the song until her throat was raw and her voice broke.

When she could sing no more, the wind hesitated, as if it loathed to part with her. She hung suspended, watching the boiling seas and raging storm settle. She looked for any sign of a struggling ship, some proof she wasn't completely alone, but the sea was empty.

She wished she could stop the storm. Although the strength of her songs had grown, Espen was much stronger. But as long as the other Witches resisted, Espen couldn't have total control.

The wind set Senna gently down.

Thank thee wind, for heading my call.
For holding strong so I did not fall.

She waited as it faded, caressing her face one last time before retreating and leaving her alone with the ever-constant thunder and rain.

She pursed her lips. She'd fought this battle many times over the past year. She always lost, but for the little good she managed.

She walked back to her tree house slowly, the weight of the decision that had pressed upon her for the last few months feeling oppressively heavy. She'd skimmed nearly every book in the library. She hadn't found the solution. But if the answer wasn't there, then where?

As she walked, she felt a presence behind her. But that was impossible. Nothing and no one could enter the island unless they could sing the Dawn Song. Still, Senna paused at the door of her tree. Unable to help herself, she turned around.

The clouds were slowly being blotted out. Like a shroud being pulled by an unnatural hand, a fog scuttled over the cliffs that surrounded her home and crawled steadily forward. Though she wanted to, she didn't flinch as it encased her, clinging to her like scum on a pond's surface. She cringed as she took her first breath of it.

"Dark Witch sends vapors. Chokes out light, kills plants and then animals," Pogg said darkly from behind her.

Senna looked at him and then at Bruke, who was standing at the bottom of the stairs. He snuffed the air with his sensitive nose. A low growl rumbled in his chest.

Senna shut the door and rested her head against the solid frame. "It appears Espen has made my decision for me."

14. Reunion

Joshen squinted at the lifeless sails. Rivulets of moisture ran down the sides of his face, stinging his eyes. He wiped them with a damp sleeve. When the fog first rolled in, he'd simply been grateful the storm had left them all alive. But after three days of no wind, he'd come to realize the endless grayness might simply be a slower death.

A voice out of the fog startled him. "Makes me right uneasy." Joshen turned as Lery, the one with the crooked teeth, settled next to him on the rail. "You hear that?"

Joshen walked to his side. "Hear what?"

Lery shook his dark head; scattering water from his braided, beaded hair like a dog shaking after a bath. "Nothing. Not even the splash of waves against the ship."

He was right. The ship was as still as if she were moored. Not a breath of wind stirred the surface of the water.

"I've never seen it so still," Joshen admitted. They might have sailed by compass and found their way out, but not without wind. A look over the edge of the ship revealed glasslike water. Joshen mustered as much confidence in his voice as he could manage. "Cap'n Parknel says he's had bad fogs. And they always break."

Lery spit into the void. "Not like this, we ain't. Came rollin' in like thunderheads. Somethin' pushed that fog in. Mark my words."

Joshen saw the hunted look plain in the other man's dark-skinned face. The same look the other sailors had—hardened sailors who had been about the sea far longer than Joshen. And he'd never known them to show fear that wasn't warranted.

Lery shifted his pipe. What with the fog, the tobacco was too damp to light, so he'd simply been chewing on the stem.

Joshen glared into the blasted fog. He liked the sea alright, but he missed his horses. He missed his family. He leaned into the rail. Could he tell Senna goodbye? Give up and go home when he knew how much she would face alone. Almost, he could hear her sweet voice again.

Today, the song in his mind sounded clearer than ever. As he always did, Joshen strained to understand the foreign words. His head jerked up. He could swear he actually heard a Witch song. He leaned as far as he dared over the rails. "Do you hear that?"

A burst of cold air hit him solidly in the face.

"Get this ship tacked into that wind!" Captain Parknel shouted.

Lery ran toward the pulleys. Still straining to listen, Joshen hesitated, but he couldn't hear anything over the sailors' shouts.

"Joshen!" Lery yelled.

Running to the other men, Joshen tugged at the pulleys.

The fog thinned. Light filtered in. As he worked, he listened for snatches of song. Then, over the shouts on deck and the hiss of the wind in his ears, Joshen heard it again—clear enough he could make out distinct words. He straightened, his eyes wide.

"Joshen! Don't just stand there! Move!"

"Witch song," he whispered, but somehow, every sailor on the ship seemed to hear it. They froze in place, fear obvious in their rigidness.

"It's Espen. Has to be," Lery cursed under his breath.

"To arms!" Parknel whispered fiercely as he ran to his quarters. Quick as a spark, he started handing out muskets.

A weapon was thrust into Joshen's arms. He stared dumbly at it. "No," he said to Captain Parknel. "It might be Senna."

The Captain didn't even pause. "Senna wouldn't bring in this fog, boy. It's Espen. Here to see the last of the sea rider's corpses coating the bottom of the ocean. Now move!"

The Captain had to be right. It was too much of a coincidence for another Witch to show up within days of this fog. Half numb,

Joshen followed the others to the poop deck. Ripping open the wadding with his teeth, he punched his ball down, filled the pan and slapped the frizzen shut. He could only hope the powder hadn't become too damp. All around him, men aimed their muskets toward the beautiful sound.

"But what if it is her?" Joshen asked Captain Parknel.

The Captain pressed his lips together. "Only on my mark," he commanded and the order rippled down the line of sailors.

Joshen held his fire, the weight of the musket straining his shoulders. Beads of sweat joined the moisture rolling down his face.

"The fog's thinning," Lery warned from his left side. "If Espen sees us, we're as good as dead."

Suddenly, the slight breeze gusted to life, shifting Joshen's hair back from his forehead. Gooseflesh pricked under his clothes. He shivered.

"There!" Lery whispered.

Joshen squinted. An outline. Someone standing in a small boat. He felt the tension of the men beside him. Ready to fire, but all hesitated, unwilling to move without the Captain's order. For a split second, Joshen wondered if he could end a song of such beauty. Even if it was Espen's.

He saw a face set against a dark cloak. Wisps of blonde hair, wavy from the moist air, fell across her breast. Her lips were full. She was dressed like the Witches, dark green cloak with a lighter green dress. An enormous wolfhound stood at her feet. His eyes widened. It had to be her! It must be her! "Stand down!" he shouted as he leaped to his feet. He glared at the other men, daring them to challenge him. "Stand down!"

Captain Parknel lowered his musket. "You sure, Joshen?"

"It's not Espen! It's Senna! Lower your weapons!"

In an instant, all the muskets lowered. As the last song faded away, Joshen gulped at what he'd almost done.

"Come up, lady," Captain Parknel called down to her. As Senna climbed the rungs, the Captain turned to the sailors. "Pull up her boat."

"How'd she move the boat?" Lery cried.

Senna took the Captain's hand and hopped onto the ship. A thrill ran through Joshen at the sight of her. "She's a Witch," he said automatically.

Senna's eyes widened at the sound of his voice. The color draining from her face, she slowly turned her gaze to him. "Joshen?" she said, as if not quite believing it. "You didn't leave?"

He could barely breathe. "No."

They stared at each other a long time. He wanted to pull her into his arms. He wanted to push her overboard. But like a fool, he stood frozen with indecision.

Senna blinked a few times, took a deep breath and turned to Captain Parknel. "I need passage on a ship."

Captain Parknel stroked his beard. "And the destination?"

Joshen wanted to shout at the man, *It doesn't matter where she wants to go. We have to take her!*

She squared her shoulders. "Southeast. Into Tarten."

Except, there, Joshen thought. "Into Tarten? Their Chancellors worship war, Senna. It's not safe." He clenched his fist, starting to wish he'd thrown her overboard.

She completely ignored him. "I know it's a dangerous passage, but you could put me ashore far from any towns. I can pay you and keep this ship safe from the storms. Will you help me?"

Captain Parknel smiled. "Even without the money or the offer of safety, we'd help you."

She cocked her head in disbelief, but eventually nodded. "Good. I'll sing for another wind. Ready the ship."

Without waiting for the Captain's order, the sailors scurried into action, their sullen mood forgotten. Some even mumbled old sea chanteys about fish jumping after drawn nets and mermaids dancing on the waves.

Senna smiled tentatively at Joshen. "The mermaids of legend were actually Mettlemots and I doubt any of these men would care to see them dance on the waves."

Even when she wasn't singing, her voice was musical. It sent shivers down his shoulders. Joshen grunted at the thought of Pogg dancing—his greenish skin, pointed teeth and webbed fingers. "Where is he, anyway?"

The smile faded from her like a wilted flower. She turned her back to him. "He consented to accompany me until this ship agreed to help. Then he turned back."

Joshen was surprised by her obvious fondness for the creature. "I'm sorry."

Senna wiped a tear that had strayed down her cheek. "It's for the best. Where we're going, he'd be of no use." She nodded to herself, as if that were the end of it. "I'll clear the way." She headed for the bow, Bruke glued protectively to her side. As Joshen hurried to help the others, she sang again, the mystifying words making him smell and hear the wind long before it actually filled the sails. It came in strong, clearing the fog before their eyes.

When they reached the harbor, many worried townspeople met the ship. Had they seen any other ships? Was it this bad farther in?

From a distance, Joshen watched as Senna stumbled toward Captain Parknel. "If I had my Keepers with me, we could banish this fog—help the other ships come in. As it is, I can barely thin it. I'm sorry."

The Captain's brow creased. "It drains you. Singing, I mean. I can see it."

She turned away. When she saw Joshen watching her, she stiffened and quickly turned back to Captain Parknel. "Singing for hours on end would drain anyone. It weakens my voice. And the weaker my voice, the weaker my songs."

"You should sleep."

She shrugged.

Captain Parknel pursed his lips. "I'll be out most of the night getting us outfitted. You can take my quarters." The Captain looked around, saw Joshen staring at them and nodded toward him. "Joshen'll go get your horses."

Senna turned to him, her eyes lighting up. "You kept Knight?"

Warmth spread through Joshen. He tried to force it down. "And Stretch."

"Thank you."

Refusing to look at her, he shrugged. "Thanks for the tailwinds."

She tipped her head in tired acknowledgement. "The least I could do."

15. SEA WITCH

Gradually, the scent from Joshen's borrowed blanket overpowered Senna's exhaustion. Opening her eyes, she breathed deep. She thought of the things she'd wanted to say last night. But he'd refused to look at her and his face had remained hard and uncaring. She couldn't help but wonder if her decision over a year ago had cost her only friend.

With a sigh, Senna took in the room. Nearly every available inch was packed with map scrolls or cases. She threw Joshen's blanket over her cotton shift and went to the window. Sure enough, she could see Pogg, just below the water, watching her forlornly.

It wasn't until leaving Haven that she realized how fond the creature had grown of her. The last of the Witches. As he was the last of the Mettlemots. She pressed her hand against the glass. "Go back," she mouthed. The thought of Haven completely abandoned made her stomach feel hollow.

A knock sounded behind Senna. Without thought, she said, "Enter." When no one said anything, she turned to see Joshen's surprised face.

He blushed and quickly looked away. "I'm sorry."

"For what?" Senna looked back over the water, but Pogg was gone. She stepped away from the glass, watching as the moist outline of her hand faded. She tried to see past the impenetrable fog. "Did you need something, Joshen?" If he could be cold, so could she.

"I, uh—I just came to get some of Cap'n's things."

Setting down his blanket, she turned, searching for her pack. "That's not necessary. I don't expect the Captain to give up his cabin for me."

Joshen stuck his hands in his pockets. "No. Cap'n says you stay here. He'll sleep below decks with the rest of us."

She crossed her arms over her chest. "No. I couldn't—"

"Would you rather sleep with a bunch of men?" Joshen interrupted. "You'd have no privacy and neither would they. Come on, Senna, they'd be as uncomfortable with the situation as you would."

He was right. Looking out the window, she rubbed her forehead. Espen unraveling centuries of songs felt like abrasive on her already frayed nerves. "I can feel her influence stronger here. Like the aftertaste of a bad meal. Something about Haven must resist her songs more than most places." When he didn't respond, she felt the need to fill in the silence—an urge she'd never experienced around Joshen before. "I hope I'm as ready as I need to be."

"You will be."

He said it with such simplicity. A fact—not yet fulfilled. He had faith in her and he'd stayed. She suddenly felt ashamed. He deserved so much more than she'd given him. "Do you still wish to be a Guardian?"

"Yes," he breathed.

"And you understand the mark can be turned to a poison, should you betray your trust?"

"My father said as much in one of his letters."

She heard him coming closer. She felt his breath on her bare neck and shivered. "Yet still you wish it?"

"Yes."

She wondered if his firm answer came from of a need to protect her or his own ambition ... and why the answer mattered so much. She shook her head. He'd earned the right, regardless.

Turning around, she found his proximity disarming. Close enough she could feel the heat from his body, smell him ... Even after all this time, he still smelled like horses.

Hurriedly, she reached for her bag and held a glass bottle filled with a pale, waxy substance between them. "A Witch's lips gather power from her songs, amplifying the strength of her potions."

She applied the substance to her lips, which had the added bonus of making them shine and rubbed it in. Pulling at his arm, she sang.

Guardian of Keepers and Witch friend decree,
But if thou betrayest, a poison be.

While she slowly rolled his sleeve, she repeated the song softly. Her lips tingled with energy as her song activated the potion. Before he could ask what she was doing, she pressed them against the skin of his forearm, leaving a perfect green imprint.

"It tingles," he breathed heavily.

Senna nodded. "It's going to feel cold. Hold still." She blew on the mark. It coalesced until it formed a perfect sphere. Senna leaned back and smiled. "There, now you're a Guardian."

Joshen fingered the raised ridges of the mark. "Thank you."

Why wouldn't he meet her gaze? After all, she'd given him what he wanted. She shrugged as she released his arm. "You deserve it."

He glanced at her before turning away, his knuckles bleached white as he gripped the empty leather bag in his hands. "Senna, could you put your dress on?"

She quickly looked away. Was that what bothered him? Her exposed skin? Humiliated, she dropped her dress over her head and secured it.

He immediately relaxed.

If Joshen couldn't even stand to look at her bare arms … Searching for something, anything, to take her mind off her shame, she unpacked the other things she'd brought from Haven. A dagger with markings of the Witches—sun rays, mountains, waves and leaves—etched on the ivory hilt and steel blade.

"It's beautiful," Joshen said as he shoved Captain Parknel's things in the bag.

If he was making conversation, maybe that meant he'd eventually forgive her. Senna ran her hands along the dagger's markings. "One thing I quickly learned is that all Witches are rich. Unless, like my mother, they choose not to be."

She felt his gaze on her. "You know we're going to find them, right, Senna?"

Tears sprang into her eyes. "If I'm strong enough." She could see by his expression he didn't understand. But she didn't feel like elaborating. She didn't feel like telling him that their entire journey would end with Senna pitted against a much wiser and more powerful Witch—a Witch who had toppled every other Witch in existence. The odds were as overwhelming as a guppy pitted against a shark. But she had to try. She couldn't hide on the island forever.

She turned back to her packed bags and carefully pulled out her most prized possession—a green and gold belt with segregated pockets. Various seeds rested in each pocket—all labeled with genuine gold thread.

"What's that?" Joshen asked.

"My seed belt." She secured it around her waist. Automatically, her fingers searched the pockets, checking the seeds.

"Seeds for dueling other Witches and healing and such?"

She shoved the dagger into its sheath on the belt. "Yes." She took a deep breath and let it out slowly. Then she said the words she'd been aching to since she'd first seen him. "I missed you, Joshen." She waited, tense, for his answer.

He grunted. "I missed you, too." He nodded toward the door. "The men will be ready. We should get going."

They walked into the fog. Somehow, it seemed even thicker today, like she was breathing water instead of air. Coughing, Senna watched the sailors hauling in ropes and bustling about. She couldn't help but wonder how many of them were here because Parknel had paid them to be. There were so few Witch friends. "Will they all come with us into Tarten?"

Joshen glanced sidelong at her. "Every one of them knows what Espen's doing to the sea. They'll help you, Senna."

She looked out across the unnaturally still waters. Would they be so willing to help her if they knew she was bound to fail?

He spotted Captain Parknel. "Wait here."

She watched Joshen walk away. He hadn't become the bulk of a man his father was. Instead, he was tall and sculpted with broad shoulders that tapered to his waist. His hair was shorter, too. She'd already noted the day's worth of stubble along his jaw. But his eyes remained the same. Gray eyes, the color of snow in the shade and his hair, the color of rich, freshly turned Earth.

He was a man now.

In the midst of their conversation, he glanced up and caught her staring. She quickly looked away to hide the blush that crept up her cheeks. He exchanged a few more words with Parknel before coming back to her. "We're ready to shove off."

She studied him sidelong, liking the pale creases around his eyes against his sun-darkened skin. It had done that before and she'd thought it made him look like he never stopped smiling.

Men stopped pulling in the ropes to watch her walk to the bow. Senna tried to pretend she was back on Haven, standing in the circle. But at the railing, she hesitated, unsure of herself. She turned back to Joshen. He nodded reassuringly. Though he wasn't as friendly as before, he didn't seem angry anymore. That alone gave her courage. With a deep breath, she placed her hand on Bruke's head and faced forward.

Oh wind, hear my plea,
From the northeast, blow for me.

She felt a breeze stirring her hair. She sang again, this time more forcefully. The ship edged forward. On her third song, the sails suddenly popped. The ship surged beneath her. Senna looked deeper into the fog. The wind should have blown their path clear. Instead, it did little more than churn the heavy vapors.

She pressed her lips together and looked back. Already the docks were swallowed whole.

Parknel came to her side. Beads of moisture streaked down his temples. "There's nothing for it, Senna. We can't sail blind. I'm sorry."

She whirled back to the southwest. Something felt wrong. The wind wasn't responding like it usually did. Closing her eyes, she listened to the things nature had to tell her. And then she felt it. Espen was singing from her circle, countering the wind Senna called and bringing in more fog. She felt Joshen beside her. "Somehow, she can feel my songs. And without the protection of Haven, she's rendering them useless."

Joshen shifted beside her. "One Witch can control something that minute from so far away?"

Senna pressed her lips together. "She's not alone. Somehow, she's using the captured Witches to amplify her songs."

Peering into the fog, Parknel scratched his beard. "So Espen wins that simply? Bars us from crossing the sea as if we were fish caught in a net?"

Senna clenched her teeth. "No. The distance is weakening her song. I can counter. It'll just be harder." She called clear air from above. A patch of blue sky appeared. A column of light pierced the waters. Senna sang again. And again. The patch widened. "Will it be enough?" she asked Parknel.

He studied the space before them with a critical eye. "Not for some captains. But I know these shores the way some men know their fields." He gave her a curt nod. "I'll get you through."

She cut off the wind from above, redirecting it behind them. The ship sped forward, but within moments, the fog began creeping in like a thief. Normally, the wind would have lasted for hours. But not while she had to continuously redirect it. Still, as long as she sang, the ship surged forward and the way remained clear, but her strength slipped away like water sifting through cupped hands.

She stopped when Joshen nudged her arm. He held a tray with salted meat, cheese and biscuits. "Lunch," he said.

Rubbing her throat, she leaned against the rails. Her head felt light and her limbs shaky. And already, the wind was weaker.

With a sigh, she slid down and ate in great, hulking bites as she watched the fog slowly strangling the light she'd worked so hard to procure. He handed her a cup. She swallowed slowly, the tepid water soothing her raw throat.

"Senna?" He looked around nervously. "I don't think the others have noticed yet, but the exposed space keeps getting smaller."

She cleared her throat and strained to speak, "My voice isn't as clear or forceful."

He picked at his food. "And tomorrow?"

She shrugged, not willing to think about tomorrow. Brushing her hand on her dress, she took her place at the bow and sang again for the wind to clear their path. But she couldn't hit the high or low notes anymore. Her voice was raspy. The Four Sisters never responded as well to a poorly sung song.

Still, she didn't stop as the sun arched blindly overhead. She didn't notice her body swaying until she tipped sideways and nearly collapsed. Gripping the rail firmly, she sang harder. Her voice cracked and wavered. She longed for the day to leave her in the cool of night. She thirsted for a cup of hot mint tea with a slice of lemon.

Was Espen as tired as she? Would she stop soon, or did her strength far exceed Senna's? She steadied herself. She'd studied and practiced for this war. This fight. There would be no saving strength, no holding back reserves. She'd take herself to the precipice and over the edge.

Suddenly, she felt the unnatural presence fade away. The Dark Witch had stopped. The ship surged forward and the fog dissipated. The first sprinkling of stars appeared on the horizon. She slumped against the rails. Strong arms gripped her shoulders. She immediately recognized his scent.

"Senna, you alright?" Joshen's voice felt as soft as down.

Not wanting to speak, she nodded.

"Come on. You need to rest." He looped her hand through his arm. Her throat was too raw to protest. The other men stopped and cast worried glances her way as he led her toward Parknel's cabin. Bruke followed them, whining the entire way.

She found a meal and hot cup of tea waiting for her beside the bed. Exhaling with relief, she kicked off her shoes. Wiggling her toes and rolling her ankles, she sipped. It wasn't mint. But it was hot and someone had put honey in it.

Joshen dropped beside her. "You can't keep doing this to yourself, day after day. You'll be in no shape for fighting her if you do."

Senna froze. She carefully set down the cup and tucked her hands under her legs. "Maybe that's her plan," the words came out scratchy.

Joshen leaned forward. "What do you mean?"

"If Espen truly wanted me to stay away from Tarten, she'd have stuck to her storms. The only reason for this fog is to flush me out of Haven and exhaust my strength so I'm in no condition to fight her."

Joshen brushed her hair back from her forehead. "Well then, find another way. I'm not going to stand by and watch you sing yourself into old age."

Joshen was right. Another day like today and she'd lose her voice. Then they'd be adrift in the middle of the ocean. Hopelessness and despair as old as her first memory rose inside her. She gritted her teeth. She had another plan. But she didn't want to face it. Not yet. "I'll not turn back."

"I didn't say you should," Joshen said.

Her gaze narrowed as she studied him. "How else can we cross the sea?" She hoped he had another way, something she hadn't thought of.

He shrugged. "I don't know, but continuing like today obviously isn't an option. We'll figure it out."

She smiled reluctantly, loving that someone cared. That she wasn't alone. The tension of the revelation faded and her exhaustion returned with full force. Ignoring the food, she finished the tea and then snuggled into the bed as he pulled his blanket over her shoulder. "Joshen?"

"Mm."

"Thanks for not leaving."

He paused, looking at her. "Thanks for coming back for me."
"Mmhm," she mumbled.

***

Senna and Joshen stood at the bow of the ship, trying to see
past the choking vapors as the sailors idly worked pointless
jobs. She felt their unease in their frequent, nervous glances.
For them, being motionless in the water felt as foreign as an
earthquake on land. If only she were stronger. "It's constantly
changing the direction of the wind that's exhausting me. I'm
sorry," she whispered.

He rubbed his eyes. "Will you stop apologizing?"

Senna sighed. If singing all day wouldn't work, that left her
with only one option. One she knew Joshen wouldn't like … she
didn't much like it herself. "You're right, Joshen."

He stopped peering into the fog to gape at her. A slow smile
spread across his face. "Course I am!"

"Espen knows fighting this fog from behind and above will
take every last ounce of my strength. I'll have nothing left to
fight her," she continued. "It's time to change tactics."

His smile faded into suspicion. He followed her as she hurried
back to the cabin. "Change tactics how?"

She sighed. "I'm going to ask for … information."

His brows remained creased. "From whom?"

She laughed. "You wouldn't believe me."

He folded his arms over his rather expansive chest. "I might."

He appeared ready to physically restrain her. And Senna knew
him very capable and very willing. Trying to act nonchalant, she
waved away his concern. "The sea creatures. They can tell me
about any snags or dangers."

"How can you ask a sea creature anything?"

"Ioa." Senna lifted the vial of topaz-colored liquid from her
belt and swirled it. "But I need you to send all of the men below
decks."

Alarm rippled across his features. "Senna?"

It had been such a long time since anyone had worried about her. She smiled faintly. "It's safe," she lied. "But painful and embarrassing."

"Painful how?"

Though it took a tremendous effort, she didn't flinch. "Like ripping your skin off with a sharpened rock. But it doesn't last long," she added quickly. At his adamant look, she threw her hands up in exasperation. "It's the only way!"

He scowled at her but finally went to Parknel. The Captain shot Senna a pointed look before giving a curt nod. "Sailors below decks!" he shouted. The men shot each other puzzled glances before obeying.

"You, too," she said to Joshen when the last had disappeared.

He widened his stance. "I'm not going anywhere."

Senna sighed. "Very well. But turn your back."

He reluctantly obeyed. She undid the clasp of her cloak, dropping it to her feet. To the pile, she added her belt, dress and last, her shift.

Joshen half turned.

"Don't look!" she warned.

His head snapped back around. Warily watching him, she settled her necklace on the top of the pile. Naked, she shivered. She was frightened of the pain. The books said it was worse than childbirth. And that was if the potion was perfectly made. She'd tried for months to make her own concoction. But it never turned out right.

Eventually, Pogg had taken pity on her and showed her to the Head of Plant's private collection. The Witch was supposed to be renowned and she had written many of the books Senna had studied. Still, if the potion wasn't exact, she'd be stuck as some half-creature. And then she'd die.

Her hands shaking, she stuck her finger in the vial and applied it to her lips. She sang a soft, low song.

Sea, I have chosen one of thy creatures,
I ask of thee, change my features.

As she repeated the song, she felt the potion coming to life. Never pausing, she took some of the oily substance from her lips, dabbed it on her forehead, the depression of her clavicle, the baseline of her ribs and at the bottom of her belly. Then she dragged her finger down, connecting the dots of oil. As she did, she sang it once, twice, three times.

The oils warmed until they grew unbearable. She dug her nails into her palms. Her song stuttered to a halt. As though connected by an invisible line of fire, the oil seared through her.

Slowly, ever so slowly, the heat dissipated. Her fingers relaxed. But then her heart sped up. She knew what came next and it was much worse. The book said the first Witch who had tried Ioa thought she was dying.

The sensation of the cold fog faded. Her flesh rippled. Her bones vibrated. The first twinges of pain exploded in her muscles. She'd promised herself she wouldn't cry out, but the pain boiled under her skin. Her first bone broke and reformed. A sob clawed its way up from her lungs. Pitching headfirst into the icy water, she screamed. Even as she writhed, her bones and muscles flamed like a roaring wildfire.

In slow, steady increments, the pain diminished before finally disappearing. Taking a moment to orient herself, she swam for the surface. She saw Joshen and knew he didn't understand. She continued to look at him until his eyes widened in comprehension. "Senna?" She nodded her head. He reeled back, his hand on his forehead. "You're a seal!"

She turned to swim away and only then did she notice the name etched and then painted on the back of the boat. If she were still human, she'd have smiled. Parknel had named his vessel Sea Witch.

She dipped into the water, searching for others. She heard them calling each other. Especially the whales, their low whines, moans and clicks articulated their displeasure with Espen's malicious songs, which approached from the east. She eavesdropped as they discussed the sea's temperament, landmarks, the Sea Witch and how strange it was that no other boats trolled the waters.

Satisfied with what she'd learned from the whales, she sought out other creatures. It didn't take her long to find a sea turtle. As she swam next to him, the urge to play with his floating shell nearly overcame her. Firmly planting her mind on human thoughts, she asked if the turtle knew of any shoals.

He regarded her with ancient eyes. His slow, flowing answer told her no dangers for boats existed for days.

"How far to the land of red flags?" she asked.

He grunted. He didn't speak with words, but long, slow movements. But Senna's seal brain was able to translate it. "Long since the Witches have swum with us. You wish our help?"

Surprised, she stopped swimming. "Yes," she barked, her lungs begging her to surface and fill them with salt air.

He nodded, his side flippers turning. "Come again. I shall spread word to those that might help the Keepers."

He wheeled and glided away. She glanced up at the gray sky and wondered which sea creatures wouldn't wish to offer their help. But she wanted to laugh. Let Espen waste her time with her cursed fog. Senna had found another way.

The urge to be a seal was so overwhelming that, for just a moment, she let her animal impulses take over. At the surface, she filled her lungs deeply and twirled around, enjoying freedom she'd never experienced on land, for she wasn't bound to the ground. Up, down, sideways. It was like flying. She shivered and leaped above the waves. She nosed a floating bit of wood, sending it flying. It landed with a splash. Giddy, she charged after it.

She played with it, taking it down and letting it float back to the surface. Then blasting up beneath it and sending it soaring. She twisted and twirled through the cold water. But then she slowed, trying to make sense of the foreboding creeping over her.

She stopped abruptly. The water felt cold.

Fear pierced her. If she changed before she found the ship, she'd die of exposure. Diving, she searched for it. There was nothing but the endless expanse of water. Desperately she swam, her mind alert for any more signs of the change.

A floating speck caught her attention. Her large eyes widened at how far she'd strayed. In this form, she could move through the water much faster than any human. Putting on a burst of speed, she reached the hulking ship as her fins lengthened.

"There she is!" Joshen hollered.

She swam willingly into their nets. They heaved her up as her legs turned from the darkest brown to creamy white. Joshen had a blanket waiting for her as fins completed their change into arms. He wrapped it around her and heaved her into his arms as her fur disappeared and her human form completely returned.

Senna tucked her head into Joshen's chest. "Please put me down. I only need a minute."

"Stop being so prideful," Joshen chided. "And let someone help you." He said it like a challenge.

Senna clamped her mouth shut. Hurrying through the men, he burst into Parknel's cabin and set her on the bed. Bruke instantly leaped up next to her and started licking her face. Joshen shooed him away, which bought him a reproachful stare.

Her wet hair clinging to her back, she lay still, concentrating on breathing.

"You turned yourself into a seal!"

A smile worked its way across her face. "It's like flying. You're not limited to the ground anymore. Up, down, sideways. Any direction you please. It's the most wonderful sense of freedom … once the transformation is over, that is."

He stared at her in wonder. "I had no idea Witches could do that."

"You'd be surprised what I can do." But then she winced as she remembered the pain and shook her head. "Creating an Ioa potion takes years of painstaking perfection. It's extremely rare. Luckily, Pogg had a good idea of where to look. The transformation itself is …" She shivered. "I would've never tried if Pogg hadn't told me of the sea creatures' hatred of Espen. I figured becoming a seal might prove useful."

Joshen shook his head. "It's a good thing Espen never thought to ask the animals. They might have accidentally led her to Haven. You'd be one of her prisoners by now."

Senna blinked rapidly. "I hadn't thought of that."

Joshen grunted. "So, could you change yourself into a whale and pull the ship through all this?"

Senna managed a laugh. "No, I can only change into something roughly the same size and weight as me. It has to be a mammal—fish are just too different. And it never lasts very long."

"No birds, then?"

Senna carefully gathered the blanket over her shoulders to spare him having to see her skin and sat up slowly. "No. I'm afraid not."

"So, what'd the sea creatures say, Senna?"

She walked to the large window that looked over the water. "Southeast, for now. Let her blind us in her fog. I'll sing us a wind and let the fish be our eyes."

16. Taste of Blood

The turtle kept its word. Sea creatures flocked to Senna. She hovered in the water, listening to their tales. Dolphins, seals, porpoises, whales. Mammals seemed to have an affinity for her ... more tolerance, or perhaps they were more intelligent than fish.

She'd heard nothing of land or other ships for days, so she was surprised when they mentioned another ship coming behind the Sea Witch. She hadn't been in the water long, so she decided to work her way in that direction. She moved at top speed, breaking the surface of the water as she plunged forward.

Joshen called after her, asking where she was going. But it wasn't like she could answer him anyway. She caught sight of the ship turning to follow her a moment before the fog swallowed it.

She hurried, not wanting to turn back to a human in the frigid waters. When she surfaced for breath, the fog was so thick she wanted to reach out and pull the film from the air. The sound of crashing waves startled her. She turned. A great hulking shape loomed out of the fog. It was coming straight at her.

Her heart pumping, she dove. The bow barely missed her. With groans and creaks, the ship passed overhead. She surfaced at the ship's side.

"Cap'n! Look, a seal!"

An unfamiliar man peered down at her. "Are we close to land?"

"No, sir. None we know of."

The ship was big, though not as large as Parknel's—but that only meant it moved faster. In gold, the words Gallant Green stood out against black and green paint. The cannon ports caught her eye, as did the heavy sails. It must have tacked onto the wind Senna had sung into existence.

The Captain pressed his lips together. "Hmm. Well, one doesn't usually see them this far out, but it isn't unheard of. Still, double the watch. I'd hate to smash against an uncharted island." Senna took a deep breath and allowed her nose flaps to close, convinced there was nothing more for her to learn.

But then a familiar voice growled, "I hate seals."

She jerked back just in time to see Wardof level a musket. She dove, her tail pumping madly. Searing pain ripped through her flipper. Less than a heartbeat later, she heard the gun's rapport. It was all she could do to keep her nose flaps closed as her whole body convulsed. With a whimper, she studied her injury. Dark blood gushed from the wound. She could taste it in the water.

Her seal senses screamed danger, overriding her ability to suppress them. Senna swam fast for the safety of her ship. But the harder she pushed herself, the more blood she lost. She grew weaker and worse, the water started to feel cold. She broke the surface and took deep, gulping breaths. Some instinct warned she needed to dive deep. But did she have time before she changed back into a human?

The instinct grew stronger, demanding she dive. Frantically, she searched for the ship, but it was nowhere in sight. She finally gave in, wasting precious moments as she worked her way deeper and deeper. It was so dark she had to rely on her keen sense of smell as she skimmed the bottom of the ocean. Then she saw why her instinct had commanded her to dive. A shark. Weaving back and forth above her as it searched for the source of the blood. Her blood. Lipless, its teeth—made for gripping and tearing—were constantly bared. Her natural enemy.

Senna put on a burst of speed she didn't know she had left. Somehow, she was safe below the shark. But she couldn't stay here much longer. And even as a seal, she couldn't hold her breath forever. Already, she could feel her skin tingling. She'd begin changing in moments.

If she stayed any longer, she'd die. Surging forward, she pushed for every ounce of speed she had. Her skin shivered. From the corner of her eye, she saw the shark dart at her. Her flippers turned into hands. She prayed to the Creators her tail would stay a few moments more.

Her fur shrank and her tail split into legs. Her speed floundered before she burst above the water. "Shark!" she screamed as she swam for the rungs on the ship. Chaos erupted above her, in the midst of which she heard Bruke barking wildly. A figure landed with a splash beside her. Joshen's head bobbed up. He lunged for her. Wrapping her in his arms, he squeezed so hard she couldn't breathe. "Pull!" he shouted

Senna felt her body jerk. She looked down. Water droplets fell on the shark's dorsal fin. They stopped moving for a moment. The shark twisted sideways. Inside its black eyes, its pupil shrank to nothing as it focused on her. She nearly screamed. With a jolt, the rope heaved again.

She found herself sprawled across the deck, Joshen covering her body with his own. "Give me the blanket!" She hadn't realized, hadn't cared, that she was naked until that moment. "Turn around!" He hadn't really even needed to say it. The men had already turned their backs.

Keeping his eyes locked on hers, Joshen lifted himself up and covered her with the blanket. "You alright?" Senna wasn't strong enough to answer. He scooped her into his arms and dashed for the Captain's cabin. He laid her on the bed and began rubbing her hands between his. "You're freezing."

She was cold. So cold. And too tired to respond. But when he tried to tuck the blanket around her, pain shot from her arm. A yelp escaped her lips. "Senna?" He pulled his hand away. It was stained crimson. Carefully, he peeled back the blood-soaked blanket. "Senna! What happened?"

Only then did she remember why she had gone back in the first place. "Wardof. Behind us." It was all she could say before she passed into oblivion.

***

Pain kept pulling Senna away from unconsciousness. Like when Joshen poured a strong-smelling liquid over her wound and scrubbed it. The moment he stopped, she passed out. And then she started as a needle pierced her sore skin. She tried to squirm away, but strong arms held her down. She recognized Parknel's solid voice, "Steady, girl. Steady."

She felt the thread inside her, tugging. The thought popped into her head that she knew what it felt like to be a quilt. "Just a few more Senna and he'll be done," Joshen's voice came from somewhere above.

Resigned that no one and nothing would help her, she gritted her teeth and endured it. When they were finally done, she felt as though her arm had been pounded flat by a mallet. She wanted to sleep, but it simply hurt too much. With a moan, she tossed, sending sharp stings and a deep ache radiating outward. Teeth gritted, her eyes fluttered open.

Joshen looked down at her. Someone was moving behind him. Probably Parknel. Joshen grasped her hand. "How bad?"

Tears spilled from her eyes, pooling in her ears. "Pretty bad."

Joshen smoothed back her hair. "Here, drink this."

She smelled it as it touched her lips and tried to pull away. She'd seen alcohol turn men into monsters.

"Come on, it'll help."

She didn't have much of a choice as the liquid burned her throat. A heartbeat later, it warmed her belly. She coughed and lay back. Bitterness flooded her mouth. They'd laced it with something stronger than alcohol. He coaxed a few more swallows into her. She lay with her jaw clenched. After an immeasurable length of time, the pain eased. Her body relaxed.

"Better?" he asked. She nodded. "Tell me what you saw."

Senna couldn't clear the horrible taste from her mouth. "Could I have some water?" she croaked.

Joshen poured her a glass and propped her up as she sipped. She lay back against the bed. "Wardof has another ship and he's not far behind. He shot me."

"That dung-licker!" He punched the mattress.

"He knew who you were?" Parknel asked incredulously.

Senna shook her head. "No. He said he hated seals and fired."

Parknel cleared his throat. "He hates anything that gets the best of him. A seal took a bite out of him once."

The two men exchanged glances, but she hurt too much to care how or what Parknel knew about Wardof.

Joshen pressed his lips into a tight line. "He must have a pretty fast ship to catch up with us."

Parknel nodded. "The question is, when will he catch us?"

Senna gestured weakly to her bags. "Bring them to me."

Joshen did. Using her good arm, she went through the contents, pulling out seeds and a small, lidded pot. She opened the lid to reveal rich, brown Earth from Haven. She dragged her finger along the surface. She sprinkled the seeds and covered them. "Give them a little water." Joshen poured some water into the pot. She cleared her throat and sang in a shaky, weak voice.

Take in light, take in air,
Spread thy roots, thy leaves grow fair.

Shoots appeared. Within moments, full-grown herbs spread their leaves. "Take all the leaves, leave the flowers," she said.

When Joshen had finished, Senna sang again and the plants aged. "Catch the seeds."

Joshen held out his hand as dried out seeds dropped onto his palm. He looked at her in wonder.

"Told you there were lots of things I could do," she managed. "Please, replace the seeds in my belt. Use the tabber for a tea. The itnot leaves are meant to drape whole over my wound, under the bandage."

Joshen did as he was told. Not long after Senna had drunk the tea, she felt the pain ebb further.

Joshen brushed the hair away from her face. "Rest now. I'll figure out what to do about Wardof."

17. SERVANTS OF THE DARK WITCH

Two days passed before Joshen would allow Senna to leave her cabin. Her injured arm strapped to her side, Senna leaned over the ship's weathered side and strained to see through the vapor. She couldn't make out Wardof's ship, but she knew it was there. And coming closer. Parknel leaned in next to her and the two listened for the sounds of waves breaking against the other vessel's hull. But she heard nothing.

"Cannons are loaded."

Senna looked at him askance before turning back to her vigil. "I'm sorry for the danger I've placed you in."

"Bah." Parknel spit tobacco juice in the water. "Sea's been listin' for years 'cause a Espen's interference. 'Bout time she got her comeuppance. I'm just glad to help deliver it." He placed a reassuring hand on her good arm and moved on.

She shook her head, amazed the Captain thought of her in any way equal to Espen's comeuppance. "Captain," she called. He turned. "All the same, thank you." He couldn't understand how much his acceptance meant to her.

He nodded again and trotted down the stairs to the main deck. Senna turned back to her vigil, not daring to move as the minutes coalesced into hours. She thought she heard something beyond the sounds of their own ship. Singing soft and low, she teased the wind into thinning the fog. Her blood turned cold in her veins. The faint outline of a ship. Even as her voice cut off, the fog swallowed it. She turned and ran, remembering Wardof's handsome, hate-filled eyes. He was perfectly capable of killing her.

Her arm throbbing in time to her heartbeat, she gripped Joshen's arm, but her mouth couldn't form the words.

He took one look at her face and then peered into the fog behind them. "Are they coming?"

She managed an emphatic nod.

His eyes darkened dangerously. "We almost made it."

In a fierce whisper, Parknel ordered the men to their battle stations.

Joshen hefted his weapon and looked down at her. "Get below decks."

"Joshen, I won't hide while you fight."

He gently grasped her shoulder. "Unless you can sing kelp to sink their ship, your songs aren't going to help us much. We need you to grow your plants for the wounded."

"Wounded ..." Senna's face paled. Heavy tears started to roll down her face. "They can't do this! Not for me!"

Joshen cast a look around before pushing her into the cabin. He slammed the door behind him before rounding on her. "This is about more than just you, Senna! This is about the right to protect their way of life. You happen to be the answer these men have been waiting for and I'll not have you shouting how unworthy you are!"

Bruke jumped easily onto the bed, obviously convinced Joshen wasn't a threat.

Senna wasn't so sure. "Joshen, they could be hurt. *You* could be hurt." Her voice was barely above a whisper. "In all the world, you're the only friend I have." She lifted her face to his. "I can't lose you."

Careful of her arm, he wrapped her in a warm embrace, the first one she'd had since her mother left. She cried harder, wetting his shoulder with her tears. Joshen didn't move. Didn't ask her not to. "I won't promise you I won't be hurt—that's a promise no one can keep. But I can promise I'll be careful."

Senna wiped her cheeks with her hand. "Promise?"

"Promise," he replied. A stealthy grin spread across his face. "Besides, there's always Parknel and Bruke."

Senna laughed despite herself. "And Pogg!"

"In a pinch, you could probably count on Lery."

Senna swiped the last of the tears from her cheeks.

The lines around Joshen's eyes softened. "See, you're not as alone as you thought you were." He brushed the crook of his finger gently across her cheek before pressing his lips to her forehead. Senna's chest ached. "Go take care of your plants." He took a step back and then was gone.

Senna grabbed her seed belt and some soil and disappeared below decks. Finding a fairly empty corner, she laid out her pots and spread numerous seeds across the top. She sang them into full maturity and then her work was done. In all that time, it had been deathly silent. She couldn't stand it. "Come on, Bruke. Let's go see what's going on."

Easing back above decks, Senna made her way to Joshen's side. He shot her a disapproving look, but made no move to force her down. Yet.

Parknel stared at the other ship's outline. "Wardof is sure to recognize me and Joshen." He turned to Lery. "You just got promoted."

Joshen leaned into Senna and spoke low, "We're going to try talking this through. Make sure they aren't merchants proving passage instead of paid mercenaries before we blow them to bits. One word from me and you disappear below decks. Agreed?"

Desperate hope clawing at her insides, Senna nodded.

He shot a commanding look at Bruke. "You stay with her." As if he understood what Joshen had asked, Bruke scooted closer to Senna's side.

Parknel addressed his men, "We're not going to outrun them. Much closer and they could rake our stern. If we bring her around broadsides, we could rake her astern before she hits us. But before we do, let's determine their purpose. Cannons loaded and touch sticks at the ready. Turn her 90 degrees starboard."

Lery flipped the wheel. Sailors disappeared below decks to man the cannons while others scurried up the masts. Much faster than any of them expected, the other ship took shape.

Joshen listened to the hull groaning in protest as their ship turned starboard into the wind. She'd stand listless, but they would have full advantage of their broadside cannons. Parknel nodded to one of his men and they pulled out a series of flags used for communication. A blue cross with a white background was run up the pole, followed by a blue flag with a white cross. They meant, "Stop what you are doing and watch for my signal," and "We are dead in the water," respectively.

The other ship must have seen them through the fog, for she pulled down her sails and turned. She paused in the water, nothing more than a dark shadow. The wind tugged her closer and he saw them raise a flag with a yellow bar followed by a blue one.

"They want to talk," Parknel said.

Joshen squinted into the fog and saw them readying a boat to lower into the water.

"Raise the affirmative flag," Parknel ordered.

As a sailor hauled it up, Joshen hefted a thick coat over his shoulders and pulled a cap down low.

Doing the same, Parknel gave the sailors a knowing look. "Lower a boat. Let's see what they want."

Nodding a curt goodbye to Senna, Joshen took his position at the back of the boat, Parknel at his side. Lery, dressed as a captain, sat at the front. As he rowed, Joshen studied the other ship. While it was true the Sea Witch had the advantage of size, the Gallant Green could claim the prize of speed and maneuverability. If there was a fight, a win could easily go either way.

Joshen kept his head tucked into his jacket as the sailors in the two boats appraised each other. Wardof sat behind and to the right of the Captain, who rose to his feet. "My name is Captain Arneth. I've a passenger here, a Mister Wardof. He's looking for a runaway girl by the name of Brusenna. We request permission to board your vessel and search for her."

The epitome of dignity, Lery stood with his hands clasped behind his back and his feet spread. "Of course, that is unacceptable."

The Captain raised an eyebrow. "Mister Wardof has paid us a good deal of money for the girl—with the understanding that the use of arms may be necessary."

Joshen doubted any of his fellow sailors missed Arneth's threat. He certainly hadn't.

"Do you threaten us, good Captain?" Lery responded casually.

Arneth's face darkened into a scowl. "I do."

Lery pretended to look back at his crew while he searched Parknel's face for an answer. From the corner of his eye, Joshen watched Parknel mull it over. He mouthed the word, "Armed?"

Lery turned back around. "Are you, at the moment, armed?"

Arneth straightened indignantly—only the lowliest of captains came to a parley armed. "Of course not!"

With a pleased grunt, Parknel stood. "Then I'll tell you the man, Wardof, is a liar, murderer and paid mercenary of the Dark Witch—she who is the enemy of all free and seafaring men alike. We're friends of the Keepers. If you align yourselves with Witch Hunters, declare yourselves now and we can dispense with the formalities and get to the fighting!"

"You!" Wardof stood and pointed a finger that shook with rage. "You left me for dead on that forsaken island! Hunting bats and seals for six months before anyone found me!"

Parknel's amused gaze fell upon Joshen.

With a grin, Joshen rose to his feet.

"And you! The horseman's son!" Wardof spat. "I know for a fact she's on that ship, Captain Arneth."

"Indeed, she is," Parknel agreed. "So I'd have to be an idiot to allow you on board to search for her."

Captain Arneth looked over the three men standing in Parknel's boat. "Which one of you is really the Captain?"

Parknel nodded to Joshen and Lery. The two sat down.

"I'm Captain Parknel. What say you, Captain Arneth? Do you follow the Dark Witch or the Keepers?"

Arneth's gaze never faltered. "My crew and I'll discuss this and have your answer." He nodded to his men and the two captains watched each other grow smaller as their sailors pulled at their oars. When the little boat bumped into the Sea Witch, Joshen scaled the rungs and jumped aboard.

"Man the cannons!" Parknel roared from behind him.

Senna jumped at the shout. Her face paled. "What'd they say?"

Joshen took a deep breath. "He said he'd think about it. Which really means, 'Give us time to fire first!'" He pointed below decks. "There's nothing you can do. Go now!"

Senna turned and rushed away. "But there is something I can do," she murmured. She held a glinting topaz vial to the sun. "Something I should've done in the first place."

"Fire at will," Parknel cried.

"Run!" Joshen screamed after her.

Senna ran, but before she'd gone two steps, a deafening boom sounded from the Gallant Green. A series of answering reports rocked their ship. The balls whistled as they cut through the air and exploded into the sea. Acrid smoke seeped up from below, stinging her eyes and making her cough. Men shouted and ran. None of them paid her any mind as she rushed toward the bow instead of below decks.

Whining, Bruke tried to block her path, but Senna simply darted around him. The cannons roared again. She heard shouts and the cannons reloaded. The Sea Witch fired again. But this time, instead of a splash, the sound of wood shattering far away.

Senna sickened. Men from the Gallant Green had just died. And even though they were the enemy, it still hurt. The Gallant Green's cannons roared in answer.

There was a massive crash. Senna covered her ears and stumbled as the deck lurched beneath. Bruke tangled up her feet.

Senna slammed into the deck. For a moment, she couldn't think through the pain in her arm. Something slipped from her hand. Even with all the noise and chaos, she was aware of a clinking sound as the small vial landed on the deck and rolled away from her. She watched helplessly as it plunged over the side.

Using her uninjured arm, she dragged herself to peer over the edge. The vial bobbed on the waves. She had to hurry. Moving carefully, she pulled the sling from her arm. She felt a throbbing ache, but didn't let it stop her from dropping her cloak and dress. She couldn't bear to take off her shift—not when it might not work.

She stood on the banister. Something jerked her shift. Her injured arm shot out to catch herself as she tumbled to the deck. She gasped as the stitches pulled against her soft flesh. Blood oozed from the wound. Tears welled in her eyes. Her shift in his mouth, Bruke whined, his eyes wide and frightened. She eased her fingers between his teeth. "I have to protect them, Bruke."

He whined louder and set his jaw.

Senna knew she couldn't waste more time. The vial could sink or be washed farther away and then it would be hopeless. Lunging to her feet, she jumped. Her shift caught in Bruke's mouth before ripping. She exploded into the ocean as another blast sent shock waves around her. Pulling against the water, Senna gasped at the bone-numbing cold. Bits of debris from the Sea Witch pelted her.

Still holding the white cloth in his mouth, Bruke paced and whined above her.

Her head swiveled desperately from side to side as she searched and then she saw it. The vial. Kicking out, she pulled herself forward with her good arm. She wasn't even sure the potion would work in the water, but she had to try. She opened the bottle and oiled her finger before stopping the cork. Forcing herself to relax, she floated on the rolling waves. Though it was awkward with her clinging shift, she dabbed the oil on her lips and body and drew a line between the spots.

Sea, I have chosen one of thy creatures,
I ask of thee, change my features.

At first, nothing happened. But then, the water didn't feel quite as cold. Her skin rippled as the familiar pain gripped her, as though her flesh were being ripped from her body. Her bones broke and reset themselves.

And then it was over. She was glad seals swam with their tails and not their flippers, letting her rest her arm. And though the salty water stung her wound, it also staunched the bleeding. Gripping the vial gently between her teeth, Senna searched for the familiar, high-pitched groaning.

Following the closest sound, she found it. An immense blue whale. Senna swam next to the creature's eye and began grunting. The whale focused on her, but it was a look of annoyance, not understanding. When she persisted, the whale flicked his enormous tail and sped away.

Senna pushed through the water, trying to keep up. But the whale quickly distanced her. And worse, the water was beginning to feel cold. Surfacing, Senna took a deep gulp of air and turned toward the now-distant battle. The fog had miraculously cleared, but smoke clung to the ships as stubbornly as the vapors had. Both vessels were damaged, but the Sea Witch looked far worse.

Senna's head swung back and forth between the whale and the battle. She was far enough away now that she could cover both of them with an outstretched flipper. If she didn't start back soon, she'd change before she could return. *I'll stay,* she thought. *It's all I can do for them now.*

Fear clinging to her, she swam after the whale. She was going farther from safety, yet she didn't slow. It wasn't long before her limbs trembled and transformed. And then she was a young woman, treading the frigid water in nothing but her shift. She sang to the whale.

Help me!
I'm the last Keeper left!
Help me!

She knew many animals understood Witch song, for it was the language of the Creators. But most had no reason or desire to listen. Senna kept repeating her song, supplicating the whale to return. But she saw nothing. Resigned, she turned to face the ship, hoping her failure wouldn't cost any of the sailors their lives.

A loud gush erupted behind her. Startled, she whirled to see the enormous eye of the blue whale staring at her. It let out a hungry call and Senna understood. Without the sun to feed the krills' prey, the whales were growing hungry.

Sadly, Senna sang.

> Witch of Black, purpose so foul,
> Wishes the whole Earth to bow,
> Takes the Keepers one by one, until—
> At the end—all comes undone.

The whale blew angrily.

Her jaw chattered as she pointed to the offending ship.

> Her Servants bent on destroying the last,
> And setting her cast.

That was all it took for the whale to flick its enormous tail. Unfortunately, that sent Senna reeling back. Now she was even farther away than before.

Racked with shivers, she unstopped the vial. Her whole body shuddered uncontrollably. The vial slipped from her grasp. The oil spread all around her. Senna immediately felt warmer, but her heart sank. Now she couldn't change. She took stock of the far-away ships, wondering if she should even try.

Joshen.

She sighed. "Well, at least I don't ache anymore." Barely managing to grab the vial before it sank, Senna skimmed some of the oil off the top of the water, recorked the vial and held it in her mouth. With her injured arm tacked to her side, she started kicking.

18. Ioa

Joshen watched in wonder as an enormous blue whale sped toward Arneth's boat. He'd never seen one move so fast. From the other ship, shouts turned to cries of panic as the enormous whale increased its speed. A massive crunch sounded. The stern of the ship crumpled as though made of spun sugar.

In stunned silence, Joshen watched as the Gallant Green's bow lifted out of the water, revealing scattered barnacles. Sailors scrambled to cut the ropes that held the boats in place. A few crashed to the water, some tipped over. Within a minute, the Gallant Green heaved a great sigh and disappeared underwater, dragging some of her crew with her.

Those who remained hauled themselves into the boats or tried to flip the swamped ones.

"Whales don't attack boats," one sailor said with fear.

"That one did," another sailor replied.

Joshen struggled to control his panic. Senna had done this, he was sure of it. Taking off at a run, he pounded below decks where Parknel bent over an injured sailor. "Is Senna here?"

Startled, Parknel looked up. "She was supposed to help with the injured. Good thing I remembered which was the itnot and which was the tabber."

Joshen wasn't listening; he was already halfway up the stairs. He shoved open the cabin door. The room was empty. "Bruke!"

The dog came from behind. He laid a piece of familiar white cloth at Joshen's feet.

As Joshen grasped the cloth, cold dread shot through him. "Senna." His mind was lost in the enormity of his fear. Something tugged at his clothes. He looked down at Bruke pulling him toward the door. Mechanically, Joshen's legs moved after Senna's dog. At the bow, Bruke looked into the water with a whine.

Joshen halted in front of Senna's abandoned sling and clothes. Bending down, he picked up her necklace. It glinted, catching the light. Unwillingly, his gaze stretched over the ocean. "What has she done?" Though he knew she wouldn't be there, he couldn't help but peer over the side of the ship. "She changed to a seal and brought the whale back, didn't she?" How long had she been gone? That potion of hers only lasted a short time and the whale had come long ago. "Man a boat!" Joshen screamed as he ran toward the crafts. "Bring arms!"

His hands bloody, Parknel appeared from below decks and shot him a questioning look. "Joshen?"

Joshen tugged the ropes. "Senna's in the water somewhere!"

Sailors sprinted to his side. Joshen jumped in the boat as others began to lower them. "Bruke! Come!" Joshen shouted.

The enormous dog jumped over the rail as the boat slammed into the water. The men loosened the ropes and hauled out the oars. Bruke pointed southwest and barked. Joshen grabbed his oar. "Pull!"

***

It was amazing how fast and far Senna had swum as a seal. Her inadequate arms flailed and tugged at the water, but for all her efforts, she wasn't much closer to the ship and her muscles were stiff and slow to respond. Shivering uncontrollably, she stopped swimming long enough to pour the remnants of the oil over her head. For a brief moment, she felt better.

She gazed forlornly at the Sea Witch. After all she had been through, it wasn't Espen who would defeat her but her own folly. "I'm sorry, Joshen. I failed you." She looked past her treading feet and searched the depths of the water—her grave. "Mother," she whispered. "Forgive me, Mother."

***

Bruke stayed at the front of the boat, sniffing the air. Whenever the animal shifted, the sailors righted their course. Joshen wasn't used to the heat or the strength of the sun anymore. Sweat rolled from the sides of his face. His shirt clung to him. He squinted into the brightness, willing himself to see something.

Bruke barked.

Shielding his eyes, Joshen leaned forward. He thought he saw something white floating in the distance. He hauled at his oar with renewed desperation. "Pull!" he growled to the others.

He kept glancing over his shoulder as the figure came closer. It was Senna. She was face down and still. Reaching over, he and Parknel gripped her under the arms and heaved her aboard. She lay still on the floor, her face as white as the remnants of her shift. "Senna!" Joshen screamed. The sailors moved aside as he maneuvered to her side. He pressed his ear to her chest.

Perfectly still and so cold to the touch.

Roughly, Parknel lifted her so her stomach rested on the edge of the boat. He thumped her hard on the back. No response.

Joshen's hands covered his mouth. She couldn't be dead. He wouldn't allow her to be dead. He rolled her back to the floor, determined to shake it out of her. As she fell back, water came free. A weak cough. Joshen grasped her shoulder and turned her to her side. She coughed harder. More water. She wheezed a shaky breath. Her golden eyes peered up at him.

"Senna?"

She moaned. "I'm so ... cold."

Not bothering with the buttons, Joshen ripped off his shirt and draped it over her shoulders before scooping her into his arms. At first, she simply lay there, but then she started shivering and Joshen knew she'd be alright. He rubbed her arm to bring back some of the warmth. She cried out and he remembered her injury.

"Don't you ever do anything like that again," he growled.

"Don't worry," she whispered. "I lost the potion."

The sorrow in her voice startled him. "I can't say I'm sorry."

She moaned. "It took someone years to create that potion and I spilled it."

What could he say? She'd been shot, chased by a shark and nearly drowned. If she had not lost it, he would have dumped it out himself.

***

Senna didn't complain as Joshen carried her toward his cabin. Parknel started calling out orders. "Sharpshooters on all sides. Sailors, man the sails and get us out of here. You, take over the wheel for me until Lery or I relieve you. And speaking of Lery, where is he?"

Joshen eased her onto the bed. "Bruke." He patted the bed next to Senna. The dog obliged and Joshen covered them both with a blanket and sat down beside her. He vigorously rubbed her hand between his. "Are you warm yet?"

Senna's whole body felt as though it were made of lead. She felt too weak to even lift her head off the pillow. She managed a frail smile. "I'm not sure I ever will be."

"Why Senna? Why did you do it?"

Senna heard the hurt in his voice and didn't understand. "I couldn't bear just sitting back while others risked their lives— died—to protect me. I might have risked my life, but no more than any other man on this ship!"

Joshen rubbed his temples between his fingers and thumb. "You still don't understand. You still don't think you're worth it." He seemed to be concentrating on keeping his breathing even. "You can't keep taking risks like this! If you die, it's over! Can't you see that?"

Senna swallowed and looked away. Didn't Joshen understand that if he died, it would all be over for her? She couldn't allow that, at any cost. She lifted tear-rimmed eyes. "And when she defeats me, what then? Will you go back to your horses?"

Joshen slowly stood. "For over a year, I waited for you and now you question my loyalty?"

Senna shut her eyes. Tears traced her temples before disappearing into her damp hair. "Not your loyalty."

"What then?" he said in exasperation.

"I can't, I can't … lose you. And I'm going to. Just like I lost my mother, father and sister. Everyone I ever care about is taken from me. Everyone."

She looked outside, reveling in the heat pouring in from the window.

"I didn't know you had a sister," Joshen fumbled.

Senna's jaw tightened. She remembered the vague drawing of a beautiful girl with brown curls in the arms of her father. "She died before I was born."

Joshen strode to the window and looked at the sunshine. Without turning, he said, "I can promise you this—I'll never willingly leave you, Senna."

"None of them willingly leave," she said. "But they leave all the same."

He turned back to her. "You have to stop worrying about all of this and focus on what you have to do."

Her voice barely broke a whisper, "What do I have to do, Joshen?"

He kneeled beside her bed and took her hand in his own. "You have to stop her."

A knock at the door sounded. Joshen didn't let go of her hand. "Enter."

Parknel came in. He was soaked in blood from his fingertips to his knees. In his hands, he had her pots, all of the plants stripped of their leaves. "We need more."

"She can't, Captain," Joshen said.

She pushed herself up. "I can."

"Senna, you almost died."

She looked away. "Actually, I think I did die. But I'm not dead yet."

Deftly plucking the seeds from the bare plants, she put them back in the soil and sang.

With a nod of gratitude, Parknel took the pots and turned to go.

"Captain," Joshen called. "Did you find Lery?"

Parknel stopped. He said over his shoulder, "He's dead."

Senna gasped and a sob caught in her throat. "How many …besides Lery?"

Parknel's shoulders sagged. "Eight."

He shut the door behind him.

Open-mouthed, Senna tried to gasp for air, but she couldn't. Her lungs froze, refusing to draw breath. The pain was so raw and devastating, she was certain it would kill her.

Crawling under the blankets, Joshen hung onto her as if she'd die if he let go. "Breathe, Senna. Breathe."

Why was he comforting her? Why didn't he hate her? After all, Lery was Joshen's friend. And it was her fault he was dead. She took a strangled, gasping breath and then a sob finally tore free.

He stroked her hair. "That's it. Let it go."

She was crying too hard to make him understand. Another person taken from her. Another person made to suffer because of her. Would it ever stop?

19. Balance

Senna awoke with a jerk. Something had wrenched her from a deep sleep, but what? She squinted in the pale moonlight, but saw nothing out of place. And then she heard it again. Musket fire. Throwing the blankets off, her feet hit the floor at a run. She wrenched open the door just as the hatch to the lower decks burst open and more sailors scrambled into sight, Joshen among them.

With nothing more than his trousers on, he pointed a warning finger at her. "Stay back." He ran in the direction of the other men, musket in hand.

Senna hefted her skirts. She had no intention of staying put.

When he saw her following, he gave her an exasperated glare before pulling her behind him. At the rail, Joshen tugged her down beside him. He loaded his musket and pulled back the hammer.

Peeking over his shoulder, she saw the stars and moon gleaming harshly on two boats filled with fleeing sailors.

Resting his musket on the banister, Parknel spoke, "Pick a target carefully and fire at will." Lifting the sight, he closed his eyes as the wind tugged at his beard. "Slight breeze from the west." He realigned his musket.

Senna couldn't help but jump as the muskets fired. Puffs of blue-black smoke plumed from the pans. Joshen and the others reloaded. Parknel was the first ready to fire again. After another round of shots, the Captain held up his hand. "They're too far now, men." He shook his head. "I wonder what that was about. They must have known we'd see them and not a one had a musket."

Joshen looked askance at Senna. "Permission to keep watch tonight, Captain?"

Parknel didn't miss Joshen's glance. "Granted. Keep a sharp eye out, boys. I've a feeling they might be planning something else tonight."

"Joshen—" she began.

"Go back to the cabin, Senna. You should stay out of sight."

She pursed her lips but didn't argue. Once inside, she shut the door softly.

Tarten must be close, she thought, *I can smell the most wonderful flowers.* She inhaled deeply through her nose. She suddenly felt extremely tired. Rubbing her eyes, she patted Bruke's head. "Why shouldn't I be tired? I almost died today." She took a step toward the bed, but her feet were so heavy her toes dragged across the floor. She blinked and barely managed to open her eyes again. Squinting, she searched the room, her mind working furiously. But she couldn't access her thoughts—it was like they were locked behind a closed door.

But just because the door was locked didn't mean she couldn't sense the chaos behind it. Something was wrong. Horribly wrong.

She had to get away. Stumbling backward, her hand fumbled for something to brace herself against. She grasped only air. She tried to right herself, but her body responded with frozen stiffness. She crashed onto her bottom. The impact jolted her. With a small whimper, she tried to crawl somewhere. Anywhere. But her limbs seemed to have lost their bones. "Help me!" she croaked.

Shattering glass. Senna looked up as a dozen vines the size of her arm snaked through her window. She recognized it as the deadly plant, barbus. Swirls of panic tried to overwhelm her, but they were distant shouts from behind the door her thoughts were locked behind. She was so tired.

Bruke stumbled sideways. Even though his legs trembled, he stepped between Senna and the plant that snaked toward them, his nose low to the ground and his tongue lolling out.

A shadowed silhouette appeared against the window frame. Even with his face obscured by darkness, Senna knew who it was. Wardof had come for her. Bruke growled and then lurched to the side. Tears came to her eyes. He should have collapsed long ago.

But she knew he was as helpless as she. Vines and flowers covered half the room now. Part of her wanted to give in to the enormous weight pressing on her. To sleep. But another part knew if she did, her eyes would never open again. Wardof leveled a musket at her.

It was over. Looking into the barrel, her body panicked and struggled to break free of the drug.

With a sudden burst, Bruke let out a vicious bark and lunged forward. The gun went off. Her ears rang. Bruke's body jerked. He slammed into the ground and didn't move.

No! her mind screamed. *No! No!* Digging her fingernails into the wooden floor, Senna pulled herself toward him. "Bruke?" her mouth formed the words, but no sound came out. Her arm slipped in a pool of warm, sticky blood. She grabbed a handful of fur and tugged.

Bruke didn't respond.

A flash of steel glinted in Wardof's hand.

Rage boiled inside her. She wished she had the strength to curse him and any spawn that sprang from his body. Every step he took, the plants around him would wither and die! The food he brought to his mouth would rot before he could taste the sweetness of the Earth!

But she was as weak as a baby as he came toward her with his knife. She was going to die.

Senna heard the door behind her fly open. A dull thud as numerous bodies collapsed. "Hold your breath!" she recognized Parknel's voice.

Wardof lunged for her. Balls whizzed around him, slamming into the wood of the ship and shattering the remaining glass. His nostrils flaring and his face red from lack of air, he ran for the window. And then he was gone with the sound of a splash.

Parknel appeared next to her, his eyes raking the room. Yanking his knife free, he dropped beside her and began cutting at something. She looked down. The barbus had snaked around her legs.

She hadn't noticed.

Senna felt familiar hands under her arms, hauling her back. Then she saw the plant had entangled the entire lower half of Bruke's body. She reached toward him, silently begging Joshen not to forget him.

The moment she breathed the clean air, the door that had closed her thoughts slowly creaked open. Someone had sent a barbus plant after her. The musket fight had been a distraction. If not for Bruke's bark, the sailors would have been too late to help her. And then he had lunged at Wardof and taken the ball meant for her. He had saved her life. She looked into Joshen's gray eyes as he leaned over her. "Bruke," she managed.

Joshen's eyes widened. He rushed back in the room. He reappeared, heaving a sleeping Parknel by the collar and Bruke by the scruff of his neck. Gasping for air, Joshen motioned to some of the other sailors. "Don't just stand there, get those other men out! And somebody fire at that escaping boat!"

Gradually, the numbness in her limbs faded away. The report of musket fire shattered the stillness. Trembling, she crawled toward Bruke. His bloody chest rose shallowly. He wasn't dead. She closed her eyes in relief. Ripping off her cloak, she pressed it against the wound.

Joshen's fingers felt for an exit wound. "I can't find it. But at least the bleeding seems to be slowing down."

Bruke whined deep, as if he dreamed.

Parknel and the others began to stir.

"Senna!" Joshen cried.

Her head jerked up. Barbus snaked through the door. Noxious orange blooms filled the air with their sweet, deadly fragrance. If she didn't stop it, the whole crew would be carried under.

Joshen took over pressing the cloth into Bruke's chest. She rose shakily to her feet and sang.

Barbus! I command thee retreat!
No more to carry out thy dark feat!

The barbus quivered and pressed on. Stepping forward to block its advance, Senna repeated her song. Trying to find a way around her, the plant arched up. She sang harder. Trembling, it backed away a little. And then a little more.

Still singing, she paused outside the cabin, unwilling to breathe in the contaminated air. When the plant had fully retreated, she called for the wind to scour the room. With it whipping her hair about her like mad, she stepped inside. A potted plant, vines straining hungrily against her song, perched on the side of the window. Without a moment's hesitation, she pushed it over. She didn't stay to watch it drop into the waves.

She ran back to Bruke. He hadn't moved and his teeth were slightly bared.

Joshen reached toward her. "I'm sorry, Senna. He's dead."

She blinked, unwilling to believe it. "He saved my life. That ball was meant for me." Pain slammed into her chest and dug vast roots throughout her body—pain so much deeper and far-reaching than a musket ball or changing into a seal could ever touch. She wrapped her arms around herself and wished for death. The inevitability of Wardof killing her and everyone she loved twisted a knot in her gut. "He'll never stop. Not until he takes everything." Tears slipped silently down her face as she rocked back and forth.

"That's not true," Parknel answered gently. "Balance, Senna. Good and evil, joy and sorrow. All things strive for balance. And that means good and bad things end. Someday, so will this." He struggled to sit up. "Joshen, take her inside and stay with her." His face lost its softness. "Everyone else, back to bed or your posts. The wind's picking up and no oarsmen could match us. Even if we are in a boat full of holes." He glanced at the stars and his features darkened. "Besides, we're closer to Tarten than we realized. I'd be willing to bet sometime tomorrow, we'll see land."

***

Numb, Senna stood at the jagged teeth of what remained of Parknel's window, staring across Tarten's vast landscape. It was truly beautiful, this land Espen had chosen to trap the Keepers.

Mountains rose, but mountains unlike any Senna had ever seen. There was no gradual climb. No hint of a mountain until one suddenly thrust itself up from the forest at an incredible angle. Nor were they peaked, but rounded across the top. Yet, as impossible as it seemed, cities crusted some of those mountains. Carpel, Tarten's greatest city, seemed carved out of the ground, the Capitol Building shining white at the top.

"It's so beautiful," Joshen said.

Senna didn't have the energy to respond. Ever since the fog had lifted, the air had been heavy and hot, leaving her sticky and groggy.

She felt his eyes on her. "After Parknel finds us somewhere remote to put to shore, how will we find them?"

The sound of his voice grated on her ears. She crossed her arms over her chest. "I'll find them. Not you. You're nothing but a liability for me." She knew she wasn't being fair. If not for Joshen, she wouldn't have made it this far. For some unimaginable reason, it infuriated her.

His jaw tightened. "And what if Wardof and Garg find you? What then?"

She shrugged. "I'm a Witch. Wardof and Garg are no danger to me."

Joshen backed away from her, his eyes glittering with anger. "Like your last few encounters with them?"

Couldn't he understand that she must continue alone? She had to be strong enough without him. "So I'll stay alert, I'll—"

"You can't be alert every second of every day! Didn't you realize that last night?"

Last night. Bruke. She tried to speak, but the words came out broken, "My fault. Always my fault." Shaking her head, she tried again, "I want to see him."

Joshen stopped pacing. "He's already gone, Senna."

She took a deep, shuddering breath. They'd already tossed him overboard? Without telling her? Without giving her a chance to say goodbye? "Why? Why would you do that?"

He rested a hand on her shoulder. She jerked away and glared at him. He sighed. "Because we thought it might be easier if—"

She clenched her fists to her side. "How dare you!"

"Senna, I—"

Rage overcame her. She pounded on his chest.

Joshen gripped her tight. Her injured arm ached, but she welcomed the pain. Welcomed any pain that stopped the all-consuming fire burning her from the inside out. She tried to push him away, but he was so much stronger. Always had been and she hated him all the more. "I never want to see you again, you detestable—"

He shook her hard. His eyes gleamed with anger. "Stop it! I'm not leaving you, so stop pushing me away. Bruke's gone. I know you loved him. I know he was one of your only friends, but that's because you won't let anyone else in, Senna. Not me, not Parknel, not Lery. No one!"

She glared at him. "Don't! You still have all your family. Your home. Your life."

He stepped back, his breath ragged. "Knowing what you know now, would you still have come all this way? Or just stayed on your land in Gonstower and hoped for the best?"

She turned her back to him. "I'd have followed my mother. Even if it meant Espen capturing me. Even if it meant the end of the Witches. At least I wouldn't be alone."

He took a ragged breath. "Yet you'll do the same to me. Perhaps you're more like your mother than you thought." He shook his head. "I left it all behind for you. All of it. And I'd do it again." Without another word, he stormed out of the cabin.

Trembling, she stared at the closed door. Was she really doing the same thing to Joshen?

Yes.

The answer startled her. She held her head in her hands. All her life, her mother had tried to protect her from danger by hiding her. But no matter what they may have faced, Senna would have gladly stood beside her mother and the other Witches rather than live among those who shunned her.

When she'd forced Joshen from Haven, had he felt as lonely and abandoned as she had?

Joshen was right, curse him. Maybe it wasn't fair to force him to stay away from a battle he'd chosen to fight. As the realization overcame her, some of her tension faded. Maybe she didn't have to do this alone after all.

Suddenly, the door swung inward. Joshen hurried in, looking relieved to see her. "I'm sorry. I shouldn't have—"

She pressed her finger to his lips. "You were right." His eyes widened in disbelief. "Am I really that stubborn?" she asked.

"Yes," Joshen said unequivocally.

Senna tried to suppress a smile.

"The last time we disagreed," he continued, "you tied me up and had the kelp drag me to shore."

She swallowed her laugh.

His face grew serious. "Promise me something?"

She paused, waiting expectantly.

"Promise you won't ever do that to me again."

Senna turned back to the window, a sigh on her lips. "The dragging you to shore part, or the tying you up part?"

He pulled up his shirt sleeve to reveal the green circle of the full moon. "Was this just some kind of meaningless symbol to you? Because it meant a lot more to me. It meant I'm bound to you. Do you take that so lightly?"

Searching his gray eyes, something deep within her stirred. To her relief, some of the pain over Bruke's death faded. "I'm trying to be angry with you, but in truth, I'm angry with myself. If I were strong enough to do this alone, I wouldn't have to endanger you. And Bruke," her voice caught, but she pushed through it, "would still be alive."

He took a step closer. "That was Wardof's fault, not yours." Senna suddenly felt uncomfortably hot. "As for me, I'm right where I want to be." He brushed her cheek with his fingertips.

A warm, almost painful burning emanated from his touch. "Do you promise to stop pushing me away?"

Some of her panic returned, battering against the soft reservoir of peace Joshen had given her. "I promise to try." She felt his tension easing as he sighed. She shook her head. "But the others must go back. They'd draw too much attention and I can't keep them all safe."

Joshen slumped in the chair in front of the bolted-down desk. "You really have no idea where to go from here?"

She shook her head.

"So what do we do?"

Senna tried not to let her fear show. "Row to shore and figure it out."

20. Witch Friends

The ground seemed to roll beneath Senna. Steadying herself against Knight's sweat-damp shoulder, she watched the tiny figures aboard the Sea Witch. At this distance, the holes in the vessel's side gaped like the ragged teeth of a giant's maw. "Are you sure you can make it back?"

Parknel was loading her saddle bags with hard tack and salt fish. "We'll patch it. Long as we don't hit any major storms, we'll be alright."

"But—"

Parknel surprised her from behind with a breath-stealing hug. "Now, don't you worry about us. We'll make it back. Have Mcbedee fix her up right in Nefalie." The wrinkles around his eyes faded. "Maybe you'll finish 'fore we do, then we can all go back together."

She closed her eyes so he wouldn't see her dread. "No. Don't wait."

He nodded. "All the same, we'll be here a few weeks." He shook Joshen's hand. "You're a right good man. Keep her safe."

Joshen looked down at his feet and nodded.

Swinging an axe onto his shoulder, Parknel disappeared in the jungle.

Her legs wobbly, Senna climbed into the saddle with a sigh of relief. Now, if only she could escape the waves of heat rolling over her like the steam from a bread oven.

Joshen grunted as he wiped his forehead with his sleeve. "Which way, Senna?"

She'd thought a great deal about this during her last, sleepless night on board the Sea Witch. She turned Knight toward the village they'd passed yesterday. "If Espen created a place like Haven, the Tartens would notice. We just have to find a way to get them to tell us."

Joshen looked away. "The majority of Tartens don't like Nefaliens. Parknel said their Chancellors imprison any Witch they find. You know that, right?"

Senna let Knight pick his way through the sand. "Well then, we won't tell them I'm a Witch. Besides, if Nefalien merchants still trade with the Tartens, it can't be too bad. We'll ask some indirect questions at the small village we saw yesterday." She hoped her voice sounded more confident than she felt. Ahead, a road traveling a little farther inland parted the dense jungle. She twisted to catch one last glimpse of the Sea Witch before the heavy foliage swallowed the ship whole.

Joshen fiddled nervously with his reins. "I suppose you're right, but I don't like it."

Senna took stock of the jungle. So different from the forests of her home. Denser and more abundant, yet at the same time more fragile. She doubted a killing frost had ever brushed across these tender leaves. Even the smell of soil and growing things was different because of the heavy undercurrent of rot.

And something else. She sniffed—a lazy fire and fish. The trees thinned, revealing a house made of white mud with a thatched roof. Laundry shifted like tethered ghosts on the lines. A small garden grew fat over cleared ground.

"Senna," Joshen said with an undercurrent of fear. She followed his gaze. She'd been so busy studying the strange house she hadn't noticed a group of mounted figures in the distance. All wore blood-red coats with gold trim and buttons. Soldiers. At least six of them. A hard ball formed in her throat. Noisily, she tried to swallow around it.

He pointed to a smaller side road that led past the house, between two of the rounded mountains. "I think we'd better get off the main road."

She didn't argue as they turned south onto the rutted path. Even though it appeared little used, she had to maneuver Knight to the side to allow a dark Tarten man driving a mule and cart to pass them. He gaped at her in disbelief.

When they'd moved out of earshot, she whispered to Joshen, "He can't possibly know I'm a Witch just by looking at me."

Joshen's brow furrowed with worry. "What if those soldiers are looking for you?" He licked his lips. "Maybe we'd better make for the ship."

A bead of sweat ran down her back. She shuddered. "With the ship damaged like it is, Parknel can't make a run for it and they're in no condition for another fight."

Twisted in the saddle, Joshen glanced back. At the look of horror on his face, Senna turned. She gasped. All six soldiers had followed them.

The man in the cart pointed at them and yelled something unintelligible. The six soldiers shouted an unmistakable command at Joshen and Senna. A few of their hands strayed toward the muskets strapped to their saddles.

Senna froze, her brain refusing to register what her eyes saw. "Come on!" Joshen shouted.

Leaning low over Knight, she booted his ribs. He pushed off hard, throwing her back. She gripped the horn to keep from falling off. She glanced back. Muskets in hand, the soldiers pounded up behind them. But why? Why were they chasing them? She shouted so the wind wouldn't whip her words away, "Maybe we shouldn't run. It might just be a misunderstanding."

A musket exploded behind them. Senna ducked. Her arm burned with the memory of being shot.

Joshen threw a look of disbelief at her. "That wasn't a misunderstanding!" He shook his head in frustration. "Knight and Stretch can outrun them over the short distance, but they haven't got their winds back! We have to hide."

She risked a glance back. Joshen was right. The soldiers had already fallen behind. "How long?"

He didn't look at her. "Not long."

The air whipped past Senna, tugging tears from her eyes as she searched for a break in the impregnable jungle. Knight's breathing already sounded ragged.

The path suddenly veered right. Pulling the reins, she leaned into the turn and spotted something half-hidden within the trees. She squinted. Buildings that blended with the shadows far beyond the path. She looked back to see how close the soldiers were. The bend blocked her view. But if she couldn't see them, by the Creators, they couldn't see her either. She pointed. "Joshen!"

Joshen brought Stretch around hard and they galloped to the closest building's blind side. Earth sprayed the walls as he jerked his horse to a stop and jumped from the saddle. He threw his weight against the door to open it. A flock of brown chickens took to the air in an explosion of feathers.

Senna burst into the barn and jumped from her horse. A wide-eyed cow bellowed and backed away from them. A couple of plow horses whinnied and stirred inside their pens.

Joshen jammed the bar home, plunging them into near-darkness. "Can you quiet them?"

Her voice barely above a whisper, Senna sang.

> Peace I sing,
> No harm I bring.

The animals settled, leaving only the sound of their horses' panting. Shafts of light shone between lashed-together reed walls, illuminating swirls of dust. Running to the other wall, Joshen peered between the reeds.

If this was a barn, the other building must be a house. If a farmer alerted the soldiers to their presence, all would be lost. Senna hurried to the opposite side. She held her breath as she waited for Joshen's cry of alarm or the sight of a frazzled farmer emerging from his house.

Joshen let out a sigh of relief. "They just passed us." He leaned his head against the reeds.

Senna let out all her breath. Movement behind the door caught her eye. Her inhalation turned into a gasp. "Joshen, a man's coming," she hissed as she ran to his side.

In one step, Joshen reached Stretch and unstrapped the musket. Senna didn't know how he managed a steady hand as he loaded the gun. She could barely grasp the pea-sized seed she withdrew from the little compartment in her seed belt.

The door flung open, half-blinding them with light. Joshen leveled the barrel at a man's chest. With a cry of surprise, the man held out his hands and said something in a language Senna didn't understand.

Joshen took a few steps forward. "Do you speak Nefalien?"

The man's eyes widened in shock before resting on Senna. His gaze raking across her clothes, lingering for a moment on her seed belt. "Witch?"

There was no point in hiding it now. Cautiously, she stepped out from behind Joshen and nodded.

He looked over their horses and pressed his lips in a thin line. He rattled off again in Tarten. Senna listened hard but couldn't understand a word of it. Jerking a halter from a nail, he threw it on one of the plow horses. Using the stall as a ladder, he jumped on. He gestured for them to follow him. *"Cheche."*

Joshen shifted his grip on the musket. "Senna?"

She weighed the farmer, his ragged clothing, dirty bare feet and wiry frame—a man who earned every bit of his bread with the sweat from his body. Would he try and sell them? But she had no sense he was a ruffian. Nor was he starving. Only overworked. "The soldiers will search for us once they realize we've disappeared."

Joshen lowered the gun. "Fine, but he stays in front."

Senna swung onto Knight's back.

Smacking his plow horse's rump with the lead rope, the man took off down the road. It started to rain. But it was unlike any rain Senna had ever experienced. More like a dam had been opened from above. There weren't any raindrops. Only sheets of water. And the rain was warm.

At least the air didn't feel so heavy.

Trying his best to keep his powder dry, Joshen kept an eye on the man while Senna watched the road ahead. Suddenly, the man veered onto a path wide enough for a single horse. They continued for another half-league before he pulled his plow horse to a stop. He motioned for them to go ahead.

Peering around Joshen, Senna saw another tiny reed home set in the trees. She turned back to tell the man she didn't understand, but he was already galloping back the way he'd come—the ground thundering a little with each step his enormous horse took.

"Well?" Senna asked.

Joshen shrugged. "He didn't lead us to a garrison of soldiers."

"It could be a trap."

He studied the house. "How? The man didn't know we'd hide in his barn." Seeming to have made up his mind, Joshen urged his horse forward.

Fear sharpened Senna's senses. Myriad sounds played on her ears—the drumming rain, pigs rooting a little farther in the forest, the garden calling softly for her song. Without really knowing why, Senna answered.

Take in light, take in air,
Spread thy roots, thy leaves grow fair.

No sooner had her song ended than a man appeared from the other side of the house, his face awash with wonder. "You're a Witch," he said in perfect Nefalien.

The groaning and stretching plants behind him seemed to emphasize his words. Senna tilted her head to the side as she studied him through the heavy rain. His skin was slightly lighter than the other Tartens. Could he be part Nefalien? "My name is Senna."

The man held his hand over his mouth as if to hold back his emotions. "For so long, we've hoped for the last."

"Who's hoped?" Joshen asked suspiciously.

The man startled when Joshen spoke, as if he hadn't noticed him. "Nefalie isn't the only land with Witch friends. And no one enjoys Chancellor Grendi's taxes." Wiping rainwater from his face, the man took off at a jog toward his home. "My name is Kaen. Come. We have much to do!"

"Hold on, man!" Joshen exclaimed. "What do you intend to do?"

Kaen shot Joshen a withered look. "Help you, you fool! The whole country is crawling with soldiers looking for her. Now move! We haven't time to delay!"

"How did they know I was coming?" Senna asked.

"How should I know?" The man disappeared into his house.

As she dismounted, Senna cast a nervous glance down the path. Were the soldiers already searching for them? Afraid they might suddenly appear, she lifted her skirts and hurried after Kaen.

Joshen blocked her entrance to the house with an outstretched arm. Adjusting his grip on the musket, he slid inside. Immediately, he lowered his weapon and gestured for her to follow. Once inside, she felt a measure of relief—from the rain at least. She didn't think she'd ever escape the heaviness. It was a small room. Woven baskets filled with fruits and salt fish lined the floor. There were no tables or chairs, only a slab of wood surrounded by more woven mats. From the ceiling, herbs hung limply. A smell she didn't recognize made her eyes water and her throat itch.

Seemingly frozen in their various tasks, a woman and five dark-eyed children shot them looks of disbelief. In rapid succession, the wide-eyed woman fired words at Kaen, who was in a side room. She gripped Senna's hand and pulled her toward the room Kaen had disappeared into. *"Cheche."*

Joshen grabbed Senna's other arm. "What are you doing?"

Ignoring him, the woman kept tugging Senna toward the room.

Senna wasn't sure why, but she trusted this man and his wife. They weren't acting like people trying to hurt them. As far as she could see, they were taking an immense risk by offering aid. "Joshen, I think they're helping."

"Her name is Valicia." Kaen gestured to his wife as he reappeared. He thrust well-worn, colorful clothes into Joshen's arms. "If you value your life, put those on."

Valicia let loose another series of words. Three girls jumped to follow Senna into the side room. It appeared to be a mass bedroom. Every available space was crammed with neatly rolled mats and lidded baskets.

As soon as the door shut, they undid her cloak and began yanking on her dress. Embarrassed, Senna pulled the dress over her head. It hadn't even hit the floor before a vibrant tunic was hauled over her shift and wide, loose trousers held open for her. The woman wrung out Senna's dress, wrapped it up tight and handed the bundle to the oldest girl. After exchanging a few words, the girl disappeared out the door.

Unscrewing a jar, Valicia scooped up a handful of brown paste. She rubbed it vigorously between her hands and smeared it on Senna's face, neck and arms as another daughter wound a cloth over Senna's golden hair. They plunked a hat over her head. The moment they'd finished, they hauled Senna out of the room.

She stopped. If she didn't look too closely, Joshen's skin appeared nearly as dark as the boy's standing next to him. The strange tunic and loose trousers fit oddly on Joshen's trim figure.

Kaen gripped the boy's shoulders and said something in Tarten. "Come! We must make haste!" The boy ran outside, jumped on Knight and grabbed Stretch's reins.

"What are you doing with our horses?" Joshen seemed more concerned than suspicious.

"Taking them as far away as he can. If the soldiers find them here, they'll know I'm helping you."

Senna watched in disbelief as Kaen's son disappeared down the jungle path. "But he's just a boy."

The man grunted. "Yes, but he's more a man than most." Diving back into the rain, Kaen took off at a run toward the mountain rising sharply behind his home. "Don't move in a straight path. Don't break the vegetation. We can't risk them seeing your tracks."

21. Deep as a Grave

Senna groaned and clutched the stitch in her side. It appeared Knight wasn't the only one to go soft over the sea voyage. But she didn't dare slow or waste her breath complaining. The moment she'd stepped into the trees, the air had grown more humid until she felt like she was breathing water instead of air. But at least the hat kept the rain off.

At first, the jungle's thick, broad-leaved plants had been nearly impenetrable. But the farther they ventured, the more scarce the undergrowth became. Senna had never seen trees like these before, with wide, buttressed bases and thin bark. They had almost no branches until high above her head. Even during breaks in the storm, no light filtered through the high canopy of trees. Strange, startling cries sounded all around them. Enormous bugs dove in from all sides to bite and sting. And there were snakes. Big ones.

By the Creators, she thought, *I want to bury my head in my arms and hide.*

Just when she'd given up all hope of stopping, Kaen halted next to a sharp incline. Bending down, he tugged at a flat rock. "Help me!"

Hunching down, Joshen heaved. After a great deal of grunting, the rock slid to the side, revealing an inky black tunnel. "Get in and don't come out until I come for you. Understand?"

Senna shot an anxious glance down the dirty tunnel. "I could sing for the trees to take us high."

"That's one of the first places they'd look for a Witch," Kaen responded. "If you want my help, you must do as I say."

Senna shuddered as she peered inside the cramped tunnel. Who knew what kind of bugs lived in the dark? Not to mention she would be buried under miles of solid rock. "I'm not sure I can go in there."

Joshen wriggled in and set his musket beside him. He held out his hand. "Come on, Senna. I'll be right here with you."

She took a step back. "Joshen, I can't."

"Yes, you can. Come on."

Her chest felt tight and she couldn't seem to draw enough air. "No, I can't."

His hand dropped. "Senna, stop it! You're not afraid to jump into the middle of the ocean and chase after a whale or traipse after the most powerful Witch in history, but you can't hide inside a hole? Now get in here, before I come out and get you!"

Senna took a deep breath and held it, then squirmed in next to him. The bottom of the hole was lined with a woven mat, which might have helped if it hadn't been musty and dirty. The man tossed Joshen a small leather bag. "There's some fruit and water inside. Use it sparingly. I don't know when it'll be safe to pull you out."

He positioned himself behind the rock. Joshen helped to roll it over them. Senna watched the last of the light disappear. As her eyes adjusted, she made out roots dangling white above them. She stretched herself out and her toes brushed the end. "Not much deeper than a grave," she murmured.

"Well, at least we're out of the rain."

Senna grunted. Then, something tickled the back of her neck. "Joshen!" Frozen, she held her breath as numerous legs wriggled over her skin. "On my neck!"

He snatched the bug. "Ouch!" He hurled it against the wall. "It bit me!" He pounded it with the flat of his hand. Senna shrieked. What other things resided, unseen, in the dark? She began to tremble uncontrollably.

Joshen sucked his finger. "A Witch afraid of bugs?"

She buried her head in her hands.

Without a sigh, Joshen gathered her in his arms and stroked her hair. "I'm sorry. I was just teasing. It's okay, Senna. It's just a little hole in the ground."

Joshen's arms were so warm and comforting. She leaned into him. Eventually, her whole body went slack. She woke sometime later and lifted her head from Joshen's chest. Her hair was plastered to her head with sweat—her whole body was sticky with it. She tried to peer into the dark, but it was pitch black. Night, she realized. And it was still raining as hard as ever. She looked back at Joshen, but could make out nothing other than his deep, even breathing. Snuggling back in his arms, she eventually fell asleep.

When she opened her eyes the second time, she caught Joshen gazing at her. He quickly looked away. "How'd you sleep?" he asked.

Feeling awkward, she pushed herself off his chest. To her dismay, it was still raining. "After I finally settled down, I did much better."

"And the arm?"

It had been almost two weeks since Wardof had shot her. She tested her range of motion with a roll of her shoulder. "It doesn't hurt unless I strain it."

The mat rustled as he pulled out the leather pouch. She smelled spices and fish. "There's some salt fish here, a few hard biscuits and ... by the feel of it, fruit. What do you want?"

"I'll try a little of everything," The two chewed in silence, sharing small sips of water. The fruit was odd stuff. Sweet and tart, it clung stubbornly to the pit and stuck in her teeth. And she didn't know what kind of grain they used to make the bread, but it certainly wasn't wheat, or rye, or oats, or anything else she was familiar with.

"We ought to save the rest. Better to have little now than nothing later."

Senna's stomach disagreed, but she didn't voice its complaints. She sang softly to herself for a while. Then, lying on her side, she drew up her knees and rested her forehead on them. "What are we going to do if Kaen doesn't come back for us?"

Though she wasn't looking at him, she was familiar enough with Joshen's idiosyncrasies to know his lips were drawn together. "Well, we can't stay here forever. Could you move the rock with one of your plants?"

Senna tried to peer around the rock. "If I could get one of the plants outside to cooperate."

"If not, I could probably push it back, but we'll deal with that if and when the time comes."

"Why does he even have this tunnel? And why does he speak Nefalien?" she asked.

Joshen shifted to his back. "We're obviously not the first people he's hidden. How we were lucky enough to find someone who knew about him, I've no idea."

"Do you really think he's trying to help us?"

"Do you?"

Senna thought about it. "Yes. His actions were nothing like a man who wanted to do us harm. What—"

Joshen clamped his hand over her mouth and pulled her to him. At first, Senna heard nothing, but then ... a slight shuffling beyond the rock. It might be an animal, it might not. Either way, she remained motionless, barely breathing. The shuffling stopped in front of them. Joshen groped for his gunpowder as she reached inside her seed belt.

The rock shifted. Clumps of mud rained down on them. Light blinded her. Blinking, Senna blocked the light with her hand. Half-crouched, Joshen held his musket like a club.

"All right below?" a voice asked.

Through her watering eyes, Senna managed to make out Kaen's face.

"We're fine," Joshen replied.

"Can you help me with this?"

Joshen handed his musket to Senna and gripped the rock. Both of them managed to push it back. Joshen hopped out and helped Senna out of the hole. Stretching her cramped muscles, she shook the dirt from her borrowed clothes.

"Earlier," Joshen asked Kaen, "you said the soldiers were searching for Senna?"

Kaen huffed. "Chancellor Grendi's been secretly rounding up Witches for years. Recently, it hasn't been so secret. Divisions have been patrolling the roads and offering rewards for Senna's capture for over a week. My Witch friends and I have been on the alert, hoping to find you first, but we haven't the resources or numbers of the army."

"By friends you mean sympathizers?" Joshen asked.

Kaen nodded.

Joshen glanced protectively toward her. "How did they know we were coming?"

Kaen shrugged. "Spies? Fortune tellers? It doesn't matter. What does matter is that we keep her safe." He handed them two packs in exchange for the old bag. "Come. This way."

Joshen trotted to catch up. "How do you plan to keep her safe?"

"We've an underground network for those who manage to draw Grendi's notice. We'll help you escape Tarten." Kaen grunted as he worked through the jungle in an irregular, almost serpentine way. He carried a weapon that was half sword, half knife. It was curved on one side. Kaen caught her looking at it. "Machete."

Senna crossed her arms and planted her feet. "I'm not trying to escape. I'm trying to find Espen."

Kaen stopped dead and whirled to face her. "Espen? The Witch? She's been an enemy of the Keepers for years—even Grendi's afraid of her. What happens when she traps you like the others? Who'll stop her from wreaking havoc on nature then?"

Senna shook her head. "You don't understand. I cannot counteract the effects of her songs. I can only moderate them—barely. The longer I hide, the more damage she'll inflict."

Kaen slowly shook his head. "Even if you do manage to free them, you'll never get out of Tarten—not with that big a group."

Senna pursed her lips. "I can't worry about that now."

Kaen rubbed his temples as if he had a bad headache. "What can you do that the others haven't?"

Senna held his gaze.

After a long silence, he sighed and headed in a different direction. "For years, I've helped others escape from Grendi and Espen. Now I'll be taking our last hope into her clutches. I hope I'm not wrong."

Senna looked away. She hoped he wasn't wrong either.

22. JUNGLE OF DARKNESS

The memory of Senna's last encounter with the soldiers still heavy on her mind, she parted the dense foliage. Fingers of dread lifting the hairs on the back of her neck, she searched the road for signs of soldier red. Her breath caught in her throat at the sight of a magnificent, white city working up the mountain like a vine growing up a lattice. Kaen pressed his fingers to his lips. She already knew they must be silent.

Kaen dropped his pack. "This is Shiok. I've a well connected contact inside. But I need to check for soldiers first. If they are here, we'll move on to the next city. Wait here." He inched forward and then waited for a lull in foot traffic before walking out.

Senna and Joshen hid behind a large fern. Her back against a tree, she rubbed a knot in her neck.

"You alright?" Joshen asked.

Her eyes closed, she nodded. "Just a kink from carrying the pack. You?"

He squatted behind her and began rubbing her neck. "We're alive, so I'm not complaining."

Senna's fatigue vanished. She felt warm and tingly all over. "How did the soldiers know we were coming?"

Joshen grunted. "Probably the same way Garg and Wardof always manage to escape. They've got to be communicating with Espen somehow."

Senna hunched over as her muscles finally began to unkink. "Across the ocean? Is that even possible?"

Shaking out his hands, Joshen slumped next to her. "There's no way the sailors from the Gallant Green reached Tarten's shore before us. Yet the soldiers seemed to know where we would come ashore. That can't be a coincidence."

Refusing to worry, Senna laid her head on his shoulder.

She woke when Joshen shook her. Kaen squatted beside them. "Come on. No soldiers this morning."

Senna paused at the edge of the jungle. The last time she'd left the safety of the shadows for the unknown had been on the road to Perchance. This was a different city on a different continent, but it felt the same—foreign and overwhelming.

Joshen looked back at her, his gaze taking in things she'd rather he didn't know. He held out his hand. "I'm here."

With a steadying breath, she took it and stepped forward.

Kaen said under his breath, "No matter what happens, neither one of you says a word. Understand?"

Senna and Joshen nodded. Kaen lowered his head like a bull about to charge and strode forward.

Senna had to trot to keep up with the with two men's long strides. The foot traffic increased the closer they came to the city. As she had done for most of her life, she kept her head down and concentrated on being invisible. If anyone appeared in her path, she ducked out of their way.

Joshen glanced at her with disapproval. "They should be getting out of your way."

Senna didn't respond and she was grateful he did not press it.

Woven into the jungle that surrounded the city were reed houses with palm leaves for roofs. People trudged through their mundane tasks with hollow eyes and sagging clothes. At the base of the mountain, Senna's steps shortened considerably as they wound up the steep, curving road. It wasn't long before she realized that Shiok was also by the sea.

Eventually, reed walls and palm roofs were replaced with white plaster and tile. About two-thirds of the way up the mountain, the road turned into steps and the plaster walls were replaced with white stone mansions encased by high walls—the inside of which could have swallowed a dozen reed huts with room to spare. Despite her efforts not to, Senna found herself staring in awe.

She was shocked when Kaen opened the side gate of one of these houses and slipped into the courtyard. Her hand feeling sweaty inside Joshen's, Senna followed. Ignoring the front entrance, Kaen made his way to the back and opened the door without any pretense. Surrounded by elaborate pillows, a table no higher than her ankle was draped with food. Restlessly, she waited for someone to appear and banish them from the house. But there wasn't a soul in sight. "Eat quickly," Kaen ordered as he sat on one of the cushions.

Her stomach growled in agreement. Trying not to dirty the pillow, she sat down gingerly. She stared at the food laid out before her. A spicy, golden soup; flat, round bread; and a bowl filled with an odd mixture of fruits and meats. She looked around for a spoon. Kaen picked up his bowl and started to sip. She blinked. Tartens didn't use spoons?

Following his example, she picked up the bowl and swallowed a mouthful. Creamy, with a mild but spicy taste. It had gone cold. Still, sweat broke across her upper lip. She coughed and looked at Joshen.

His eyes widened with his first taste. "This is good." With a grin, he took several gulps.

Raising the bowl, she took another tentative taste. If she sipped, the spiciness was bearable. But when she stopped, her mouth burned. The sweat above her lip spread to her forehead. Taking one last swallow, she set the bowl aside and studied the meat and fruit mixture and circular bread. Without any utensils, what was she to do with it?

Kaen must have noticed her hesitation. He tore the circular bread into wedges and used them to scoop up his fruit and meat. "*Hun'eden.* It means 'bread spoon.'"

She carefully tore the bread and pushed it into the mixture. When she tried to take a bite, the bread collapsed, covering her chin with sauce. Her face burned with embarrassment.

Joshen didn't have better luck. But he didn't seem to care. Licking his fingers with relish, he lifted his bowl to his mouth and stuffed the bread back into the mixture. "This might be the best meal I've ever had."

"That's because you can eat with your fingers," Senna grumbled.

Joshen laughed. "You're probably right."

Kaen cleared his throat. "Hold the bowl under your mouth."

Doing as instructed, she took a tentative bite. Tang hit first, followed by a sharp sweet. A squishy fruit flooded her mouth with juice. Her eyes widened in disbelief as she rolled the strange combination on her tongue. Already on his second spoon bread, Joshen watched her reaction with amusement, "Good, isn't it?"

She shook her head as she took another bite. "It's delicious, but so odd! Meat served with fruit?" In Nefalie, meat was seasoned with salt, herbs and vegetables. Never had she eaten sweetened meat.

Joshen tipped the bowl and used his bread to scrape the remainder into his mouth. "I know. Why Mother never thought of it, I can't understand." He filled another bowl and devoured it.

"More?" Kaen asked.

The thought of trying either dish again made her lip curl. She shook her head. Joshen leaned back, rubbing his belly. "If only I could find the room."

Kaen shook his head, amusement twinkling in his eyes. "Come with me." He led them up a beautiful set of stairs to a covered patio, within which was a tiny lake enclosed by stone. "Senna, if you'd like, you may bathe."

Senna gaped at the stone lake. "That's a bathtub?"

"Yes." He pointed to a small table, upon which sat an enormous towel and various types of soaps.

Too amazed to do anything else, she nodded.

"Joshen, if you'll come with me."

They disappeared, leaving Senna alone. Self-consciously, she studied the large, airy space. She stripped her clothes, but she hesitated before entering the bath. It was large enough for six or seven women. Bending down, she skimmed her fingers across the top. "Cleaner than well water," she murmured.

Holding her breath, she dropped in. It was cool, but not cold and a very pretty blue. It felt so strange to bathe in something so large. As she used the soap, the brown paste ran down her skin in rivulets. She felt guilty that it stained the pretty water. Her body ached to relax and enjoy the coolness after the sticky heat of the jungle. But she hurried, afraid the men would return before she could finish.

She was so paranoid that she nearly jumped out of her skin when a dark-skinned woman rushed in. An outrageous purple tunic with an overlay of gold gauze flitted about her like adoring butterflies. She was easily the most beautiful, exotic woman Senna had ever seen. And young. She couldn't have been more than a few years older than Senna.

She smiled easily. "I'm sorry, did I frighten you?"

Shielding herself against the bathtub wall, Senna stammered, "That's—that's alright."

"My name is Ciara. I had thought to join you, but I had things to see to. You understand, of course?" Senna nodded. "Well, are you almost finished then?" Senna nodded again. "Very well. Come out and I'll help you dress."

Senna swallowed hard. "Help me?"

Ciara gripped a wide towel, a look of amusement on her beautiful face. "Well, I know maids usually do that sort of thing, but I can't have them finding out about my little hobby, can I?" She laughed before she grasped Senna's hand and pulled.

Afraid to offend her, Senna allowed herself to be hauled out of the water. But instead of wrapping the towel around her, Ciara vigorously rubbed Senna's hair and skin.

Senna gaped, her body frozen between wanting to run and shoving the woman away. After running the towel through her hair once more, Ciara threw it aside and headed for a different door. "Come, dear one, we mustn't delay."

Senna snatched the towel and held it to her chest. "But I'm not dressed!"

Ciara turned, surprise written across her features. "Well, you're not chilled are you? I thought it was rather warm, but perhaps ..." She trailed off and then her eyes widened. "Oh, you're ashamed of being naked?"

Senna managed a miserable nod.

The woman's brow creased. "Even in front of other women?"

Senna nodded again.

Ciara sighed in exasperation. "My room is just inside. There are clothes for you there." She tsked as she pulled out a pretty, well-made tunic. "In Tarten, all women bathe together, as do the men. I'm sure that's what Joshen and Kaen are doing now. And to think," she chuckled, "I worried you'd be offended because I didn't join you."

Just as Valicia had, Ciara helped Senna dress in a tunic that rivaled her own. "I'm afraid this is fairly elaborate traveling garb, but the soldiers are looking for a Nefalien man and woman dressed as Boors, so Class clothing should elevate you beyond suspicion. It will also give reason for your silence. Class women are not encouraged to speak to Boors or Middlings—that includes soldiers. In addition, the soldiers believe you're moving away from Espen's realm, not toward it. You should make it through fine."

Senna was fairly certain Ciara was speaking Nefalien, so why couldn't she understand a word she'd said? Judging by the pounding going on outside, it was raining again. "Where are my clothes?" she asked miserably.

Ciara directed Senna to an elaborate cushion. "Your Witch ones or the Boor ones Kaen brought with him?"

"The Witch ones."

Ciara poured a viscous, brown liquid on her hands and rubbed it into Senna's skin. "My brother probably has them with him somewhere. It wouldn't do for you to carry a Witch's garb. If the soldiers decide to search women's packs, as I'm sure they will, it would certainly be found."

"Your brother?"

The woman smiled as she lined Senna's eyebrows and eyes with a darkened stick. "Yes. Kaen and I are brother and sister."

Senna couldn't understand how this woman and Kaen could be related; the meager two-room, dirt floor farm hut seemed little better than a chicken coop compared to this.

Guessing Senna's thoughts, Ciara grunted. "He had a great deal more than I before the government began to suspect him. They could never prove his involvement with Witch friends, but they ruined Kaen financially anyway." She sighed and styled Senna's hair in an elaborate cloth that hid its color. "With the Council watching him, the danger he's placing his family in ... Well, I suppose if he has to go into deeper hiding, I could care for his wife and children here. Valicia made a very public show of disapproval to throw off any suspicion. Everyone still believes she never knew of his involvement."

Ciara smiled broadly. "We can both be pretty good actresses when we need to!" She laughed at her own joke before growing serious again. "Well, there's nothing I can do about your eyes, but it's not unheard of for a Tarten woman to have something other than brown eyes." She looked Senna up and down before nodding. "You're a very pretty girl. Not one of the great beauties, perhaps, but a fair thing nonetheless. That could work to your advantage, you know."

Senna blushed furiously before looking away.

Ciara laughed, a tinkling sound like water over crystals. She threw open her door and flowed out. From a distance, Senna followed the woman into a broad room. Senna halted and stared at Joshen as he stared back. He smiled. "Tarten nobility?"

Senna blushed and was glad no one could see it under her new skin color.

Ciara placed a dainty hand on Kaen's shoulder. "Come, big brother, I must throw you out now."

Kaen smiled ruefully. "Do make a good show of it, dear sister."

Ciara's happy demeanor evaporated. She began screeching in Tarten. Kaen grunted in amusement before his face contorted into equal amounts rage and desperation. Their shouting match moved to the kitchen, where Kaen shoved armloads of food into his pack. With a wink to Joshen and Senna, he exited the back door just as the dripping servants began showing up.

One of the male servants grabbed Kaen's arm. Kaen wrenched free and shot the man a look of contempt before straightening his tattered tunic and huffing away. As soon as he was out of sight, Ciara crumpled on Senna's shoulder and began repeating the same meaningless words.

Ciara's act must have worked, because her servants studied her with a great deal of pity. Struggling to regain her composure, she gave them a few calming words. Her large eyes glimmered like dark pools. Though Senna knew better, she found herself believing that sincere gaze. With a few heartfelt bows, the servants went back to their duties.

When the last had moved on, Ciara gestured for them to follow her. Senna watched her, wondering what kind of trouble she'd put herself in to aid them. Only when they'd gone a good ways into the house, did she address them in Nefalien, "I told them we arrived home to find Kaen here. After denouncing his actions, I lamented how hard it was to turn him away—he is my brother after all. I asked them to give me some time alone. I think the servants believed it, do you?"

"I almost believed it," Joshen commented, clearly impressed.

Senna's gaze darted to Joshen. He stared at Ciara with a mixture of admiration and respect.

Ciara smiled coyly. "You must be Joshen, Senna's Guardian?"

Joshen squared his shoulders. "I am."

A twinge of envy pulsed in Senna's veins. Ciara was everything she wasn't—beautiful, poised, rich. How could Joshen not compare her long, slender curves with Senna's short, small frame? Her flowing dark hair, perfect skin and rich brown eyes with Senna's yellow-green eyes and muddy, straw-colored hair?

"Come then. I told my servants we only paused here long enough to refresh ourselves before traveling to your home in Zaen, the last city before Espen's realm."

"And will you come with us beyond that?" Senna asked with a touch of heat.

Ciara's joviality vanished. "I dare not pass Zaen's border. Not just because it is forbidden, but because that jungle is darkness."

23. Man of Nightmares

Umbrella over her luxurious hair, Ciara lead them to a covered carriage with cushioned seats and a fine pair of matched palominos. Spicy smells wafted through the open door, making Senna's nose tingle. The carriage barely rocked as Ciara climbed in and settled beside Joshen. Senna looked at the two, talking and eating Ciara's delicacies and wanted to strangle them both. Taking the opposite seat, she sank into her corner. With a gentle lurch, the carriage started forward.

Joshen and Ciara continued eating and laughing, neither noticing Senna. In fact, Joshen was having so much fun whispering with Ciara—so the driver wouldn't hear them speaking in Nefalien—that Senna wished she could melt into the walls and disappear.

But more than anything, she wanted to go home. The closer she came to Espen's realm, the more seconds of her life ticked away.

The road wound around the enormous, domed mountains. With nothing else to do, Senna studied the countryside and its people through the gauzy rain. It seemed in Tartan, there were few Middlings and almost none of the Class. Most everyone was Boor.

"Ciara," Senna entered their conversation. The two seemed surprised she was there. "Where did you learn to speak Nefalien?"

Ciara sighed as she looked away. "My father was a Guardian. He married my mother during the war in Nefalie. After his Witch disappeared, he brought us to Tarten."

"He brought you back here?" Senna asked incredulously.

"Yes, but Mother was a Nefalien, so their marriage wasn't recognized. Officially, she was his concubine, which is why I never married. You see, though I have money and to spare, I haven't a legitimate birth." Her sad countenance melted like butter in the hot sun. "And now you know my ignominy," she said melodramatically.

Joshen and Ciara immediately restarted their conversation where they'd left off. Senna went back to her window. Eventually, the rain stopped again. Homes grew more frequent, the road more traveled. Soldiers passed them. She found herself trying to hide from any gaze that might stray through the window. The carriage slowed. "We are coming closer to the city gates. Both of you remain silent and act as conceited as possible," Ciara whispered. She looked Senna up and down, her brows creased in disapproval. "Poise, Senna. You're Class, remember?"

Grudgingly, Senna sat up straight and squared her shoulders. She didn't want to act like Ciara's 'Class'—snobbish and rich.

The carriage rolled to a stop. Senna's heart shot in her throat as a guard with a soldier's red tunic leaned in and spoke. Ciara lifted her dainty nose and replied. Senna did her best to act uninterested in the soldier's questions as her blood pounded in her fingertips. His face darkening, he motioned for them to step out. The huffiness in Ciara's voice increased. The guard jerked the door open and shouted an order.

Ciara faced them. The lines around her eyes betrayed her anxiety. She said something. Senna caught one word. *"Cheche."* The same word the farmer had used when he motioned for them to follow him, the same word Kaen's wife had used as she'd dragged Senna into her room. She suspected it meant "come."

The guard held open the carriage door as they filed out. Joshen stayed close to Senna's side. She saw his hands flexed into fists and his legs in a fighter's stance. She kept her betraying amber eyes down. Still, she couldn't help but notice the city shining from the top of the hill.

While one guard went into their carriage, another lowered the bags from the roof while yet another rifled through the trunks.

One guard grabbed Ciara's arm and pushed her toward an official-looking building. She wrenched free and pressed her lips to Senna's ear. "Don't sing! No matter what, don't sing!" The guard viciously jerked Ciara away.

The realization they meant to separate her from Joshen blossomed in Senna's head like thistle flowers. A hand gripped Senna's injured arm. She gasped as pain clawed through her flesh. She struggled to twist away from the guard and reach Joshen.

With an enraged roar, Joshen lunged toward the guard. His balled fist met the man's temple with a thud. The guard crumpled. Shouts rang out. More soldiers gripped her. Joshen fought with the strength of a bull, throwing the soldiers off Senna. Taking her hand, they ran. With a yell, two soldiers fell in behind them. She couldn't move in these shoes! Heavy hands clamped down on her arms. She gritted her teeth as the pain flared in her arm again.

The two soldiers threw their weight into her small frame and grappled her to the soggy ground. One pressed himself on top of her. She squirmed beneath him, hating his body on top of hers and his breath on the back of her neck. Gripping her jaw, his lips brushed her ear as he spoke. She didn't have to speak his language to understand his meaning.

Her gaze met Joshen's horrified stare. He squirmed, but at least four men held him. Blood seeped from his mouth, mixing with the dirt his face was pressed into.

Senna's voice ached to sing. But Ciara had warned her. Perhaps these soldiers simply wished to question her? Perhaps they didn't know who she was? She clamped her mouth shut until her jaw ached. Joshen's desperation mirrored hers. Neither said a word.

Hauling her to her feet, the soldiers jerked her toward what she guessed was the guard house. She dug the heels of her finely made shoes into the ground, but they weren't made to handle abuse. Only look pretty. The straps broke and though her bare feet grappled for traction on the slick grass, she couldn't get away.

Once inside, they threw her into a small room. The soldier pushed her toward a chair and forced her down. Hunching protectively over her arm, she glared at him. A commander paced in front of her, speaking that confounded language of his. The only thing she caught was his name, Methen. Remembering Ciara's words, Senna lifted her head and refused to acknowledge him.

As he continued pacing, his voice rose until the spittle flew from his lips. Senna trembled in fear, but she didn't respond. A door creaked open behind her. She dared not look. A hand gripped the wrap around her hair and ripped it off. As her light hair tumbled down her shoulders, words, crystal clear and superior, hit her. "She's not responding to you, Methen, because she doesn't understand Tarten. Do you Brusenna?"

Senna clenched her eyes shut and willed her ears to lie. Begged the words not belong to the man who haunted her nightmares. But he slowly came to stand in front of her. Wardof. His demeanor cold and condescending. Triumph was written across his features. "If you wanted to face Espen, all you had to do was ask. I would've brought you here and we could've avoided all this."

"Bound and gagged, I'm sure," she responded in a voice that sounded far away.

He shrugged. "Of course."

Her eyes darted to the small window. She opened her mouth to sing. Wardof's fist cracked against her temple. She slammed into the floor. The world swirled. Her stomach rolled. She blinked, trying to force the objects in the room to hold still. When she could bear it, she looked up to see Wardof shaking his hand. "Corner a Witch and they'll start singing. It's that simple."

Before Senna knew what was happening, Methen forced something between her teeth. She bit his hand. Another fist cracked into her eye. Her vision turned red amid fragments of exploding light. Her eye tingled. But little pain. At least, so far.

She tried to resist the cord forced between her teeth, but her jaw refused to obey. Strong hands wrenched her arms behind her. A sharp sting blasted through her shoulders, the sting of her muscles tearing. A rough cord dug into her wrists. She cried out, but they didn't relent. Her hands felt swollen and hot. Wardof glared at her. "We'll put you in a cell for a while. See if that doesn't loosen your courage."

Two men dragged her down the hall and threw her in a dark room. They tossed her to the floor like a sack of grain. She landed on something hard. Her back screamed in pain. She groaned and rolled off it.

"Senna?"

Joshen. She tried to push herself up, but the world tipped to the side. She crumpled. Concentrating on breathing, she rested her forehead against the cool dirt floor. Squinting through the eye that wasn't swollen shut, she saw faint traces of light that grew stronger as her eyes adjusted.

Something brushed against her leg. She smelled the sea and horses—Joshen. "Senna! What did they do to you?" She heard the anger and hurt in his voice. She glanced up at him. His arms were bound behind his back. Easing beside her, he curled himself around her. "I'm so sorry I could not protect you," he whispered.

"You 'ried," she fumbled through the cord in her mouth. Her words sounded strange to her—strange because, despite her failure and inadequacy, she could still speak. "How 'id dey know?"

Another figure emerged from the shadows. It was Ciara, her eyes swollen from crying. "I thought my status would get us through. I was wrong."

Joshen hunched over Senna's face. She felt his lips working at the rope around her mouth. She shivered. Eventually, he got it off. He immediately went to work on the cords around her hands. "Can you sing us free?"

Her head hurt so much she could barely think. Her gaze followed a shaft of light to a high window. "I might," she rasped. She felt the ropes around her arms go free. Her blood pulsed angrily in her hands, which burned as though stung by nettles. She brought them around carefully, her shoulders groaning in protest. She rubbed the circulation back into her hands as Ciara scooted closer. "I have a knife. Above my knee."

Senna found the knife and cut the rope from Joshen's hands. Her headache was growing worse, as was her nausea. With a careful shake of her head and a groan, she handed the knife to Joshen. He shot her a look of concern before cutting the rest of the ropes. When he was free, he gripped her shoulder. "Senna, can you sing now?"

She tried to sit up, but the room swirled like someone stirred it. She tipped forward and was sick. It did not ease her nausea.

"Senna?" Joshen's voice had an edge of desperation she recognized all too well.

Forcing her hands under her, Senna pushed herself up and faced the window. Her voice felt weak and shaky.

Plants, with strength and swiftness, come to me,
For with my companions I must flee.

As she repeated the song, she felt the plants respond before she saw a vine snake through the window. She tried to hold on to consciousness, but the song drained strength she simply didn't have. She faded to blackness.

When she came to, the room jerked wildly. She closed her eyes, but the dizziness didn't fade. "Senna, I can't carry you. You have to climb."

"I don't think I can. Go, Joshen. Get away from this. Go raise your horses. Marry Ciara; she's so beautiful. You deserve that."

"They must have hit you really hard," he said in disbelief. "Ciara, you go first." His arms gripped her. She felt herself rising upward as he guided her hands with his own. "Grab it, Senna. Just grab it and hold yourself up."

Somehow, her arms obeyed. Joshen was always beneath her, pushing her so she had only to grip the rope and hold on. She reached the window and looked down. The ground twisted violently. She swayed and barely caught herself from falling. "Joshen, I can't … ." she closed her eyes and worked desperately to simply stay on the windowsill.

"It's alright, Senna. Just stay there, I'm coming around you."
She felt him climbing over her and lowering himself down. "Just
let yourself fall. I'll catch you."

She opened her eyes. In front of her, Joshen seemed to jerk
from one side to the other like a pendulum. But she figured
gravity would do most of the work for her. She let go of the
windowsill and tipped forward. It felt like a long time before he
caught her.

Then he ran.

**

Wardof grimaced as he lowered his hand back in the cold
water—curse Tarten and their abominable lack of ice. It had
already swollen to nearly twice its size. "That girl has a harder
head than I thought."

The door eased open. Garg's head appeared, his gaze fixed on
the floor. "How's the hand?"

Wardof rather liked that Garg was terrified of him. "Tell the
soldiers to send someone to wrap it. You idiot."

The door shut quickly, leaving Wardof alone again. He closed
his eyes against the pain throbbing in his hand, but then a worse
pain touched his ears. Witch song, clear and unimpeded.

In two strides, he wrenched open the door. He sprinted down
the hall. Methen whipped in beside him. "Did you put her with
the others?" Wardof screamed in Tarten.

He seemed affronted. "There's no way they could escape."

"She's a Witch! You imbecile! Of course there's a way!"

Methen fumbled with his keys. On his third try, he finally
managed to open the door. The cell was as empty as a hollow
egg. "She wasn't even lucid—" he began.

"Find her! Spread out and find her, or I'll have every last one
of you whipped and run until at least three of you die!"

Methen took a menacing step forward. "I'd like to see you
force my garrison to do that."

"I won't force anyone. Espen will," Wardof hissed.

The man's eyes widened in genuine fear. White-faced, he
hollered, "Search everything! Bar the city gates!"

24. Under

Senna caught fleeting glimpses of her surroundings. The houses sagged and the people grew less frequent. They circled the bottom of the mountain—the Boorish part of town. Sweat rolled down Joshen's face. His breathing rasped through his throat. He kept readjusting his damp grip. Even though she was small, she knew he couldn't last much longer. "Let me down."

"Humph," Joshen replied, hoisting her up again. The jostling thrust her stomach in her throat. She moaned. His arms tightened around her. "Hang on, Senna. I'll get you somewhere safe."

She opened her eyes when Ciara let out a startled gasp. Leaning against a wall, she lifted her bleeding foot. "I'm not used to being barefoot," she mumbled as she yanked out a sliver.

"Where are you taking us?" Joshen asked harshly.

Senna pressed her palms into her eyes. The jerking was getting worse. Her stomach rolled.

Gingerly, Ciara tested her weight on her foot. "Somewhere I'd much rather avoid."

Shouts came from behind them. Joshen's grip tightened as he twisted toward the sound. Ciara peered down the street ahead before bursting from the alley, Joshen right behind her. They crossed two more streets and Senna watched helplessly as they ran full-speed into a reed house that hunched like a withered old man. Under normal circumstances she would have thought twice about entering, but she wasn't going to complain now.

No sooner were they out of sight than she heard the unmistakable sounds of running soldiers. Carefully, Joshen and Ciara moved deeper into the shadows. The three of them held their breath until the footsteps faded into the distance.

Joshen gently set her down, his arm hovering around her shoulders as if to make sure she didn't tip over. Senna glanced around. Bits of blue sky gleamed through the ragged palm ceiling, casting warm shafts of light upon plants and even a small tree that had managed to grow inside. With a start, she recognized the plants. Witch plants. "Where are we?"

"Desni's place." Ciara shivered. "Apparently, she's not here, but I'm sure she'll be along as soon as she hears of a Witch escaping the soldiers."

Through her jerky vision, Senna noted a few shelves along one wall. By another, a woven mat and some sort of wash basin. The hut smelled of strong herbs and rotting wood. "Someone lives here?" she asked in disbelief. The whole room twirled around her. She clenched her eyes shut, glad to at least be still.

"We're just lucky I remembered how to find it. Kaen said if there was trouble, I should come here. I met Desni once and I can't say I understand why he trusts her. Her mind seemed as muddled and mixed up as an imbecile."

"Quite true," a heavily accented voice cracked the stillness.

Pulling Senna behind him, Joshen whirled. From the doorway, a haggard woman peered at them from under the great sag of her eyelids. Senna felt Joshen's muscles tense, ready to flee or fight.

"Settle down, young one. No need to fear old Desni." Her teeth were as brown as aged wood and her hair was matted with bits of leaves. Her sallow flesh seemed as transparent as onion skin. What little Senna could see of the old woman's eyes settled on her. She moved with surprising agility to the woven mat. "Lay the little one down."

Joshen hesitated.

The old woman didn't look up. "Don't let my appearance deceive you. I may be old and ugly, but I wasn't always."

Senna rested her hand on Joshen's chest. "It's alright, Joshen. This woman knows something of Witches. I recognize her plants." One who embraced a Witch's plants embraced the Witch. Or so she hoped.

He lingered, his body tense, before moving. His arms trembled with exhaustion as he helped her to the old woman's bed.

Senna clenched her jaw, her whole body tight with pain as she lay down. The woman kneeled over her and pulled open her bruised eye.

"Ow!" Senna groaned.

Desni merely grunted and probed at the swollen spot on her temple. Senna forced herself to hold still, though she felt like there were shards of glass under her skin.

"Not broken. How do you feel?" Desni asked.

"Dizzy and nauseous," Senna managed.

Desni leaned back on her haunches. "Hit her pretty hard, he did. To mess up her balance like that."

"Her balance?" Joshen clearly didn't understand.

Desni handed Ciara a little pail. "Get some water out back and be careful no one sees you."

The woman grabbed a handful of leaves from the plants and disappeared outside with an armload of sticks. The whole room whirled. Senna groaned and shut her eyes again. "It's worse when my eyes are open."

Sloshing water announced Ciara's return. Senna heard them working over the fire outside. She started to sweat amid the strong smell of herbs and smoke. Someone slurped.

"More itnot," the old woman announced.

The next loud sip brought a satisfied smack of lips. "There we are!" Liquid splashed into another container. "See she drinks every drop."

Easing her up, Joshen rested her head on his legs. "Kinda reminds me of when you nursed me back to health at Haven."

"Hmm," Senna managed. She smelled the tea, hot and strong. Her lips met smooth glass. She managed a small sip. The bitter liquid burned her lips. "Itnot, tabber, honey." She sipped again. "And a few others I'm not familiar with."

The old woman's scratchy voice answered, "That's because you can't grow them in Nefalie. Too cold. But they're used for the same thing. Just like your eye, your brain is swelling. If we can't get the swelling down, you'll be dead in a few hours." Senna choked on the tea then took a big gulp. The old woman went on, oblivious, "Bessil tames the hurt. Candor helps with dizziness and nausea—give that to all my expecting mothers, I do."

Senna's stomach suddenly rebelled at the liquid. She pushed the glass away and laid back, her face hot and sticky. She felt Joshen leaned worriedly over her. "Senna—"

She held up her index finger. "Just give me a minute."

He sat back on his haunches. Eventually, the queasiness faded. She tried again. This time, the tea settled her stomach. Before long, she'd downed the whole glass. In barely discernible increments, the jerking of her vision steadied. The tension in her body eased. "Mush be'er," she slurred, her tongue thick with fatigue.

"You won't think so when the Under wears off." She was barely cognizant of the old woman arranging boiled leaves over her eye and temple. "That will help with the swelling and bruising. Now all of you, get some rest."

When Senna woke, it was because her dizziness had returned. Though not as bad as before, it was bad enough that a moan escaped her.

"You'll be wantin' some more of this," Desni held out another jar of tea. With a whimper, Senna sat up. The soggy leaves slipped down her cheek. It was raining again. Drips fell through the tattered roof, splashing her. She gulped, not really caring that the liquid scorched her mouth.

First, her stomach eased away from the nausea. Then the room stopped whirling. Exhaustion pulled at her. She lay back, enjoying the feel of Joshen's back pressed against hers. The last thing she remembered was Desni's soft chuckle. "You'll sleep the rest of the day away with as much Under as I gave you."

When Senna woke again, she blinked and waited for the room to swirl. It held still. Tentatively, she eased to a sitting position.

Desni handed her more tea. Senna looked at it suspiciously. The old woman smiled. "Don't worry. No Under in this one."

Senna sipped slowly, enjoying a room that held still and a stomach that didn't revolt at the merest provocation. She swallowed the last and pulled the remnants of the mushy leaves from her face. She could see through her eye again.

Joshen came in with a load of water. "The swelling looks a lot better and the bruise is already starting to fade."

"How long have I been asleep?" she asked.

Desni leaned in and toweled away the remaining leaves. "This is the evening of your second day." Senna swallowed at her suddenly dry mouth. Desni took the glass from her. "If you're well enough, it'll be best to leave tonight."

Senna tentatively probed the puffiness with her fingers. It certainly felt better. She looked around and sighed with relief when the room stayed put. The light filtering through the slats had softened to a grainy gray.

Desni handed her Tarten flat bread. "I'm sure you're hungry."

Suddenly, Senna was. She took a bite. Other than tough and hard to chew, it wasn't bad. Better than the stuff Ciara had given them. Holding fresh leaves to her face, Senna sucked on the bread until it dissolved before she carefully swallowed. "Where will you take us now?" she asked around a mouthful.

"Well, for Ciara, it's off to live with her brother. I'll take you two to the edge of my land. Then, I'm afraid you're on your own."

"Your land!" Ciara huffed. Senna hadn't noticed her in the corner, her knees tucked into her chest.

Desni turned slowly. "All of Espen's forest was once mine. Mine and my daughter's. She was Espen's first captive. She took my home as her own."

Ciara's gaze fixed on the roof. "I'm sorry."

Desni turned back to Joshen and Senna. "Nefalie wasn't the only land blessed with Witches and it hasn't been the only land to lose them."

A hush crept over Senna. "So …you're a Witch too?"

Desni harrumphed. "I'm a Wastrel. Though if anyone said it to my face, they'd find I'm meaner than a cornered constrictor."

Senna's brow furrowed. "I-I don't understand."

Desni rubbed her forehead. "I can't sing, Senna." Tears stood out in the old woman's eyes. "Can't carry a tune, tone deaf, helpless when it comes to understanding a score and a voice even the plants cringe away from."

"I'm sorry. I didn't even know—"

"That such a thing as a Wastrel existed? Well, Senna, there's all different levels of Witches. If you manage to free the others, you'll find out how strong your song is soon enough."

Absently, Senna tore off pieces of bread and stacked them in a neat little pile. Years of struggle drawing to an end. What if the end meant the last of the Keepers—of Senna. And she no longer had her seed belt ... her dueling seeds. She took a deep breath and forced herself to focus on something else. "How is it you came to speak Nefalien?"

Desni smiled. "All Tarten Witches learn Nefalien so they can communicate with the Witches at Haven. I learned from my daughter. She was one of the best singers."

"What was her name?" Ciara asked softly.

"Tiena. The Dark Witch took her ten years ago." She tossed them two packs.

Senna gaped at the pack—the same one she had taken from her home so long ago. Eyes wide in wonder, she pulled out her green dress, cloak and golden seed belt. Reaching into a pocket, she sifted tiny Yidd seeds through her fingers. "How ... How did you get these from the soldiers?"

Desni smiled as she handed Senna a damp towel and a basin of water. "One of the maids recovered them for me."

Senna immediately set about scrubbing off the brown paste. When she had her own skin back, she cast a look of disgust at the gaudy tunic Ciara had given her. If it was possible, it looked even worse now—ripped in numerous places and stained with blood and dirt. With a knowing smile, Joshen closed his eyes and turned his back. Senna stripped the ridiculous tunic and dropped the familiar green over her head. She sighed as the sturdy fabric settled into the curves of her body.

Desni handed Ciara a scarred tunic and a pair of practical shoes. With a look of mortification, Ciara pulled it on.

With a pleased grunt, Desni handed Senna a small bag. She pulled open the strings to find a mixture of leaves. "Drink a handful with every meal. In between, if you really need it. Gradually, you should be able to reduce your body's demand for it."

Taking the bag, she glanced up to see that Ciara's face had paled her eyes fixed on something behind them. Whirling, Senna saw a man at the doorway. Joshen pulled her behind him.

Her hand up, Desni put herself between Joshen and the stranger. "This is Tren. He'll be seeing Ciara home safely."

Ciara stepped in front of Joshen and Senna, her eyes sad. "I'm sorry I could not do better for you both."

"You aren't the only one who failed her," Joshen said softly.

Senna's gaze darted from Joshen's downcast face to Ciara's. "We made it out alright, didn't we?"

Ciara nodded a little too quickly. Tren looked her over, as if gauging her. Then he turned and disappeared. Ciara cast one last look at them before hurrying to follow.

Desni shook her head. "About time that girl fell in love." She winked at Senna. "And Tren's the kind of man to show her how."

Senna felt her face flush, but the old woman had already headed for the door. She paused at the threshold. A man dressed in rags leaned in and spoke to her in Tarten.

Gently, Joshen lifted Senna's hood over her head. "Tartens don't have golden hair," he said softly. Reaching down, he clasped her hand in his. Senna studied their intertwined fingers— his flesh melding with hers. Warmth spread from their touch. Despite the danger all around them, she felt safe.

The Tarten man's gaze met Senna's. In his eyes, she saw a mixture of sadness and hope. He nodded once before moving past the doorway. Desni motioned for the two of them to follow. "Gilden will lead us. Come. Now."

Joshen led Senna to the door, peered both ways and eased out. Halting between the shadows of the withered huts, they followed Desni with Gilden leading a little farther on, his head swaying from side to side as he searched for danger. Another man darted out of the shadows. Senna started and gripped Joshen's hand tight. The man merely whispered to Gilden and shot away again.

"They're tracking the soldiers for us," Desni whispered.

"They?" Senna wondered how many people were helping them.

A woman wandered past with a basket of linens on her head. She peered into Senna's hood. A soft sound of surprise escaped. She bowed to Senna and rattled off something to Desni before dropping the linens and taking off at a run.

"What did she say?" Joshen demanded.

Desni didn't pause. "That she'd follow and warn us if soldiers started trailing us."

Senna looked back to see the woman round the bend and vanish. "I don't understand. Why would they help us?"

Desni shook her head. "Since the Witches have gone, most of the Middlings have become Boors. Hungry people are angry people."

Another man darted in to speak with Gilden. Senna noted the clothing hanging limply from his lean frame. So … it was the Boors who helped them. Those who had suffered the most without the Witches' protection. Coming back to them at a run, Gilden rushed them down a side street. Senna and Joshen waited in the shadows while he checked for soldiers. After what seemed forever, he eased forward. *"Cheche."*

Senna let out a tense breath and hurried after Joshen. But they hadn't passed three houses before she recognized another of their guides darting from the shadows. He spoke in low, frantic tones and then ran off again. Gilden shoved them into the closest hut. He shut the reed door behind him and leaned against it.

Senna stared into the room. A young man stood with eyes wide, an angry crease between his brows. Behind him, a woman sat on a reed mat, her breast bare, a suckling child in her arms.

Desni whispered to the man. His gaze shot to Senna—a gaze filled with fear. He shook his head and pointed to the door.

Gilden spoke softly from behind Senna.

She wanted to scream with frustration. What was happening? What were they saying? Was he going to hand them over? At the sound of shouts, she turned to see flashes of red tunics between the reeds.

What if they found her? Wardof would kill her! And Joshen! Her head pounded and her arm ached. The Creators protect them. With a soft whimper, she gripped Joshen's shirt in her fists and clenched her jaw to keep from sobbing.

Before any of them could react, the young father strode past them toward the door. She read the determination on his face as plain as if he'd uttered the words. She felt Joshen preparing to lunge for him. Gilden spread himself to block the door. But a soft voice from behind Senna stopped him.

The young mother stood, her back stooped in the cramped hut. She stared into Senna's eyes and though her gaze was wild with fear, it was calm, too. Shifting her child, she spoke low.

In the same low tone, her husband argued with her, but his voice lacked the determination Senna had seen earlier.

Someone whispered through the reeds. Gilden eased the door open and peeked outside. *"Cheche."*

Senna cast a look of gratitude at the mother, wishing she could give her something in return for saving them—to somehow repay her for the danger she'd willingly shouldered.

There wasn't time. With the sounds of the soldiers fading behind them, Gilden ran.

Senna struggled to keep up. Desni's tea had tamed her dizziness and nausea, but her head pounded with the effort. When they finally reached the last house before the city wall, she wanted nothing more than a place to lie down. With a grim nod, Gilden left them to walk toward the empty space before the wall. More men filtered from the streets to join him.

With a jolt, Senna noted the slings in their hands. She realized what they were doing. What if one of them died? Bruke's and

Lery's deaths flashed in her mind. "No." She started toward them.

Joshen pulled her into his chest, crushing her against him. "Don't," he whispered. "Not again."

His arms engulfed her. She buried her face into his chest. Though she tried to block it out, she heard the insults thrown out. The clatter of stones from the slings. More shouts and pounding feet as the soldiers gave chase. What if they were caught? She tried not to think of it, to remember that it had been their choice. "I could've done it with the plants," she whispered.

"But that would've brought the entire garrison down on us instead of drawing them away," Desni said. Moving cautiously into the moonlight, the old woman searched for any sign of remaining guards. With a satisfied nod, she hurried forward and pulled aside some low brush. On the other side was a tiny hole.

Casting worried glances at the high wall, Senna and Joshen hurried to follow. Desni wiggled in and disappeared. Senna didn't hesitate to hit her knees. Using her feet and hands, she wormed her way under the wall. One rock hung down lower than the others. She managed to get her head under it. But halfway through, it dug into her back, pinning her. She squirmed. It seemed to push back. She was stuck. The air left her lungs. Sweat coated her skin. The ground seemed to rise up, compressing her. She stopped, unable to catch her breath. "Senna?" Joshen whispered.

She began backing out. "I can't, I—"

"Hurry, Senna," he urged. "An enormous spider just crawled in after you."

How close was it? How far had she come? Her fingernails dug into the ground as she scrambled forward. At last, she saw Desni. The old woman gripped her hands and pulled. Scrambling a safe distance from the hole, Senna lay on the ground, staring into the night sky and wishing she could go home.

She turned at a vicious grunt. Joshen's head poked out of the hole. "My shoulders are stuck."

"Back in and come out one arm at a time," Desni said.

Joshen wiggled back. One arm appeared. Keeping a careful eye out for the spider, Senna took his hand and pulled while Desni pushed his broad shoulders in. The rough wall tore his shirt. Senna gasped at the sight of his blood. "Give me a minute to catch my breath," he rasped.

Desni shook her head. "No time." Grabbing his wrist, she heaved. He broke free, his face white.

Desni dusted off her hands. "Just like having a baby."

Ignoring the old woman, Senna leaned over him, carefully inspecting the cuts on his shoulders. "Joshen?"

"I'm alright." He grinned sheepishly. "Sorry about the spider."

She rocked back on her haunches. "You lied to me?"

He pushed himself up heavily and gripped her hand. "Come on. Let's go before those soldiers get back."

She gave him a dirty look but kept her retort behind her teeth. She had a feeling she'd need the energy before they were through. Once inside the jungle, the three of them ran for what felt like hours. Her breath whistled through her lungs. Her lips tingled. She felt her heart pounding in her hands. Without asking, Joshen hoisted her on his back and gripped her legs around his middle.

Too tired to complain, she rested her head against his neck. "I can't even run."

"Stop your whining," Joshen chided. "I'm carrying you; do you hear me complaining?"

Desni wheezed and panted behind them. "Well, this old woman is complaining plenty enough for the three of us." She rested her back against a tree. "Some outlaws we make. An old woman, a tiny, injured Witch and a boy."

Joshen bent to pick up Desni.

She waved him away. "Don't be ridiculous. You can't carry us both." She pushed away from the tree and plowed forward, albeit at a slower pace. For a long time, all Senna heard was the tramping of Joshen and the old woman's steps. Then Joshen stiffened beneath her and half-turned toward the city.

Senna strained to hear what he had. Her heart dropped to her toes. Baying dogs. Joshen and Desni exchange worried glances.

Senna scrambled from his back. He moved to pull her up again. She neatly sidestepped him. "I can run for a little while."

He hesitated before nodding for her to follow Desni. "I'll take the rear." The three of them ran flat out.

After only a few minutes, Desni stumbled and her breathing came in great, wheezing gasps. When they rounded the last of the domed mountains, she collapsed beside a fallen tree. "From here, you can find it on your own." Shakily, she pointed to the right of the next mountain. "Get past the Tangled Trees. If you can make it that far, not even the dogs will follow."

"We can't leave you!" Senna exclaimed.

His face grim, Joshen said, "I'm going to create a false trail. You two rest here." He took off in a different direction.

Desni smiled weakly. "He loves you. As much or more than any man has ever loved a woman. Seeing it brings me hope."

Senna felt the blood drain from her face.

Desni chuckled at the look on her face. "Too insecure to believe it? The way he looks at you, as if daring anyone to harm you. Yet he is as gentle and loving as you'll allow him to be."

A pain began in Senna that had nothing to do with Wardof's fists—a deep, throbbing longing. She tried to rub it away. "I'm small and plain. He is so strong and handsome."

Desni shot her a look of disbelief. "You're a beautiful girl, Senna. More so because of how rare your features are. Those golden eyes—"

"But when compared to someone like Ciara—"

"Bah!" Desni exclaimed. "You compare diamonds to rubies. Rubies may be a bit more flashy, but diamonds are made of tougher stuff and are more rare."

Senna looked up as Joshen crashed into sight. "That should buy us some time."

Grabbing a gnarled stick, Desni struggled to her feet. She jabbed it in the direction they were to go. "Follow the slope of the land." Using her makeshift cane, she hurried off in the opposite direction. Senna grasped her shoulder. Desni shook her head and smiled. "Don't you worry about me. They'll give me a lift back and feed me until you defeat Espen. Then you can break me free."

Joshen tugged on Senna's arm. "She's right, Senna. I can't carry her and she can't run anymore. Let her go."

Images flashed in her head. Lery, Bruke, Ciara, the young mother, Desni. Countless other sacrifices. For what? Releasing her, Senna gave Joshen a look that said, "If I fail, see to it."

He looked away in exasperation but nodded anyway.

Desni hurried away. Senna wanted to call her back, tell her to hide, anything. But her words congealed in her throat. Hiking up her dress, she ran ahead of Joshen. The leaves whipped her.

Plants of the forest, make a path for me,
For through this forest, I must flee.
After I pass, hide my trail,
For an enemy I must quell.

The plants gathered behind them, blocking the path to those who might follow.

She forced herself to keep going, but she wondered how much longer she could push herself before her body stopped obeying. The sound of dogs drew steadily closer. When it split and shifted, Senna guessed the soldiers were following Joshen's false trail and Desni. But it wasn't long before the sound was behind them again. Senna clenched her fists. The soldiers wouldn't hurt a little old Tarten lady? Would they?

Suddenly, a bark sounded close behind them. Turning to look, she tripped over a vine and fell. Joshen pulled her up. She looked into his eyes and knew they couldn't outrun them. But there was something else in his gaze. Tenderness. She couldn't deny that Desni was right—he loved her. But did the old woman mistake brotherly love for the love a man has for a woman?

Senna struggled to her feet. Her legs felt numb and her lungs raw. Sweat ran down her temples before streaking down her neck.

Joshen must have seen her exhaustion. He ripped a limb from a dead tree and rounded. "Go on, Senna! I'll keep them off!"

If she left him alone, he'd die. At that moment, saving everyone else from Espen seemed trivial in comparison to saving Joshen. Her chest heaving, she stood shoulder-to-shoulder with him.

"Senna! I said go!"

She glared at him. "You made me promise not to leave you, remember?"

He waved the stick at her. "This isn't what I meant!"

"Then you should've phrased your words more carefully!"

There was no more time for arguments. The dogs streaked through the trees, their baying increasing to a fevered pitch as their quarry came into view. Reaching inside her belt, she drew a barrier seed. She forced a hole in the soil and pressed the seed down. "Back up." She gripped Joshen's arm and pulled. As she moved, she sang.

Take in light, take in air;
Spread thy roots, thy leaves grow fair.

She repeated the song over and over. A green shoot burst from the Earth. Within moments, it was taller than Joshen. *Just a few more songs,* she thought. The first dog sprang past the tree. Joshen swung the tree branch, catching it in the ribs. With a yelp, it backed out of his reach and barked like mad.

Too late to grow it to full maturity! Senna's song changed into something deeper and darker. It wasn't a song so much as a chant—this was where the insult "Chanter" came from. She cringed at the animosity and menace in her voice.

Let nothing pass.

The dogs slowed, sensing the danger, but not understanding it.

They didn't have time to do more than flinch as the tree's branches wrenched them from the ground. Barks of excitement changed to howls of terror as they writhed to free themselves. But the tree didn't pause as it flung them back in the direction they'd come. Tails between their legs, the others fled, terror in their eyes.

Senna sang again, forcing the barrier tree into full maturity. It became oddly quiet and then the rustling of brush reached through the stillness. Patches of red appeared through the trees. The soldiers were here. Her mouth went dry. She swallowed hard and cleared her throat in preparation for her song.

Joshen tightened his grip on the branch. "I wish I had my musket!"

Through the shadows, moonlight slanted across the face she feared more than Espen. Wardof sifted through the jungle, his gaze pinning her in place. He came into full view. He lowered his shoulders and pressed forward. Senna waited until the men around him were in the shadow of its branches. "Senna?" Joshen warned, but she didn't budge as she timed her next move.

Understanding dawned on Wardof's face. Fear replaced his malice. Senna gave him no time to fully understand his danger. Her song burst free.

Let no one pass!

As if a sudden wind whipped the branches, the tree came alive, snatching up red-coated soldiers. For the briefest moment, it seemed to bear strange, red fruit, before it hurled them into the air. No sooner had it loosed one than it picked up another. Everywhere, men were running, dodging tree branches and shrieking.

Bullets whizzed past Senna's head. She didn't stay to watch. Clutching Joshen's arm, she ran.

25. TANGLED

"Did the tree get Wardof?" Joshen panted.

Too out of breath to answer, Senna slumped to the ground. Her head ached like someone had dumped gravel into her ears and shook her.

Joshen took one look at her and started gathering kindling. "You need some more of that tea."

The jungle seemed to slide sideways. Her stomach twisted. Wardof. Was he still after her? "I didn't see," she managed after a few deep breaths.

Joshen dropped handfuls of leaves in a little jar of water and nestled it in the fledgling flames. His gaze kept darting from the tea to the jungle that surrounded them. "That was really amazing, Senna. What exactly can't you do?"

Senna grunted, her throat too raw for a proper laugh.

Joshen dipped his finger in the tea and sucked in his breath. "Yup. Plenty hot." Using the corner of his blanket, he pulled it from the fire and wrapped it up before handing it to her. Without bothering to strain it, she sipped. She fished out a few itnot leaves and held them to her eye. Within moments, she felt better—as if her body healed itself as she drank. Tipping the jar, she drained it and wiped her mouth. She leaned back against a tree as the remaining ache lifted from her head. She sighed with relief.

Her relief was short-lived.

A cord yanked across her neck, cutting off the blood to her brain. She clawed at it. It tightened. She choked and gagged. She scratched at the sausage-like fingers holding the cord. Garg.

Joshen lunged for him, but Wardof grappled him from behind. The two rolled to the ground. Senna twisted. Garg pulled her in tighter and wrapped his legs around her torso.

Air! She had to have air!

She rammed her elbow into Garg's paunch. He let out a gush of air, but managed to hold tight. Senna scrabbled to gain her footing, but Garg had the advantage of position and size. Her vision turned red. In a cascade of sparks, blackness edged in.

The cord around her neck went limp. She gasped and coughed. Garg forced something between her teeth. In one quick jerk, he tied a gag.

After a few deep breaths, her panic receded and her senses returned. Garg had feared her song. But he'd underestimated the rest of her. Her fingers searched through the rotting foliage. She found something hard and rough. Twisting, she smashed the rock into his temple. He reeled back, stunned.

Rock still in hand, she ran, but she hadn't managed two strides before he grabbed her from behind. Scraping her shoe along his shin, she stomped on his foot and threw her head back. She felt his nose crunch.

Garg released her and stumbled back. Twin ribbons of blood flowed from his nose, forming a crimson mustache.

I should've finished this long ago, she thought grimly.

He lunged for her, grasping her forearm. But this time she was ready with a small seed. As he came at her, she stepped into his arms and shoved the seed into his mouth.

His eyes widened in fear. He desperately started spitting and clawing at his tongue. But the seed imbedded itself on contact with a human mouth. If he wanted it out, he'd have to carve out his own tongue and it was fast becoming too late. Vines sprang from his mouth. Garg clamped his jaw shut, but it was too late. He vomited vines that circled his body like a green shroud.

Senna watched, her anger mounting. What had she ever done to Garg, Wardof, any of them? They'd taken everything from her! Everything! They would not take Joshen! She yanked at the gag. But Garg had tied it so tight her jaw ached. Her lips cracked and bled, but it wouldn't budge.

She whirled to see Joshen and Wardof still struggling. Frantically, her fingers flew to the knot—a hard, unyielding ball. She couldn't see what she was doing! She wanted to scream in frustration, but all she could do was work at the knot as she watched Joshen and Wardof pummel each other.

Joshen broke free and shoved Wardof. Before Wardof could recover, Joshen was on his feet, careful to position himself between Wardof and her. Wardof charged. Joshen stepped forward and twisted until his back was to Wardof. Senna's heart sank, but Joshen simply gripped Wardof's arm and heaved while bending over. Wardof slammed into the ground, stunned. Joshen's fist smashed into Wardof's temple. He went limp. It was over.

Joshen glanced at Senna. The fury in his eyes melted. Rushing forward, he pulled his knife and sawed at the knot until it came free. Easing her jaw open and shut, she rubbed her neck.

"You alright?"

Wiping a trickle of blood from the corner of her mouth, Senna nodded. "You?"

He groaned. "Few broken ribs. Could be worse."

Senna's eyes fell on Wardof. Hate simmered inside her. Reaching inside her seed belt, she drew a seed exactly like the one she'd used on Garg. "By the Creators, I should've taken care of this long ago." Stepping forward, she crouched beside the man who had taken so much from her. It wasn't hard to slip the seed between his open lips. She watched while it took root, covering his entire body. When it was finished, Senna sighed and stood.

"What was that?" Joshen asked, a trace of fear in his voice.

Senna didn't take her eyes off Wardof. "Bindweed. It's more like a parasite than a plant. It feeds off its host, but in return, nourishes him. There are only two ways to escape."

Joshen bent down and touched the hard shell. "And they are?"

"For the Witch who entrapped them to sing them free. And I'll never release them." Senna found her pack and walked in the direction Desni had pointed.

Clutching his ribs, he hurried to catch up. "And the other?"
She paused. "Death."

***

So this was what Desni meant by the tangled trees. Senna
studied the wall that stretched higher and wider than the
surrounding jungle. Branches knotted together in snarled clumps.
An impregnable barrier. One that should have taken dozens of
Witches to create. Espen had done it alone.

Senna shivered. She could feel Espen's taint strongly here.
The harmonious rhythms of nature felt off-key and jumbled.
Senna was so tired her toenails hurt, but beyond the tangled trees
lay safety—from the soldiers, at least. She sang a rather simple
song.

> *Plants of the forest, make a path for me,*
> *For through this forest I must flee.*
> *After I pass, hide my trail,*
> *For an enemy I must quell.*

The branches unraveled, leaving a low, narrow tunnel.

"Of course," she muttered. "Another dark, bug-infested hole."
Too exhausted to care, she stepped inside. The branches wove
closed behind her, cutting her off from Joshen. She could barely
see him through the thick growth. Singing, Senna stretched for
him. The branches parted from her. Joshen gripped her hand and
the branches widened enough for him to step inside.

She let go. The branches closed on him, binding him like the
strongest ropes. Surprised she stopped singing. The branches
closed on her as well. She grabbed his hand again and sang hard.
The branches retreated. Clever. Espen had made it so even a
Witch with an army couldn't pass.

With Senna holding Joshen's hand tightly and singing, she
peered into the gloom and tried to guess how far the tangled
trees went on. Nothing but the unnatural darkness. With a sigh,
she started out. Hunched over as she was, it wasn't long before
her back began to ache. She could only imagine how much worse
it was for Joshen, tall as he was. Breathless, she paused. The

branches closed on them—binding her, stealing her air, cutting her off. It felt worse than the tunnel Kaen had hid them in.

Though her mouth felt like parched Earth, she didn't stop.

How long she plodded forward, Senna didn't know. When they suddenly stumbled free, she blinked rapidly at the blinding light. She snatched the canteen and drank hard and fast. Wiping the water from her cheeks, she turned to see Joshen frozen in place, his eyes glassed over. And then she smelled it. Heady, sweet, tropical. Exotic orange blossoms sent her eyelids plunging downward. Barbus.

With a sharp intake of breath, she shook Joshen. "Breathe through your mouth!"

"Hmm?" His eyes were already closed, his breathing deep and regular. The barbed vines stretched toward him.

She couldn't go back. Not into the darkness again. That left no way but through. Gritting her teeth, she sang.

Barbus, I command thee retreat.
No more to carry out thy dark feat!

Gripping his hand, she hauled him forward. Automatically, he stumbled after her, eyes still closed.

Though she was careful not to breathe through her nose, her feet grew heavier. Each time she blinked, it was harder to open her eyes again. Her head ached, her body ached, her very soul seemed to ache. All she wanted was sleep. Her grip on Joshen's hand weakened. He slipped from her grasp. Shaking her head and forcing her eyes open, she saw him lying peacefully among the barbus, its poisonous vines reaching for him.

If she didn't do something now, he'd die.

Collapsing, she tried to lift him. He didn't budge. "Joshen. Joshen, wake up."

Her breathing unnaturally deep, she watched the barbus encircle them like a snake. "I can't shleep," she slurred. "Josshen'll die if I shleep."

Through the heavy fog in her mind, she searched for a song to wake him. Then she remembered a lullaby her mother had sung to awaken Senna as a child. Stirring herself, she sang.

Awake my love,
Open thy eyes and rise above.
Come to me, come to me, come, come along.
For my love will keep thee strong.

His eye lids fluttered before he settled back to sleep with a sigh.

It wasn't strong enough. How could she make a Witch song stronger? Some deeply buried memory surfaced. Her lips gathered a residue of power from the song. What if?

Bending down, she pressed her lips to Joshen's.

His eyes flew open. Senna pulled back, her heart hammering wildly inside her. A slow smile spread across his face. "Now that's something to wake a man up!" He pulled her mouth to his.

Joshen's lips were like every other part of him. Strong and gentle, caring and protective. He tasted like wind and musket powder. She found herself wanting to stroke his chest, his arms. But she held back, unsure what his reaction might be.

Something prickly like a squash vine gripped her wrist. She gasped and pulled away. In one wrench, Joshen snapped the vine.

"I needed to keep you awake," she said shyly.

"Senna, I've never been more awake in my life." He jerked free of another vine circling his knee. "Come on, let's get out of here." He took her hand and they ran through the barbus as the plant reached lethargically toward them; both of them afraid if they stopped or slowed, they'd fall asleep.

The barbus ended as suddenly as the tangled trees had begun. Warily, Senna scanned for any other dangerous plants, but all she saw was a jungle. Rubbing at her burning lungs, she glanced skyward. Like a great amethyst seamed with gold, the dawn spread along the horizon.

They had been running all night.

Senna stumbled the last few steps to the base of an enormous tree. Joshen collapsed beside her and immediately set about making her tea. Absently, she handed him fruit from her pack.

At the touch of his hand, the memory of his kiss vibrated in her. She brushed her fingertips along her lips. Could he ever long for her as she did for him? Tears came to her eyes. She realized Joshen was staring at her. The desperate look on his face unnerved her. Was she mistaken, or was their genuine panic in his eyes? "What's wrong?"

He stabbed the fire with a stick. "That kiss—it was just to save me?"

Senna felt her face grow hot. He didn't love her back; his panic confirmed that. It was just like Joshen to protect her. She closed her eyes tightly. She could never again pretend she didn't love him. She knew it and now he knew it. She shook her head violently. Pain shot through her skull. She cried out. Sobbing, she tried to scramble away, but his hand snaked out and held her. "Senna?"

"Why?" she choked, the words coming through her raw throat. "Why is it that I'm me? If I'd been anyone, anything else, perhaps you could love me back ..." She forced herself to meet his gaze.

A disbelieving smirk crossed his face.

Her temper flared. She tried to jerk free, but Joshen pulled her to him, his smirk gone. He studied her lips like they were a riddle he desperately needed to solve.

All her senses were inundated with him. She felt the heat of his body next to hers, his breath against her skin. Somehow, he always smelled like leather, horses and the sea. But now, there was a hint of jungle and clean sweat. She couldn't get enough. She could never get enough. Her whole body ached for him.

Slowly, he inched toward her. When their lips were so close she could almost feel his, he paused and changed course. She held perfectly still as he kissed the edge of her jaw. She gasped softly as he moved to her neck. She wanted to lose herself to the heat blazing through her, but doubt still stung her. Determined to ask him, she pushed against his chest.

He chuckled dryly. "I guess I'm lucky. If you knew how incredible you are, you'd never settle for the likes of me."

Senna's body lost all resistance. Joshen guided her to the ground. He paused to tuck a piece of hair behind her ear. "I've been wanting this every day since the moment I met you. I love you, Brusenna. And I need to hear it from you, because I couldn't bear it not being real."

Senna wanted to say it, but she just couldn't. "I've wanted it since then, too."

It must have been enough. Joshen pulled her into his arms and kissed her. She felt the weight of his chest, the steady thrumming of his heart against hers.

Was it just her imagination, or did they tangle together and beat as one?

26. Goodbyes

Drowsily, Senna watched as light and shadow played hide and seek through the leaves. She'd wanted more, but Joshen had stopped it before they'd gone too far. Still, her lips felt bruised and her cheeks slightly tender from the few days' growth on Joshen's face—but it was a welcome pain. She was within Espen's realm now and she didn't care. Nor was she afraid. In fact, this was the happiest she'd ever felt.

"How could a woman like you love a man like me?" Senna turned to see Joshen watching her as she'd watched the shadows.

"I've been wondering the same about you."

He lifted himself up on his elbow. "You can't mean that."

She shrugged as she traced the outline of his jaw, loving how strong and muscular he was.

He watched her carefully. "What you said about Ciara, you actually meant it? I thought it was just the bump to your head?"

Senna sighed. "She is so beautiful—"

He pulled her roughly into his arms. "You are the most beautiful woman I've ever laid eyes on, Senna. And I won't hear you berate yourself. You do it far too often."

"You really think I'm beautiful?" she murmured.

"Yes," he said tenderly.

Senna waited for a sign he didn't mean it, but she saw only naked honesty in his eyes. Desni had been right. And if this was her only day left, she'd spend it in Joshen's arms. When evening came, everything would be different. With a sigh, she fell asleep listening to Joshen's heartbeat.

Just after sunset, she lifted her head and studied Joshen's peaceful face until his eyes blinked open. He looked at her with a smile. "Mornin' beautiful."

She rested her chin on his chest. "Actually, I think it's night."

He stroked her hair. "So, what do we do tonight?"

Senna sighed and looked away. The enchantment was over. Brushing herself off, she stood. "I need you to trust me."

He eyed her warily. "And the catch?"

"I've had nightmares every night for over a year. For the first time in a long time, my dreams have been untroubled and I ... I want to thank you for that."

"Senna," he warned as he stood to face her. "It sounds a lot like you're saying goodbye."

She forced herself to hold her ground. "I am."

His brows drew down dangerously. "Senna, you promised—"

"I won't stop you from coming," she interrupted. "I'm just asking you not to." His stance relaxed. She hurried on, "If you come with me, I'll have to protect myself and you." She took a deep breath and blew it out. "If she captures you, I'll surrender. It's that simple."

"Senna, you can't. Everyone needs—"

"What everyone else needs won't matter. I can't watch her torture and kill you any more than you could watch her hurt me."

His eyes widened. "You love me that much?"

"Yes," she replied. "And knowing that you're alive somewhere ... would comfort me during my imprisonment."

"You say it like it's already happened," he said in exasperation.

How could she make him understand? "Somehow, Espen is gleaning strength from the other Witches. She's much stronger than I. And more experienced in a duel. She's defeated every Witch, alone or in groups, who has ever crossed her path. This was never about winning, it was about ending it." There, she'd said it. The truth she'd been avoiding for so long.

He gestured back the way they'd come. "If you can't win, come with me. We'll hide from her and—"

"No." She shook her head, her voice gentle, but firm. "I won't be a coward. Her defeat is not impossible, only difficult. I must try." She felt the tears in her eyes and wished she could banish them. "For my mother. And the others."

Joshen wrapped her in his arms and kissed her in a way that almost convinced her to run with him. To spend whatever time remained loving him. But the magical day had ended and reality was staring her down. When their lips parted, Senna rested her forehead against his. "Please, Joshen. Please stay. Wait for three days. If I don't come back, find a way out of here and live your life."

"I'll stay," he finally managed, though his voice broke. "But I won't leave. If you don't come back, I'll come get you, even if only to join you."

Senna looked away, knowing he still didn't understand. "You can't come where she'll take me. Understand ... if she wins, I'll only see you again if I agree to join her. And I never will."

"Senna, I can't abandon you."

She gripped his arms. "You have to. It will be all I have left."

He bowed his head and Senna could tell he was trying not to cry. It tore at her heart, but this, her fate, had been awaiting her for years. She was beyond mourning it now. In a way, it was a relief. The end drew near. All that mattered was Joshen's safety.

"All right," he finally relented.

Relieved, Senna gripped him tightly. "I need to hear you promise it, Joshen. Please."

"I promise," he managed.

Drawing herself up on her tiptoes, she kissed him. She stepped back and tried to burn his image into her mind. It would be both a comfort and a torture; but not being able to remember his face would be worse. "Goodbye, Joshen."

"Goodbye, Senna."

It was hard, so very hard to pick up her pack and walk away from him. But each step she took made it easier. She paused to look at him once more before he was obscured by the trees. He stood like granite, his fists and jaw clenched tight. Tears flowed freely down his face. He made no attempt to brush them away.

A sob caught in Senna's throat. After all they'd been through, she'd never seen him cry. But he had cried for her. He loved her. And it made what she was about to face that much easier and that much harder. Easier because she wasn't alone. Harder because now she had something to lose.

27. WITCH FIGHT

Evening faded into dusk and dusk into night. A full moon shone down, casting the world in silver and slate. Everything grew to gigantic proportions, from the ferns to the flowers. It was an odd, intoxicating mix of the forests of her home and the jungles of the Tartens—beauty that belied the danger Senna faced. A Witch's habitation, if ever there was one. She found no comfort in this. The flows of nature were all wrong, grating against her like a high-pitched squeal.

The deeper she wound into Espen's lair, the more the trees shifted and groaned, as if whispering furtive secrets. But no matter how hard she strained to catch the words, the meaning escaped her. More than once, she paused to study them. They were unlike any other trees she'd ever seen. Sort of like a weeping willow, except the leaves formed a faultless circle. Each tree bore one piece of perfect, white fruit. In wonder, she reached out and cupped one. The fruit vibrated like a beehive inside her hand. The whole tree trembled and pulled away. Senna jerked back. That wasn't fruit—and these weren't trees. Not really.

But if not trees, what were they?

The possibility drove away her gaze. But then she caught sight of one tree. It, more than all the others, seemed somehow familiar. Unable to look away, Senna moved toward it as if in a trance. She stretched out to touch it. The whole tree strained forward. Branches wrapped around her shoulders, holding her tenderly against bark that felt as soft as skin. A hauntingly familiar scent warmed her. She suddenly understood. "Mother," she said breathlessly. "It can't be!" But it was. Senna had no doubt. She rested her forehead against the unnaturally pliable bark. "What has she done to you?"

The limbs caressed her back, stroked her hair. Stepping back, she surveyed the other unnatural trees. Each of them must be a Witch. Some, like her mother, trembled in excitement, reaching toward each other, whispering. Others stood stiff. Carefully, Senna approached one of the still ones. She held her hand against its rough bark. It showed no signs of recognition. "You've been here much, much longer, haven't you?" That's why Espen couldn't search for her. She had to watch her new prisoners.

Senna backed away with a shudder.

How had Espen done this? No seed Senna had ever heard of could turn flesh into trees. Perhaps it was some kind of potion— something like Ioa. Espen must immobilize her prey and then force them to consume it. So the key would be defensive seeds. Seeds that would keep Espen at bay … at least at first. After, Senna would have to find a different way to combat her.

A wisp of hope grew within her. Perhaps this knowledge might help her where the other Witches had failed.

She felt a branch at her back, gently pushing her back the way she had come. She turned to face her mother. "No. You couldn't stand back and watch her capture your friends. And I can't leave you like this. Not while I have the strength to fight. Besides, maybe, just maybe, I'll defeat her."

Her mother sagged, her lovely, gleaming branches trailing on the jungle floor.

Senna's heart sank. Sacra had sheltered her from this fight her entire life. She'd always believed her mother was trying to protect her, but what if she was simply afraid Senna's song wasn't strong enough … and never would be? She turned away from her mother and the others. Senna felt the call of the Ring of Power. With tears welling in her eyes, she moved to answer it. Shafts of light appeared, growing into beams the closer she came to the clearing. At the edge, still in shadow, she paused and thought ruefully how exactly her dream mirrored reality.

Her dream. Terror squeezed the air from her lungs. In the dream, Espen always defeated her.

Squaring her shoulders and lifting her chin, Senna forced herself to step into the moon-bright clearing. Willing her stride not to falter, she climbed the gentle rise toward the center. Just like in her dream, Espen emerged from the opposite side and strode out to meet her.

A few paces apart, both women stopped and faced each other. Senna was surprised by Espen's beauty—somehow, it seemed wrong that someone so evil should be beautiful. Her waist-length, dark hair shifted softly in the wind. Her skin was impossibly clear, with a smattering of innocent-looking freckles across her nose. Senna was dressed after the manner of the Witches, in shades of green and gold—the colors of life and growth. Espen wore a black cloak with a red dress—the colors of death and blood.

Desperate to make the first move, Senna threw a barrier seed and started singing it to maturity. Not very original, perhaps, but the tree would protect her from anything physical Espen grew. Espen smiled—the smile of a starving woman about to delve into a table of delicacies. She also threw down a barrier seed.

Senna would have liked to grow her barrier tree a little bigger, but she didn't want to lose the advantage of her slight lead. Her deft fingers dove into a pocket of her belt and grabbed a handful of seeds as small as sand. Her song changed.

> Wind, carry my seeds upon thy back,
> Toward the Witch with purpose black.

The wind gusted past her, twisting her hair around her face. She threw the seeds high into the air. It caught them and carried the majority past both barrier trees, where they pelted Espen like the gritty wind before a storm.

Senna immediately switched her song.

> Thine, with vine of thorn,
> Bind up Espen, her song to scorn.

The vines shot up around Espen's ankles. Espen ignored them. Instead, she focused on Senna, her song a soft murmur.

The Witch threw something in the air. Senna saw the wind catch a white powder as fine as flour. She had time to do little more than suck in a deep breath before the powder engulfed her.

The powder seemed to stick to Senna's sweat. It burned and stung as though driving needles through her skin. The worst pain was in her eyes. She barely had the presence of mind not to gasp and fill her lungs with the toxic stuff. She wasn't sure what the powder was, but she knew she had to get away from it. She couldn't sing if she couldn't breathe.

Senna stumbled back, her eyes on fire. Without any other option, she shut them and ran blindly away from the defense of her barrier tree. When she'd finally freed herself from the choking vapor, she turned frantically to find Espen. Through her tear-filled eyes, she saw the Dark Witch nearly covered in vines. Only her face remained uncovered, her mouth working frantically.

Desperately trying to catch her breath, Senna staggered on her feet, her hands reaching inside her seed belt. But before she could form a song on her lips, she felt a presence behind her. Eyes wide, she whirled to face this new threat.

In an instant, she realized what Espen had done. The powder had driven her away from her barrier tree—her physical protection—toward another barrier tree. One Espen had been busily singing to life while Senna's thine had been binding her.

The great tree stretched toward her. Senna dove to the side. She felt the whoosh of air as a branch barely missed her. She scrabbled madly to get away. Feeling another branch coming, she dove. But this branch whipped out at the last second, cracking across her ribs.

She felt like she'd been branded by a white hot, iron rod. Gasping, she twisted away from the scrambling branches' hold. She was nearly out of the tree's reach. She'd just managed to get her feet under her for the second time when the tree stretched out, wrapping one of its longest branches around her ankle. It snatched her up so fast it felt like she'd left her stomach on the ground that was fast falling away from her.

It flicked like a whip, sending her careening end over end through the air. She saw ground then sky, ground then sky, moving together so fast they blurred together.

And then her whole body hit the ground. She felt herself flatten, her bones vibrating and stretching to absorb the shock. The blood in her veins sloshed madly. The air was forced from her lungs in an inhuman cry. Then all was blackness.

She wasn't totally unaware of herself, though. She knew there was pain, but in the same way she knew the sun was hot. It was far away and only tendrils of it reached her. Gradually, she became aware of movement all across her skin. A kind of cold slither. She tried to make sense of it, but making her mind work brought her closer to the pain.

Still, she knew she had to wake up. Had to or die. As she forced herself to think, she realized suddenly the cold, slithering feeling was vines moving around her.

And then her mind formed one word—*Espen*. That shocked her out of unconsciousness. She opened her eyes. Her body did a quick assessment of its injuries. Nothing broken. But terribly strained and bruised.

She tried to push herself up, but the vines had been hard at work. She knew instantly that these were not Thine vines. Those had vicious, hooked thorns to discourage their prisoners from wiggling free. No, these were simple bindweeds and grasses. But they'd been circling her by the score.

Still at only half-strength, she strained against them. A few popped free of their roots, enough that she could sit up slightly. She searched for Espen. The other Witch was covered in blood, her skin caught in the barbs that stretched it cruelly.

The Dark Witch must have freed enough fingers to reach her seeds, for Senna could see a gray plant growing between Espen and the Thine. It was bulky, thick and soft. This accomplished two things at once. One, it was putting a soft barrier between Espen and the thorns. And two, it was pushing the thorns away. Any second now, Espen would free herself.

With renewed determination, Senna strained against the bindweeds. More popped free. Her right hand broke free. She shook off the weeds and reached for her seed belt. But her hands only encountered her green dress.

Panic lanced through her. She searched frantically and finally found the belt lying near the circle's center. Tugging with all her might, she managed to free her left hand. She jerked and kicked at the weeds binding her legs like a too-tight blanket. Finally breaking loose, she stumbled toward her belt.

She heard Espen's song changing and knew the woman had reached her seed belt. She ran furiously for her own, but as she did, she felt the wind howling at her, felt seeds pelting her. When she was a mere few steps away, a plant shot up all around her. She knew it immediately, though this variation was darker than the kind in her belt. Kine—a low-growing cactus. But instead of leaves, it had millions of razor-sharp blades the length of her thumb. And it had completely encapsulated her seed belt.

Senna took one final step forward. She felt the blades pierce the soles of her shoes, stabbing her foot. She cried out and forced her hand toward her belt. The vines shredded her skin. She felt a poison working through her flesh from her wounds. But she had to reach her belt. She shoved her hand forward again, straining, stretching. She felt the belt's smooth surface under her fingertips. But a voice stopped her.

"You may as well stop."

Senna winced and turned to see Espen standing free of the Thine, a handful of seeds in her hand.

She'd lost.

Withdrawing her shredded hand, she cradled it against her and felt the blood soak through her dress and run down her belly. Her hand and foot stung and burned. But it didn't matter. Trees didn't feel pain like people did. She waited for Espen to turn her into one. Part of her was coldly curious to find out how Espen did it.

But Espen surprised her by speaking. "No other Witch has had the courage to face me in my domain." She cocked her head to the side. "I'll admit, your song is amazingly strong. Stronger than I ever anticipated. Stronger than my own was and I had no equal. Which is why I actually dueled you instead of just ending it immediately. You see, I wanted to put you in your place."

Espen laughed. Senna tried to wrap her mind around the Dark Witch laughing—or holding a conversation, for that matter. Somehow, in Senna's imaginings, Espen had never seemed capable of something as bright as laughter. "A Witchling. Untrained. And you very nearly had me."

Espen sang a simple song and the Kine vines curled up, though the ones around Senna's belt stayed firmly in place. Senna felt the blades leave her feet and nearly sighed with relief. But she still felt the poison spreading a strange lethargy through her limbs. Odd, since the Kine she knew had no poison.

Espen's bright eyes shone with excitement. "The two of us would be a force so great, the other Witches would have no choice but to join us. So, the question is, does your intelligence equal your strength? Or would you rather join your Keepers?"

Bitter panic rose in Senna's throat. She considered lifting her skirts and running, but Espen wouldn't allow that.

Her life suddenly seemed precious. If she accepted, Senna could even have Joshen. But the thought was fleeting. She refused to consider it any longer. Clamping her jaw, she searched one last time for something so simple she might have overlooked it. If only she could have a few moments more. She had to stall. "What do you offer me?"

Triumph leaped into Espen's eyes, but she kept her face impassive. "In all the world, you will answer only to me. Of the riches, one eighth. Lands are negotiable. I prefer…"

Espen continued, but Senna had stopped listening. Desperately, she searched for a way to save herself from her mother's fate. Joshen's words of long ago echoed in her head. *You don't have to do everything alone.*

She shook her head to clear the memory. She was alone! The last of the Witches. Her belt was trapped beneath an unreachable layer of Kine. Her body was battered and shredded. There was no one and nothing left to help her! How could she have thought she could defeat Espen when all the others had failed?

Perhaps the only ones left with the power to stop Espen are the Creators themselves, she thought bitterly.

That notion stopped her frantic thoughts cold. She gaped at the Ring of Power as if she'd never seen it before. It could work. It might work. Even if it didn't, she had nothing to lose.

Espen was watching her expectantly. Taking a chance, Senna limped forward. Espen moved into a defensive stance, but she didn't prevent Senna from overtaking the circle's center.

Senna took a deep breath. She would only have time for one song before Espen retaliated. Lifting her face, her song began.

> Wind lift me high,
> That my words reach to'rds the sky.

Espen's eyebrows arched in surprise, but she made no move to halt the wind's slow swirling. "And who will you call for, little one? There are none left. Even if there were, they wouldn't come in time to save you."

But there are some left. If only they can hear me. If only they will come, she thought. The trees bent and swayed as the wind lifted her higher than she had ever been before. "Higher," she sang, until she was dizzy from lack of air and chilled to her bones.

Her song changed.

> Givers of life! Creators!
> The Keepers have failed,
> Their hold dispelled,
> Heed my call,
> Or our Earth shall fall!
> Help us!
> Help us!

The whirlwind caught her words and bore them away, but whether they would ever reach their destination, or be answered if they did, she couldn't say.

She looked beneath her dangling feet. The Ring of Power seemed so far away. A small, lighter dot amidst leagues of darker green.

Small, but not insignificant.

Below, Espen waited for her.

As the wind's hold over her lessened, she could do nothing but watch as the clearing rose toward her and Espen's features clarified. She was suddenly very tired.

"A fool's choice," Espen said as Senna returned to hearing range. The respect that had been in her eyes was gone.

"But one that all, excluding you, have made," Senna replied as her feet touched the ground and the wind calmed.

Espen gestured to the unnatural trees. "Obviously. That's why I called it a fool's choice."

Why did Senna feel it was already over? It seemed her fate had been sealed before her birth—that this end had always been inevitable. She closed her eyes and thought of Joshen. She'd tried. For him. For her mother. That was all that mattered. "You might call me a fool. Others would call me courageous."

In response, Espen flung a black seed into the air and sang.

Her body consume!

Senna waited for Espen to continue the song, but the Dark Witch remained silent.

Senna followed the older woman's gaze. Her body went cold. The black seed had not fallen.

It should have. It was too heavy for even a strong gust. And Senna felt no wind at all. But instead of falling, it floated in the air as if held by an unseen hand. Slowly, it floated toward her. It seemed to steady and travel incrementally faster. Even as she tried to wrap herself around this impossibility, her doom dawned on her as it must have on all the other Witches. There were plants to counteract other plants, potions to change her form, plants to protect the singer, but there were no weapons to defend against something as small as a single seed.

The seed was gaining speed. Senna couldn't help it. Even if it was hopeless, she had to try. Whirling, she ran as fast as her battered and bloody body would let her. How many before her had done the same? Just before she reached the edge of the clearing, Joshen burst into the moonlight. "Senna!"

Her soul shattered into a million pieces. "Joshen, you promised!"

"I couldn't leave you! I just couldn't!"

Just as she reached him, a sharp pain hammered her spine, pitching her forward. Joshen caught her in his arms. The pain spread. Her body suddenly went rigid.

"Senna?" Joshen tugged at her, trying to force her to run. But her feet were already rooted to the Earth.

With the last bit of dexterity she had, she tipped her face to his, "I love you." She'd finally managed to say it. As soon as the words left her, her lips grew together, sealing everything else she wanted to say behind them.

Joshen's face screwed up in anguish. At last, he understood. "Oh, Senna no!"

Senna felt Espen coming up behind her. She ached to scream for Joshen to run, but with each passing moment, her body grew more unyielding.

Espen came into view. She glanced at Joshen before turning to Senna with a look of relief. "You realized what was coming sooner than most, but there was nothing you could do. Nothing any of them could. You should've joined me."

Senna couldn't answer as her body grew more wooden. Joshen gripped her, but she could no longer feel his touch. Only see him. And even that was beginning to fade. With a groan, her body stretched toward the night sky. Of their own accord, her arms grew and splintered into main branches while her fingers shivered and split into smaller ones. As she grew upward, her feet separated and her toes plunged into the cool Earth. Leaves burst from her fingertips. She groaned and fought, but it was useless. She was no longer human. If her shoulders remained, they would have sagged. As it was, she could simply stand stiff and still, only her thinnest branches capable of movement.

In front of what used to be her face, a beautiful white flower appeared.

Espen sang.

> Oh little flower, change for me
> Into a seed with ripe fruit be.

Senna had no choice but to force nutrients and water into the flower. She felt her Witch song gathering inside as the flower changed into a fully mature fruit. It was finished. Every part of her that was a Witch now dangled before her face. She groaned in despair.

As the last of her hope leeched from her, Joshen snatched the fruit. Whirling, he ran toward the jungle.

"Run, Joshen! For the love of life, run," she tried to scream but couldn't.

Espen waited until he reached the line of trees before singing. A tree snagged him in a tight embrace. He cursed. The tree wrapped a branch around his mouth, silencing him. Senna cried out, but the sound came out as little more than a wooden groan. She fought to pummel Espen, but her branches refused to obey. Instead, they gently shifted in the breeze.

Espen sauntered toward him. Taking the fruit from his hands, she inhaled its aroma. With a look of intense satisfaction, she took a juicy bite. Smiling as she chewed, she sauntered toward Senna.

Senna wanted nothing more than to squash her, but she was Espen's servant now. As were all the other Witches. Had it really ended so quickly, so completely? Watching Espen consume her song, she yearned to weep.

Espen licked the juices from her fingers and then held up a black seed. A seed that mirrored the one in Senna's back. "It took dozens of my Servants' lives to create Lathel—a seed that could hold a Witch captive and give me her song. After consuming dozens of Witch songs, I had strength for a song strong enough to micromanage a wind to propel my seed. The Keepers had no hope after that. Really, it wasn't me at all. Just an undefeatable plant." She slipped the seed into her seed belt. Another flower bloomed on Senna's branch. Espen handled the blossom tenderly, "And this is the reason I'm trapped here. I have to consume your Witch song daily to glean your power. What a relief it is to have the last of you captured. I'll be able to leave now."

She sang again and the tree pushed Joshen toward her. She tipped her head as she studied him. "Such a loyal one,

Brusenna. And so strong. Really. I'm impressed." She ran her fingertips across one of his straining muscles. "It's only fair you recompense me for Wardof and Garg. Two bumbling idiots for the price of one competent servant. A fair trade." She pulled a waxy substance from her belt.

Senna stretched and groaned and wept anew. Through her foggy vision, she recognized the potion. Yarves. All records regarding its creation had been destroyed long ago, but the violent blue could be nothing else. Espen had either found a missed record or discovered how to create it herself.

She smeared the substance on her lips and rubbed them together. She circled him, her eyes taking him in as a buyer does a horse.

> Desire most fervent
> To be Espen's servant.
> To heed my call,
> You will give your all.

As she repeated the forbidden song, Joshen struggled and fought, but he couldn't break free. Espen sang the branch from his mouth. "No!" he cried as Espen leaned forward to kiss him.

Unable to bear it, Senna refused to watch. When she forced herself to face it, she wished she hadn't. A vacant stare had come over Joshen's face. He was no more Joshen now than Senna was herself.

Espen sang him free. He stood dumbly before her. "Who is your mistress?" she asked him.

"Espen," he said hollowly.

28. Earth, Water, Plants and Sunlight

The breeze tugged at Senna's leaves, reminding her of when the wind had caressed her hair. She wished she could close her eyes to block out reality. But at least her sight was dim and fuzzy; it made it easier to believe none of this was real. She struggled to move her thinnest branches. How long would it be before she took the path the other Witches had and forgot everything? How long before Joshen's memory no longer existed for her? How long before she was fully a tree, a woman no more?

Espen had disappeared for a while. She returned with an axe in hand. Senna suspected she wouldn't have to wonder much longer. Espen handed the axe to Joshen. "Come." She stood before Senna, her arms folded across her chest. "I don't need you anymore. Only your continued interference stopped things from progressing. Besides, I need to test the loyalty of my new servant. You understand. And even if you don't, I forbid you to stop him." She pointed to Joshen. "Chop down the tree. Burn the wood."

Senna wanted to lash out with her branches. Wring Espen like wet laundry. As best she could, she sang for Joshen, but it came out as little more than the rustle of her leaves.

Joshen took a step forward then stopped. Sweat broke out on his face.

Espen circled him, her eyes gleaming. "I see I'm going to have to be very specific with you. Using the axe, cut down this tree. Do it now."

Arms trembling, Joshen lifted the axe into the air. Senna longed to cringe, close her eyes, scream. She couldn't.

His whole body shaking as uncontrollably as if fevered, Joshen lowered the axe.

Espen's gaze narrowed to a fuming glare. "I command you— CUT DOWN THE TREE!"

Joshen quaked. His skin turned a magnificent shade of red. His eyes bulged. Through clenched teeth, he said, "No."

Espen reeled. She glanced at Senna and then back to Joshen. "Then you are of no use to me." She removed a small vial from her seed belt. Senna recognized it. A simple poison. *We'll both die this night,* she thought. *But at least we'll die together.*

The selfish part of Senna wished she could go first. So she wouldn't have to watch Joshen die. But at least her sorrow wouldn't last long. Nor would she fear her own death, but embrace it. She didn't wish to remain in a world Joshen wasn't a part of … one Espen ruled.

Espen unstopped the vial and tipped Joshen's head back.

The vial touched his lips. Senna stretched and groaned, trying to struggle as hard for Joshen as he had for her. The liquid shifted toward his waiting mouth. Then Espen suddenly stopped. Senna could have cried with joy as the evil little container lowered to her side. But then she saw it, too. Though it was still deep night, the sky was brighter. Much brighter.

Shoving in the vial's stopper, Espen pulled a seed from her belt, her stance defensive.

With a shimmering pulse, the sky flashed, blinding Senna to anything but light. Espen and Joshen shielded themselves from the intensity, but Senna's weak eyes were able to look into the brilliance. At first, she saw nothing. And then colors appeared. Long thin shapes of green, blue, brown and very last, gold.

The long, thin shapes clarified into the curved shapes of women. The Creators. They had come after all. The light faded, or perhaps Senna simply became accustomed to it. There were four of them. Everything but their skin was a single color whose tint varied by the moment. The brown one had hair of black Earth that brightened to the light red of clay. The blue woman's hair and dress went from turquoise to nearly green-black. The green Creator's color varied from the color of baby grass to the deepest evergreen. But the golden one—whose hair and dress varied from sun yellow to corn silk to ripe wheat—studied Senna.

The brown one examined Espen's cowered figure. The blue one's eyes were closed and the green one considered the forest beyond the clearing. After a moment, the blue Creator sang like the rush of wind over breaking waves.

The seas are in havoc, their creatures tortured.

The green Creator answered.

The plants are weak, sick and dying.

The brown Creator sang.

All the Earth is in torment.

The three turned to the golden Creator. She hadn't taken her eyes from Senna. Senna wished she could shuffle her feet or look away, but her roots held her fast.

She is the last.
For a long time, she's prepared to fight an unknown weapon.
A seed the one in black and red wields.
A plant forbidden by its very nature,
For it goes against everything we endowed the Keepers for.

Singing, the Green Creator came forward and pressed her lips against Senna's bark. Almost immediately, Senna felt her branches shrink. The wooden stiffness of her body softened to flesh and bone once more. And then she stood as a woman, fully healed of her injuries, a dress of white as pure and soft as the petals of a calla lily wrapped around her. In her unblemished hand, she held a piece of white fruit.

All of them set their faces and looked at Espen. Senna hadn't noticed that the Dark Witch lay curled up, her forehead pressed to the dirt. The four Creators circled her. The golden one sang.

Of all our worlds and all our creations,
Only here has a Keeper so grievously betrayed her Keepers.

Espen looked up. Though she made no sound, her eyes were desperate. Frantically, she reached inside her seed belt.

But before a song could leave her lips, the golden Creator stretched out her hand.

We take from thee that which was freely given.
No longer a Keeper, but a woman.

Espen's back arched as if she were in pain. The seed slipped from her grasp. Her mouth opened in a silent scream. Sinuous light twisted from her body and gathered into a sphere above the golden Creator's spread fingers. When the last tendril slipped away, Espen collapsed like a spent coal.

Joshen gasped as though released from a vice. He staggered to Senna's side and embraced her, nearly crushing her in his joy. Senna held tight, tears leaking from her eyelids. "Joshen," she whispered. Nothing else existed in that moment. Just Joshen.

When she finally let go, she saw the golden Creator, her eyes sparks of reflected light from the sphere's brilliance, watching her with amusement.

Senna fought the urge to look away. "What is your name?"

The Creator smiled. "We have many names." Her hair flashed to a vibrant orange. She held out the sphere.

Drink and gather the power to restore thy Keepers.

Senna's eyes flicked from the orb to the Creator. "I ... I don't want anything that was Espen's."

The golden Creator's amber eyes shifted to the sphere.

Espen's evil was her own, nothing gifted her by us.
Only the power given was taken. Nothing else.

Senna hesitated before bending down and touching her lips to the pool of light. She sipped. It tasted as warm and pure as sunshine. When the last of it slipped inside her, she straightened, marveling as the warmth of the Creator's power filled her.

So rarely have we bestowed more power upon one.
Guard its use well,
For we shall require an accounting
When thou hast joined us again.

"Join you?" Senna asked in disbelief.

The golden Creator's hair seemed to burst into flame, though her face and body remained serene.

All Witches join the Creators at their passing.

She leaned forward and pressed her lips to Brusenna's forehead.

Light guide thee.

One by one, the other Creators followed suit, pressing their lips to Senna's forehead and singing a blessing.

Earth obey thee.
Plants honor thee.
Waters heed thy call.

And then they were gone, leaving Senna alone in the shadows once more. When her eyes finally adjusted to the lack of brilliance, she saw that dawn smeared the horizon with gray. Not darkness then. It only seemed so after the loss of the Creators' radiance.

What had begun at midnight had ended before daybreak.

And it was raining again. Hand in hand, Joshen and Senna stood, too overwhelmed to speak. Espen was the first to move, lunging for Senna's hand.

Suddenly realizing she held her song in the form of the Lathel fruit, Senna jerked away.

Before Espen could retaliate, Joshen put her in a choke hold and forced her to her knees. "You would've had me murder her! You're still trying to murder her!" He pushed her into the mud.

Espen trembled from head to foot. She suddenly looked much older to Senna. "Mercy," she whispered.

"Don't ask for mercy. You've no right!" Joshen growled.

"You hurt those who most deserved your protection." Senna shook her head, water dripping from her face. "Not death. You deserve so much worse than death." Unable to bear the woman's pleading eyes, Senna looked away. She felt the weight of the fruit in her hand. Studying it, she took a hesitant bite. It tasted the same as the light the golden Creator had given her.

She was suddenly starving for it. With each morsel she consumed, the song within her magnified until her lips tingled. She suddenly understood what the Creators had given her. She had the power of her own song plus Espen's. The power of two Witches. Her head soaring above her body, she turned the seed in her hand. "Will you open your mouth, or should I force you?"

Espen flinched. "I could teach you things other Witches have only dreamed of! Songs, potions, plants. I may no longer be able to sing myself, but—"

Unwilling to listen to another syllable, Senna lifted the seed. Espen backed away, her hands raised. "Wait! You don't understand. I've never worked alone. You won't escape Tarten unless I help you."

Uncertain, Senna paused.

"I'll tell you everything in exchange for my freedom."

Senna's eyebrows flew up. "Freedom? After all you've done?" Her whole body trembled with rage. "You're a liar!" She shoved the seed into Espen's mouth.

Her body consume!

It imbedded itself in Espen's throat, halting her poisonous words. She coughed and gagged. "You—don't—understand—" her voice broke. She convulsed. Her body elongated. Her skin went from pale and soft to rough bark. Her arms shot up and grew into limbs and her legs into roots. Leaves burst forth— perfect orbs that danced beautifully.

But there was no white flower, for Espen was no longer a Witch. When it was done, all that remained was her broken seed belt, seeds scattered across the Earth.

"But the others," Joshen cried. "The Creators didn't free them!"

Senna whirled toward the trees, cursing herself for failing to ask. Now it was too late.

"I'm the last. The last Witch," she realized. She shook her head in despair, but then she caught sight of the black Lathel seeds that had spilled from Espen's seed belt. The echo of a hauntingly beautiful song resonated in her memory, "so that you may have power to restore your Keepers."

What if? Bending down, she held one up. Rain circled it. "What are seeds if not the containers of life?" Digging a little hole, she shoved it into the Earth and sang, her voice shaking with desperate hope and fear.

Take in light, take in air,
Spread thy roots, thy leaves grow fair.

A pale shoot burst from the grass as she repeated the words. However, it wasn't a sapling that grew, but the folds of a green dress and darker cloak. As Senna repeated the song, flower buds burst open, revealing a face and hands.

Her eyes closed, Coyel appeared. In her hand, she held a piece of white fruit. She drew breath and her eyes blinked open. Her face full of fear, her gaze darted about. She caught sight of Senna. A slow smile spread over her face. "You defeated her?" She laughed in relief. "Sacra's daughter! Brusenna!" Without hesitation, Coyel devoured her song like a starving woman. She breathed deeply, stretching her arms skyward as the rain washed her face. "My song!" She tipped her head back and cried, "I'm free! After nearly two years, I'm free!"

Her mother, the other Witches, they were still trapped. Senna whirled toward Joshen. "See if you can find my mother's tree!"

He dashed away.

Searching the scattered seeds, Senna found another Lathel seed. Shoving it into the soil, she sang again. Another Witch grew. An older Witch, with a multitude of shining spectacles surrounding her face, making the woman look like she had a miniature peacock sitting on her nose. With a sagging breath, the woman came to life. Twisting down a rose-colored glass on her spectacles, she stared at Senna in disbelief. "Am I to take it that I'm no longer a seed?"

Coyel ducked to catch the shorter woman's gaze. "Prenny? Are you alright?"

Tipping back a head full of wiry gray hair, Prenny glared at Coyel. "Of course I am," she snapped. "Espen preferred to keep troublemakers' seeds close."

Coyel smiled with forced patience. "I only meant—"

"I know what you meant! Awful woman cut down the trees of the other Heads as well. Burned them to the ground and then carried us around in her seed belt." Prenny sniffed loudly and rubbed her eyes beneath her heavy glasses. "Thought I was dead."

"Heads?" Bewildered, Senna looked between the two Witches. "Does that mean my mother's seed is in Espen's seed belt?"

Prenny twisted down another glass from her spectacles that made her eye look ten times larger than it actually was. Kneeling, she began searching the seeds. "Of all the Witches, a sprout frees us."

Coyel shot Prenny an exasperated look and spoke to Senna, "The Heads of the four Disciplines. I'm the Head of Sunlight, Prenny is the Head of Plants—"

"Coyel!" Prenny interrupted. "History lessons later. Yes?"

Coyel took a deep breath and murmured under her breath, "Being a seed had some advantages, it seems."

Senna couldn't help the small smile turning up the corners of her mouth. She ducked so Prenny wouldn't see it.

Coyel squeezed her hand. "Sacra may be here. There's only one way to find out."

Prenny sang to the next Lathel seed. Senna watched as a slight Witch with perfectly curled hair and bits of lace sewn into her dress appeared. She had a different-colored gem on each finger and heavy gold chains around her neck. Coyel whispered to Senna, "That's Drenelle. She's the head of Earth."

His shirt bulging with fruit, Joshen came running back. "I grabbed as many as I could."

Taking one, Senna split it with her thumbs and pressed the seed into the Earth. A young Witch appeared. She was beautiful.

With rich dark hair that brushed her waist and large, soft brown eyes. But she didn't speak or move and her eyes had a faraway, glazed look. "Coyel," Senna said. "Something's wrong."

Prenny elbowed her way in. "Don't ask for a diplomat when a healer's needed."

Senna backed away. "I'm sorry, I didn't—"

"Know? Yes, I'm aware." She lifted the Witch's eyelid and peered into her pupil. "Arianis? Can you hear me, child?" Arianis blinked slowly. Prenny gently led the girl to the side. "Arianis was turned years ago. It may take her a while to adjust."

Coyel led over another Witch who wore a similar vacant expression.

"Will they come around?" Senna asked.

Prenny pressed her hands to her hips. "I'm a healer, not a soothsayer, girl!"

Coyel straightened. "Prenny Bonswiky, if you cannot keep your temper ..."

Prenny waved away Coyel's threat. "Yes, yes. Not helping." She pointed her finger at Senna. "Make yourself useful and stop asking pestering questions."

Tears stung Senna's eyes. It had been a long night and a longer few months. She felt exhausted and overwhelmed and ... After all, she'd saved them! In return, she was insulted. Lifting her skirts, she made her best guess at where her mother's tree was and started running. As she neared the edge of the clearing, Joshen appeared with another armload of fruit.

One look at her and he dumped the fruit in heap and ran after her. "They all look the same to me," he huffed as he came alongside her. "I'm sorry."

She shook her head. "I should've been the one to look for her." So why hadn't she? The answer was embarrassingly simple. She was still angry at her mother for leaving her behind ... and in the dark. For so long.

Her eyes fell from one tree to another, searching for the one she'd recognized the night before. And then she saw it. Her frenzy faded as the sun peaked through the clouds and filtered through the heavy canopy, revealing bits of pollen and dust clinging to the air like honey. She walked toward the fruit as the tree stretched it toward her. With a snap, it pulled free. She sank her thumbs into the juicy flesh. A black seed shone against the white. Her hands shaking, Senna pulled the seed free and forced it in the ground. With a dry mouth, she sang. A dress and cloak appeared. A face blossomed into being. Her mother took a sharp breath and opened her eyes. "Brusenna," she breathed.

Senna closed her eyes as her mother's voice enveloped her anger like a warm blanket. Her mother's arms encircled her. Wet tears streaked down Senna's hot face. "Mother."

"You did it!" Sacra laughed.

Senna's tension faded. She wanted nothing more than for this moment to last forever. She wanted to study her mother, to drink in every feature. She'd forgotten about the small mole on her neck and the wisps of gray at her temples. The dark freckle in her green eyes and the dimpled scar on her right cheek.

Her mother's eyes lighted on Joshen. "And who's this?"

Joshen had been hanging back, but he came forward and gripped Sacra's hand. "I'm Joshen, Senna's Guardian. My father is Wittin."

Sacra stepped back in surprise. "A Guardian? Senna you're not even a Witchling, how can you have a Guardian?"

Senna's skin felt hot. "You told Wittin to send Joshen with me."

Her mother held her hand over her lips. "Yes, but not for you to make him a Guardian! Only Heads can approve Guardians!"

Senna's mouth felt like it was sealed shut.

Sacra didn't seem to notice Senna's anger. Her eyes darted from Senna and Joshen's clasped hands to their faces. "Even if they let you keep him, you're not supposed to be involved with your Guardian."

Senna wanted to scream, cry, hit something—hard. "Yet again, something else *no one* told me." The fury in her voice surprised her. When had she become so bitter?

Joshen squeezed her hand. "It'll be alright. I'm sure of it."

The exchange seemed to surprise her mother. "Oh Senna, you're not a little girl anymore." The rain came down harder. Sacra looked away, into the forest. "I've missed so much." She shook her head as tears plummeted down her cheeks, mixing with the rain sheeting down her face. Wiping them, she forced a smile. "It's obvious he is in love with you. Are you in love with him?"

At the sight of her mother's tears, Senna's anger ebbed. "Yes."

Sacra's gaze fell to the fruit in Senna's hand. Taking it, she began to eat. When she finished, she sighed in relief. She looked around once more, as if searching for something. "How did you defeat her?"

"I called for the Creators."

A thin line appeared between Sacra's brows. "And they came?"

Was it so hard to believe the daughter she'd left behind had been capable. Of anything? "Yes. All four of them."

"You saw them?" her mother breathed. She shook her head as if to stop herself. "There will be time for questions. First, we must right Espen's wrongs before it's too late." Without looking back, she hurried toward the Ring of Power.

29. Apprentice

Back ramrod straight, wrists resting on her knees, Senna sat inside the Ring of Power. Spaced at even intervals all around her were the Witches who had recovered from their imprisonment, while those not yet in full possession of their minds docilely waited where they'd been led, eyes glassed over.

Arianis was among them. Senna had learned from one of the other Witches that, though Arianis wasn't much older than Senna, she was the second-most powerful Witchborn in the last century.

Coyel stood in the circle's center, in command of the proceedings. Though her hair fell damp down her back and her dress hung heavy with water, she was still an imposing sight. Drawing herself up to her full height, her eyes zeroed in on Senna. "I remind you all, our ceremonies are sacred. We do not discuss them with outsiders or even our own Witchlings. Failure to obey this rule will have serious consequences."

Shame burned Senna's cheeks. She knew the words had been for her alone and the other Witches knew it, too. Her ignorance of the workings of the Witches felt like a brand on her forehead.

Coyel spread her arms skyward. "Keepers, we have a great deal to repair this day. Much of our world has gone awry since last we fought to preserve it. And while it will take years, we must begin restoring the lands to their former rhythms." Her gaze rested upon Senna. "But first, we must choose a Witch to serve as our channeler."

Surprised eyes turned toward Senna. She itched to squirm under the heat of those penetrating gazes.

Sacra lifted a hand in protest. "She's not ready, Coyel."

"To be a channeler, she must be a full Witch. She hasn't even been initiated as a Witchling," Drenelle added.

"Does she have strength enough to serve as a channeler? If not, the act itself could kill her," said the Head of Water, a woman Senna had heard the others call Chavis.

Coyel turned to Prenny. "Well, does she?"

Prenny twisted down a rose-colored glass as though dreading what it might tell her. "She's got the strength," she said reluctantly. "She's a Level Seven."

Gasps and exclamations shot around the circle.

"A Level Seven!"

"We've only had one Level Six in the past decade!"

"She can't be stronger than Arianis! It's impossible!"

Senna felt her mother's shocked gaze on her. Coyel squatted in front of her mother. "Why didn't you tell me this?" she whispered.

"I saw no signs of a Level Seven."

"What's her affinity?"

Sacra shrugged. "Plants."

Senna leaned toward them. "I don't understand."

Coyel shot Sacra one final look of exasperation. Then she whispered to Senna, "Only one other Level Seven was born in the last century." Her lips were pressed in a grim line.

Senna's eyes widened. "You mean … Espen?"

Sacra looked away. Coyel nodded. "Your song is the strongest one here. It makes the others nervous."

For the first time, Senna wondered if the Creators had given her a gift or a burden.

"Well, then," Chavis said with a shrug, "let the girl. She's certainly earned the right,"

"I'm with her mother," Prenny said. "She's not ready."

Coyel turned to Senna. "The vote is split. That leaves it in my hands." A murmur of protest rose from Drenelle and Prenny.

Coyel silenced it with a wave of her hand. "She entered her apprenticeship when she defeated Espen." The two pressed their lips together but offered no further protest. Senna sensed the other Witches in the circle exchanging uneasy glances.

Seeing her supporters go silent, Sacra's raised hand fell.

Coyel stood before her. "But I know so little," Senna whispered.

"All are naïve before knowledge finds them," Coyel whispered back. Taking her hand, she pulled Senna to her feet and claimed the patch of grass she'd vacated. Settling her damp skirt, Coyel looked up expectantly.

Senna searched for signs of disapproval from the other Witches as she made her way to the center. Most held no expression aside from intense concentration. The moment Senna reached the center, the Witches gripped each other's forearms. With a boom, the ground beneath her surged. The shockwave whipped the trees, nearly laying them flat. A great cylindrical barrier rose into the night sky. Shimmering like an aurora, it stretched to the highest levels of the atmosphere. Senna felt the strength of the barrier, pulsing with power as unyielding and tough as the strongest fortress walls.

A tendril of thought brushed her mind. Surprised, she concentrated on the strange presence. Coyel's voice vibrated in her head, *When the time comes, I'll supply the songs you must sing. For now, remain silent.* Senna realized the joining of the Sisters' arms connected more than their bodies. Their minds were now linked.

Coyel provided the song they should sing. As a single voice, the Witches sang softly.

> Espen's betrayed us and plotted our demise,
> Filled the Earth with her enclave of lies,
> And so we release from her previous calling,
> Espen the Witch, her authority falling.

A feeling like a string being plucked from a tapestry twisted inside Senna. Espen had been cut off. But it was more than being blotted out. It felt more like the Dark Witch had never existed.

As the echo of their songs faded, another song rose.

Brusenna risked her all
So the Witches would not fall.
For her courage, we seal her birthright,
A Keeper after the Discipline of her choosing this night.

The vibrations of the Witches' voices rolled toward Senna in waves. The waves condensed within her, filling her with song until her whole aura glowed and her body tingled.

The songs burned to be set free. The knowledge of what she needed to do came as naturally as breath to a newborn. She had to hold them. Tightly. She waited, knowing she didn't have enough song, not yet. The Witches' cadence increased, as did their volume until Senna couldn't bear it another moment. Her body went rigid and her face flung upward. The other Witches abruptly stopped singing as Senna's own song began. Even to her own ears, the sound was sweeter than any she'd ever heard.

I am a Witch. Mark me.

With the power of a dam breaking, Senna's consciousness expanded through the other Witches to include the Four Sisters—Earth, Water, Sunlight and Plants. With minimal effort, she felt her connection to them as naturally as her fleshy appendages. For their part, the Four Sisters accepted her dominion naturally—the Earth like a shovel in its flesh, the waters like a net cast into their depths, the plants like a fruit plucked from their boughs and the sun like another creature to shine upon.

A tingling began on the side of Senna's navel. Without seeing it, she knew a crescent moon now adorned the right side of her navel. Knowledge of what it was grew within her. The crescent moon—one piece of the whole. Senna was now part of the Witches.

The mark of an Apprenticed Keeper.

She finally belonged somewhere.

The power of the first song grew cold, a feeling like the warm sun setting on a chilly day. But the Witches weren't finished. Another song began, one with a much different purpose than the first. This time, Senna felt the Witches gathering power from their songs—directing that power to right the wrongs Espen had committed. It was similar to the songs Senna had sung many times, but now she had the strength to see it was done.

> Four Sisters—Earth, Water, Plants and Sunlight,
> Our order and control upon thee's been scant.
> But now with authority and power irrefutable,
> We command thee to return to order most suitable.
> Seasons stay in place,
> Winds blow in pace.
> Weather hold to thy climes,
> Plants keep thy times.
> Chaos and disorder cease,
> All settle and return to peace.

The song continued, growing stronger. As before, Senna sang its release. As her last note settled, she felt the song travel across the Earth through her newfound connection—a connection that also told her the Witches could never undo all the damage Espen had inflicted. Many, many of the creeping, crawling things had died, or would in the coming months. And more would fail before the song could take full effect. A crushing sadness shrouded her. Never again would those animals and plants be found upon the land.

Only two songs and already Senna felt exhausted. Still, more work remained. Smaller matters that needed attention. The singing wore on long into the day and Senna sensed a wholeness beginning to return to the Earth. Their work here was done—at least until spring, when their powers would reach their apex and they could finish the work they'd started in Tarten.

She waited for the circle to break. Her Keepers were tired; she could feel their exhaustion through their connection. Everyone was wet and hungry. But they didn't release their grips. Not understanding, Senna's gaze rested on her mother. Finally, Tiena, Desni's middle-aged daughter, broke the silence with her heavily accented voice, "Tell us of the Creators."

Ah, that was it. Tipping her head to the side, Senna concentrated on the heat from the sun warming her neck. "There were four of them—Earth, Water, Plants and Sunlight. Each was a living, breathing emblem of their respective domains. Earth appeared as a woman of ebony, Water had the slanted blue eyes and russet skin of the north, Sunlight was as fair and blonde as the rays of the sun and Plants was covered in freckles. From their long sinuous dresses, to the shade of their hair, to the tint of their eyes, the colors varied by the moment."

All the Witches were silent. Senna's mind was so full of the memory, she couldn't have spoken anyway.

"How much pain could they have stopped?" Sacra's words held a bitter edge.

"Don't, Sacra," Coyel said. "This life is not one to be without heartache."

"No," Prenny agreed. "That is for the next."

Coyel turned back toward the city of Zaen. Worry lines creased her face. "For now, we have finished our songs, but we still face Tarten. If only they'll let us pass unmolested."

In response, Prenny snorted.

30. Witch War

Alongside the Discipline Heads and her mother, Senna was in the first line of Witches to flow from Espen's jungle toward the city of Zaen. She flinched when the soldiers atop the wall shouted a warning. On either side, her mother and Coyel packed a little tighter. Senna glanced behind her and saw the other Witches do the same—their grim faces looking steadily forward. All of them were barefoot to better feel the Earth, the first Sister.

The Witches were at war.

Senna felt the plants trembling in anticipation of a Witch song. As they neared the main road, the people of Tarten shrank from them, calling for the soldiers as they ran for safety behind the city wall. She wished she could be closer to Joshen, but that would sever her connection with the others. Instead, he walked unarmed beside them.

As Head of Water, Chavis led in battle, which also meant she served as their channeler. She struck up a song. Senna and the others joined her.

> Take in light, take in air;
> Spread thy roots, thy leaves grow fair.

All the plants within the sound of their voices stretched upward and flaunted their leaves; behind them, the land grew more lush.

Without pause, they marched to the guard house where Senna had been pummeled by Wardof. There, the Witches' progress halted with their voices. She felt the gaze of the soldiers and she couldn't help but remember her trips to Gonstower market as a girl. She yearned to shrink deeper into the protective lines of bodies behind her. But she'd accepted when Coyel had offered her a place in the first line. She wouldn't shame herself by backing away now. *I've faced worse,* she told herself as she planted her feet. *And I was alone then.*

Chavis spoke while Tiena translated for the Witches who didn't speak Tarten, "I'm Chavis, Head of Water and War General. I come seeking Desni. Release her and you have nothing to fear."

The main door cracked open and a commander came out—the same commander who had caused Senna so much pain. "I'm Methen, Commander of Zaen," Tiena translated. The commander's eyes flicked to the Witches flanking Chavis on every side. Recognition touched his eyes when he saw Senna.

Unconsciously, her hand wandered to her temple. Anger swelled within her like a bruise. Her throat burned with a song that could hurt him as badly as he and Wardof had hurt her. Methen was gauging them. And he was afraid. She longed to justify his fears.

He signaled toward the building. Soldiers rushed out, forming ranks beside him. He spoke and once again, Tiena translated, "There are warrants for the arrest of all Witches, so see her you shall." He strode forward, his soldiers behind him.

Chavis threw a barrier seed. The Witches packed tight and gripped forearms. The connection of their bodies also intertwined their minds. With one voice, they sang.

Barrier tree, strengthen thyself and fresh courage take;
Our warrior thou art and our enemy, thy enemy make.

Fuelled by their collective power, the tree shot up like a lightning bolt, wider than a horse is long and deeply in tune with Chavis. Groaning, it stretched forward and gripped the building. With a sharp crack, the mud walls fractured and slowly arched forward. With eyes full of horror, the soldiers ran for their lives as the entire side of the building crashed down on them.

Dust and debris rushed toward Senna like a tidal wave.

Don't let go! Chavis' words echoed in her head.

Clenching her eyes, Senna turned away as the cloud overtook them. Her mother and Coyel gripped her arms tighter. Senna gripped them back. Something sharp stung her cheek. She felt warm blood trickle down her face. As the dust cleared, she searched for Joshen and was relieved to see him covered with dirt, but unhurt. Soldiers lay at the foot of the tree. Methen rose to his knees. With a sharp command, he grabbed his musket.

"He's ordered them to open fire!" Tiena warned.

She'd no more than said it than Senna felt Chavis channeling the Witches' energy toward the tree. It snatched muskets the moment the soldiers lifted them, breaking them as easily as if they were brittle pine needles. Hefty branches encircled the soldier's waists and hauled them aloft. But the tree didn't throw them. Not yet.

Senna pressed her lips together in frustration when she saw the same look of hate and anger in Methen's eyes that had so long been present in Wardof's. She shook her head, dust from her hair pluming around her like a veil. Chavis' dark hair appeared to have been combed with an ash-coated brush. "Tell him if he, or any other soldier, chooses us for an enemy, we will kill them. Complete surrender and an oath to let us pass in peace. No pursuit."

In response, Methen drew his knife and stabbed at the branch. Some of the other soldiers followed his example, while others struggled to set themselves free.

Chavis simply thought and the tree tightened its grip around the soldiers' middles. Sharp cries of surprise and grunts of pain pierced the air. "Drop them," she ordered the soldiers.

After a brief hesitation and another squeeze, knives clattered to the ground. Methen took a deep breath as his shoulders slumped. "I'm not your enemy," Tiena finally translated.

The Witches sang and the tree dropped them. Rising to their feet, the soldiers cast furtive glances at the branches. As if the Witches very nearness might burn them, they shied toward the ruined building. Methen backed away with the rest of them. "We surrender."

Chavis nodded.

The Witches had taken the entire city without shedding a single drop of enemy blood. Senna signaled to Joshen, who ran toward the ruined building. When he emerged, he held Desni's blue-veined hand in one hand and in the other, a musket. He had a smug smile on his face.

A cry erupted from the Witches. Tiena rushed forward and wrapped her arms around her mother's withered frame. Both had heads of gray, both were bent with age, one more so than the other. The two women cried and hugged each other. Desni pulled back and faced Senna, "Thank you. Now I can pass on in peace."

Senna inclined her head toward the old woman.

"I'll stay here with my mother and heal my own lands," Tiena stated.

Coyel exchanged a concerned glance with Chavis, who touched Tiena's shoulder. "Methen's loyalty is to the government. You know this."

Tiena glared at the commander. When she spoke, Desni translated, "Your loyalty should be to your people. I can help."

Methen squared his shoulders, obviously drawing courage. "If my superiors order me to apprehend Witches, I'll do so."

"Cowards hide behind orders," Coyel murmured. With a shake of her head, she spoke to Tiena, "It won't be safe for you here. Perhaps the best weapon we can wield against Tarten is our absence. Espen has kept these lands in fair order; let us see how long Tarten lasts when that is gone."

Chavis turned back to the Captain. "The Witches will be in Nefalie when your government is ready for us."

Desni stood rooted to the spot, staring at the city. Finally, she shouted something in Tarten. Softly, her daughter translated, "These are our lands. We must fight for them; the Witches cannot do it for us." Without a backward glance, she walked away from her home.

As Senna turned to follow the departing Witches, she saw Boors lining the city walls, despair obvious by their slumped posture. Senna searched the faces, hoping she might recognize some who had helped her. But there were too many and she dared not fall behind.

***

Senna looked up as Joshen burst through the trees and ran toward them. "Tarten has sent its army this way!" he cried.

Chavis rose from beside the flames, her face bathed in firelight. "How many?"

"It was hard to tell, it's so dark, but I'd say at least a thousand," he replied, his face white.

Senna looked at her mother. There were less than two hundred and fifty Witches. A formidable opponent to be sure, but a thousand soldiers armed with muskets pitted against the Witches and their plants?

Prenny's gaze swept the gathered Witches. "If we fight, some will be lost."

"And so soon after regaining their freedom," Coyel said.

Senna dropped her head. It was miles upon miles to the coastline. Was Captain Parknel still there, or had he long ago repaired his ship and retreated? "What can we do?"

Chavis fingered the seeds in her belt. "There are moments when you act and there are moments when you react. I'm afraid this is the latter. If the Tartens attack, what choice have we but to fight? If however, they allow us passage out of their lands, we'll take it gladly."

"What chance do you stand against so many?" Joshen asked.

Chavis's smoldering eyes studied him. "A Witch war is not a pleasant thing to see, Joshen. But be assured, we hold our own very well."

Coyel must have seen the uncertainty in Senna's eyes. "Don't worry. Just as you did in the Ring of Power, you will know the songs when the time comes for you to sing them."

***

Senna stood on the clear ground on the slope of the rounded mountains. Before them waited vast fields of red coats. Joshen had only counted the first battalion before running back. There were not a thousand, but ten thousand. All were armed, their muskets gleaming in the sun. Joshen stood beside her, their sole firearm resting across his forearms. A look to the left and right revealed women of all ages and races—all clad in the traditional green. *I have only just found them,* Senna wanted to cry.

"Could you call upon the Creators again?" Coyel whispered.

She felt the answer ringing in her breast. The Creators wouldn't interfere if man chose to damn themselves; only welcome their Keepers with open arms as the world slowly died. "No."

A small company of mounted soldiers separated from the main group. One of them held a white flag attached to a pole. The sickness twisting inside Senna expanded as the company grew larger and took shape. Four men—the decorated one in the center was obviously the commander. Coyel, Chavis, Drenelle and Prenny strode out to meet them.

Unable to bear it, Senna hurried after them. Her mother snatched her hand. "No Brusenna. You haven't a place there."

Jerking free, Senna hastened on. Seeing her, Prenny rolled her eyes. "You've no business here, Sprout."

Chavis studied her. "Let her stay. She came through Tarten undetected. Perhaps her knowledge of the terrain can help us."

Coyel nodded in agreement.

Two of them. Senna breathed a sigh of relief. Two was sufficient.

"That's far enough," Chavis said as Tiena translated.

The commander took them in, searching for their leader. Just as Chavis began speaking in Tarten, he held up his hand for her to stop. "I speak fluent Nefalien, though the weak language grates upon my ears."

He waited for a response, but the Heads refused to let him bait them. He shifted in the saddle, obviously still unsure which of them was the leader. "I am Reden, General to the kingdom of Tarten. You have been accused of Witchcraft, among other charges. I'm under order to bring you in for trial."

Coyel cocked an eyebrow. "And what 'other numerous charges' have we unwittingly gleaned?"

"Our borders have long been closed to Nefaliens; your presence alone is against our laws. In addition, lawlessness, recklessness, evading arrest, trespassing."

"Would you like to add stealing Tarten air while you're at it?" Prenny said through clenched teeth.

"We didn't come here of our own will," Drenelle added in her shrill voice.

Coyel rested a warning hand over Prenny's arm. "We only wish to depart your lands. Let us pass in peace."

"That's not for me to decide. The Chancellors make those decisions."

"And if we threaten to curse your land?" Chavis said while studying her fingernails.

Reden lowered his head, his lips curving down disapprovingly. "I'm a soldier, Witch. I follow orders. I'll bring you in, one way or another."

"What chance of fair trial would we have?" Coyel exclaimed.

The man's determined eyes shifted to her. "I say again, that is not for me to decide. I'll guarantee you fair treatment while under my care. Though you will of necessity be gagged and bound."

The Heads exchanged glances. "We'll discuss your terms and return with an answer."

Senna studied the man as the others moved a few steps away. His gaze shifted to her, evaluating her as she did him. But his unreadable expression revealed nothing.

"Senna," Coyel called.

Reluctantly, she turned away. The Heads had moved out of earshot, forming a tight circle. She bent her head with theirs.

"What are we to do?" Drenelle asked in a low voice.

"I'm a healer, not a warrior. We have no chance against so many," Prenny growled.

"I'll not rot in another prison. This one probably worse than the last!" Drenelle countered through clenched teeth.

"We must run!" a Witch cried from the crowd behind them.

The Heads ignored it. Chavis's eyes darted from one face to another. "You know as well as I that we cannot outrun horses on foot. We are in the middle of Tarten; where could we hide? There are thousands of them! Most of us would be captured immediately. The others shortly thereafter. Many would die."

Senna glanced back at Joshen. "There is an underground network to hide Witches. They helped me."

Chavis nodded slowly. "That could work. A few might escape unnoticed. Young Witches. Runners."

Coyel's brows gathered in concentration. "This network, you could find a contact?"

Remembering Kaen, Senna nodded. "Joshen and I both could."

"Our only chance is if all of us run," Drenelle interjected, a touch of panic around her eyes. She must have known she would not be included in the small group to run for it.

Prenny groaned in disgust. "Don't be a fool! If we all run, the whole army will come after us. If we fight back, they'll kill us in droves. Those left will either be locked away or killed."

"Being locked away and killed is inevitable," Drenelle cried.

"Maybe not." Senna hesitated as Drenelle shot her a murderous glare. For a woman wrapped in lace, Drenelle could look as dangerous as a gut-shot bear. She was obviously set on escaping and didn't like Senna interfering with her chances.

"Go on, Senna," Coyel said.

Senna moistened her lips with her tongue and avoided Drenelle's glower. "We're miles inland with ten thousand soldiers blocking our way. The capitol, Carpel, is near the shore. We stand a better chance of escape from there."

"She's right about the capitol," Tiena agreed. "It's Tarten's main port. There are hundreds of ships."

"I see no other viable choice," Chavis said, looking at Coyel.

Coyel nodded. "I agree."

"Well, I don't!" Drenelle hissed. "And don't you pull that, 'I hold the sway vote,' nor the 'Witch General' nonsense. Prenny and I have equal weight. I demand a council be convened."

"There's no need," Prenny said with a shake of her head. "I agree with them." Drenelle balled her lace trimmed skirt in her fist. Prenny merely shrugged. "I can't order my Keepers to suicide. Much as I hate admitting it, the sprout has a point. The soldiers will take us where we want to go. We stand a better chance of escape from there than here."

Chavis straightened. "It's agreed, then. Two groups stand a better chance of survival than one. Joshen will lead a company of five Witches to this network. The rest of us will try to escape from Carpel. I'll round up some good candidates for escape." Lifting her skirts, she strode toward the Witches with a critical eye.

Senna stared blankly after Chavis. Joshen. Leaving. She ran after her. "I'm young. I can run. I'll go with them."

Chavis shook her head. "No. We might need you to lead us to that Captain Parknel you told us of. Now, where is this Joshen?"

Senna's heart fell to her feet. "Let me tell him?"

Chavis nodded curtly. "Yes. That would be faster." She turned away.

Senna froze when she saw Joshen rushing toward her. Tears brimmed her eyes. She angrily wiped them away. He slowed and approached her cautiously. "I know that look," he growled.

She couldn't meet his gaze. "You're to lead a group of Witches to Kaen and have him help you get them to Parknel."

He gave a quick nod of approval as he studied the mountains. She could see him planning the route already. "That's smart."

She winced and finally met his gaze.

He took a step back as understanding dawned on his face. "You're not going with us, are you?"

She shook her head.

"But Senna, I'm your Guardian! They aren't supposed to separate us."

"They're the Discipline Heads. They can do what they want.

Besides, whether or not I'm even allowed a Guardian hasn't been decided yet."

"Cow dung!"

She couldn't help a small smile at Joshen's cursing. "It might not be fair, but you know it's the right thing to do."

Joshen gripped both her arms. "I haven't left you yet. I'm not going to start now!"

"If they imprison us, you must go to Nefalie and appeal to the city-states," she whispered fiercely. "If you don't, no one will ever help us!"

"As if Nefalie would interfere!" he shot back.

She flinched, knowing he was right. His gaze turned from angry to pleading. "Come away; we'll escape the same way we came."

Senna looked away to hide her fierce desire. No. She wouldn't deny she wanted to run. Wanted it desperately. She closed her eyes as the fear overcame her. "Understand, Joshen," she said breathlessly, "I came all this way to free them. And I did. If that leads to their deaths, I'll never be able to live with it." She thought of adding that her mother needed her, but the words wouldn't come. "Please, Joshen. If not you, who else?"

Agony in his gaze, Joshen looked away. "All right," he finally relented. "I'll lead them to Parknel. But then I'm coming back for you." He kissed her, his lips hard. "Stay alive. I don't care what you have to do, stay alive." With another kiss, he sprinted toward Chavis and a small knot of Witches gathered around her. And one very withered woman. Desni. Without looking back, they disappeared into the crowd. Senna knew within moments they'd be in the jungle.

And one of the women had been Arianis. Senna couldn't help the fierce jealously gnawing at her breast. She didn't know how long she stared after him. But at the sound of thundering hooves, she turned.

So, General Reden wasn't waiting for their answer. He was coming for it instead.

31. Enemy

Senna waited with the Discipline Heads. They all knew it was useless to fight. Against a thousand, they had a slim chance. Against ten thousand, they were little more than a mantis pitted against a horde of ants.

Mounted on a sleek, gray horse, General Reden cautiously approached them. Grudgingly, Senna had to admit he was handsome, in a brutish way. He was broad, built like a wrestler, with a long, puckered scar across his jaw. His eyes gleamed so dark they bordered on black, with hair to match. She couldn't venture a guess on how old he was. He might be in his mid-twenties or early forties. When he stood mere yards away, he paused, his musket trained on the ground. "Your decision?"

Coyel held out her hands in surrender. "You've given us little choice."

He gestured to the men at his sides, who stepped toward them. "That was my intention. Your name?"

"Coyel."

"Very well, Coyel. Allow my men to bind your hands and mouths and I'll ensure you receive fair treatment. Agreed?" The men approached them, cords in hand. Senna eyed them warily.

"And what assurance will you give me that you will honor your word?" Coyel asked.

He chuckled. "Asking you to surrender was a courtesy. If I had wanted to take you by force, I'd have done it already."

"And if you had, a great many of you'd be dead by now," Chavis said.

Did the woman have no fear? Senna wondered.

Coyel shot Chavis a warning glance. "Fair enough, Reden. But I'll hold you to your word."

Reden nodded to his men—two for each Witch. The soldiers who approached Senna stripped her of her seed belt. They tied a soft cotton rag across her mouth. The man who bound her hands did it strong enough she couldn't pull free, but loose enough she didn't lose circulation. A small part of her dared to hope Reden might keep his word.

The men took positions, one on each side. With their mouths covered, did Reden really think them dangerous enough to warrant two guards per Witch? Senna thought it excessive, until she began to move through the host of soldiers, who glowered at them as they passed. Only then did she understand they were the Witch's protectors just as much as they were their guards.

"I'm assigning my most trusted men to guard you," Reden said as they moved. "You'll be allowed to remove your gags while you eat, but they will have loaded muskets trained on you the entire time. I have given them instructions to shoot should one syllable leave your lips." His gaze rested on Chavis. "Understand there will be no mercy granted should this rule be broken."

When they were surrounded by ten thousand Tartens, they were strung together like pack animals. She and her mother were separated, Sacra in the back. All Senna could think of was Joshen—somewhere in the jungle without her—so she didn't notice she was first in line until Reden dismounted in front of her and signaled for her gag to be removed.

The Heads frowned at her suspiciously. She shrugged. Her hands tied in front of her, she waited.

He studied her. "How is it a mere girl came to free the Witches?"

How could he know it was me? she wondered. She wanted to look to Coyel for help, but she feared giving something away.

When she didn't answer, he continued. "And a single man traveled with you. It doesn't make much sense. What use would the Witches have for one man?"

"I don't see why it matters," Senna replied hotly.

"It doesn't," he replied. "I'm just trying to satisfy my curiosity. We have little else to do while we wait."

Senna felt the heat of the soldiers' stares. She forced herself to remain stoic. What was he going to do? "Wait for what?"

He stepped back and gripped his wrists behind his back. "For my soldiers to find the five Witches and the man you sent away." He leaned toward her. "I have been a warrior for my entire life. Don't think you can outsmart or outmaneuver me. I don't want to kill any of you. But I will. Do you understand?"

Senna backed away and looked toward the jungle. "I'm not a leader; why are you telling me this?"

"Because it was your idea." Reden followed her gaze. "Don't worry. My men will not kill anyone unless they use deadly force."

Joshen would certainly try. She swallowed hard. "How many soldiers did you send after them?"

Reden caressed his musket with his palm. "Send? I sent no one. You were surrounded long before you saw us coming."

Gunfire echoed off the side of the mountain. Senna whirled toward the jungle. Reden began rattling off commands in Tarten. Within moments, a group of armed men headed toward the sound.

Senna's hands flew to her mouth. *He's right. It was my idea,* she thought. Even now, were bullets piercing those she'd helped escape? "Oh, Joshen," her lips mouthed behind her fingers.

***

Joshen felt torn in more ways than one. Splitting up gave them a better prospect of someone making it through. But how could he leave them? He was a Guardian and if giving his life gave them a better chance, he wouldn't hesitate—though he hoped with every fiber of his being it wouldn't come to that.

At the sound of voices, he flattened himself. The others followed his lead. He studied the thick tangle of trees, watching for movement. He didn't have to wait long. Soldiers were riddled throughout the trees. Waiting for them. The only way they could be in front of them so quickly was if they'd been there all along. *Cow dung!* His plan disintegrated.

As a group, they'd all be caught. "Split up! And if you're captured, don't give them a reason to kill you!"

He darted hard to the right. He'd try and avoid them along the outskirts, hoping they'd focused their strength on the most obvious path of flight. He was a fast runner. He ran low to the ground, taking long, sweeping strides. He knew how to move quietly. Above his own soft noises, he watched and listened.

He paused at the sudden sound of a Witch song. At least one of the five was in trouble and fighting back. He wanted so badly to go back and help, but he had to get through. He had to get help!

He darted around a large tree and saw a cluster of red. Diving under a fern, he pressed himself flat against the ground and waited. He counted to fifteen before chancing a look. They hadn't seen him. But if they didn't find him soon, they'd start tightening the noose and sending more soldiers. If he wanted any chance to escape, he had to take it now.

He was grateful for his dirty shirt and even more grateful the soldier's red tunics made them so easy to spot. He waited for his breathing to quiet before crawling forward. Placing his hands and feet with extreme care, he inched away from the pocket of soldiers. A little farther, the ground disappeared before him.

At some point, the rains had cut a deep swath through the soft Earth. Dry now, it would provide excellent cover. He looked back at the soldiers. If they'd discovered it, they'd watch it. But if not, he could run flat out. *Too tempting,* he thought. *Senna would be more cautious.* At the thought of her, he had to fight the impulse to run back to her. *They better keep her safe, or they'll have more than Tarten soldiers to worry about.*

He peered up and down the wash. *The faster I find Parknel,* he thought, *the faster we can get Senna out of here.* Jumping down, he jogged forward. But the sloped sides also blocked his vision. Voices. Close. And coming closer. He pressed his back against the dirt and lifted his musket. He counted every time the blood pounded in his head.

The voices moved closer. Had they heard something and come to investigate? He wished he spoke Tarten!

Rocks and dirt rained down on his shoulder. He heard them shout for others.

He had to get out of here! Not caring how much racket he made, Joshen sprinted full-tilt down the wash. Gunfire followed him. Musket balls whopped into the dirt around him. He darted to avoid being an easy target. *If I make it out of this, I'll never shoot another deer again. I swear I won't!* he thought.

After the soldiers had spent their first round, he chanced a glance behind him. He saw a sea of red. He cursed silently. For the briefest moment, he considered surrendering. But he tossed the idea quickly. They were unlikely to take mercy upon a Guardian with a musket. Especially since he planned on taking a few soldiers with him. No, he had to keep moving, keep ahead of them.

He ran as hard and fast as he could. Before long, the shouts and flashes of red fell behind and disappeared altogether. He changed course, cutting out of the jungle and sprinting through meadows and past farmers' huts.

He had little but water to fill his belly in the days to come. When he could, he stole a piece of fruit from an accommodating tree. Occasionally, he found nuts and more than once he borrowed food from a farmer's field—or the fire in front of their homes. He didn't know how many miles he covered in those few days, but it had to be over a hundred. And it rained every single day.

That's how he found himself, filthy, half-starved and ragged in front of a familiar home. Even from a distance, he could smell tantalizing food wafting toward him. Without knocking, he pushed the door open to find Kaen and his family with Ciara and

Tren. Not caring what kind of meat it was, he tore off a chunk and swallowed.

Kaen stood, wide-eyed and afraid. "The Witches? Senna didn't free them?"

Joshen shook his head as he tore off another chunk and began hammering it with his teeth. He was pretty sure it was snake. It wasn't too bad. "She 'reed 'em alright. But the 'oldiers didn' let 'em get 'ery far."

Kaen ran a hand through his hair and quickly translated Joshen's garbled explanation. He shook his fist toward the rafters. "This will start a war, mark my words. The Boors have suffered enough. If the Class imprisons Witches who are perfectly capable of healing the land, there will be an accounting. We have to let Nefalie know of this!"

Joshen swallowed. He didn't see how a Boor who could barely feed his family could afford a musket to fight with. Let alone what Nefalie had to do with anything. But that wasn't his problem. Senna was his problem. "I need my horse back."

Kaen said something to his son. The boy and Tren disappeared through the door. "What else?"

Joshen tore a hunk of spoon bread and topped it with mashed fruit and the other hunk of meat and headed for the door. "Some travel food and some more balls and powder if you've got any."

Kaen nodded and prattled something off to his wife, who was at her feet in a moment, throwing up the door to the cellar and shouting at her children, who scurried about in response.

"What are you two going to do?" Joshen asked before stuffing half the bread in his mouth.

"We're going to lead the resistance." He said it like he really thought he might pull it off. Joshen had to give him credit for his determination, at least.

A fully saddled Stretch emerged from the barn. Joshen's eyes swept over the animal. He looked healthy enough, not fat or weak. His coat gleamed. Obviously, Kaen had put the animal to work, but fed him well.

Good, Joshen thought, *'cause you're gonna need your wind.*

Jumping into the saddle, he lifted his half-eaten meal in farewell and dug his heels into the horse's sides. With the horse, things went much faster. Joshen only hoped he could remember the way and Parknel had neither left nor was too far out from leaving. Witches or no, Tarten or no, he was getting Senna out of here.

32. KEEPERS

Woodenly, Senna put one foot in front of the other. She had a feeling Reden had put her at the front of the line so he could keep an eye on her. She couldn't fathom why. She was filthy, hungry and had needed to empty her bladder for hours. But after two days of marching with the Tarten army, she'd learned there would be no stopping until the evening meal. It was hard to judge in the rain, but she was sure supper had come and gone and Reden showed no signs of stopping. Yet.

It had taken less than an hour for Reden's soldiers to round up the fleeing Witches. Other than bruises and one turned ankle, all of them had returned intact. Even Arianis. At least Joshen and Desni hadn't been among them. More soldiers had set off in search of them. Senna missed Joshen fiercely. She hoped he wasn't caught.

Senna glanced back and saw Tiena stumble and nearly go down. She looked pale and weak. Some of the other Witches didn't look much better. Apparently, recovery from their imprisonment wouldn't come all at once. "Weden!" she shouted through the damp gag. Either he didn't hear her, or he chose not to respond.

Her anger flaring, Senna planted both her feet. Chavis plowed into her from behind and then grunted as Coyel ran into her. With grunts and scrambling, the whole line of Witches came to a shuddering stop. Immediately, her guards trained their muskets on her. Giving both men an angry glare, she mumbled, "I'll not go 'anover wep until I weap to Weden."

"General!" one of her guards shouted.

Reden surveyed the situation before pivoting his horse and coming back to them. "What is it, Paner?"

"This prisoner refuses to go any farther," he said with a heavy accent.

Reden cocked a single eyebrow. "Is this true?" "Wake out the wag," Senna managed.

Amused, he nodded to Paner. After the gag was out, Senna worked her jaw, enjoying the ability to close her mouth and have wet cloth away from her skin. "Well?" he prodded.

"We're hungry, tired and desperately need to relieve ourselves."

Reden flipped his reins in irritation. "We're an army. Not a caravan. I want to reach Carpel in two days. That means we have to push ourselves. You'll survive until I say we stop." He began to turn his horse around.

"Reden!" Senna shouted. "You promised us fair treatment— we are women! Some of us old! Where's your honor?"

He whirled around and fixed her with a fierce stare. Senna knew she'd gone too far. But she refused to take any of it back, or cower in fear—by the Creators, she was done cowering! She raised her head higher and squared her shoulders. Something in Reden changed at the sight. The harsh lines around his mouth and eyes melted away and a chuckle surfaced. "Very well, Witch. Go relieve yourself. It means another night sleeping on the ground for all of us, but we'll make camp here." He brought a stern finger to bear on her, "But in exchange, you must give me something."

Senna stiffened with sudden dread. "And what is that?"

He tipped his head to the side. "Answers."

She remembered Coyel's warning at the circle. "There are many things I'll not tell you."

Reden leaned forward. "I promise, your craft secrets are safe."

Senna looked back at the other Witches. Directly behind her, all the Heads but Prenny nodded. Prenny's shoulders were drooped, but she still managed to look fierce. "I 'an mar' all nigh'."

Senna shook her head; she was past finding Prenny's stubbornness annoying. The woman was like a hive of angry bees. To Reden, she said, "All right, but we want to bathe as well. And a chance to wash our clothes," she added as an afterthought.

Reden held up his hands. "It's raining."

"That's not the same."

Reden roared with laughter. "Bathing will depend upon your answers!"

The meal Reden delivered was little more than filling, but it was a stark improvement from an hour ago, so Senna didn't complain. She wanted desperately to converse with the Heads about her upcoming meeting with Reden, but they weren't allowed to speak. When Paner came for her, she could only shoot an apprehensive glance at her mother and the others before following him.

He led her to Reden's massive tent, which wasn't far away. Holding back the flap, Paner gestured for her to enter. It was a sparse affair; Reden had obviously chosen functional over grand, lightweight over sturdy.

He rose when she entered, dagger in hand. Eyes wide, Senna backed away. He laughed. "If I wanted you dead, it would've happened long ago." Behind her, he jerked the dagger through the cords at her wrist and gestured to a chair in front of his battered desk.

Rubbing her wrists, Senna thought perhaps under better, friendlier circumstances, she might actually like this Reden.

"Now," he said as he sat in his own chair opposite Senna. "I know you won't try anything, simply because it would be fruitless and all of your fellow Witches would die. But I'd like your word."

Senna nodded once—what choice did she have? "You have it."

"Good. Well then, about this bathing thing. In order to do a proper job, you'd have to have your hands free, which would render your gags useless. I might be willing to allow it if, like mealtimes, my guards were allowed to point primed weapons at you. But I doubt you, or any of the other women, would find those terms agreeable. And even if you did, my guards are men and some of your Witches are rather fair to look upon. The whole thing is a bad idea."

Senna shrugged. "One at a time, allow us to use a tent. You can line the front with all the primed weapons you want."

Reden stroked his chin. "Not a bad idea. But I want your word that none of the Witches will try anything."

Senna grunted. "I think you misunderstand my role. I'm not a Head. By the Creators, I'm not even a full Keeper—just an Apprentice. I don't have any authority."

His eyebrows rose. "Then why do they listen to you?"

For a moment, words escaped her. "They don't."

"Mmm." He steepled his hands under his chin.

He obviously didn't believe her and she didn't know how to change his mind. "If you want the Witches' word, you'll have to ask them individually."

He crossed his arms and leaned back into his chair. "Seems like a waste of time to me. They should fall in line with their leaders."

She felt her hands begin to tingle with anger. "Like the Boors should fall in line behind the Class?"

"Don't get bigheaded with me. Every nation has Boors. Including Nefalie." He arched a brow, obviously enjoying this exchange, much to Senna's increasing frustration.

Senna shook her head. "Not like here. Nefalie has different problems. Mostly involving squabbles between the city-states. Civil wars, that sort of thing."

He grunted. "And what role do the Witches play in all this?"

She shrugged. "Ask Coyel. She's our diplomat."

"So, you condemn us for our treatment of the Boors and yet not many years ago, the Witches sold their songs for money."

Senna sighed and sat back in her chair. She knew the history well. After all, she'd scoured the libraries at Haven looking for any clues history might give her to defeating Espen. "All of that was before my time, but Espen came up with the idea. It led to a faction among the Witches and hate and mistrust by the people."

"And the man? The one with you?"

Afraid her feelings would show, Senna looked away. "Have you found him?"

"No."

Senna tried to tell if he was lying, but she couldn't read his blank face. "And if you do?"

"That all depends on whether he fights us." He paused. "You didn't answer my original question."

Her gaze narrowed. "Why don't you ask me the questions you referred to earlier?"

He smiled in open amusement. "I'm getting there."

"You're a strange man."

"And you are an honest woman," he shot back. "Now, who was the man?"

Senna crossed her arms over her chest and sat back farther in her chair. "Are we done?"

"Not yet." He leaned forward. "How did you defeat her? All of Tarten is afraid of Espen and a young, untrained Witch defeats her when all others failed. How?"

So he'd finally asked his real question. Senna looked away. She couldn't talk about it. Especially not with Reden.

"Even if I deny your baths?"

Clenching her jaw, she twisted her skirts in her hands and refused to answer.

He studied her for a long time before he called for Paner. "Have the cooks set out the pots to boil. Station men at the front of my tent, muskets loaded. I have promised the witches a bath."

Though it was an uncomfortable thing, to bathe inside a tent with men pointing primed weapons at her, it was worth it. After she'd washed herself, she plunged her dress and cloak in as well. When she'd wrung them out as best she could, she draped them back over herself and went outside to shiver herself dry.

With a great deal of discomfort, she noted Reden watching her with a mixture of curiosity and respect. His attention didn't escape her mother, or the other witches. Senna saw sparks of distrust in more than one pair of eyes. She bit her lip and tried to pretend she was somewhere far away.

***

As Reden had said, they didn't reach Carpel until early morning on the third day. As the sun peaked over the city's domed mountain, it cast the mountain in stark shadow—like someone had upended a bucket of pitch over the city. Her eyes smarting, Senna squinted at it until she came under its shadow. Then, amid the smells of fire, fish and filth that came with the Boorish part of town, she saw the precision and prestige of the Class atop the mountain like a lofty nest. All traces of green jungle had been snuffed out, replaced by cold, dead stone. Cobblestone streets ran down the mountain like white rivers. Encased by stone walls, marble homes seemed to say, "Here, where no eye can avoid, see us in our glory and loath our success, but do not think to touch. Our walls and our wealth will keep you out."

Her lips were cracked and her cheeks chafed from the gag. Even with all the care Reden took to see they were not bound too tightly, her wrists were raw. She was beginning to comprehend what a lifetime as a prisoner would feel like—silence, pain, boredom and hate building every day until she'd eventually burst from it.

With a sigh, she watched as the city grew ever larger and the smell of sea foam and fish became stronger. Long before they reached the mountain, Tarten's Class appeared among the Boors, throwing curses as they came. For once, Senna was glad she couldn't understand their words.

By midday, they reached the bottom of the mountain and began their ascent. At the pinnacle, a square building sat like a pompous aristocrat. Senna climbed the harsh stone steps that led past the pillared entrance. The scraping of their feet echoed off the stone walls of a great hall. Senna took in the room. From their high perches, enormous windows let in shafts of light. The walls were white and crisp, adding to the hollow feeling. The angles were harsh, unnatural. The room was a dichotomy against the soft curves and flowing sinews of nature.

She understood at once. This was the Class' way of flaunting its perfection, its control. There were little adornments, save four stone chairs lined with cushions. Upon these chairs sat three men and one woman. All wore a grim expression, the kind of look Senna received when, as a child, she disobeyed her mother.

The Witches entered the building one at a time and they stood shoulder-to-shoulder in a line. Unbeknownst to anyone in the room, the connection allowed them to move and act as one. Senna instinctively felt that Coyel was in the lead. Their steps perfectly matched, like a dance, they stopped at the same moment.

The woman was picturesque in her statue-like stillness as she said in perfect Nefalien, "Unstop their mouths."

"Chancellor Grendi, I would strongly advise against removing their gags. Their mouths are their weapons," Reden said.

She fixed him with a cold stare. "Did I ask for your advice, General?"

If Reden was affronted, he showed no sign. "The safety of Tarten is my charge, Chancellor Grendi. I would be shirking my post had I not spoken."

"There is no soil or seed here," she said with a dismissive wave of her hand. "I shall consider myself warned."

One soldier went along the line, cutting the cloth that had kept them silent for so long. When Senna was free, she worked her jaw, wishing she could rub her cracked lips. She looked over the four Chancellors as they, in turn, studied the Witches. Of the four, Senna was quite sure they had the most to fear from Grendi.

"We are unstopping your mouths because we know you will not try anything here, for that would bring a sentence of death." The woman said it kindly enough, but the harshness in her eyes couldn't be denied—almost like she wished they would sing.

"I'm Chancellor Grendi," she said before she gestured to the others. "These are Chancellors Argun, Netis and Serben. You have been accused of Witchcraft, lawlessness, resisting arrest, trespassing, theft, treason, insubordination," the woman went on until Senna's tired mind drifted. She snapped back into focus when Grendi ended with, "What have you to say for yourselves?"

As one voice, the Witches answered, "Witches we are."

The other Chancellors all leaned back and exchanged nervous glances. "As for the rest?" Grendi asked.

"The rest was thrust upon us," Coyel answered.

A slow smile spread across Grendi's face, followed by a dangerous chuckle. "Well, then. The rest doesn't matter. I confer upon each of you the life sentence required for witchcraft."

"Yet Espen roamed unchecked across your lands. Why did you not seek her?" Coyel said it like she was speaking to a small child.

Grendi leaned back in her chair. "Because we paid her to catch the rest of you. I'm really quite disappointed she failed. I'd hoped to rid the world of Witches once and for all." She snapped her fingers and a small goblet was brought to her. She took a slow sip. "Still, it worked out for the best."

Senna stared in open amazement. So Espen hadn't worked alone. Suddenly things began to fall into place. Espen had been telling the truth. But Senna had been too angry to listen. *Oh, Joshen,* she thought. *Everything's my fault!*

Senna felt the Witches at her side bristle, felt the question from Chavis. *Shall we attack now?*

Senna weighed the consequences. The army surrounded them. They couldn't escape. Cautiously, she pushed her consciousness toward the others. *Could we wait for a better opportunity?* she asked.

Other thoughts flooded her mind.

Grendi's right. There are no seeds or soil here.

If we fail, she'll kill us.

That's her plan. Look at her. She wants all of us dead.

There's nothing we can do.

"No. There is something," Chavis' whisper halted the thoughts. Immediately, the song came to the front of Senna's mind so horrible, no Witch, not even Espen, had the animosity to deliver it.

Coyel bent her head to send words from her mind to the other Witches' minds. *Can we even release it? This room is no circle and our hands are bound.*

Drenelle answered with her mind, *Chavis knows as well as I that we can. It's in the War Histories. Both of us have access.*

Chavis nodded. *The location will diminish the song's strength, but there are enough of us to compensate.*

Senna squared her shoulders and narrowed her focus on Grendi. It had to be done. *Yes.*

The answer echoed up and down the line.

Yes.

Yes.

Yes.

No. Prenny's thoughts sounded just as demanding as her voice. *By nature, we're healers, growers, protectors. Keepers! If we unleash our bindings in Tarten, how many will die? How many will hate us all the more?*

Coyel squared her shoulders. *I'll give them one warning, one chance, but no more.* She faced the Chancellors. "Would you make war upon all Witches until they are eradicated?"

Grendi's eyes shone with a luster of malice. "Witches are an abomination on the land and its people. None should have more power or grace than another."

Senna cocked her eyebrow. "Yet you sit atop your throne, while thousands of Boors suffer." More than one of the Witches glared at her for overstepping her boundaries, but she didn't care.

Grendi's pinched expression transferred to Senna; the woman was obviously unused to anyone questioning her authority. "I am a leader, a protector. You are a meddler."

"Your words are a justification for your cruelty," Coyel said.

Senna saw it now. Grendi was mad. Her thoughts were a poison spreading like dye leeching into white cloth. The realization came upon her suddenly and the other Witches felt it, too: Espen was not their greatest enemy. She was merely a pawn.

Coyel's voice was solemn, pierced with sorrow and strength, "Then the Witches declare war upon the land of Tarten! Let all who oppose us shudder in fear and beg forgiveness before the end." She transferred control of the circle to Chavis. With the speed of their desperateness, the Witches quickly formed a circle. Grendi and the Chancellors beckoned to more than two dozen soldiers who ran to break them up.

Senna's bonds wouldn't allow her to grasp the others' forearms, but she was able to huddle next to Tiena and Coyel, their shoulders touching. Even as her lips opened, Senna felt strong arms around her, hauling her back. Bracing herself, she sang all the more desperately and the shield responded, springing to life and hurling the soldiers back.

Chavis was right. The room was wrong, stone instead of plants and square instead of circular. It diminished the circle's power. But the Witches' numbers made up for the faulty design—besides, utter desolation and near destruction were kin enough.

The Witches' song began—a song Senna was surprised had ever been written down. The melody was beautiful, intoxicating—like a poisonous flower. But the words—more chant than song—raised goose flesh on her arms and sent her whole body shuddering,

> We, Keepers of the Earth, withdraw.
> We speak to the First Sister:
> Soil harden thy crusts,
> Let no sickle or seedling enter thus.
> We speak to the Second Sister:
> Water seal thy clouds and hide thy rain,
> Let not a drop fall upon the plains.
> We speak to the Third Sister:
> Plants hide up thy fruit,
> Seeds to wither and refuse to root.
> We speak to the Fourth Sister:
> Sun, bake the mud, scorch the lands,
> Death to follow at every hand.
> Only one check we ask of thee,
> Not forever, but until we revoke our curse decree.

The song ended and four ribbons of color—blue, green, brown and gold—arched upward like an oddly hued rainbow. They were beautiful, surreal and more deadly than a bolt of lightning. The bands segregated, each leaping from a high, slanted window.

Slowly the power of the song faded and the barrier began to shimmer, but the Witches shored it up again. Their song fell into humming; keeping the shield took far less song than creating it.

Senna hung her head in shame. She wasn't the only one. How many had they condemned to death? Certainly far more Boors than Class. She searched the circle and found her mother to her left, about twenty Witches down. Senna read her expression as easily as the printed words on her journal. Would this act seal their fate and the fate of an entire nation?

Chavis began another song and the other Witches joined in.

Oh wind, to Nefalie carry our song,
For the ears of her people must hear 'fore long.

The vibrations from the Witches' throats swirled, gathering strength and power as it twisted in a slow moving whirlwind. Had there been a channeler, the wind would have carried her up. As it was, it did little more than tug at all of them like the wind trying to rouse a bird from its roost.

"We must be in perfect harmony," Drenelle warned. "If not, the message will be garbled beyond recognition." When the wind had the required velocity, the Witches' song changed into their message.

Tarten holds the Witches captive,
Forbidden to sing or leave or live!
Awake Nefalie and for the Witches fight,
Or all the goodness of the Earth turns to blight.

Senna felt sure it worked. Even to her own sensitive ears, their song was so harmonious she could have sworn it came from one voice.

The wind snatched the last of their words and barreled from the room like the gale of a hurricane. The Witches began again, this time sending their cry to the people of Tarten. But a good many of the Witches didn't speak Tarten; only half as many voices joined in that song. It would have to be enough.

The barrier shimmered. Senna looked outside of the circle for the first time since they'd begun. A soldier's broken body lay atop one of the Chancellor's chairs. Beneath him, Chancellor Netis lay dead, his head badly misshapen. The soldier must have been hurled with enough force to shatter his skull.

"As long as we keep the circle, none can touch us," Drenelle said.

Yes, but how long can we hold on, Senna wondered. If even one Witch broke contact, the barrier would dissipate. The move had bought them time, but how much?

Grendi's face was deathly pale. As she met Senna's gaze, her face blotched red with rage. Her voice cracked like brittle leaves, "Shoot them all!"

Reden stepped between the Chancellor and the Witches. "Chancellor, you don't know what firing into that thing will do."

She held up her hand to silence him.

He ignored it. "Let one man try it first. There's no need to risk more. Those Witches aren't going anywhere."

She shoved him aside. "Not another word or I'll have your tongue cut out!"

With a shake of his head, Reden stepped behind the dead Chancellor's chair.

A grim line of soldiers formed before Grendi. Senna watched as a soldier across from her loaded his musket. Sweat trickled down her face. She felt stiflingly hot—as if the air were too thick to breathe. The man seemed to move in slow motion as he rammed the ball home. He filled the pan, shut the frizzen and trained the barrel on her. She looked into the dark abyss of the barrel.

Do not break contact! Chavis warned. *If anyone moves, the balls will break through and we'll die.*

But had the shield's strength been tested against musket fire?

Oh, Joshen! her mind cried. *I don't want to die!* Unable to watch death come for her, she clenched her eyes shut.

"Fire," Grendi shouted.

Even with the warning, Senna couldn't help but jump as the report sounded.

A repercussion. Screams of pain. But Senna felt nothing. The man must have missed her. Tensed to run, she opened her eyes.

What she saw stopped her cold. The soldiers lay on the ground, blood gushing from their wounds.

The barrier had more than held. It had sent back all the balls.

A nearly uncontrollable urge to help overwhelmed her, but she knew she couldn't. Knew to do so would only lead to her death. Senna felt dizzy and realized she'd been holding her breath. She forced the air from her lungs and inhaled quickly. Using her shoulder, she wiped the sweat from her brow, being careful not to break contact with Tiena or Coyel.

Reden seized Grendi's arm. "Why didn't you listen?"

She jerked from his grip. "I've given you enough soldiers to spare a dozen." She glanced around in disgust and shouted to a nearby servant, "I want this mess cleaned up before my return."

His fists clenched at his sides, Reden watched her storm from the room, the other Chancellors in tow.

"Perhaps the sight of so much blood bothers her," Prenny said darkly. "Especially since she caused it."

Reden started shouting orders. Senna felt a surge of pity for him. "Reden," she called. His eyes flicked to her. "If you bring us our seeds and some dirt, we'll grow healing herbs for them."

He froze and stared at her in bewilderment.

"We will?" Chavis asked.

Prenny kicked her. "Of course we will!"

Coyel looked at Drenelle, who had gone deathly pale. "Do what you wish," she said.

Coyel nodded with finality. "Yes. We'll help."

"They just tried to kill you," he said cautiously. "How do I know you won't poison them?"

Senna rolled her eyes heavenward in exasperation—Reden seemed to have that affect on her. "Because we aren't murderers!" She made no attempt to keep the accusation from her voice.

He debated before grabbing a soldier by the collar and speaking softly. The man shot the Witches a dubious glance before moving to obey. After women healers bound the wounds, other soldiers began moving them out on long stretchers. Still, Reden didn't approach the circle. Servants came after them, wiping up blood, vomit and feces.

Senna refused to watch. Her head felt light and her stomach on the verge of rebellion. It could have been her, her mother, any of them … but the thought did little to ease her abhorrence.

When the last soldier had left, Reden ordered all the remaining servants out, though a few protested about leaving before their jobs were finished. When the room was empty, he placed an enormous, soil-filled pot beside the circle. "If you try anything, I'll see you regret it." He held a couple seed belts. She breathed a sigh of relief. He'd listened.

Prenny told him which seeds to use. Senna began to sing. The song was as gentle as a lullaby, the sound itself a healing balm. The pot blossomed green. When she stopped, she looked at Reden. Something monumental had changed. He stared at her as if he finally understood something profound. "Our foe cares more for my men than our own Chancellor. You've never been the enemy. All this time, it's been Grendi."

"Will you help us?" Senna asked.

He stroked his musket with his thumb. "What would you have me do?"

"What can you do?"

He looked away. "My officers wouldn't support me if I tried to usurp Grendi. They're too afraid."

She exchanged glances with Coyel. *Go on. He seems to have an affinity for you.*

Senna inwardly cringed. Everyone was looking at her. Listening to her. *Wouldn't someone else be better?*

He trusts you.

She had to repress a sigh. Her Keepers still needed her. And as long as they did, she'd help them. "Can you get us out of here?"

The muscles of his jaw bulged. "Perhaps two, at the most three. But certainly not all of you."

"It's all or none," Senna replied.

"I'm sorry, but the whole army is guarding the State Building."

Chavis shrugged helplessly. "Then we must destroy the city."

The Witches set their mouths in tight lines.

"We are not killers!" Prenny cried.

Senna tried to force her tired mind to think. How could they destroy the city without killing? And then she knew. "Can you clear the city? Get everyone out?"

He mulled it over. "The civilians, yes. But not the soldiers."

Chavis nodded. "See it's done. By morning, there won't be one stone sitting atop another."

Reden shook his head. "I'm not letting you kill my men."

Senna bit her lip. "Reden, you don't understand. If we die, there will be nothing to break the curse. Nothing to change the seasons, call in the storms ... It's not just your soldiers who will die—your entire country, the whole world—will die."

Reden did not gape. Senna didn't think he ever would. But he'd automatically moved into a defensive stance. Slowly, he deflated.

"Our capitol, our beautiful city." But he departed at a jog.

After he left, Senna and the others began another Calling Song. There were others they needed to speak to—Joshen and Captain Parknel.

33. MESSAGE

Stretch leaped over a fallen tree and hit the ground at a dead run. Foaming sweat ran down his shoulders and dripped from his belly. Judging by his breathing, his lungs were burning. By the time they finally left the trail and hit the sand, the animal's legs trembled like they might collapse at any moment. Joshen knew if he did, the horse would likely never get up again.

His heart wrenched with every stride he pushed from the horse. He would die running if Joshen asked him to, because the animal loved him. But Joshen felt Senna's danger. He had to hurry. Even if he had to run Stretch to death to save her.

Joshen rounded a patch of trees and his whole body sighed in relief. Parknel's ship was anchored not far from shore; fresh patches of new wood stood out against the black paint of the old. Barren stumps lined the shore, where swirling sawdust mixed with loose sand. It appeared all the fruit-bearing trees had been lightened of their load; Joshen suspected the reason the ship was still here was so the sailors could gather more food for the return journey.

He pulled Stretch to a stop. The horse trembled and shook beneath him. Joshen cupped his hands over his mouth, "Parknel! Captain Parknel!" He waved his hands over his head. But at this distance, the sailors appeared to be little more than bugs crawling atop a toy ship. It was a long way to swim. "Parknel!"

To his relief, a boat was finally lowered into the water. As it grew closer, he saw Parknel's grim face standing at the front of the boat. He cupped his hands over his mouth, "Senna?"

Joshen shook his head emphatically. "Captured!"

"The other Witches?" Parknel shouted back.

"Captured!" he said as he dismounted.

Parknel jumped from the boat and waded toward Joshen. "So she freed 'em?"

"Yes sir, but the Tarten soldiers caught them. We have to go back to Carpel and get her out of there."

Parknel rubbed his red beard. "How?"

Joshen looked away. He simply didn't know the answer.

Parknel surveyed Stretch. "You've abused your animal."

The horse's ears hung limply and his head dropped as if it were too heavy to lift. Joshen stroked his neck. "It couldn't be helped."

Parknel grunted. "Well, I suppose we'd better find some fodder before we make for Carpel."

Before they could step into the water, the wind picked up, gushing past him, even though only moments before the day had been as calm as morning. It blew straight toward him, flattening the trees in a line—a line that came straight from Carpel. Witch song drifted down. Joshen thought he heard the inflection of Senna's voice and some of the tension seeped from his muscles.

> Joshen, to Carpel thee must come,
> For our destruction cannot be undone.

The wind faded and picked up again.

> Captain Parknel, from Jarten we must flee.
> In Carpel, we have need of thee.

"They didn't know we'd be together," Joshen murmured.

"If I take our ship to Carpel, we'll be captured." Parknel set his jaw. "You'd better let that horse go, son. We haven't enough hay to feed him over the journey and no time to gather any."

Joshen's face lost all color. After all he'd been through with Stretch, could he just abandon him? His mouth set in a grim line, Joshen loosened the cinch, pulled it from the horse's back and set it gently in the sand. His hand trailed along Stretch's neck and then rested on his poll. He hesitated and then tugged the bridle over his ears. Stretch opened his mouth and shook his head as the bit came out and then stood chewing tiredly.

He'll survive, he told himself. Joshen rested his forehead against his horse's neck, knowing he'd probably never see him again. "Goodbye, old friend." Draping the bridle and stirrups over the saddle horn, he hefted its sweat-soaked weight on his shoulder. He sloshed through the water, handed the tack to one of the sailors and looked back. Stretch still stood at the shore, looking at him. Joshen couldn't help but notice the horse looked confused, lost. He didn't understand why his master was abandoning him. Why he was being left in a strange land, alone.

Quickly wiping his cheeks with his sleeve, Joshen pulled himself into the boat and watched as Stretch's features grew increasingly indistinguishable. He stood at the ship's banister until he couldn't see the horse at all. Stretch never moved.

34. Ring of Power

Grendi paced the barrier, her gaze raking across each and every Witch, as if searching for the weakest among them. "You cannot hold it forever. Eventually, one of you will break and then I'll see to it you are all executed. I'll burn your bodies and bury your ashes in the deserts of the south. None will mourn your passing."

She paused. "But for one of you, I'll grant a pardon. I'll give you a small allowance and a home of your own, with the condition that your tongue be removed and any spawn drowned."

Senna's fists clenched until her nails pressed half moon circles into her palms. What kind of monster thought that was generous?

"Your offer isn't freedom," Prenny said, "but isolation in some run-down shack with songs stripped and children murdered."

Senna felt like cheering the woman on.

"Each of us has already faced imprisonment, many for years." Coyel said. "A half life isn't much of a life."

"Nor would we betray our Keepers," Drenelle added. "We saw what Espen did."

Chavis glared at the woman. Tiena leaned against Senna.

Grendi moved to the edge of the barrier. Senna found herself hoping the woman would take one more step, just one, so the barrier would send her careening into the far wall.

Unfortunately, Grendi could see the barrier's boundaries. "Some of you are considering it. And why not? You're all bound to die. Why not allow one to survive? Someone will bow before the end, why not you?"

"Your words are poison" Senna said. "And we all know it. You aren't talking to common women, Grendi. We're Keepers."

An evil smile spread across Grendi's face. "Everyone has a vice, Brusenna, daughter of Sacra. For your mother, it's you and for you, her. The woman to your left, Coyel, she'd not break. But the woman four down, her aging mother fled into the woods when you were captured. I've had my men looking for her. Would she not break the circle to save the old woman's life?"

"No," Tiena replied. "You don't understand, Grendi. But in time, when you are starving like the Boors, you will see what Witches do for you."

"I don't fear your curse!" Grendi shrieked. "I turned one of you once and she nearly destroyed you! I'll turn one of you again!"

"I would leave the city if I were you, Grendi," Senna said.

"And why is that, Brusenna?" Grendi asked. "Is your curse going to blow in a storm?"

The Witches brooded until Chavis spoke inside their minds, *Let's destroy it now.*

Coyel gave her a withering look. *Not until Reden comes back and tells us the city has been evacuated. Besides, we have to give Parknel enough time to reach us. Reden said he'd inform us when the ship came into sight.*

Drenelle shifted uncomfortably. "My hands are numb." She wiggled her fingers, working to increase the blood flow.

Senna had already noticed her hands were a dusky blue. "It won't be much longer," she promised. She tried to calculate how far the ship had gone after they'd spotted Carpel. But she hadn't been paying much attention. Perhaps half a day, perhaps more?

Glancing at the other Witches, Senna knew they wouldn't be able to wait much past nightfall. Their fatigue was obvious. Senna felt dizzy from lack of food and water. Under the cover of darkness, their plan must be set into action.

At dusk, Reden returned with his musket in hand, two pistols strapped to his sides and a large bag. In Tarten, he spoke to the guards. When they left, he said, "Most of the city is gone. Grendi is in a fine fit about it, but I told her about your evil plants and how I feared you'd put up a fight before you gave up. She finally allowed it. But I must warn you, not a single soldier has left."

"They will," Senna said solemnly, for she didn't wish to kill them. "Are you ready, General Reden?"

He checked his musket and pistols. "As ready as I can be."

Senna and the other Witches began their song.

> Forests and trees, lend me thy seeds.
> Over the city Carpel, spread thyself well.

The sound of rushing wind began from far away. When it hit the city, it pelted every surface with seeds, branches, even rocks. When the gale finally settled, the Witches began singing, but this, like their curse, was more chant-like.

> All of the seeds within the city,
> We ask of thee, take no pity.
> Crush rock, shatter stone,
> Topple building, streets groan.
> Grow with power ripe,
> For on this night,
> The Witches take flight!

A deep-throated groaning began, like the moans of a thousand ghosts. It echoed strangely from the square building's walls. New shadows appeared in the moonlight. Senna felt a jungle sprouting within the city. In every crack, in every crevasse, a plant was growing, expanding, heaving. At the corner of the room, a small green vine grew stark across the cold stone floor.

Within minutes, the groaning was pierced by fierce cracks followed by crashes as weaker walls gave way. Outside, the frightened shouts of the soldiers rang out, until the sounds of cracking and crashing overpowered them.

Grendi rushed in, her hair frazzled as if woken from sleep. "Stop! I demand you stop!"

As if in response, the Witches' song reached its apex. The walls around the State Building shivered and groaned. A deafening crack fractured the air. A fissure shot up the side of one of the walls like ice splitting. Reden took flight, lodging himself between the two thrones. Grendi scampered across the rock-strewn floor after him. With a shiver, the wall crashed down. Trees and vines tugged, pulled and pushed. Grendi cowered.

The cries of the soldiers again reached Senna's ears, but they grew more distant. They were fleeing.

As the Witches sang, more seeds blew in and took root, springing up around the Ring of Power and pressing against the roof. With a circle of trees around them, the power of their song intensified and the three remaining walls collapsed. The plants continued to grow, shattering the chunks of rock into shards and covering them in green. Grass and flowers sprang up, completely covering the ruined capital in green so thick and lush no one would guess a city had ever stood atop the mountain. Only the most beautiful jungle in all the world.

The Witches went silent. Within moments, the barrier shimmered and slowly dissipated. Senna's limbs were stiff and cold from sitting on the hard granite floor for hours and their songs had drained her. Shakily, she struggled to her feet. A look around revealed they were all weary—some much more than she.

Senna peered in awe at the world around her. The Witches had created their own Ring of Power, encircled with full grown trees. In the center, a perfect granite floor. Of the State Building, only the four thrones still stood stark and white against the deep jungle green. Reden emerged from behind one, his musket still in hand.

Grendi rose to her feet, her eyes wide with rage. Spit flew from her mouth as she pointed and screamed, "I want them DEAD!"

Reden gave her an odd look. "Yes, Chancellor Grendi."

She snatched a knife from his belt and rushed forward, murder bright in her cruel eyes. Reden rammed the butt of his musket into her skull. She crumpled. "That felt good." Reden shook his head as he retrieved his knife. Rushing forward, he jerked his blade through the cords binding Senna's hands. When she was free, he handed her the other knife and the two went to work.

Within moments, all the Witches were free. He pointed to the bag. "Your seed belts are inside. Put them on and then pull your hoods over your heads. And stay together!"

After she'd found her seed belt, Senna tugged her hood up and followed Reden away from the Capitol Building. What used to be a road was pockmarked with rubble and jungle. Reden had lost his landmarks and the trees made it impossible to see the docks below the city. They had to rely on his sense of direction and their noses to lead them toward the sea. Senna's heart hammered wildly with fear. This time, there would be no quarter and no General Reden to see that they were protected from the other soldiers. They'd be shot.

Senna's legs felt like rubber as she rushed through the heavy trees. She hadn't the wind to sing for the jungle to hide their path and some of the older Witches struggled to put one foot in front of the other. At least their way was downhill, harder on their muscles, but easier on their lungs.

Senna knew Reden was frustrated with their pace. He was used to the speed of a trained army, not exhausted women. He kept glancing nervously behind him. The fact that his weapons were primed and ready didn't escape her.

Beside her, Tiena tripped over a root. No sooner had her body hit the ground than Sacra and Coyel pulled her back to her feet. She looked back and realized why Reden had insisted they wear their hoods. In the dark, they were little more than blurs of green.

It seemed her whole life had consisted of running. A cry erupted behind them. The Witches unconsciously increased their pace, some bracing others up. A shot rang out and the Witches tucked their heads and rushed faster. Senna could smell the sea stronger in the air, but she wasn't sure they'd make it.

"Hurry!" Senna dropped back. Her blood pounding in her ears, she shoved a seed into the Earth, ran a few yards to the side and plunged in another. She sang the barrier trees to life. It seemed to take forever for the shoots to mature. She could no longer see the others. She had to slow the soldiers, had to give them more time!

She could hear footfalls. They'd come close enough she could see the triggers of their muskets. She ducked deeper into her cloak and prayed they wouldn't see her. "Let no one pass!" She cried as she bolted to her feet and ran for her life.

Shouts. Shots rang out. She heard a ping and saw a spark as one ricocheted off a rock at her feet. Another smacked into a tree at her side. Splinters exploded in her face. Her feet flew over the Earth. One of the soldiers reached toward her. Her cloak choked her and her hood fell back. He dragged her to the ground and shouted in triumph.

Just as she filled her lungs to scream for help, a branch wrapped around his middle. His shout of triumph turned to a shriek as it sent him flying. Her stomach in her throat, she scrambled to her feet and ran. More shrieks followed as other soldiers went flying like rocks from a slingshot.

Where were the others? Had she lost them? What if they left her behind? No one had noticed her drop back. No one would be looking for her. Her chest burned with every breath she took and her lips and hands tingled. Her head felt light and though she hadn't eaten for nearly a day, she felt like she might vomit. Yet she knew stopping to rest might very well mean death. Or worse. She couldn't bear to think what Grendi would do to her.

She surged through the trees, little more than a dark shadow passing through the starlight. When she finally caught a glimpse of more dark figures ahead, she nearly cried out in relief. Her fear had left her weak and shaky, but other than that, it was like she'd never left.

Reden raised his hand for them to stop. His breathing was labored as he pointed through the trees. Inky black water, crested with starlight. Senna had never seen anything so beautiful. "There are the docks. Go to pier seventeen. It's the longest."

"What are you going to do?" Chavis asked breathlessly.

"Stay here and keep them off."

"You only have three shots before you have to reload!" Senna cried.

"And a saber," he reminded them. "That's at least four kills. I imagine up to seven, depending on how many rush me. And that's only if they don't obey my orders to search elsewhere."

But Senna doubted the soldiers would believe Reden. If Grendi wasn't already awake, she would be soon. Reden had betrayed her. If he stayed here, he would die. Senna made a quick decision, one she knew posed a huge risk. "Those of you with the breath, create a boundary. Barrier trees and barbus. Anything you can think of to hold them off! Those of you who can't, get down the pier and wave in Parknel's ship; it's called the Sea Witch!"

The Witches obeyed her as if they'd done so their entire lives, dividing into two groups. The larger group scurried to the forest, plunging myriad seeds into the ground and singing them to life. They created a semicircle around the piers, as wide as possible. Senna knew it wouldn't take long for soldiers to come at them from the water; there was little she could do about that. Few defensive plants grew in the sea, besides kelp that could drag them to their deaths and flip over boats. But all the kelp in the harbor wouldn't stop ten thousand soldiers. Not for long.

Reden wandered among them, his musket and pistols ready. They planted barbus behind the barrier trees, so any who managed to get beyond the trees would fall into slumber. Soon the air was heavy with the smell of the enormous orange blossoms—a smell that would plummet almost any man into slumber.

Thorny plants were also abundant, to scratch the men who might pass the barbus and barrier trees. And beyond that, every plant imaginable with the ability to irritate and burn the skin. The effect would be double because the poisons would seep into the cuts and enter the soldiers' blood streams. Any who survived the quickly erected forest would itch for months.

When the first explosion and flash of light erupted, the Witches huddled and finished the task at hand before running to the pier. But Senna hadn't reached as close to the water as she'd hoped. She kept plunging in seeds as she sang in desperation.

The soldiers hit the barrier trees. Soon, their bodies were flying through the air. Seeing the danger, the others backed away and concentrated on firing.

A plume of sand erupted beside Senna and then another. A strong hand gripped her shoulder and hauled her back. "Come on! You're no use to any of us dead!" Reden half-dragged, half-steered her toward the pier. A ball ripped through her cloak. Senna jumped and froze. Her arm burned at the memory of being shot by Wardof. Reden kept her going.

They both floundered in the sand before they hit the wooden planks. Senna covered her head with her hands as her footsteps echoed across the boards.

"We're out of range," Reden said.

Her step felt lighter. The other Witches had made it to the edge of the pier. Some faced the shores. Senna saw soldiers coming at them in small boats. The Witches were sending the wind into their faces, forcing them back with every stroke. Others sang to the kelp, which flipped the boats.

But even with their desperation, their voices were faltering. They were drawing upon reserves already drained. Senna felt her own exhaustion keenly. Her body was numb with weariness and her lungs and voice raw. She searched through the darkness. Parknel would come from the north. Standing at the end of the pier, she sang to the wind to bring their ship in.

"The soldiers are abandoning the boats," her mother said.

"What are they up to?" Chavis asked.

Light flickered behind her. Senna turned to see blue flames.

"They're burning the barbus!" Prenny cried.

The barrier trees wouldn't be far behind.

"Please Joshen," she whispered. "If you don't come soon, it'll be too late."

35. Wind Song

Joshen felt the wind picking up behind them, blowing harder than it had since noon. It was pitch dark and every sailor among them was scanning the shore for signs of the bay. "Fire!" the man in the crow's nest cried. Joshen saw the eerie blue flames licking the starry sky. "Is it the city burning?" he asked.

Parknel's eyebrows nearly drew together. "I don't see any lights. No signs of the city at all. Surely, that's the bay."

Joshen studied the rounded mountains, trying to remember if these were the same ones he had seen days ago. But this had to be the inlet; it was the only one they had seen before they had thrown anchor.

"To port!" Parknel cried; the ship groaned as it turned into the bay.

Joshen heard distant popping sounds and saw smaller flashes of golden light. "Musket fire!"

"To arms!" Parknel screamed. "Load the blasted cannons!"

Sailors tore open the door to the Captain's cabin while other men thundered below decks to load the cannons. Joshen grabbed his own musket, ran back to the bow of the ship and loaded it. But he wasn't in range yet. All he could do was watch as a cluster of Witches at the end of the pier struggled to rip up the planks so the soldiers couldn't reach them from the shore. Some were singing desperately to the wind that drove their ship, others were intent on stopping the soldiers in boats. There was a man with them. Three Witches took turns loading his musket and pistols. He fired as rapidly as he could at the advancing soldiers. It seemed all the soldiers of Carpel had converged on them.

Joshen couldn't help but wonder who the man was and why he was helping. The ship wasn't in musket range yet, but it wouldn't be long. "Prepare the gang plank and the stern cannon! Force those soldiers back!" Parknel screamed. "And disable the other vessels so they can't follow us!"

The ship bucked as the cannons fired. Some of the balls slammed into docked ships, while others careened toward boats filled with Tarten soldiers. The musket fire forced the soldiers to shift focus onto the Sea Witch, but it didn't halt their advance. The sailors aboard the Sea Witch had the high ground and a rail to shield them. Steadily, they managed to curtail the Tartens' progression.

Not much farther in, Joshen recognized Senna, Coyel and an unfamiliar Witch loading the man's muskets. Grasping ropes as thick as his arm, Joshen and a handful of men jumped from the ship. He hit the pier with enough force to send painful shudders up his shins. Fast as he could, he tied the rope to the pier. The ship groaned and the hull nose-dived. Water exploded from the stern, throwing sailors and cannons helter-skelter.

His fellow sailors wrestled with the awkward gangplank while the ship bucked like a colt. The moment it touched the pier, Witches ran up. Joshen saw the danger immediately. He opened his mouth to shout a warning when shots began popping, hitting the exposed Witches as easily as chickens on a fence post. More than one crumpled. The sailors rushed to help, but there was little need. The Witches behind the women simply heaved them up without so much as a break in stride.

The very last to come were Senna, Coyel and the man. Joshen was tempted to throw him overboard, but there wasn't time for it. All the while, the cannons never stopped firing as the cannoneers took aim at whatever targets they could find.

"Quick!" He heard Senna say. "Before one of them tacks onto our wind song!" With the Witches singing, the ship turned and jerked forward, rendering all but the stern cannon useless. It continued firing. Breathlessly, Joshen waited to see if the Tartens would follow. Parknel's ship wasn't up to another sea battle.

But no other ships surged forward. He sagged in relief and then went to see if Senna was safe. He found her bent over a Witch who was obviously Tarten. Her hands pressed over the wound in her leg that gushed warm and red between her fingers.

"Tiena, can you feel the ball?" Sacra asked.

The woman's voice was strained and accented, "In my bone!"

"It has to come out!" Prenny said gravely. "We'll never be able to control an infection if it doesn't." She gazed up at Joshen. "You and Brusenna hold her. Sacra, help me."

They gave her the hem of her cloak to bite down on. Joshen and Senna gripped her arms while two others laid themselves over her legs. Tiena screamed as Prenny's fingers disappeared within her flesh. Her face white and strained, she pulled back her crimson fingers. "It's too slippery, I can't grasp it."

Parknel appeared with a pair of pliers. Prenny dug back in and finally came out with a ball. The Witches went about healing the injured and calling upon the wind.

As exhausted as they all were, their work was not yet finished.

36. Circle of Keepers

The wind gusted hard, whipping Senna's hair around her like a thing alive. It stuck to her tear-lined face. But she was too exhausted to care. If not for Joshen shoring her up on one side, she wasn't sure she could withstand even the swaying of the ship. A good many of the Witches weren't strong enough to come; many had wanted to.

Coyel began the funeral song.

> One of our own has passed from our sight.
> We know not whence her soul took flight.
> We trust in the Creators' tender care,
> That Tiena may find a better fare.

The song was high and keening; the sailors couldn't hold their tears. They lifted the plank and Tiena's body slipped into the sea. Senna heard a splash and choked on a sob. Desni didn't know her daughter was dead. Years of waiting, only to be parted like this.

The process was repeated three more times.

She knew they were lucky. Tarten's strongest army had captured them; Grendi had sworn to murder them all. It was a miracle any had survived. But the thought was little comfort. Four Witches were gone. And that was four too many.

Senna blamed herself. She'd freed them. It had been her plan to escape from Carpel instead of fighting Reden and his army inland.

When the last of their songs slipped over the rolling waves, the Witches slowly moved away. Only Sacra, Coyel, Senna and Joshen remained.

Sacra stared at Senna's hand intertwined in Joshen's. She sighed heavily. "When I was young, I met a man. A man who made my heart sing. We brought two children into the world. Of the three members of my family, I only have one left." Her bright eyes bored into Senna. "Make your decisions well, for you may not be able to keep everything you bring into this world." She pressed her lips against Senna's forehead and turned to stand at the stern of the ship, for it was her turn to coax the wind.

Senna tried to understand the sudden urge she felt to scream. Joshen's arm tightened around her. "Come on, Senna."

Her mind was too muddled to protest as Joshen led her below decks. With a gentle kiss to her lips, he left her alone. Of their own accord, her feet carried her to Coyel's side, where she lay beside the older woman and fell asleep.

***

Senna woke to shouts from above. It was no longer pitch dark, which meant daylight had come. Senna blinked through her bleary eyes and worked her sandpaper tongue over the roof of her mouth. Oh, but she was thirsty! And hungry, too! During the long night when they'd fought for the lives of the injured, she'd had little more than a few hard biscuits and some water.

Rubbing her dry eyes, she climbed back up the stairs and stumbled above decks. Judging by the sun, it was early morning. She'd slept through the remainder of yesterday and all of last night. She heard another round of shouts and recognized Joshen's voice. Her eyes widened at his words. "Back off him!"

"He's one a' them ain't he!"

"The Witches trust him, what more do you want?"

Senna was running now, up to the poop deck. Untroubled, Reden leaned against the rail, while Joshen and another sailor shouted at each other. Other sailors had gathered; most wore hateful expressions that she'd been the recipient of all her life.

Her eyes met Reden's and she couldn't be sure what she saw—
something akin to calm acceptance? But there was something
else. Her eyes widened as she realized he was appraising her.
Half the sailors on the ship wanted to throw him overboard and
Reden was still trying to figure her out.

"Reden is a Witch friend," she said calmly.

The sailors shot her incredulous looks.

It infuriated her. "I'll say it again, he's a Witch Friend. If you
want to remain one, leave him be."

She stood breathing hard as the other sailors slowly moved
away. Eventually, she was left with Reden and Joshen. Joshen
clapped a hand on Reden's shoulder, "Sorry 'bout that. As a
general rule, Nefaliens don't trust Tartens."

"Nor Tartens Nefaliens." Reden didn't take his eyes off Senna.

Joshen studied her disapprovingly. "Have you had anything
to eat?" She shook her head wearily. "I'll get you something."

He left her alone with Reden. The Tarten General was still
contemplating her, as if he couldn't quite understand something.
"You're a leader," he finally concluded. "I've trained soldiers all
my life, so I know the difference between the type of man who
gives orders and the ones who follow them. You, Senna, give
orders."

She looked away quickly, shame burning her ears. "No. I'm
not any good at it and I hate it. I've always hated it when people
look at me." She'd never told anyone that, not even Joshen.

Reden only chucked. "Perhaps it was crushed out of you
when you were young. But it was always there, waiting for you
to find."

Senna looked Reden up and down. "Find what?"

He shook his head and started to pass her, but he paused long
enough to say, "Your calling in life." He trotted down the steps.

Her heart was still pounding as Joshen handed her some
food. She sank to the deck. As she ate, she puzzled over Reden's
words. Joshen, however, didn't seem to notice her distress. "I've
never been on a ship moving this fast. We'll be in Nefalie in
days."

Senna drained the cup he brought and began stuffing food in her mouth. Joshen chuckled. "And you said I eat fast!"

Senna shot him a dirty look as she took another bite.

***

Senna had taken her turn singing to the wind. As dawn approached, the sun emerged from the waves, wet and shimmering.

> Oh morning light, hear my cry,
> To Haven, I must fly.

The mist rose before them, leading to the northwest. It had done so for days. Before the sun reached its zenith, Senna saw black cliffs jutting out of the churning sea. Coyel, Parknel in tow, came to Joshen, who rarely left Senna's side. "The other Heads and I have discussed it. We wish your presence on the island as we usher in Fall."

Joshen grinned from one ear to the other as he slapped Parknel's back. "It's the most amazing place."

Captain Parknel dispatched numerous fully loaded boats. In the last boat to make the underwater journey, Senna counted to two hundred before calling to the sea.

> Oh sister sea plants, I ask of thee,
> Take me to the place none but Witches see.

The kelp pulled the boat under the cliffs and into the caves within. The Witches emerged into the light. The island was a bit unruly after their long absence. Pogg met them at the entrance, tears dripping down his mottled cheeks. "Pogg knews Senna brings Witches backs! Pogg knews!"

He threw himself into Senna's arms and then moved down the line, hugging Witches while wailing and keening. Parknel gaped at the Mettlemot.

"Now, we go to sing to the gardens, but at midnight, we meet at the Ring of Power," Senna told them.

***

As the tendrils of moonlight lit the island, Senna waited with her Keepers outside the Ring of Power—something that hadn't happened for four years. All emerged from the trees at once and grasped forearms.

To the lands that winter touches with frost,
Shed thy leaves and turn to dross.
Slumber now and in sleep remain,
Until in spring we call again.

The wind whipped their songs away, pouring them across the leaves and plants. Heeding the Witches' call, the trees would soon drop their leaves. It would take months of singing in shifts to even begin returning things to how they'd once been. But it was a start. Senna smiled with joy and ran to Joshen. "Come on! There's something I want to show you." Taking his hand, she led him through the valley to the sheer side of a cliff. There, a hidden stairway led up a ridge.

Up the flight of stairs, Senna's feet flew to a high balcony. Here, they could see the whole valley, with the Circle of Keepers in the center and the evenly spaced waterfalls that lined the cliffs. Lanterns lit the treehouses like hundreds of tiny stars.

Senna closed her eyes to concentrate on the warm wind on her face. She turned to see if Joshen approved of the view. But he wasn't looking at the valley. His eyes were fixed on her. "You are the most beautiful woman to ever live. You know that, don't you?"

Tears sprang to Senna's eyes. He meant it. She could see it in his face. It made her dizzy.

Clearing his throat, Joshen looked away, embarrassment touching his ears with red. "I know your mother doesn't approve of us; not with how dangerous things are. And I have to agree. Marriage would lead to children and they would certainly be targets, helpless ones at that." His gaze turned back to her and there was a fierceness there, a need greater than any Senna had ever seen in a man's eyes. "But just because we can't marry does not mean we can't be engaged."

Senna's eyes widened and her breath caught in her throat as Joshen took both her hands in his own. He pulled something from his pocket. A ring made of a willow tree's thin branches woven around a single pink pearl. "Coyel sang its shape," he apologized, "and Parknel gave me the pearl. I promise, we'll get you a real ring when we get to shore, but I couldn't wait any longer. I had to know. Will you promise to marry me?"

Senna took the ring from Joshen. She slipped it over her finger and admired it in the moonlight. A pearl. Like a tiny moon. A smile broke across her face. "Yes, Joshen. I'll marry you."

Joshen sighed in relief.

Senna tipped back her head and laughed. "How could you possibly think I'd say no?"

Scooping her up, he swung her around and then set her down and smothered her laughter with a kiss.

Pure joy, Senna thought as tears slipped from her eyes. *In this moment, I know pure joy.*

THE Eɳd

ACKNOWLEDGEMENTS

There are many people who had a hand in not only creating the books I write but also the author I have become. To acknowledge them all would be nearly impossible. So I'll attempt a brief overview.

Thanks to those who told me how amazing my writing was—even when it wasn't. Especially Kent, Alice, Ellen, Gordon, Gayle and all the members of my book club.

Thanks to my critique groups for telling me my writing needed work—because it did. Especially JoLynne Lyon (for listening to me whine), Cami Checketts (for saying my books are as good as Hunger Games), Janet Jensen, Marion Jensen (for making me laugh), Chris Loke, Michelle Argyle and Kathy Beutler.

Thanks to my educators—true philanthropists who endeavor to pull themselves up with one hand while pulling up everyone else with the other. Especially Jeff Savage, David Farland, James Dashner, a host of librarians and my own teachers (Lonnie Kay, Reed Eborn and Ralph Johnson).

Thanks to Rhett and Emmaline Hoffmeister, Kara Klotz and Eve Ventrue (for the awesome cover).

And most of all, thank you to those who love me—Derek, Corbin, Connor and Lily. Because without you, none of it matters anyway.

1. SHADOWS

The night was so deep the shadows seemed to bleed darkness. Senna glanced toward the hidden sky, searching for the moon that would not come. Not tonight. Even the strongest starlight was strangled by the dense canopy of trees. The temporary blindness was frightening, but it ensured no one would notice her slipping away.

With each step she took, the roar of the waterfall grew louder. Finally, she reached the staircase carved into the side of the cliff. Mindful of the slippery steps, she climbed upward until her muscles burned and sweat broke across her skin despite the chill.

When she'd crested the top and crossed the bleak expanse, she glanced at the frothing sea far below. Sea spray misted her skin. She faced westward, towards the distant land of Tarten. Closing her eyes, she cast her senses across the vast ocean, searching and feeling the faraway echoes of the Four Sisters—Earth, Water, Plants, and Sunlight. She concentrated until she could hear their pain, an aching melody.

Senna's tears started again, wetting the salty tracks already on her cheeks. At night, her dreams haunted her. Dreams of a withered land and a dying people. With all the strength she had, she sang.

> Let not the curse of Witches
> Destroy a land of natural riches.
> Plants, preserve life in thy roots,
> Seeds sleep in earth, send forth no shoots
> Until the Witches shall disperse
> This terrible and unjust curse.

She came to the cliffs every night she could manage to slip away. Hoping to right the wrong she'd done, she sang for Tarten—the lands she'd helped destroy months ago.

When her throat was scratchy and she could no longer hit the high notes, she stared at the land she knew was struggling to hold onto any life at all. Because of the Witches' curse, no rain had fallen in Tarten for over two months—death to any jungle, but this one held on deep in the ground, waiting for the promise of her song to be fulfilled.

She withdrew her senses back to her home, Haven. Above the crash of waves, Senna thought she heard the scuff of a boot against stone. She whipped around and peered in the direction she'd come, her heart pounding in her throat. If the Discipline Heads discovered she was subverting their curse, the punishment would be severe.

"Who's there?" Her whisper sounded like a shout in the darkness.

No answer. She wished Joshen were here. The Discipline Heads had done their best to keep her apart from her Guardian. She hadn't seen him in two months. Not since he and Leader Reden had gone on a recruitment assignment.

Hugging herself, Senna trotted back to the staircase and began the long descent into the uninhabited quarter of Haven. At the base, she plunged between trees that towered above her, the tallest over eight stories high, the smallest just over two. Some were so wide it would take twenty witches stretched arm to arm to encircle one. Each tree was hollow and had once been inhabited by a Witch. Now they were empty, proof of the Witches' lingering decline into ruin.

Here, everything still bore faded signs of the Witches' final battle with Espen. A door in a tree creaked on its rusted hinges, a hole yawning where the latch should have been. Broken windows gaped like mouths with hungry, serrated teeth. The destruction was at odds with the life bursting all around.

Still, Senna couldn't shake the feeling she wasn't alone. There was no indication anyone had marked her sneaking away, no indication she'd been followed. But some instinct inside her seemed to chant a warning—through the gloom, someone was watching.

The feeling grew, and with a start, Senna heard music again. But this wasn't the distant music from Tarten. This was closer. *Here.*

She halted and tipped her head toward a sound so soft and natural she realized she must have been hearing it for a while and mistaken it for the sounds of nature.

But there was no mistaking it now. The melody carried a warning.

The wind picked up, snaking along the path and tugging at her cloak. Senna held her hood close. The thick vegetation before her shifted against the breeze. Someone was coming. Trying to calm her ragged breathing, she reminded herself she was safe on Haven. The Witches' headquarters were an impenetrable fortress—surrounded on all sides by cliffs that were in turn surrounded by the frigid ocean. The only way in or out of the island was for a Witch to sing you through an underwater cave.

So this was simply another Witch out for a stroll in the middle of the night in the abandoned part of Haven. The witch would see Senna and wonder why she was out for a stroll in the middle of the night in the abandoned part of Haven.

The tempo increased, matching the pounding of Senna's heart. She backed off the path and hid behind a plant with leaves the size of her chest. Her hand strayed to her seed belt, her practiced fingers automatically finding the pouch of Thine seeds. She waited, as motionless as a mouse at the mere whisper of a wing.

A figure emerged onto the path, features hidden by the dark. Coming level with Senna, a muscular hand brushed some of the overgrown vegetation out of the way.

The hand was distinctly male, but there were no men on the island. They weren't allowed, not without the Discipline Head's permission. If this man shifted a mere fraction, he would touch her cheek. She gasped softly.

He paused and cocked his head as if listening. Holding her breath, she closed her eyes so they wouldn't catch a stray bit of light and reveal her. The man hesitated before moving forward, his pace faster this time.

Senna let out her breath in a rush. She bit her lip as the man disappeared back into the shadows that had birthed him. Steeling herself, she stepped onto the path.

A man where no man should be? Perhaps she was mistaken. After all, it was so dark. But there was a way to find out. Obscured by time and neglect, the gravel path held a perfect imprint of a boot. She eased her foot inside. It was easily half a dozen sizes bigger.

She hadn't been mistaken. But why was a man here? The music changed, luring her forward. Her fingers buried in Thine seeds, Senna slipped after him. She kept him just in sight—the solid darkness of his form, the scrape of his boots. He rounded a bend. She crept forward, but when she glanced down the path, he was gone.

She paused, listening. The hollow tap of a boot on wood. There. He was slipping up the steps to a tree house. Dropping into the shadows of the plants, Senna parted a leafy branch and peered upward.

The man glanced around before tugging the door closed behind him. It shut soundlessly, as if someone had oiled the hinges recently. Senna heard voices that were too muted for her to make out the words. The tempo of the music picked up, pounding out a savage beat.

Something was wrong, and she had to know what. Her breath catching in her throat, she eased silently up the steps. At the top, she couldn't help but notice the creepers had been carefully pulled away from the doorframe. Whoever this was, they'd met here before.

Senna peeked past the vines that partially covered one of the broken windows. Through the gloom, she could only make out two distinct silhouettes. That meant there wasn't just one man on the island. There were two.

"Why?" asked a bass voice.

A tenor answered, "Because I had to know for certain."

"And *now* you're certain?"

"Yes. She'd put the rest of us to shame. Even Krissin." He paused. "Have you spoken with our contact?"

The bass grunted. "She'll make sure we're clear to depart with our captive tomorrow. And she guarantees our forces will breach the island."

Senna gripped the sill until her fingers ached. Why would anyone attack Haven? And who would help them?

"Good. I'll be glad to go home and stop pretending."

The other man chuckled. "Easy for you to say."

A sigh left the tenor's lips. Senna saw movement and thought he must have stood. "We'll meet again tomorrow after sunset."

A vague shape started toward the door.

The music grew louder, pounding a warning.

Senna gathered herself and rushed down the stairs. She heard the door behind her swing open, followed by a startled cry. "We have to stop her!"

Hauling her skirt above her knees, Senna ran. Her cowl slipped off her head. She glanced back. Her hair swept over her face and partially blocked her view, but she could see two hooded figures chasing her.

The smaller of the two stopped and swung something around above his head. A rhythmic, whooshing sounded around her. Before she could understand what was happening, something solid smacked into the back of her head.

Lights exploded behind her eyes. She pitched forward and hit the gravel hard. And then he was on top of her. Senna didn't have time to think. Acting on reflex, her mouth opened and a song poured forth.

> Plants, stop the man who'd halt my flight.
> Bind him, though he flails and fights.

A rustling slither filled the air as the plants responded. The man yanked her into his chest, into his arms. His breath washed over her face—he smelled of something dark and sweet, like licorice. Repeating the same verse, she tried to kick free, but his grip was too tight.

A vine shot past her and snatched his arm away. More plants responded, twisting around him and pinning his other arm. Still singing, Senna kicked her way out from under him. One more song, and he'd be wrapped up completely.

Something snapped behind him. She had forgotten about the tenor! She clambered to her feet, a song on her lips. Before the first syllable fell, he barreled into her. She slammed back into the dirt.

Plants, stop–

He shoved a gag into her mouth. Knowing how vulnerable she was without her song, Senna drove her elbow back, catching his wiry frame in the gut. The attacker grunted in pain. His grip loosened enough for her to spit the gag out. But she didn't have enough breath to sing. She twisted until she was chest to chest with him. All she saw was a face wrapped in shadows, dark eyes glinting. She punched as Joshen had shown her, putting all her strength into it.

An explosion of pain spider-webbed through her hand. Her attacker tottered. She shoved him. The man tried to hold on, but his movements were slow and clumsy. Senna kicked her way free and started running. She panted out a song.

Plants of the forest, hide my trail,
For an enemy, I must quell.

She was too winded for the song to be very effective, but it was the best she could manage. At the sound of a sawing knife, she knew the smaller attacker was freeing the larger. They'd be after her soon.

Even with her song weaving the plants behind her, Senna didn't think she could outrun two men. She needed some kind of weapon. Her head whipped from side to side as she searched for something.

All she saw were enormous plants, broken doors, and *windows!* She darted into the dense foliage. Plants whipped her face, stinging her eyes. She erupted onto another of the hundreds of Witch-sung paths that wound between Haven's trees. She followed it for half a dozen steps before darting back the way she'd come.

Beneath a tree's broken window she flattened herself against the ground, her face pressed into the damp soil. Her movements slow and even, her fingers searched for a piece of glass to use as a weapon. All she could find were worthless bits.

She froze as footsteps pounded past her. The men paused uncertainly, but they were good at this game, better than her. Without a word, they split up. Senna could hear them hunting for her.

She tried to slow her breathing. Sweat soaked through the back of her dark green dress. She started searching again. Something sliced her finger—a shard of glass about the size of a knife blade.

Keeping her movements smooth, Senna wrapped the edge of her cloak around her hand and picked it up. She chanced lifting her head. Sweat rolling down her temples, she listened for any sign of the men before she scooted backward. When she bumped into the tree house, she eased to her feet and edged to the other side.

Now she was near where they'd first attacked her, hopefully the last place they would think to look for her. Her heart pounding in her throat, she waited. Nothing. She moved away from the tree, toward home, her senses straining for any sign she'd been spotted.

Some instinct made her turn around. By then it was too late. The gag bit into her mouth and the knot pulled tight. But the attacker had underestimated the rest of Senna. She whirled and struck with the glass shard.

A gasp slipped from his lips. Under his hood, the bass's eyes went wide with shock. A gush of warm blood soaked Senna's hand, and she stumbled back in horror.

The attacker fell to his knees, his large hand on his stomach. Senna retreated, fear clawing her insides.

He watched her, the skin around his eyes creased with pain. "You're not safe, Brusenna. Soon, all the Witches will be dead."

About the Author

Amber Argyle grew up with three brothers on a cattle ranch in the Rocky Mountains. She spent hours riding horses, roaming the mountains and playing in her family's creepy barn. This environment fueled her imagination while she was writing her debut novel.

She has worked as a short-order cook, janitor, and in a mental institution, all of which gave her great insight into the human condition and has made for some unique characters.

She received her bachelor's degree in English and Physical Education from Utah State University.

She currently resides in Utah with her husband and three young children.

CPSIA information can be obtained
at www.ICGtesting.com
Printed in the USA
LVHW091023260320
651275LV00001BA/258